The Laura Principal Series

'*Nights in White Satin* is the best book yet in this amazing series . . . If you're not intrigued, go check your pulse' Ian Rankin

'Cambridge-based Laura Principal is one of the more believable and astute private investigators' *Sunday Telegraph*

'Michelle Spring joins the ranks of our best crime novelists . . . Her touch is deft, her insight enlightens and the suspense grips' Helena Kennedy, Q.C.

'A major new novelist whose literate, intricately patterned storytelling will be warmly greeted by fans of P. D. James and Minette Walters' Sandra Scoppetone, author of the Lauren Laurano novels

'Splendid combination of old fashioned teaser and new fashioned social criticism, and a lovely feeling of a writer getting into her stride' Jill Paton Walsh

'Genuinely chilling undercurrents, and above all that authentic page-turning quality' Michael Dibdin

'The author, with great skill, makes us love the characters we cared for least' *Mail on Sunday Review*

'A female private eye comparable to V.I. Warshawski and a twisty psychological plot worthy of Elizabeth George' *Alfred Hitchcock's Mystery Magazine*

'Subtle, highly charged evocation of menace . . . extraordinary skill' *Washington Post Book World*

'With each book, Spring is maturing as a writer, discovering how far she can push her talent and exploring the darker recesses of the human psyche' *The Times*, designating Michelle Spring as a Master of Crime

Nights in White Satin

Michelle Spring

ORION

First published in Great Britain in 1999 by
Orion
An imprint of Orion Books Ltd
Orion House, 5 Upper St Martin's Lane, London WC2H 9EA

A CIP catalogue record for this book
is available from the British Library

Typeset in Great Britain by
Deltatype Ltd, Birkenhead, Merseyside
Printed and bound by
Clays Ltd, St Ives, plc

The characters and events in this book are fictitious
Any similarity to real persons, living or dead, is coincidental

For the Cambridge girls –
Mary Hamer, Terri Apter and Janet Reibstein

Author's Note

The City of Cambridge is much as described in this book. St John's College and Midsummer Common have a full existence outside the pages of this novel, as does the Arts Cinema, the Casualty Department at New Addenbrooke's and the Fort St George. However, the characters in the novel were born in my imagination, and the events described in these pages are fictitious. Astute readers will notice – and, I trust, forgive – the liberties I have taken with the area adjoining New Square and with a certain road in Fulbourn.

Acknowledgements

I would like to thank Sarah Epstein, of Girton College, Cambridge, Dr Simon Franklin, of Clare College, Cambridge, Professor David King, Master of Downing College, Cambridge, Inspector Chris Bainbridge of Essex Police, and Superintendent Kate Gooch of Cambridgeshire Constabulary, all of whom gave generously of their time and expertise to help me in the preparation of this book.

Thanks also to the staff of The Cambridgeshire Collection at Cambridge Central Library for maintaining the archive on the Spinning House. Among these papers, Enid M. Porter's concise article, 'For unruly and stubborn rogues', *East Anglian Magazine*, vol. 18 (1958/59), proved a particularly useful starting place.

Assistance, information and inspiration came from a variety of other sources. I would especially like to acknowledge the help of the following: Pamela Gillies, Yvette Goulden, Rosa Held, Anna Hont, Alan Kerzey, Pamela Lee, Jane Lichtenstein, George E. Moss, independent forensic scientist, Gill Motley, Caroline Oakley, Susan Peters, Sue Pope, Anita Healey Porter, Dr Janet Reibstein, Selina Walker, the Cambridge Women's Resources Centre, the English Collective of Prostitutes, and individual women who talked to me about their work in the sex industry but who wish to remain anonymous.

A particular debt is owed to David Held and Frances Pine, and to Jane Selley, the copy editor, for their meticulous attention to the manuscript in its final stages; and to Joe Blades of Ballantine, Yvette Goulden of Orion and Jane Chelius, all of whom read the manuscript in more than one version and offered wonderful suggestions.

Above all, thanks to my family – David, Rosa and Joshua – for being there, even when the going gets rough.

Prologue

The ball had taken place, as May Balls should always do, on a warm night in the middle of June – a champagne and oysters kind of night, following a strawberries and cream kind of day. By the early evening, even a stranger to the city could sense that something extraordinary was about to occur. There was a low sun glazing the spires of King's College Chapel, and a pulse of excitement in the air.

Three young women alighted from a taxi on King's Parade. They debated briefly and then tottered off towards Market Square, their high heels click-clacking as they went. They circled past the silent face of the workaday world. Past Great St Mary's Church, where the bells were muted. Past the Guildhall, locked and still. Past the market, like a ghost town, the stalls shut up tight for the night.

Tourist numbers and Mediterranean weather had tempted Don Pasquale to push the frontiers of the pizzeria out on to the pavement. The result was a makeshift sidewalk café. The young women took possession of a table. They seated themselves with elaborate precaution. They slid their frocks up their thighs, so the silk and satin and organza didn't crease; they crossed their knees and stretched their long stockinged legs away from the table to reduce the risk of snags. In full-length gowns and high-heeled sandals, with pale backs and silky shoulders gilded by the sun, the girls glittered against their drab surroundings. They checked their make-up, plucked at pastries, sipped cappuccinos, and giggled in equal measures of nervousness and pleasure. It was

I

going to be a special night. Each girl was buoyed by the conviction that she was special enough to be a part of it.

Nearby, in Rose Crescent, in front of a shop selling designer hats, a young man stopped to review the angle of his bow tie. His pals looked on from a distance. A fleeting comparison with Pierce Brosnan flashed into their minds; they revelled in what they fancied was a sophisticated image. The woman who was rearranging the window display observed their starched white shirts, their formal suits. She thought of her eldest boy who would soon, like them, be at university. For their fresh good looks, for their fragile confidence – for fantasies of her son's future – she accorded them a smile of pure indulgence.

The 007 look-alike misread this response. 'She's after me,' he boasted.

His companions cuffed him on the shoulder. 'Try to control yourself,' they teased, 'those trousers have to last all night.' There was a moment of scuffling and pummelling, of thinly disguised masculine warmth, before the undergraduates tugged down their cuffs, reclaimed their dignity and hurried on to the café.

These were the first groups whose appearance on the streets punctured the quiet of the evening. Within minutes, others had appeared – a trickle, and then a stream, of bright young things. The men stood out sharp and clean against the soft grey stone of Cambridge; the women looked bright and exotic. They filled the narrow streets with their scent, the clatter of their heels, their laughter, their high spirits. Cocky and loud they came, or tight and restrained; in parties of ten or twelve, or intimate cliques; loosened up with drink already, or holding out for excesses to come.

All exuded the wild energy of freedom. Many of them had just finished the three most demanding years of their lives. As undergraduates at Cambridge University, they had been pushed and pressed and challenged; they had been coddled and cared for; they had been ignored, patronised, criticised and overlooked. A few of them, with exceptional talent, had been singled out for stardom. All of them had been made to understand that, however banal their individual achievements, they were better by far – better qualified, better informed, better taught and better connected – than those who'd attended universities of the lesser rank.

And now, at last, the ordeal had ended. Examinations were over. Results – with their baggage of success and disappointment, their dashing of hopes, their imperatives to action – had started to be posted. It was May Week and, for the first time in years, these undergraduates were unburdened of academic demands. The May Ball was their chance for a final wild fling. They faced the opportunity with arms wide open.

And so, eventually, did Katie Arkwright. She was only a first-year student, and not at Cambridge; as she perched amongst a group of more confident party-goers in a café near Magdalene Bridge, she found the prospect of the ball faintly intimidating. She had one small glass of wine to take the edge off her nerves. She pricked up her ears to the cheers of the crowd queuing for admittance to St John's College. She went to the ladies', and checked her make-up; she smiled uncertainly at her impeccable reflection in the mirror. Finally, Katie too was gripped by a pleasurable excitement. Everyone – the other girls in their party, and especially the men – had been so nice to her, so full of compliments, that her diffidence drifted away. By the time they left the café, and made their way towards the college, she felt a part of the occasion.

Almost as if she belonged.

And by the time they entered St John's – streaming through the gate, at the tail end of twelve hundred party-goers – Katie was more optimistic, more excited, more elated than she had ever been before in her life. She made a promise to herself: she'd have a night to remember.

After that, it all happened so quickly.

At nine fifteen, they toured the college grounds, milling with the crowds from courtyard to courtyard, marvelling at the

3

entertainments that lay ahead. They helped themselves to champagne and smoked salmon and melon.

At ten o'clock, there was the fireworks display. Katie sat on the grassy riverbank and scanned the skies. She was entranced by the starbursts over the tower of the University Library, bewitched by their shimmering, watery echoes in the Cam.

Katie Arkwright was seen at eleven o'clock, tossing her soft gold curls to the insistent rhythms of Hot Chocolate. More than one person watched how she moved, noted how the deft shrug of her shoulder echoed the deeper pulse of the music.

At eleven fifteen she was gone for good.

Katie Arkwright left, apparently of her own accord. She abandoned the May Ball quickly and decisively, as a person might walk away from a bus queue. As if the money that Jared Scott-Pettit had forked out for a ticket meant nothing. She took her splendid young self – the elegant white curve of a dress, the silver armlets, the dainty sandals, the corona of curls – and disappeared.

Not even a glass slipper remained behind on stone steps to signal she'd ever been there.

Chapter 1

It was back in January when I'd been asked to co-ordinate security for the May Ball at St John's. I didn't play hard to get.

'We'll do it,' I'd said. 'No problem.'

For a private investigator, security work is bread-and-butter. Doesn't tingle the taste buds, but keeps the stomach full.

'Piece of cake.' That was Sonny's response. He's my partner at Aardvark Investigations – the man to blame for getting me into this line of business in the first place. His heart was set on expansion, and – as he never tired of saying – expansion calls for capital.

Sonny knew a job that couldn't be turned down when he saw it.

'Easy peasy,' echoed Stevie, our right-hand woman, during the week-before planning session. 'Maybe Geoff could help.' She reached for the telephone.

But by the time I asked, 'Geoff?' she was deep in conversation with a client.

No problem; piece of cake; easy peasy. Two parts business and one part bravado, these responses.

St John's College lies more or less in the centre of Cambridge. The ten green acres that make up its grounds are bounded by busy roads – Northampton Street, Bridge Street, St John's Street. The River Cam runs through St John's, providing a conduit to Trinity College on one flank and to Magdalene Bridge on the other. Our brief was to keep college property intact, keep revellers safe inside, keep gate-crashers out. This might sound simple. But anyone who thinks they can coast their way through security with logistics like this is long on optimism and short on sense.

It's part of the wayward tradition of the Cambridge May Balls – just as staging them in the month of June is part of that tradition – that there will be gate-crashers. Their exploits are the stuff of local legend. It's whispered through college corridors how a pair of students equipped with climbing gear scaled an outer wall, changed from tracksuits to black tie, and managed to reach Third Court before they were accosted by security men. How a party of women from Newnham wrote themselves into history by scuba-diving up the Cam. They infiltrated John's from the river. Their presence was betrayed only by the slapping of their flippers on the lawn. How a Churchill man, stowed inside a brewery van, had been pinned under three hundred pounds of draught lager when a barrel detached from its moorings. He emerged with broken ribs and a greatly enhanced reputation.

Or that's how the stories go.

Our job – Sonny, Stevie and I – was to hold firm in the face of siege. To secure the beachheads of the ball. To guarantee that the mock-Gothic portals of New Building would not be breached. It might not be a heavyweight assignment, but it had an element of challenge. On the evening of the ball itself, even I felt a surge of excitement.

By the time I'd escorted all the suppliers out of college, and checked the store rooms for stragglers, there was a queue awaiting admission that stretched from St John's gatehouse all the way to neighbouring Trinity. With three-quarters of an hour still to go before the party began, the crowd grew by the minute. Their voices bounced off the buildings on either side of the street. Echoes magnified the sound until a hundred people seemed like several thousand. I heard the raucous cries that greeted new arrivals; heard a football commentary conveyed by radio to the crowd. And every few seconds, massive and mysterious whoops of delight.

'What's going on?' I asked Stevie, whose territory included the

6

'Nice to see you in formal dress,' Sonny whispered, and planted a gentle kiss on my neck.

The worst thing about working posh occasions is trying to do security with satin flapping around your ankles. I'd opted initially for a turquoise halterneck, vaguely Egyptian in shape, with lots of room to swing my arms. But it called for high heels. The thought of chasing an intruder down a staircase on stilts made me think again.

So I'd settled instead on a black dinner jacket and trousers. The jacket had jet beading on the lapels, and a skinny silk chemise underneath, so it wasn't quite Radclyffe Hall. But I could fit a walkie-talkie in the pocket, and get away with glittery hightops. And in spite of the glitz, I could still do a six-minute mile.

'How about a dance?' Sonny asked. He was moving gently to the music, carrying me with him into the sway.

'Have we time? Before the hordes mount the horizon?' I didn't really mean it as a question. I wanted more than anything in the world to snuggle up, to slow-dance. To imagine that this fairy-tale setting had been magicked into existence for the two of us.

I turned slowly, guided by the circle of his arms, until we were face to face. Until I was staring straight into Sonny's warm brown eyes; until his lips brushed the side of my mouth. Until our legs were entangled, and there wasn't space between our bodies for the night air. Until his breath stroked my hair, and my breath stroked his. Until I couldn't tell whether the pounding I felt was his heart beating in his chest, or my heart beating in mine.

Until we were dancing slowly, slowly. Barely dancing.

Cheek to cheek.

'Do you play?' Sonny whispered in my ear. As he had the evening in the jazz club, when we'd first met. When he'd put away his clarinet and turned up at my table.

As he had, again, much later, when we'd teetered on the edge of a new relationship – fearing to damage the old, the purely professional one, but drawn to something more powerful. 'Do you play?' Sonny said. Left it to me to decide. And I did.

We ignored the bass beat from the band. We shut our ears to

9

the clamour of the queue outside. First Court, still unpopulated, was elegant and tranquil. If it had been left to me, I might have forgotten obligation. Might never have allowed the ball to begin. Might have stayed all alone – just me and Sonny – slow-dancing the night away.

But Stevie, at least, had her mind on the job and her eye on the clock. She stepped out into the open, near the gatehouse. I could see her across the court, and in the laser lights, her sequins spat fire. She was waiting for a signal.

'Are we ready?' Sonny asked. He kissed me and began to pull away.

'Aye-aye, Captain,' I joked. 'Everything's under control. Except for the multitude lined up outside, all itching to be first at the food.'

I allowed sixty seconds in which to steel ourselves for the chaos to come . . . fifty-nine, fifty-eight, fifty-seven . . .

Sonny headed back towards the Bridge of Sighs.

. . . three, two, one. 'All right,' I said, sending Stevie a thumbs-up. 'Do it. Let them in.'

And in they came. Dressed to the nines. Coasting towards delight. Pausing only long enough for Stevie's crew to clamp each wrist with a luminous security tag.

The rest of the evening – that is, the night; my stint didn't end until eight a.m. – went by in a haze of duty. There was no shortage of incident – such as the moment when a young classicist, gripped by a tablet she'd been given as a gift for graduation, removed her harness at the top of the bungee tower and prepared to fly. It took forty minutes to talk her down. Afterwards, I had a quick glass of champagne – my only alcohol of the evening – and returned to work.

And my only break came early on, when the fireworks started, and the first Silver Dragon arced above the night sky. I took moments out for the spectacle, as all the guests turned their eyes above the tops of the trees.

And then, as I turned back to duty, I came across a small group of men in formal attire, standing quietly, watching the tangle of dancers. From their age and air of confidence, I'd have guessed they were senior academics. But then, I'd met the Master of St John's earlier. His walking stick gave him away.

'Dr Patterson?' He swivelled on his good leg, and looked at me with appraising eyes.

He had been at an evening meeting. 'With colleagues from St Bartholomew's,' he said, by way of introduction. 'This is Stephen Fox.' Fox had a shrewd face and a nod that was far from friendly.

'And this tall fellow,' the Master continued, 'the one who looks as though he's about to take a turn on the dance floor, is John Carswell.'

'Not just yet,' Carswell demurred, and restrained the tapping of his foot. Fox gave a quiet snort, almost certainly a rebuff. Carswell ignored it. He transferred his attentions to me.

'What's it like being in change of security, Ms Principal?' Carswell offered a convincing show of interest. 'Are the guests giving you a hard time? Or do John's students, as the Master boasts, know how to behave themselves?'

'There's been far more fun than trouble, up to now. And,' I added, excusing myself, 'I'd like to see it stay that way.'

I headed towards faint sounds of a scuffle from the other side of the courtyard. I figured it would be bad for business to let a full-scale fight break out under the Master's eye.

'Let's get the sequence straight,' I said.

He went over it again. Katie Arkwright arrived at the ball just after nine o'clock; popped off to have a dance shortly before eleven; disappeared – for no apparent reason – minutes later.

'This sudden departure,' I interrupted. 'You've no idea what triggered it?'

Philip Patterson stood by a tall window in the Master's Lodge overlooking the gravelled drive below. He'd recently had an operation to replace a hip joint, which explained why he used a stick. But if surgery had slowed his movements, it hadn't dented the habit of command.

'It wasn't me who was in charge of security arrangements last evening, Ms Principal. It was you.' He said this in the mildest, the friendliest, of tones. Yet the rebuke was unmistakable. 'I had hoped you would supply an explanation for Ms Arkwright's absence.'

The Master of the college had called me to account.

It wasn't what I'd expected. When Patterson's secretary turned me out of bed with her telephone call that afternoon, I'd envisaged a more conventional grievance. Maybe the fountain that had been imported from Italy to add an air of authenticity had been damaged. Maybe there'd been more complaints than usual from townspeople about the volume of the music. Maybe – in spite of my best efforts – there'd been boisterous behaviour from one or two of the student security men.

To be interrogated on any of these wouldn't have surprised me.

But Katie Arkwright came at me out of the blue.

Aardvark Investigations' brief, I reminded him, was to maintain order at the ball. To keep crashers out. To ensure that the only students who danced their socks off in the music marquees, or chuckled at the comedy tent, or heckled the hypnotist, were those who'd forked out the money for a ticket. That only those with a right to the night would pose at six a.m. for the survivors' photo. That everyone who punted to Grantchester for breakfast would have preceded their eating, drinking and merry-making with the requisite surrender of cash.

Well, Katie Arkwright hadn't gate-crashed. She had come, on the arm of her boyfriend, in a spirit of elation. And then – with seven hours of festivities still to run – she had turned and walked away.

And Philip Patterson seemed to expect me to know where she'd gone, and why.

I was worn out. I'd paced the grounds of St John's all night, straining to hear anything untoward over the blaring of the bands. My ears still felt as if I were underwater. I was not in the mood to be bullied.

'Dr Patterson, I'm sorry that this Arkwright girl's gone AWOL.

12

And it's odd, I agree, that there's still no sign of her fourteen hours later. But to be perfectly frank, twelve hundred people partied in this college last night, and it's hardly surprising that I can't recall this particular individual. Frankly, I don't see what help you can expect from me.'

Maybe I should have stopped there. But lack of sleep made me less than circumspect. 'Nor is it clear to me, Dr Patterson, why you should take an interest.'

Philip Patterson turned from the window. He made his way with halting steps to the leather chair that was angled beside his mahogany desk. Sitting down appeared to be an ordeal, requiring careful positioning, and a gradual shifting of the leg to minimise pressure on the hip. He didn't once wince with pain. The journey, from standing by the window to sitting nearer me, took only half a minute, but it worked. By the time he'd positioned his stick on the rug, within reach, and shot me a rueful smile, I'd been won over. I'm a sucker for a limp – especially when it's endured with such stoicism. Sure, I had a ringing in my ears; but what was temporary tinnitus compared to what he was going through?

'Ms Principal,' Patterson said, 'I fear I haven't made myself clear. You and your colleagues did an excellent job last evening. I took a short stroll around the grounds this morning and everything was ship-shape. I make no complaint.'

'Then what . . .?' Damn these all-night sessions. My daylight hours in bed had left me groggy.

'Just this. Jared Scott-Pettit is a final-year student at John's. He was Katie's escort. They have been – dating' – Patterson paused, as if expecting me to offer a trendier word. I didn't have one – 'for several weeks, and are, apparently, fond of one another. Scott-Pettit was shocked by Katie's disappearance, and when he saw his tutor today, he mentioned his concern that Katie had not yet returned to her house. His tutor passed the details on to me.'

'But why? Why would the absence of an undergraduate's girlfriend be a matter for the Master?'

Patterson did what officials do in this sort of circumstance. He rolled out the rhetoric.

'Everything is a matter for the Master,' he declared. 'Everything that might reflect on the reputation of the college. It is my job to safeguard the college and its standing in the community. Especially these days.'

These days? 'You mean now that fund-raising is such a priority?'

'Precisely.' He gave me a one-of-the-boys smile – confiding, inclusive, but without real warmth. 'I knew, Ms Principal, that being a Cambridge graduate yourself, you'd understand. These days, one cannot depend for contributions even upon one's own alumni. The faintest whiff of scandal can send the bequests of potential donors into someone else's pocket.'

It was beginning to make sense. But not quite. 'So you want to be reassured that Ms Arkwright's disappearance is a simple matter – no scandal, nothing that might embarrass St John's? Nothing that might cast a dark light over the end-of-term celebrations? And you haven't rung the police because—'

Patterson gave an impatient wave of his hand.

'For one thing, we have no direct responsibility for Miss Arkwright. She's not a student of the University, let alone St John's. As I understand it, she's studying modern languages at Anglia University, on the other side of the city. So, you see, it isn't really our place to report her disappearance.' He paused, hoping that would satisfy me.

'For another?'

'Surely you know, Ms Principal, that it's not a criminal offence to make yourself scarce. When an adult like Miss Arkwright – she's nineteen, I understand – goes missing, the police work on the assumption that she has gone of her own free will. Has relocated. Or is merely seeking solitude. Missing adults aren't high on police agendas.'

'Not unless there's foul play.'

'There's no question of foul play.' Patterson shot this back with a firmness that raised its own questions. But I pursued a different line.

'Of course, the police might have the right idea.'

'I beg your pardon?'

'Dr Patterson, you're a conscientious servant of the college. You intend – I take it – to hire me to look into Katie's disappearance?'

Patterson nodded, a small, careful movement of the chin. Not committing to too much too soon.

'You trust me because of my connections with Cambridge. You see me as a safe pair of hands.'

Patterson was smiling, and for the first time, it was with a trace of warmth. He liked assertiveness. Cambridge teaches respect for a combative approach. I'd almost forgotten.

'You want me to be discreet. To come to you first with any information I turn up – particularly information that could be disquieting for the college. Right?'

'Ten out of ten, Ms Principal. But you're losing your thread. The police, you said, may have it right. You think I'm rushing things, by instigating an investigation now?'

'That's precisely what I think. The most likely scenario is that Katie and her boyfriend – what did you say his name was?'

'Scott-Pettit. Jared Scott-Pettit.'

'That Katie Arkwright and Jared Scott-Pettit probably had a lovers' quarrel. Odds are that Katie has gone somewhere to dry her tears and that she'll turn up in a couple of days, wondering what all the fuss was about. If you hire me, you'll waste your money and my time. Unless, that is . . .'

'Go on.'

'Unless, as I believe, you have some other reason for suspecting the worst.'

He paused for a long while. Groped for his stick, gripped the arm of the chair with his free hand, and slowly, awkwardly, lifted himself to a standing position. I made a graceless gesture of help. He shook his head – no. Then he replied.

'There may well be a special cause for concern in the case of

Katie Arkwright. But it is not my place to explain. It is a deeply private matter. Another college is involved. I know some of the details because the Senior Tutor of St Bartholomew's has confided in me. You do remember meeting Stephen Fox last evening, Ms Principal?'

'No, I . . .'

I didn't remember. And then I did. With the shrewd face; with the manner that was far from friendly.

'Yes, I remember now.' Stephen Fox, as I recall, had watched after me as I left to check out a disturbance on the other side of the courtyard. He had shown more interest in my going than he had in my company. 'Senior Tutor at Bart's, is he? And just what did he tell you that throws light on the girl's disappearance?'

'It's a delicate matter, Ms Principal. The information should come directly from Bart's. I'll ring Stephen Fox, shall I, and say you'll be popping in to see him?'

There was a pause while I thought it through. While I relinquished my hope of a couple of quiet days, catching up on administration. While I acknowledged to myself that a job like this – clean, on home territory, and with a customer known for paying promptly – couldn't be ignored.

'Any time tomorrow,' I said.

From then on it was straightforward. Patterson passed me to his very competent secretary. She handled contractual matters. She even dialled Katie Arkwright's boyfriend for me.

'Any luck?' she asked, when I'd replaced the receiver. 'Can he see you now?'

'He's tied up at the sports hall this evening. We're meeting tomorrow.'

I left the college by the front gate and headed home, taking the long and lovely route that would lead alongside the river and on to Jesus Green. The evening was too glorious for rushing back indoors. I took off my linen jacket, looped it around my waist, and welcomed the caress of the warm evening air on my arms. Bought an ice cream on Quayside. Swished barefoot through the grass. And as I strolled, I shook the sleep out of my brain.

Allowed myself to be engulfed by memories of the previous evening, hoping to spot Katie Arkwright – to know her, at least a little – in the archives of my mind.

The Master's description left a great deal to be desired. A long white dress, he'd said; some sort of shiny material. Scouring my memory, at first I could conjure up only flashes of silver, patches of pale – a spaghetti strap on a tanned shoulder, a bow of snowy silk – flitting among the guests. Then, as I concentrated, individuals began to separate from the crowd. To shift into focus.

I saw a girl with a dress that draped delicately over a full bosom, trailing her hand in the fountain. She beckoned to two men to join her; they acknowledged her with a gesture, and resumed their conversation. Noticed another young woman whose gold ankle chain flashed beneath a white hem; she searched for something, distractedly checking under chairs, and the panic in her eyes suggested that the loss was more than she could bear. A pair of women in white embroidered dresses strolled by, wearing enough jewellery between them to stock a Christie's sale; they had their arms around each other's shoulders, and were happily, boisterously tipsy. Saw a skinny woman feeding salmon parfait to an adoring companion; her dress was draped low in the back, so that her shoulder blades stood out harshly in the light. Recalled a stunning girl with a halo of bright curls standing dignified and serene at the bottom of a staircase. Her dress splayed out at the hem in pale pleats. A man came down the stairs behind her and took her arm, and as she turned, I'd had a shock as I'd seen that her eyes were unfocused.

Was one among these girls the missing Katie? Had I actually seen her? It would have been strange if I hadn't; after all, I'd milled among the guests all evening – and everywhere I went I watched. My mind was like ultrasound, scanning for little blips of trouble. How could I not have skimmed over Katie once or twice, maybe dozens of times?

And somewhere, presumably, my brain had filed her picture away, one small part of a mass image. Like an old school photo – merely waiting for someone to point to the little girl, third from the left in the back row, and say, *That's her! That's my old pal Katie!* A face can shift from one of the crowd to someone special in a matter of seconds.

But in the case of Katie Arkwright, who could do the pointing?

Chapter 2

When I first took up my position at the viewing window at Kelsey Kerridge, there were five men limbering up on the climbing wall.

One took a break, and then there were four.

'Which is Scott-Pettit?' I asked the fellow who'd made a dash for the drinks machine. He turned and pointed. Then he scooped up his Lucozade, and trotted back to the practice hall.

Scott-Pettit was the kind of guy who'd be described in certain genres as well formed. He was strong-looking, but not ostentatiously so. He had square shoulders, good posture, regular limbs, a firm chest. Nothing about him offended the eye. To my mind, nothing quite compelled it either.

I watched with interest as he spidered up the wall. He inserted one foot into a depression about fifteen inches off the ground. One hand found a grip, and then the other. His free leg edged its way over the moulded surface of the wall, knee bent, seeking a foothold, and finally embedded. Like a stick figure, he hung for a moment, arms bent at the elbow and outspread to left and right. Before I had properly registered the position, he was off again, searching for a higher base. While his companions did complicated things with ropes and pinions and overhangs, Scott-Pettit ratcheted himself to the top. He looked down the twenty feet to the floor and paused. Then he extended his arms, pushing his upper body away from the wall, and hurled himself backward. He landed with a whump on the springy surface below, and was back on his feet in seconds.

I've always applauded climbers, all the more perhaps because I haven't got a head for heights. I can't help but be impressed by people who ascend into ludicrous positions, dangerous positions, high in the clouds – or in this case, the practice hall – and then pause to consider the next move. The thrill for the spectator doesn't come from speed – as in downhill skiing, say, or motor racing; it doesn't come from overt power or from split-second skill. The excitement comes from the cool-headedness of it all. From the bizarre combination of precise calculation, mundane equipment – the minor bits of engineering, the clips and spikes and hammers – stunning locations and death-defying feats.

So when Jared Scott-Pettit finished his session on the wall, and left the practice hall – mopping his arms and neck with a towel, snapping off his wristbands, as if the whole exercise had been effortless – I was prepared for a hero.

What I got was a pompous ninny.

I interrupted him as he was padding off towards the showers. He stopped in his tracks. 'Friday, eleven a.m. That's what we agreed. It's now' – he made a show of checking his watch – 'seven o'clock on Thursday.' And he added, for the benefit of his climbing comrades, 'Don't they teach you to tell the time at private detective school?' His companions shuffled around uncertainly. They didn't find the joke as funny as he did.

'Most private investigators learn good manners,' I said. 'After all, rudeness is a business liability. Don't they teach you that at Cambridge?' I smiled, to soften the impact, and saw the ghost of a smile flit across the face of one of Scott-Pettit's cronies.

'Look,' I continued, 'you told me you'd be busy this evening at the sports hall. I was passing by. Thought I'd see if we could fit in ten minutes now. I rather imagined that it might suit you to have your girlfriend's disappearance looked into as quickly as possible. But if I'm mistaken . . .?' I looked enquiringly at Scott-Pettit's climbing companions, enlisting their support.

'Ten minutes then.' His tone was sullen. He dismissed the others with a wave. 'I want Katie to be found as quickly as possible,' he said. It was more than an addition; it was an afterthought.

I suggested that we retire to the bar for our chat, but Jared

Scott-Pettit leaned back against the wall. 'We're fine here,' he declared. He lifted his knee, placed his right foot in its trainer flat against the wall. He spread his towel out across his upraised thigh. Not everyone would look comfortable in a position like that, but Scott-Pettit did.

'Tell me everything that happened last evening,' I said. 'What time did Katie and you meet up?'

Scott-Pettit and Katie had met in the Café Rouge on Bridge Street, very near St John's, at eight o'clock. She had looked beautiful, he volunteered. Quite the most striking girl around. Her costume might have come straight off the cover of *Vogue*, and a gratifying number of male heads had turned as she entered the café.

'No one would have guessed,' he said, with obvious satisfaction, 'that Katie wasn't a Cambridge girl.'

'She's not from around here?' I asked, feigning innocence.

'She's from some dull village on the edge of Cambridge,' Scott-Pettit said, with a trace of petulance. 'You know perfectly well what I mean. She doesn't attend the University.'

If I had wanted to be difficult, I might have pressed him on what he meant by 'the University'. After all, Katie, as I understood it, was a student at Anglia University. And Anglia University was certainly in Cambridge. But I knew that Scott-Pettit was not alone in believing that Cambridge was the only local institution that deserved to be called 'university.'

'And Katie's mood?'

'Her mood?' he repeated, as if I'd asked a question in Swahili.

'Was she looking forward to the ball? Did she seem anxious, worried about anything?'

Jared assumed the irritated expression of someone compelled to waste time on trivialities. 'Of course,' he said, 'she seemed anxious when she first arrived at the café, but that's to be expected. She doesn't have much confidence, you know, for all her good looks. It's her background, I suppose. But after I'd commented favourably on her appearance, she relaxed. And by the time we set out for John's, she was exhilarated. Excited at the prospect of the evening.' He offered an expression that was intended, I believe, as an ironic smile. 'One wishes it were possible still to use the word "gay".'

'Try me. I'd probably get your meaning.'

We moved forward to the early hours of the ball. Katie and Jared hadn't contributed to the eager queue outside the gates of St John's. Katie was intrigued by enthusiastic voices from that direction, but Jared had vetoed it. There'd be a lot of jostling and pushing, he'd explained, and nothing really to be gained. So they'd passed the time in the café with friends of Jared's and made a relatively decorous entrance to the college just after nine p.m.

'And then?'

Jared rearranged the towel on his thigh and gave a shrug. 'A May Ball is a May Ball,' he said. And looked at me, as if there were nothing more to say.

Now, I'm not a devotee of May Balls myself. But I liked even less Scott-Pettit's studied indifference. He couldn't be older than what – twenty-one? – and already to him the biggest social event in the Cambridge calendar was a been-there, done-that affair.

So young, so lacking in fervour. What would he be like when he was thirty? I wondered.

But the question I actually asked was more straightforward. 'How did you and Katie pass the time after your arrival?'

Scott-Pettit stared at his knee for ten seconds, as if it had the answers; and when he glanced up again, he seemed vulnerable for the first time. I wondered whether I'd misjudged him. Perhaps he wasn't indifferent. Perhaps his gruffness covered a reluctance to confront painful memories. Perhaps his distress at Katie's disappearance was deeper than it seemed.

'Katie had to see everything, immediately,' Jared recalled. 'So we did a whirlwind tour. Popped our heads into the marquees. When the fireworks began, we sat on the lawn on the far side of the river to watch the display. Aterwards Katie wanted to dance, but I was determined to have a photo taken in front of the hot air balloon, and insisted we should do it early. We joined the dreadful queue. Then, while we were waiting, Hot Chocolate began their gig. Katie begged me to let her have a dance. Just one. I agreed. And' – Jared slapped his hands on the towel, on either side of his thigh, as if marking a decisive moment – 'that was where it all unravelled.'

I looked at Jared, trying to decide what was odd about his appearance. You couldn't easily fault his face. The nose was good, shapely even; the lips were full and firm, the eyes a solid grey. But the face lacked the humour that might give it animation and make him really attractive. It was a face with handsome features, not a handsome face.

'Unravelled how?'

'I don't know what to say,' Jared said, twitching the towel. 'It was all over in a flash. *Look*, said someone in the queue, *isn't that your girlfriend?* And I looked, and sure enough, there was Katie, running pell-mell across the lawn. She was distraught; she looked terrible. All that – gaiety – had gone. *Jared*, she urged, *we must go. Go where?* I asked. *Home*, she said. *We've got to leave. It's horrible here, it's not safe. I can't stay.*'

He paused and stared at his knee again. And for just a fraction of a second, he closed his eyes, blocking something out.

'You didn't take her home, Jared.'

'Of course, one always ought to escort a lady home. But I didn't think Katie really intended to leave. It's easy with hindsight,' he protested.

Ought to escort a lady? It was as if he had broken a rule of etiquette, rather than abandoning someone he cared for.

Jared cast around for a way to make me understand. 'Surely you can see what a waste it would have been to leave at so early an hour. How to explain it to one's friends? Perhaps if Katie had given me a reason . . .' Jared shrugged. 'But she didn't.'

'So you let her go, all by herself, in that distressed state?'

'I believed it would all blow over. Don't you understand? I didn't believe she would actually leave. I tried to get her to stay with me. But she wriggled out from under my arm. Well, then, I said, perhaps you could get us both some ice cream – that would keep her busy, I thought, until we reached the head of the photo queue, and by then she would have forgotten whatever had upset her.'

'And when did you realise that she hadn't got over it?'

'When I got to the head of the queue, there was no sign of her. I was annoyed, I don't mind telling you. I'd queued for an hour, for nothing. I went looking for her. One of my friends, Baz, told me he had seen her being let out of the gatehouse shortly after eleven. He'd asked Katie if anything was wrong.'

'Did she reply?'

'Yes, she did.'

'And?'

He looked directly at me now, made eye contact, with that vulnerable expression. But I could read it now. It wasn't vulnerability, it was puzzlement. Puzzlement and injured pride.

'Everything. That's what Katie said. *Everything is wrong.*'

Everything?

Everything is a lot, especially for a girl who's only nineteen.

There she was at the event of the year. She looked lovely. She had an escort with features that were hard to fault. And she was excited by the prospect of the ball. Even making allowances for the overstatement of the young, it was hard to see how these elements would add up to an evening where everything was wrong.

'May I go now?'

Like a child in reception class waiting to use the loo, Jared asked permission to end the interview.

'Up to you. I do have a couple more questions.'

Scott-Pettit remained where he was, and ran with me through the possible places where Katie might be found.

Since her disappearance, he'd made two trips to her house off Mill Road, but had found neither hide nor hair of his girlfriend. There was no sign that she had returned from the ball, and the girls she shared with seemed to be away.

I gathered from Jared's tone that Katie's accommodation didn't meet with his approval. 'She deserves something better,' he claimed, when I pursued it. 'It's a junkheap. And she deserves better housemates, too. I don't like to go there. They're rather difficult girls to get on with.'

'Difficult for Katie?'

'Difficult for me,' he admitted, with a scowl.

Jared provided the names of the difficult housemates for my notebook. The address and phone number of the house. Some leads on Katie's family – a mother in Histon, a father on the outskirts of Cambridge. Scott-Pettit hadn't a photo, but he gave me a description so detailed – from the fleck in Katie's eye to the stud in her navel – that the boy could put Polaroid out of business.

At last he made his move. Folded the towel, and slung it over his shoulder. Straightened up, returned his foot to the floor, and prepared to take an uneventful leave.

'One more question,' I said.

Jared nodded.

'*It's her background*, you said. Tell me what you meant by that.'

His explanation was brisk and revealing. 'Katie had a decent upbringing,' Jared said. 'Not a council flat, not a comprehensive school, or anything like that. She went to St Mary's, here in Cambridge. But all the same, there wasn't much money – the school fees soaked up everything. And she was rather – unsophisticated, shall we say. I have the impression that her mother and father are not really from our sort of circle.'

'Does Katie mind?' I asked.

Jared cocked an eyebrow at me. 'Mind?'

'Does she mind having parents who are not from – our sort of circle?' I held back a grin, thinking of the meaning that my mother Dorothy, who runs a small hairdressing business from the kitchen of her house in Bristol, would give to that phrase.

'Not as much as I do,' he said.

Honest to a fault.

Chapter 3

Browns Restaurant – where I was due to meet Helen Cochrane that evening for supper – is a meeting place that moves with the seasons. It sits on the edge of the old Addenbrooke's Hospital site, on the other side of the street from the Fitzwilliam Museum.

In winter, as you bound up the stone steps, you get a blurry image of golden light from behind the slim blinds, and a rush of warmth and clatter as you push through the revolving door into the restaurant. But in June, the door of Browns no longer revolves. It is fixed at an oblique angle, the better to admit a breeze, and some of the side windows open to convert the bar area into a patio.

Bustle and chat from inside the restaurant reached out to greet me on Trumpington Street as I approached.

I checked for Helen in the bar first, among the green wicker and the soft-cushioned armchairs. Scanned for a dark-blonde woman with a sunglow on her face. Blinked with astonishment when instead of Helen, it was Sonny I saw. Sonny was supposed to be in London. In spite of my surprise – perhaps because of it – I stepped up without stopping to think and laid my hand on his shoulder.

'Hello, gorgeous,' I said.

Time stood as still as I ought to have done. Two seconds felt like ten, like twenty, as the shoulder beneath my hand stiffened; as the girl sitting opposite – a child of fourteen or so, fresh and gawky, with hair in a pixie cut and purple-painted nails – raised her mascara-laden lashes; as the woman at his side sent me a tentative smile. As Sonny turned, and I snatched back my hand, looking in consternation upon a stranger's face.

When I had first seen this man, there wasn't room for doubt. He had the thick straight hair, fair and floppy, with darker shadow at the crown, that is Sonny's. He had the broad shoulders, the pale grey jacket, the long lean legs, the sinewy wrists.

But this man's hands were broader at the knuckles than Sonny's, and, when he turned to me, his face was nothing like. Sonny has a long face with a good strong nose; he has eyes that look straight at you, and a generous smile. The face that shifted towards me now had wary eyes, and a mouth that kept itself to itself.

I'm not a blusher. But as he looked at me – with irritation; and then, up and down, with a glint I didn't like – the colour sprang into my cheeks and trickled down my neck. It raised the temperature of my walk-warm skin to a slow burn.

Gorgeous? Had I really said that?

I stumbled, made a feeble comment about doppelgängers. He relished my discomfort; I could see it in his eyes.

I addressed my apology to the other people at his table. 'I've made a ridiculous mistake. Sorry to have disturbed you.' The pixie glared through prickly lashes, but the woman's smile was shaded with sympathy; I had the impression that embarrassment was an emotion she knew only too well. The doppelgänger – he who had Sonny's hair and legs and wrists, but who carried an unfamiliar smugness on a face that resembled Sonny's not at all – announced that what I needed was a cocktail. He signalled for the waitress and drew up an empty chair.

I escaped. Took a drink of iced water at the bar, and, turning, spotted Helen. She strolled in through the open door like a letter from home.

When you're squirming inside from an awkward encounter, there's nothing like a friend to wipe it away. We'd been undergraduates together, Helen and I. And from the moment we moved into adjoining rooms at Newnham College, until now, we've had plenty of occasions to administer anaesthetic to each other's emotional wounds. I confessed to Helen that I'd said *hello, gorgeous* to a complete stranger; Helen converted my humiliation into laughter. By the time we'd ordered lagers, and the lagers had arrived, I was myself again.

'Cheers.'

It was summer-hot inside the restaurant. The large-bladed ceiling fans did little more than shift heavy air from one part of the room to another. Helen lifted the hem of her dress and shook it to cool her legs.

'So tell me,' she said, 'what was it that this creep had in common with Sonny?'

At first I took the question literally. 'Well, his hair was exactly—' I said, and then stopped dead in my tracks. 'Maybe the common factor, Helen, was that he was Sonny one moment, and then the next moment, not.'

'Lost me,' Helen said.

I took a long sip of beer, and debated whether or not to continue. Is it disloyal to tell your best friend about difficulties with your lover? Was Helen Cochrane the kind of public I should keep my dirty laundry from? Should I try to work things out with Sonny – quietly, on my own – or should I talk with her about our troubles?

Talking would mean that I'd have to acknowledge to myself – and that would be a first – how bad the past few weeks had been. How even our moment of closeness at the May Ball had ended in disappointment.

'Sonny's difficult these days,' I said. 'When's the last time you spoke to him? In detail, I mean. At length.'

'Let's see. Four or five weeks ago, I suppose. Sonny dropped in with a birthday present for Ginny. I persuaded him to join me for a drink.'

'Did he tell you what he had in mind for Aardvark Investigations?'

'You bet. He was full of it. An office in Amsterdam to pick up more of the inter-European trade. This could be just a stepping stone, he said. Amsterdam today, Brussels tomorrow.'

'And next week, the world.'

I felt the familiar discomfort descend on me again. When the topic had first come up, over a year ago, expansion was mentioned as a vague possibility. Sonny had been picking up more and more contracts in air freight security between Britain and the Netherlands, and more of his work originated on the continent now. An office there, with a Dutch colleague, seemed an option. Something to think about – not an overriding commitment, as it seemed to Sonny now.

'It's become an obsession, Helen. Sonny can't let it go. The only thing he seems to care about is the money for this project. Without it, he says, we'll stagnate. Go nowhere. In his view, it's expand or go to the wall.'

'Can things really have got that bad?'

'Not in my book. I like things the way they are. As far as I'm concerned, if we want to expand – note the *if* – there are far less risky ways to do it. We could find another freelancer in Amsterdam, someone who wanted to work out of their own home. That way our overheads wouldn't skyrocket. If we open up a new office, and hire new staff, and then it doesn't work out—'

'You could end up spending the following two years working your butts off just to pay off your Dutch investments.' It's easy to see why Helen's been successful in university management; she may have trained as a librarian, but she has a damn good head for business.

'So you two are locked in dispute over this?'

I nodded. 'If we screw up, Helen, we could lose the business. Lose everything we've worked for. We might end up owing great chunks of our future income to the bank.' I hesitated, and then told Helen the worst of it. 'Sonny thinks I should use my share in Wildfell as collateral on a loan.'

Helen planted her forearms on the table and leaned towards me. Her voice fell to a whisper. 'You're not going to do it?'

Helen and I are co-owners – and Stevie is co-tenant – of Wildfell Cottage. It is a holiday home near the north Norfolk coast, a getaway, a retreat. But it's more than that too. Helen knows – and she knows Sonny knows – that Wildfell is central to my sense of self.

'Don't want to,' I said. Which was not quite an answer to her question.

'Listen, Laura. Surely Sonny – the Sonny we know and love' – Helen waggled her eyebrows, trying to lighten the tone – 'surely Sonny wouldn't make a mistake like that. In all the years I've known him, he's never been a reckless kind of guy.'

'Knew and loved.' I sighed. 'Sometimes these days I'm not sure I know him at all. He seems driven. Any caution on my part he takes for hostility. If I'm not with him on this, I'm against him.'

Helen stopped fanning herself with the menu and looked at me, hard. She'd got the picture now. 'Things are seriously bad between you two,' she said.

I nodded, and swirled the few remaining drops of beer around in the bottom of my glass. 'Yep.' I drained the glass.

Helen cast around for a ray of hope. She doesn't abandon her cheerful outlook easily. 'Sounds like you and Sonny need to talk it out. Away from work. Why don't you hole up at Wildfell for a few days? Remind him of how easy it is to relax there. Or throw caution to the wind – fly to Paris for the weekend?'

'Believe me, Helen, I've tried.'

What can you do if someone doesn't want to talk? I wondered. If he's set his mind on keeping you at a distance? In recent months, I'd proposed weekends, day trips, overnighters; always Sonny gave the same response. *Can't afford to take time off.*

'How the hell am I going to make him talk, Helen? I can't even get him to come home with me.'

'Meaning?' Helen looked at me over the rim of her lager, puzzled.

'Oh, nothing,' I said.

Last night, in spite of our recent quarrels, in spite of the distance between us, when I'd seen the courtyard all laid out for the ball, and picked up the first strains of music from the band, I'd been taken by a sudden powerful urge to forget our differences. Sonny must have felt it too. For just a few minutes there in the courtyard, when we'd danced, we were close again.

'Come home with me,' I'd whispered. 'In the morning, when we're finished here. Spend the day with me. Spend the night.

'How about it, Sonny?' I asked again, touching my cheek to his. Swallowing my pride.

He turned me down.

'I'd love to, darling,' he said. 'But I've got things to do. You know that. Things to do, places to go, people to meet.' It was supposed to be amusing.

I could still feel the emptiness that had rushed in as he'd disengaged himself from me. As he put duty before pleasure, again.

'Laura?' Helen asked. 'What's this about going home?'

'It's nothing, Helen. Really.'

But if it was nothing, it was the kind of nothing that feels bad when it hits the pit of your stomach.

It took a few anecdotes from Helen's work – she always manages to make the library seem like the setting for a sit-com – and another bottle of lager before I shook off my melancholy and joined the conversation as an equal partner again. Helen interrogated me about the previous evening.

'Was it as good as May Balls of the past?' she asked.

'What do you mean by "good"?' I challenged. My feelings about the balls have always been more ambivalent than Helen's. She's the party girl.

'Oh, don't be exasperating, Laura. You know what I mean. That very first ball is a magical experience. You emerge from your student room—'

'Your small and shabby room,' I took up the tale, 'with a private food supply limited to Pot Noodles and Nescafé . . .'

'And then you waltz into this astonishing world of beauty and abundance. We were all wide-eyed, don't you remember? Trying to look nonchalant – but more or less bowled over.'

'It's still like that,' I said.

During those first few minutes, after the guests had begun to stream in through the gates last evening, you could tell the May Ball virgins at a glance. By the way their eyes widened, in spite of efforts to appear insouciant. By the way they lunged for the drinks, as if the champagne might be snatched away before they'd had their money's worth.

They needn't have worried. May Balls evolved so that students could let off steam after exams and, in spite of their differences, they all occupy a cusp between enchantment and excess. Clare College has a reputation for May Balls spiked with romance. Trinity, with follow-up flights to Paris for breakfast, cultivates an aura of decadence. But at John's the atmosphere is boisterous and matey, with elegance edged out by indulgence.

'And the food?' Helen asked eagerly. She all but licked her lips. I decided to play to my audience.

'There was a torrent of food,' I began. 'A landslide, an avalanche. Eats on the scale of a natural disaster.'

This was true. It had taken the catering staff hours merely to put the refreshments in place. To heft the crates of mineral water, to carry the cases of champagne. To stack the fruit – the peaches, pears, plums and apricots, the strawberries, the melons. To lay out the smoked salmon parfait. To arrange the stalls by which donor companies planned to impress themselves on the palates of a future élite – the tower of Twiglets, the crater of Covent Garden soup, the mountain of Movenpick ice cream.

There were hot provisions, too, to satisfy a thousand hefty appetites. 'You could tuck in to roast hog, Helen, fresh off the spit. You could eat oriental prawns with your fingers, or chomp your way through chicken-in-a-bap.'

'Quantities?' As if she didn't know.

'Gargantuan, of course. That hasn't changed. No limits. No rules. No restraints.'

'What, no one to make you finish main course before you take dessert?' For Helen, this has always stood as the epitome of adulthood.

32

I laughed. 'Imagine, Helen, if you can – and I'm sure you can – an entire table dedicated to chocolate delights: chocolate chip brownies, Death by Chocolate, chocolate mint mousse, Black Forest gâteau, Belgian chocolates, Mississippi Mud Pie, chocolate-covered ants. And more. Some diners made their way along the table sampling a single bite of each item and then chucking the rest away. What do you say to that?'

'Let's order!' Helen said.

We quizzed the waitress closely on the specials, before settling for scallops on Helen's part and a warm salad with roast peppers for me. 'A bottle of house white?' Helen suggested.

'Not for me. I've got one or two calls to make when I leave here.'

Helen ordered a half-litre anyway, and returned to the interrogation. 'And was there really – or have I misremembered? – a never-ending stream of alcohol?'

'Never-ending,' I confirmed. 'Glasses of champagne, bottles of imported beer, pints of draught – as many as your body could accommodate.' Far more than some bodies could accommodate, if the state of the loos was anything to go by.

'They do say,' Helen said, 'that there's no excuse for sobriety at a May Ball.'

'No?' Alcohol poisoning might do for starters. Hangovers. Liver damage. The injury to your love life that follows from puking up on your partner's shoes. But maybe this sudden identification with the themes of Alcoholics Anonymous was merely a reflection of my slightly sour mood. I changed the subject.

'Helen, do you know a man named Fox? Stephen Fox, Senior Tutor at St Bart's? Or John Carswell?'

Helen thought for as many seconds as it took to pour herself a glass of wine. 'No to the Senior Tutor,' she said. 'But Carswell – isn't he the one who wrote that amazing book on viruses?'

'You tell me. I met him briefly last evening. Didn't ask for a CV.'

'What did he look like?'

I recalled how Carswell had stood, smiling at the dancers and tapping his foot. 'Comfortable with himself,' I said. 'About six foot one, nice taste in jackets. A much smarter dresser than your run-of-the-mill academic.'

'It's all those royalties,' Helen ventured. 'Anyone can have good taste in clothing with enough surplus cash. Face?'

'He could hardly get by without one, Helen.'

She raised her hands in mock exasperation, and stared at me until I succumbed.

'All right, quite attractive, since you ask. Warm blue eyes, good laugh lines, photogenic jaw. Brown hair that is going a great shade of silver on the temples. Conventional, certainly, but nice.'

'That's him,' Helen exclaimed. 'I've seen him on telly. More than *quite* attractive, if you ask me. Come on, Laura, you must have heard of Carswell. His book was a best-seller on both sides of the Atlantic. Not a huge best-seller, but a best-seller all the same.'

'What's it about?'

'About the drama of virus research, the quest for a cure for Aids, that sort of thing. When he talked about it on Clive Anderson's show, he made viruses sound like the sexiest thing since Leonardo DiCaprio.' Helen held a large stuffed olive poised near her lips and looked at me coyly. 'So how about an introduction?'

'I don't know DiCaprio.'

'Carswell,' she growled.

'I met the man once, Helen. That hardly qualifies me as a matchmaker. And now, if you can drag your mind away from Carswell, what can you tell me about Stephen Fox?'

'Never heard of him.' She shrugged, setting her olive pit in the ashtray. 'Why the interest? Is he quite attractive too?'

'Not unless you believe that still waters hide a lot of passion. In my opinion, more likely to be a breeding ground for algae.'

Helen noticed the waitress threading her way towards us with two steaming plates of food. She shifted the candle and the carafe to one side, clearing room for the vegetables, and carried on talking. 'What's all this about Carswell and Fox, Laura? You wouldn't be so interested in them unless something happened last night, during your tour of duty at John's. So tell me . . .'

The food looked delicious. I road-tested a sliver of roasted pepper. 'Mmm,' I said, 'not bad.' And tucked into my salad in earnest.

'*Bon appetit.*' Helen was temporarily distracted. But once she'd got the measure of her scallops, she pointed her fork in my direction and challenged me again.

'Now you've cut a path through that salad, Laura, perhaps you'll take the trouble to answer my question. Did anything happen at St John's May Ball?'

Had anything happened?

'The night had its lively moments. What May Ball doesn't?'

There was the group that tried to surge through the gates with tickets that were wonky – forgeries, of course. There were the three or four punts that Sonny repelled, and the gate-crashers who got dunked in the process. And, of course, there was that poor young woman who'd threatened to imitate Icarus from the bungee jump. But none of those incidents was the one she wanted.

'Laura?' I could tell by the set of her chin that Helen wouldn't let go.

'A girl named Katie Arkwright disappeared.'

'Disappeared? What does that mean?'

'She was a student at Anglia – your place.'

'Never heard of her.'

'No reason why you would; she was only a fresher. Her date was holding their place in some interminable queue, while she danced. Then she came to him, in some distress, and insisted on leaving. She didn't say why. And she left, all on her own.'

'Maybe she felt ill?'

'She didn't say so. *It's not safe here*, is what she said. And anyway, if she had been ill, that wouldn't explain why she never turned up at her house.'

'Listen,' Helen said, 'a girl can't just disappear from a May Ball

35

without someone noticing. For one thing, all the exits and entrances are secure. Aren't they?'

I nodded. 'Until five a.m., there was only one way out – past the Porters' Lodge, in the forecourt – and Stevie was in charge there. I'll ring her later tonight. If Katie appeared distressed when she left St John's, Stevie might have talked to her. She might be able to tell us what was up.'

'I'm not sure you'll find Stevie at home,' Helen said.

'Meaning?'

'Just that I saw her this morning – I'm pretty sure it was Stevie – getting into a car on the Backs. I was on my way to work. Couldn't help but notice, since she was wearing a full-length dress studded with sequins. Not the usual thing for a morning jaunt. Or for Stevie, for that matter.'

'So?' I said. I'd assumed that Stevie had driven herself back to London after the May Ball. We hadn't actually talked about it, and she had left St John's rather quickly when duties were over, but it wasn't like her to make elaborate social arrangements and keep them from me. 'Maybe she was getting a lift. She was tired; maybe she didn't want to drive.' I brightened. 'Maybe she was taking a taxi to the station.'

Helen shook her head. 'It was an old sports car. With some camping gear strapped to the roof. Funny kind of taxi.' Then she changed the subject. 'Why on earth would someone up and leave in the middle of a May Ball?'

'You tell me,' I said.

'Pour me another glass of wine, and I will.'

'Are you driving, Helen?'

'None of your business. Now listen. Here's theory number one. Katie became ill. She had a pounding headache. Or she was dizzy.'

'Perhaps she'd just drunk too much,' I added, joining in the game, 'and felt she'd disgrace herself in the hot air balloon.'

Helen gave me a warning glance, then returned to her topic. 'Two. She had a quarrel with what's-his-name – her boyfriend. What's he like anyway?'

'Jared Scott-Pettit. A man convinced of his own superior place in the world. He admires Katie for her looks; despises her lowly origins.'

'Well, there you are then,' Helen said, as if that explained everything. 'Let's say he was flirting with someone else. Katie had to get away, to the privacy of her room, before she burst into tears.'

'Is that all?'

'Not in the least. Those are things that would make her want to beat a hasty retreat from the ball – the pushes, if you like. There's also the pull factor. Theory number three: something at home demanded her attention. Maybe she'd left a pot of pasta simmering on the cooker.'

'Perhaps,' I interrupted, 'she needed to pick up some medication – some sanitary towels—'

'An Ecstasy tablet!' Helen exclaimed. 'Katie was exhausted by the dancing and decided on amphetamines.' Helen thought it over and withdrew the last suggestion. 'Too melodramatic. Let's go for something simpler.'

I heaved a sigh of relief.

Helen ignored me. 'How about this? Number four: a straightforward case of someone who tried a May Ball and found it not to her liking. Let's say Katie's a quiet sort of girl; she likes long, intimate conversations and dinners for two. She wasn't a student at Cambridge, so she might have been virtually friendless that night. Maybe the crowds made her uncomfortable. She might suffer from claustrophobia, even – that could be why she felt unsafe. Maybe, feeling lonely and alienated, Katie concluded that the game wasn't worth the candle. Home she went, to watch a video and get some beauty sleep. There,' Helen said, looking just a shade off smug. 'What do you think?'

'Very inventive, Helen. But ingenuity won't take the place of solid information. This has to be the most holey set of explanations I've ever come across.'

'Holy?' Helen asked. She folded her hands under her chin in a gesture of prayer. Then she poured more wine for herself, and took a sip.

'As in full of holes. If Katie Arkwright were ill, she wouldn't have gone off by herself. She wouldn't have left St John's to pick up drugs or anything else, knowing she wouldn't be allowed to return to the ball. And in any case – and this applies to all four explanations – it's not the going that's the mystery; it's why she hasn't turned up yet. Leaving a May Ball is eccentric. Disappearing is more sinister.'

'Do you think she might have come to harm?' Helen asked. Suddenly real danger took the place of a puzzle.

'I hope not,' I said. 'But the police station and the casualty ward are on my agenda for later tonight.'

'A sobering thought,' Helen said, and set her wine glass firmly on the table.

When I was eight years old in Bristol, I challenged a friend to a cross-over race down the lane that ran behind my house. Cross-over meant that you had to ride your bicycle with right hand clutching the left handlebar and left hand clutching the right. I won. It was my first experience of what a teacher at the grammar school termed a Pyrrhic victory. As we crossed the finishing line, level with Mr Candleford's greenhouse, I hit a bump and flew off the bike, cracking my collarbone on the rutted surface of the lane. I was driven to hospital. The scents and smells and sensations of that day are still with me. I was pinioned by the pain; fearful of needles; wide-eyed at being the centre of attention. But I had every faith, as did my parents, that the National Health Service would see me right.

The NHS was still, in those days, the glory of the nation. It had been a triumph for the people, a reward for their sufferings during World War II. By my own generation, it was applauded still. The National Health Service was the institution that softened the hard edges of the British class system – that minimised the impact of ferocious inequality on the facts of life and death.

Whatever shortcomings have become visible in recent decades – however un-patient-friendly the procedures of the NHS, however unresponsive its consultants, however trifling its commitment to preventive care – the NHS stands for a noble attempt to create a nation in which no one need die for lack of medical insurance.

The kind of nation, that is, in which I prefer to live.

But this attachment to the NHS doesn't make me sanguine when confronted with an actual hospital. At busy times of day, in casualty departments, I find the distress and derangement, the anxiety, the crowds, the indignity – above all, the impotence in the face of suffering – to be more than I can bear.

I timed my arrival at the casualty department of New Addenbrooke's carefully so that the automatic doors opened to admit me just after ten p.m. It's a quiet time: beyond the hour when domestic accidents push family members to seek emergency help; before the stream of injuries that flow from pub closing time.

I got it right. When I rolled in, there were only three other visitors in sight. The nurse who checks patients in and assesses their level of need was speaking to a girl whose baby lolled listlessly in a pushchair; on the infant's pale, plump cheek was a hideous-looking cluster of blisters. From where I was standing, they looked like burns. Probably the nurse saw it that way too; although the mother demanded in a furious voice to see a doctor about her own medication, the admissions nurse was quietly insistent on examining the child.

Beyond the nursing station, an elderly woman sat rigidly upright on a metal chair with a face made desolate by the prospect of loss. Her husband, I later overheard, was being treated for heart failure.

Near the drinks machine sat a youth wearing a scruffy Kappa sweatshirt and an even scruffier beard. He looked me over as I entered, consulted his clipboard, and jotted something down.

A notice warned that the current waiting time for treatment was half an hour.

39

I chose not to queue up behind the blistered baby. Instead, I got a Coke from the machine and seated myself next to the fellow with the flimsy beard. He shifted uneasily and kept his eyes glued to the clipboard.

'Sorry,' I said. 'Am I crowding you?'

'Pardon?' He asked the question as if he hadn't, until that second, registered my presence.

'By sitting here, when there are empty seats all around?' I offered him an explanation. 'You see, I reckon you're keeping track of the comings and goings in the department – doing research. And since I'm looking for someone, I wonder whether you can help.'

He dropped his pencil in astonishment. 'How did you know?' he asked.

'Well, you're not a reporter.' I picked up the pencil and returned it to him. 'Not dressed for it.' Besides, what reporter would be so scrupulous in recording mundane events? 'You're not a hospital auditor – not with that *Trainspotting* clipboard. So what's left?'

'How do you know I'm not a novelist, soaking up local colour?' he asked hopefully.

I considered. 'Most writers I know do their medical research by watching *ER*.'

'Well, you're right,' he said, lowering his voice. 'I'm a student. This is a project for my research methods class. Non-participant observation.' He jerked his head towards the front desk. 'Do you think they've figured it out?'

'If they've noticed you at all, they've figured it out.' The anxiety that flashed into his face at the thought of their reaction took ten years off his appearance, making him look – even with the beard – like a little boy in fancy dress. 'They won't mind,' I assured him. 'Most people – honest people – are flattered to be the subjects of research. Next step, they hope, will be a fly-on-the-wall documentary, with them in a starring role.' I looked towards the front desk. 'But most likely, they haven't even noticed you.'

'I've been here for twelve hours,' he protested. No man likes to be invisible. He'd gone, in less than a minute, from uneasiness about exposure to anxiety at being overlooked.

'Don't take it personally. People who work in Casualty learn to focus only on the patient they're dealing with at that moment. That way, they can't be overwhelmed by the distress in the room. Mind if I ask you a question?'

'Sure,' he said. 'Just a second.' He scribbled, *Interrupted, 10.09* on the bottom of his notes.

'While you've been here, has a young woman wearing a white evening gown come into the department?'

'What, walked in, do you mean? Or been carried in on a stretcher?'

Either would do.

'Not that I can recall,' he said. 'But it's been a long day. The best thing is if I go through my notes.' There were pages and pages, all carefully clipped together.

I promised to check back later.

The nurse was trying still to get a coherent story from the baby's mother. I by-passed her and went straight to reception. A heavy-jawed woman with a brown Cleopatra bob, every hair glazed into position, was running through entries on a database. I rested my elbow on the counter and waited as she scrolled through. She seemed to pause occasionally to scan an entry in more depth, and then move on. She didn't do anything with the material. Just kept flicking through.

After a full minute – carefully monitored on the departmental clock – I interrupted. 'Excuse me,' I said. I might as well have been that fly on the wall for all the attention I got. Another twenty seconds and four more screenfuls of data passed, and still no reply.

'Can you help me?' I couldn't keep my voice free from the gritty edge of irritation.

She looked up at me, through a dark fringe of hair. She didn't smile. 'Number,' she said.

'I beg your pardon?'

'Number. From the assessment nurse.'

'I didn't see the nurse. Don't need a doctor. But I'd like to ask a question.'

She said nothing – not yes, not no – but she did remove her fingers from the keyboard. I slid my question through this window of opportunity.

'I'm making inquiries on behalf of St John's College. A student has gone missing.' Katie wasn't a St John's student, but a little ambiguity wouldn't hurt. 'Have you admitted a young woman named Arkwright – Katie Arkwright – at any time since eleven p.m. last night?'

'I only came on duty this afternoon,' the computer addict said. Her glance yearned in the direction of the screen.

'You have records. Could you check them? Please.'

She sighed with such force that her fringe actually fluttered above the unfriendly eyes. Medical confidentiality wasn't mentioned. Can't-be-bothered seemed to be the issue here. Then – rather to my surprise – she checked. Katie Arkwright's name didn't appear.

'Any unknowns?'

An elderly man with a shaky grip on his own identity had been brought in. But that was all.

I exchanged thumbs-down signals with the bearded student on my way out. He'd not found her; nor had I. If Katie Arkwright had come to harm after leaving the May Ball – if she had been injured or maimed or fallen ill – she hadn't, apparently, ended up in Addenbrooke's.

Was no news good news? Not necessarily.

But at least it wasn't bad.

At Parkside Police Station, I bumped into two uniformed officers whom I knew slightly, lurking about after the end of their shift. They entertained me with highlights from May Week.

There'd been silliness enough to last a lifetime.

At the Mill Pond, in the wee small hours of the morning, three people who had overdone the champagne had been lectured on the dangers of swimming while inebriated. The biggest danger, of course – as they'd find out soon enough – was a bacterium that would leave them with a raging fever almost as soon as their hangovers had passed.

On East Road, a woman who might – or might not – have been soliciting had been hassled by a group of party-goers, until a passing patrol car moved them all on.

And on Coe Fen, police officers had responded to a report that a man was abusing a cow. The cow in question, they discovered, had got its head firmly wedged in a garbage bin. The man – a postgraduate student with a penchant for operetta – was serenading it with tunes from *The Mikado*.

Standard stuff for May Week. If it had ended here, the police would have been cynical – *silly buggers*, they would say – rather than heartsore.

But there were other, less easily managed, complaints.

Two caterers coming off shift had been road-raged; a car had driven alongside, threatening to bump them, after they'd slowed down for a moped on the Madingley Road. They'd been inches away from collision.

A couple who were strolling home from a ball had been savagely set upon by an attacker who seemed not to share the party spirit.

And police had been called to quell trouble after a spontaneous gathering on Grantchester Meadows finished in uproar. So many students had drunk themselves into a stupor that the ambulance services were tied up for a considerable time carting them off to hospital. A nurse had been assaulted and the language of the students had – that was the claim – shocked even the medical staff.

So it hadn't all been good clean fun.

But no young woman answering to the name or description of Katie Arkwright had come to police attention. The police, like the hospital, provided me with no bad news.

My final job that evening was on the telephone. I rang Stevie, intending to find out whether she'd opened the gates of St John's

43

for Katie's exit. I fancied a sip of whisky, and wasn't averse to a late-night gossip, either. Before I dialled, I poured a thimbleful of Macallan into a tumbler and set it next to the telephone, just in case.

Prudent. But, as it turned out, unnecessary. Stevie wasn't in. Or she was in and she wasn't answering. Maybe she was down the local disco, eyeing up the talent. Maybe she was in the shower and couldn't hear the phone. Maybe, as Helen had suggested, Stevie had gone in sequinned splendour on a camping expedition.

After the tenth ring, I abandoned my guessing game, drained my whisky, and climbed into bed. I felt a little lonely, but in spite of that, fell asleep within minutes.

And in my dreams, I slow-danced the night away.

Chapter 4

My mobile phone rang – wouldn't you know – as I was dodging traffic in the middle of Mill Road, just up from the East Road junction. I made it safely to the pavement. Behind me a car horn blasted a complaint. Instead of offering two fingers to the driver, I scrambled in my shoulder bag for the telephone.

It was Sonny. 'You're looking for me?'

'Hang on,' I said, scanning for a better spot to. carry on a conversation. A homeless man with a litre of cider and an absence of teeth was urging me with sweeping gestures to join him in the bus shelter. I declined and headed for the centre of Petersfield. On the green, all the benches were occupied. Students from Anglia – catching an early lunch and a late tan – had bared their bodies to the sun as if they'd never heard of melanoma.

I shooed away a stubborn squirrel and settled myself at the base of a chestnut tree. 'It's about the May Ball, Sonny.' It only took a minute to describe what little I knew about Katie Arkwright. 'I'm on my way to talk to her tutor at Anglia, if she's about. In case she has any idea where Katie's gone. And failing that, to get addresses for her family and friends. And then there's Katie's house. She shares with two other girls in Great Eastern Street. No one answers the phone, but I thought I'd nose around a bit and see what I can see.'

The squirrel edged towards me, reared on its hind legs, and made indignant noises. In a cartoon, this squirrel would have had its fists on its hips.

'Piss off,' I muttered. I've not been a fan of the little rodents since the time one ran up my leg at the University Botanical Gardens and gnawed on my knee. 'No, not you, Sonny.'

He let it pass. 'You've checked the hospital?'

'And the police. Nothing. I suppose we should be pleased about that. But Philip Patterson – he's the Master – suggests there's some shady goings-on.'

'Shady goings-on? He didn't actually use those words, did he?'

I was forced to concede. '*A special cause for concern*, that was Patterson's phrase. *A deeply private matter.*'

I was pleased to hear a faint sound over the chatterings of my little rodent, a sound that might just be a chuckle. We'd had few conversations over the past weeks; and even in those, Sonny's sense of humour had been muted. I'd been finding that a chat without a chuckle, let alone a laugh, wasn't quite the same.

Sonny was amused, apparently, by Patterson's choice of phrase. In our line of work, *cause for concern* is as common as muck – why else hire an inquiry agent? And any problem that can't readily be referred to official agencies is likely to be labelled *private*. Sonny wasn't any more impressed than I.

'I suppose it was *delicate*, as well?' he asked.

'Delicate as Dresden china. The skeletons in this particular closet have to be dusted with care. Before I do anything much, I'm instructed to lend an ear to Stephen Fox, who has a story to tell about Katie Arkwright.'

'Who's Stephen Fox?'

'Senior Tutor at St Bartholomew's.'

'But I thought Katie disappeared from—'

'You thought right. St John's. I don't yet know how Bart's comes into the picture, but I should be able to tell you later this afternoon, after I meet up with Fox. Anyway, this is a two-college case. Or perhaps I should say, a three-college case, since Katie Arkwright isn't a Bart's student, she's—'

'At Anglia. Yes. You said.'

No chuckles now. Was that a touch of impatience in Sonny's voice?

'So?' he asked.

A graceless question. I didn't grace it with a response.

'So,' Sonny continued after a second's silence, while the squirrel advanced on me with menaces, 'what do you want with me?'

At that moment, a high-pitched siren started up on the other side of the junction. The doors of the fire station rumbled open, just out of my line of sight, and one and then another fire engine careered out into the traffic, and jumped the lights on to Mill Road. The noise of the sirens was in keeping with my own sense of alarm.

What do I want with you?

Well, if you don't know by now, Sonny . . .

I didn't say it. I retreated instead to my just-the-facts voice. Stuck to the case in hand.

'Wednesday evening, Sonny. Cast your mind back. Did you see a girl who fits the description—'

'There were six hundred girls, Laura.'

'Nineteen years old?' I persisted. 'Blonde curly hair, dressed all in white?'

'Uh-uh.'

'Katie Arkwright left the ball just after eleven o'clock. Taking off early like that, she might have stood out. I've been hoping that you or Stevie noticed her departure. Better still, saw what happened to prise her out of the party mood.'

'Not me,' Sonny said. 'Every guest at the ball passed by me at some point during the night. But I can't put a face to the name.'

Sonny's voice was wearing its time-to-go tone.

'Got to ring off, Laura. I'm just turning into Stansted Airport. Catching a flight to Amsterdam, remember?'

I couldn't think of anything to say.

'See you,' Sonny said. 'Love.'

The word hung in the air like a wet sheet on a windless day, heavy and flat. When Sonny said *love*, he wasn't referring to me. Love in this case was like *best wishes* or *ta-ta* – nothing more than a signing-off phrase. And like *kiss-kiss* – another signing-off phrase that I detest – it was no substitute at all for the real thing.

Suddenly a figure stood over me, blocking out the sun. The squirrel was forced to find another base. It was the toothless man again, the one who had offered me a seat in the bus shelter.

I could have done without this, now, in my current undecided state. 'You want something?' I asked, more abruptly than was fair.

He wanted money. For a drink, he said.

Part of me recoiled from buying a cider for a man who was in such obvious need of a solid meal. But maybe, I thought, maybe even I would opt for booze over mince and two veg if I'd lost my home and my teeth. I stood up, found a rare two-pound coin in my jacket pocket, and passed it over.

If he'd had teeth, he might have bitten down on the coin, like a pirate in an old film. As it was, he examined it closely and then tossed me a big gummy smile. 'Oh, you are beautiful, my darlin'.' He laid his weather-worn hand on my shoulder. 'Here, darlin', lovely lady, here's a kiss to thank you.'

The last person to kiss me when I wasn't looking to be kissed was my Uncle Stuart, and that was a long time ago. I had no intention of waiving the rules of consent for present company. I warded him off. His self-esteem seemed to survive my rebuff, since he shuffled off cheerfully enough in the direction of Cambridge Wine Merchants.

But the old fellow's invitation had a useful side-effect. It propelled me towards a decision.

I pulled in to Stansted Airport not long before boarding time. Sonny was still in the main concourse. He was working at the coffee bar, legs stretched out, chewing in time to his thoughts. He appeared to be studying a photograph. I watched him for a moment, torn between a rush of affection, and the wall that his coldness had built between us. But while I stood there, rooted in uncertainty, Sonny looked up and spotted me.

'What happened to Katie Arkwright's tutor?' he asked. For someone who seemed to be avoiding me lately, he'd taken very keen notice of my schedule.

'She can wait,' I said. 'And Katie Arkwright can wait too. I'd rather see you.' I climbed on to the stool next to his. The barman was hovering as if he wanted to join in the conversation. I waved him away, and helped myself to a calamari from Sonny's plate.

Sonny asked me one or two desultory questions about Katie Arkwright. I let the half-hearted interrogation peter out, and then got down to business.

'It's a funny thing, Sonny, when a woman has to travel all the way to the airport to spend a bit of time with her bloke.'

He was expecting this. Didn't have to marshal an answer, it was ready and waiting. 'Nonsense, Laura. We were together, more or less, all Wednesday night—'

'Not what the Rolling Stones meant by spending the night together,' I interrupted.

'Pardon?' he said. A stalling tactic.

'You – stationed on the Bridge of Sighs. Me – careering from crisis to crisis. It was work, Sonny, not play. And you left Cambridge – you know you did – the moment the duties were over.'

A trace of guilt shaded his features, but it was quickly chased away by irritation. 'Someone has to look after the London office, Laura. Someone has to keep things ticking over – make sure the wages are paid, answer enquiries. What do you think would happen to the business if I lolled around Cambridge all the time too?'

Loll?

When Sonny and I had become business partners, I'd been reluctant to give up my house in Cambridge and my networks there. We'd agreed that I would try to build up a caseload in Cambridge and work from there as much as possible. So far, the strategy had been a success. I pulled in more and more jobs from the city and from surrounding areas, and I'd thought we were agreed that this arrangement was a good thing.

But the term *loll* suggested something less than a consensus.

'Are you implying that I don't pull my weight, Sonny? Who deals with the Inland Revenue, then? And VAT? Who takes care of advertising? Who trained Desiree? Who chases overdue payments? Who—'

The barman was swishing his cloth closer and closer to our spot along the stainless-steel counter. 'Get you anything?' he asked.

I stopped my series of questions. Ordered a roast beef sandwich with mustard mayonnaise. There's nothing like a quarrel to make me hungry. 'And a green salad, with French dressing.'

'Nothing more for me, thanks,' Sonny said. 'I'll have the bill.' He began putting his papers away in the briefcase.

'I hoped we might talk, Sonny.'

The barman leaned towards me, trying to catch my eye. 'Anything to drink?' he asked.

'It's overdue,' Sonny said. He was referring to the prospect of our talking, not to the flight. 'But I've got to go through to departures now.'

I pointed to the departures monitor above the bar, to the space where *DELAY* had just settled on to the screen. Sonny checked it out, and then folded himself back on to the stool. I could see, in the shape of his shoulders, that he was steeling himself for a row.

'Orange juice,' I ordered, hoping the barman would drift away before there was an explosion.

And then I decided to try and steer a more peaceful course.

'That photo you were looking at when I arrived. Was it Amsterdam? Have you found a site for the office?'

Only a second's pause. Then Sonny's posture relaxed. He opened the briefcase, extracted a large folder, and replaced his briefcase beside the stool. He took a photocopied image from the folder and passed it to me.

The image proved to be an enlargement of a black-and-white photo. It was pale and cloudy, short on definition. There was a bed – a hospital bed, judging by the narrow gauge and metal headboard, and by the sharpness of the sheets. A pair of arms emerged from tightly folded linen. They were not a smooth colour as flesh should be, but deeply blotched with black and grey and charcoal. One wrist seemed to be bound by a bracelet, the mark of which stood out bright and hard; on closer inspection, it was a line of darkly discoloured flesh, not a piece of jewellery. The fingernails on both hands were ragged and darkened. And the face. It was a woman's face. Probably young. That's judging by the chinline. You couldn't read her age, or anything else for that matter, from her features.

A black-and-white image isn't only black and white, of course, as everyone knows. It consists of many shades – dozens, hundreds, in some cases, thousands – blends of black and white producing subtle differences in effect, making it possible to pick out the ghosts of colours even without knowing precisely what they are.

That's what the face was like. Crowded with ghosts. Ghosts of cheekbone; phantoms of eyebrow and chin and lip. It was a spectral face, hidden beneath contusions and bruises, within splits of skin where raw flesh was exposed, drowned in the reservoirs of blood that pooled beneath the surface.

Whoever she was, she'd been beaten to a pulp.

One thing was obvious. 'That wasn't done by fists alone.'

'There was no weapon used. Not directly, anyway.' Sonny paused.

'Meaning?'

'Her attacker wore a large ring. With a raised metal surface. The effect, according to the doctor, would be like one of those ridged hammers you use to break down the tissues in a slab of steak.'

'You mean a meat tenderiser,' I said.

The barman brought my roast beef sandwich. I pushed it to one side.

'Who is she?'

'She was christened Linda Parfleet. Better known to clients as Cindy Sinful. Cindy the Saucy Schoolgirl.'

'Schoolgirl for real?'

'What do you think?' Sonny's tone was the verbal equivalent of rolling his eyes. 'Ms Sinful left her convent school a full five years ago. She's twenty-one.'

'It's amazing how many punters are persuaded by a gymslip.'

'To be fair' . . . Sonny said.

Fair? To punters who go for little girls?

. . . 'before this happened to Cindy, she looked awfully young for her age. With puppy fat, and crooked teeth, and huge round eyes.'

I glanced again at the photo. Cindy's eyelids were swollen to such an extent that there was scarcely a depression marking the eye sockets.

'Yeah,' Sonny said, following my drift. 'If they'd got to it sooner, they might have saved her right eye, in spite of the damage. But he locked her in the boot of the car. She wasn't found until morning.'

'She's alive then.'

'In a way.'

He picked up my sandwich and nibbled on the fringe of beef that laced the edges. 'Your lunch, Laura,' he reminded me.

I wasn't hungry any more. 'Is Cindy a client?'

Sonny looked in the direction of the monitors.

I checked his flight number – it was still marked *DELAY* – and prodded.

'Why are you carrying her picture?'

Sonny took the roundabout route to an answer. The attack that cost Cindy her right-side vision occurred last October, he explained. For Cindy, business had been slow, not many telephone callers. She needed extra money quick, so she decided to do a few cars. When a newish BMW pulled up, clean-cut guy inside, open and friendly, Cindy thought her ship had come in. She agreed a price and settled into the leather passenger seat. 'She directed him to her room, which was only half a mile away,' Sonny explained, 'but he turned towards the open road. She objected. She struggled. She smashed a side window with her high heel.'

'Cindy put up a decent fight.'

'She did. But then the punter ended her resistance with a blow that flattened her. Probably the blow that did her cheekbone.

Here.' Sonny pointed to the photo, his finger gently stroking the lurid discoloration that was once a cheek. 'Then, in a lay-by near the start of the motorway, he did the rest to her. It looks as if that's what he'd wanted from the start.'

'And then?'

'Then he tipped her into the boot of the car, and abandoned them both.'

'The BMW was stolen?'

'Yup,' Sonny agreed. 'And Cindy's a lucky girl to have been found alive. A truck driver stopped, very early morning, to stretch his legs. He was surprised to see an abandoned BMW in the middle of nowhere.'

'And even more surprised when he heard scraping noises coming from the boot?'

'How did you know that?'

'Look at her fingernails,' I said.

Sonny still hadn't told me what his connection was with Cindy. Then, with a sinking feeling, I knew.

'You're acting for the guy who drove the BMW?' I wanted Sonny to deny it, but he didn't. 'For the punter?' I couldn't keep the astonishment from my voice. 'For the bastard who did this? Sonny, for Christ's sake, what is the point?'

'What do you mean, what is the point?'

'Of having our own agency. Sure, you take a job with Microsoft, you do as Bill Gates says; you work for Murdoch, you ignore human rights violations in China; you get an executive position with McDonald's, you don't join a march against meat. But God damn it, Sonny – one of the perks of working for yourself is that you can choose your cases. You don't have to represent every bastard who waves a cheque in your face.'

'Hold on a minute, Laura. You're jumping the gun. I'm looking for defence evidence to clear an innocent man. The fellow who's been charged is Trevor Wallace. He's not a bastard, he's a respectable businessman—'

'Respectable businessman,' I snorted. I held up the photo of

Cindy. 'You think this little performance deserves a Queen's Award for industry?'

Sonny stood up and shrugged himself back into his jacket. He picked up his briefcase.

'Wallace didn't do it,' he said.

I checked the monitor. Gate 8 was indicated, alongside his flight number. Now boarding.

I took a deep breath. The alarms were ringing once again in my head; I was shaken with the sense that something irreversible was about to happen. We used to talk about everything, Sonny and I. Disagree, yes. Sometimes even shout at one another. But always talk, talk, talk – until the disagreement itself was a link between us. Something we'd gone through together.

'Got to go, Laura.' He started to move in the direction of Gate 8.

'Sonny,' I whispered. I grabbed my bag and raced after him. 'Haven't finished,' I called over my shoulder to the barman. 'Be right back.'

I caught up with Sonny as he reached the gate. 'Wait. Sonny, I'm sorry. Like you said, we need to talk.'

He didn't seem to soften, but he did stand still.

'How about coming up to Cambridge next weekend?' Into the barely perceptible pause that followed, I inserted a quick plea. 'Bring the boys.'

Sonny's children, Dominic and Daniel, live during the week with their mother, Morag. Before his current bout of workaholism, they had spent more weekends than not with their father. And occasionally – trying, difficult, wonderful times – with me.

'You know how keen they are to try go-karting. We could do that. It would be like a holiday, Sonny. You've been so busy lately. They must have missed you too.'

Sonny set his briefcase down on the tiles, and as if with a sudden decision, gathered me in his arms. Maybe the fact that he was about to fly away made it easier for him.

'Only four more months, Laura. It won't be forever. Four more months to get the money together. If we don't succeed – well, we

54

might as well go back to twopenny-halfpenny cases. Or find some other line of work. One way or another, it'll soon be over.'

He kissed me. At that point I might have considered a job in a BSE-infected abattoir to get him the money he needed. But he quickly disentangled himself, picked up the case again, and turned to go.

I touched his arm. 'Next weekend?'

Sonny smiled enough of the wide, generous smile that I used to know to make me feel hopeful. 'Can't manage the go-karts,' he said. 'Morag's taking the boys to their grandfather's place at the weekend. And anyway, I've got stuff lined up in Amsterdam. But I've got a couple of days clear next week. How about if I come Tuesday evening and stay the night?'

I returned to the counter, smiling a little. I expected to find – at best – that my food had been whisked away, and, at worst, that they had alerted airport security about my failure to pay.

Instead, my roast beef sandwich sat primly in its place. Cutlery stood to attention on either side. There was fresh ice in the orange juice. The salad hadn't wilted. I felt like Beauty when she wanders into the Beast's palace and finds that dinner has been served.

I banished from my mind the image of Cindy Sinful's face, and tucked in.

OK, I'd jumped the gun, I acknowledged to myself. Been too quick to assume that the man arrested for doing Cindy over had to be the perpetrator. But it's easy to make a mistake like that. The fact that Trevor Wallace had been charged indicated that there was enough evidence stacked against him to convince the Crown Prosecution Service, at least. And Sonny couldn't have been on the case more than a few days. What could he have learned that would make him so certain that Trevor Wallace was a respectable businessman rather than a criminally violent one?

I wished I'd had time to ask this question. Wished Sonny'd hung around to tell.

The barman was moving down the counter again, eddying his cloth rapidly towards me. Glancing at me sideways, through lashes unusually long for a man. He was probably looking for an explanation of why I'd dashed off with my food still untouched – and that fresh ice in my orange juice meant that he was entitled.

'You didn't tip my lunch in the bin,' I said, when his cloth reached my spot on the counter. 'Thank you.'

'That's because I was hoping you'd return.'

He shuffled a little, maybe with embarrassment, and then he popped the question. It was so unexpected, I had to ask him to repeat it. But it came out more or less the same the second time around.

'That girl you were talking about,' he said. 'It was Katie Arkwright, wasn't it? From Histon?'

'That's where her mother lives. Must be the same Katie Arkwright. How do you know her?'

'We grew up together in Histon,' said the barman. 'We used to go out when she was fifteen, I was sixteen. Go to the cinema together.'

An expression came over his face – nostalgic pride? It was like the look you see on the faces of Manchester United fans when they're reminded of Eric Cantona. 'She was really something,' he recalled.

'Something? What's your name, by the way?'

'Matt Hamley.'

'Laura Principal. What do you mean by *something*?'

'What I mean is, Katie was – you know – not just pretty. She was spectacular. The kind of girl that guys think, a babe like that'll never have anything to do with me.'

'She liked you?'

Matt Hamley – who was no slouch himself in the looks department – blushed. 'We were – you know – good friends,' he said.

I compared descriptions with him, and sure enough, the details matched. It was my Katie. I asked him to tell me about her.

Matt did a quick survey of the counter, confirming that he wasn't neglecting his customers. 'What do you want to know?'

I went through a list. 'How long you went out together. When

56

you last saw her. About her friends, or boys she goes out with now. What kind of girl she is. That's for starters,' I said.

'Just a minute.' Matt picked up the coffee pot, and went to the other side of the kidney-shaped counter, where he poured fresh cups for two men who were eating fishcakes as they checked a pile of receipts. He was back in half a minute. 'Sorry about that,' he said over his shoulder, depositing the coffee pot once again on the hotplate. 'Why are you interested in all this? Do you mind me asking?'

'Not in the least.' I showed him my identification. Katie had not been seen since she left a party unexpectedly two nights ago, I explained. I was trying to track her down. I wanted to find out where she'd gone, make sure she was all right. 'Would leaving a ball like that have been in character with the Katie that you knew?'

'Hard to say.' Matt took up a fresh cloth and polished a bundle of cutlery while he considered Katie's character. 'In a way, no. You'd have to feel pretty independent to go like that, to leave your friends behind. And Katie – well, Katie didn't really like to do anything that made her stand out. She liked to be the same as the other kids. You know what I mean? In a café, she'd wait until everyone had decided, more or less, what they were going to order before she'd say what she wanted. And she'd always have the same as everybody else.'

'She needed to fit in?'

'Well, I guess we all do. It was more than that, really. She seemed almost – well, fearful, of being different. I never could make much sense of it. Like, there she was – a knock-out, with a face like an angel, and legs up to here—' He paused, bowled over, once again, by his mental image of Katie.

'But still unsure of herself, you mean. Low self-esteem.'

'That's it. She thought she wasn't good enough. Like her hair wasn't right. Or she was fat. Or she wasn't bright enough. To tell you the truth, it got me down. One of the things I learned, dating Katie, is that I kinda prefer to hang out with girls who are a bit more—' He paused, searching for the right word.

57

'Confident?' I suggested.

'Uncomplicated,' he said.

'Matt, you knew Katie for – how long?'

'We went out together for a few weeks,' he said. 'But I knew her, as a friend, you know – around – from primary school until . . . Well, I suppose until I got the job here, and she went to university. I haven't bumped into her recently. But before that, I guess I knew her pretty well.'

'I'd be interested to know why she felt so unsure of herself. Any ideas?'

'Dunno. Well, the thing with her dad didn't help,' Matt said. 'Last year – did you know this? – her parents split up. She was really attached to her father, you see, thought the world of him, and she always thought that if her parents ever separated, he'd take her with him.'

'And he didn't?'

'No. He just moved out one day. Said Katie had to stay with her mother, that her mother needed her. Katie seemed – sort of crushed.'

A customer caught Matt's attention, a man in a stiff grey suit. 'Bet he wants soup of the day and a white roll,' he said in a low voice, before he nipped around the counter to take the order. Being a betting woman – sometimes – I strained my ears. Sure enough, cream of broccoli soup and a roll with butter.

'How did you do that?' I asked when he returned. 'How did you know what he was going to order?'

'Easy,' Matt said. 'He comes in every day. Order never varies.' He pointed to the departures monitor. 'That man you were talking to, earlier on. He's in the air now.' A chime of curiosity crept into his voice. 'Is he a private investigator, too?'

'We're partners,' I said.

'Partners?' Matt said, as if that were really something to think about.

Chapter 5

Cambridge enjoys world renown. Its ancient university is an internationally recognised symbol of scholarly excellence. The city glows in reflected glory.

Every year, as a result, three and a half million tourists come to visit. They gaze at the colleges, catch the choir in King's College Chapel, meander along the Backs, or ride in the open top of a double-decker bus. They take afternoon tea – a practice more or less abandoned by the English – in Aunties Tea Shop, or The Little Tea Room, or Henry's. They browse in the bookshops and purchase postcards. Then they go off on further jaunts to Stratford-upon-Avon, or Edinburgh, or Cornwall.

You can find people the world over who are familiar with the image and sometimes the detail of the city of Cambridge. Who possess miniature jars of jam from the National Trust Shop on King's Parade or hand-stencilled T-shirts from Magdalene Bridge; who recognise the lions on the flanks of the Fitzwilliam Museum; whose minds drift to the thought of a punt on the River Cam – and who know enough to populate that punt with a young man in a waistcoat and straw boater, and a girl in a floppy-brimmed hat.

But these same people, these admirers of the city, would be hard pressed to recognise the part of central Cambridge that Katie Arkwright called home.

It's not that Great Eastern Street is far from the tourist route on King's Parade. A brisk walker could cover the ground in twenty-five minutes. Could cut through the market and then follow St Andrew's Street; cross Parker's Piece on the diagonal; pick up

Mill Road at the crossroads and then trace its length until it forms a hill beneath which trains rumble in and out of Cambridge station. Ascend this hill – this railway bridge – and at the peak, if you crane your neck, you see the backs of the houses on the near side of Great Eastern Street. When Mill Road dips down again, take a left along the side of the Earl of Stamford public house, and you're there.

Great Eastern Street is a dead-end street that runs at right angles to Mill Road. Its terraced houses, dating from the 1880s, are built to a narrow, no-nonsense design. Each has a door that opens directly on to the pavement; each has a sash window on the ground floor and another window, of identical size and shape, above. The houses on one side back on to the railway; those on the other side, where Katie lived, have long, narrow gardens that are divided by a brick wall from those on Cavendish Road.

Cambridge has grown steadily in recent decades. Homes like these, near the city centre – homes that enable their occupants to walk or cycle to work, rather than to spend the rush hour in traffic jams – have become increasingly desirable. In the mid-1970s, you could buy a house around here, not yet done up – that is, without central heating or modern wiring, perhaps even without an indoor toilet – for £7000. Today, even on a street where the sounds of the railway encroach on the peace of a summer's day, £70,000 would be nearer the mark.

These changing fortunes can be read within the street itself. Some houses look from the outside as if they might be waiting for photographers from *Architectural Weekly*: doors glossed an aristocratic blue; handmade louvred shutters; arrangements of petunias and aurelia in terracotta tubs; skylights puncturing newly slated rooflines. Others have the net half-curtains and the fractured paintwork that suggest they might just be waiting for modernisation still. On Great Eastern Street, hard-up students and old people with paltry pensions rub brick shoulders, so to speak, with up-and-coming professionals. For the civil servants and computer analysts, house purchase here is a step on to a rising escalator; they will soon move up and away to Mawson

Road or Victoria Park, to other streets in other parts of Cambridge where their middle-class credentials need never be in doubt.

The house that Katie Arkwright rented was blatantly a student house. All the signs were there: the sitting room converted to a bedroom now, the length of Indian madras tacked over the window, the wall scored at waist height where a sequence of students had scraped their cycles against the blackened brick.

There was no doorbell. I tapped. I removed my loafer and used the leather heel to make a more insistent noise. I waited. In vain.

The upper part of the door was pierced by a vertically mounted letter-box. It was big enough to spy through. I held the metal flap open with my fingers and took a long, hard look.

The front door of Katie's house gave straight on to a narrow hallway. There was a scattering of bills and flyers splayed across dark-stained floorboards. Hooks to the left of the door held a jacket and a clutch of carrier bags. The place had a musty, shut-up feel. The upstairs area was dark, without sign of light or life. At the end of the downstairs corridor, the door to the kitchen stood ajar; beyond, there was silence.

I put my nose to the opening. Recoiled from a sharp, unpleasant scent – the acrid smell of urine, and something else. Something darker and meatier and more unpleasant.

Suddenly, from inside the house, there was a high-pitched quarrelsome sound. A staccato complaint. Then a quick thumping rhythm, like a forefinger on a bongo drum. It was moving fast in my direction. I turned my gaze back towards the stairs, as a cat – a long, skinny cat, with a strange sway-shouldered gait – padded down the last few steps. She stopped a metre away from the front door and stared up at me, demanding my attention. Then she turned and trotted down the corridor. There on the floor, halfway to the kitchen, was a small mound of black fur, the size and texture of a chick. The cat nudged the fur with its nose, stepped back and looked at me over her shoulder. The querulous wailing started up again.

You didn't have to be a cat-lover to know that something was dreadfully wrong.

I put my mouth to the letter-box and shouted a hello. Not that I expected a reply. The background silence continued. The cat continued with her keening.

I gazed up and down the street, but could detect not a single sign of life. The inhabitants of Great Eastern Street were out – at work, at school, at the shops; or they were indoors, and unwilling or unable to be roused. Yet, only steps away, along the length of Mill Road, the traffic nudged and pressed and dawdled its way towards town. There was the sound of a train as it ticked along the tracks below. I could see the cyclists, pressing jerkily up the hump of the railway bridge, or coasting down towards the Broadway.

But in front of Katie's house, within sight and hearing of this hustle and bustle, the street was as silent as siesta time in an Andalusian village.

The gate that gave access to the back gardens of the terrace had a new lock with a bold metallic gleam. But locks only work if gates are closed, and this one was ever so slightly ajar. I pushed. Something an inch or two behind the gate blocked my way. I slid my hand around the edge and groped until my fingers made contact with the lip of a metal wheelbarrow. I bent over and thrust my shoulder against the lower panel of the gate. The wheelbarrow inched backwards. The movement produced a scraping sound, metal grating on rough cement, that moment-arily drowned out the grumble of a passing train.

Then the gate edged open.

Though I'd shifted the wheelbarrow backwards, its bulk still blocked the narrow passage that ran between two houses. I took a quick step up on to the barrow, crunching on a pile of cuttings, and down again on to the ground. The wheelbarrow wobbled; before it tipped, I was off and out into the sunlight at the back of the terrace.

The path ran beside and then behind eight long and narrow garden plots. Each, like the house it served, was a mere ten feet in width. The gardens were every bit as varied as the houses at the front. One was brightened by bold rows of runner beans and tubs of impatiens and petunias. You knew, even before you spotted the miniature windmill, the crazy-paving path, that this patch belonged to a dedicated gardener. Another was a grassland, wild and unkempt, but among the weeds a magnolia tree hinted at an earlier history of care. Next to it was a plot that put such a premium on privacy – the boundary marked by a tall stockade, the windows of the shed blacked out – that a mistrustful type might be moved to suspect some criminal intent. Further along was a family garden, all a-clutter with climbing frame and tricycles and rabbit hutch. At the far end, someone had begun to clear an overgrown garden. A long-handled machete was lying on a massacre of brambles, but the person doing the clearing must have gone inside to escape the afternoon heat.

As far as I could tell, every garden was empty. No gossips stood, elbows on fence, shielding their eyes from the sun and exchanging scandal. No one tended the petunias or staked the runner beans. No one picked their way along the crazy paving. No one unlocked a shed or buried bundles in a dustbin.

I was, in short, alone. Free to explore.

Katie's back garden was shielded from its neighbours. The neighbour on the right – the one who had used regal blue glosswork on his front door – had rebuilt the high brick wall between their gardens, giving it an undulating edge. The wall was pocked with portholes, each opening curtained by ivy.

This elaborate design put the decrepitude of Katie's garden – the dirty milk bottles, the bicycle for sale, the abandoned spade, the broken deckchairs – into sharp relief. Only one feature saved it from the status of wasteland. A climbing rose tumbled over the wall. Its extravagant blooms gave a lush, decadent, summery feel. When you looked at that rose, you could sense the heat of the sun, see the butterflies, hear the bumble bees.

I waited in the shadow of a ramshackle shed, to check that my movements had gone unremarked. Then I made my way to

Katie's back door. A trellis hazy with honeysuckle screened her kitchen from the neighbour.

I knocked, but not too loudly. A light breeze lifted the corner of the top newspaper in the bundle beside the door; it stood the tendrils of the honeysuckle on end. It may even have shifted the ivy in the portholes, for something seemed to whisper there.

But no one came in answer to my knock.

Through the glazing in the top half of the door, I saw the long, skinny cat trot towards me. Its eyes were frantic with need.

I went to work on the back window. Quietly, quietly, just in case. Just in case someone was sleeping in there, someone who might hear me slide a stainless-steel card into the slender gap between the two sashes. Someone who might stir. Someone who might snap awake as the latch cracked open and the sashes ran free.

That part was as easy as pie.

But the sash slid only inches and jammed. Someone had inserted screws in the frame. The window couldn't be fully opened. Very prudent, I thought. Who knows when an intruder is going to chance her arm?

The screws slowed me down, but they didn't stop me. It wouldn't be pretty, and it wouldn't be clean, but I determined to squeeze myself through. I took a deep breath, and snaked my head and shoulders through the gap between the window and the ledge. With my head and arms inside, I craned my neck up like a lizard taking the sun, and glanced around.

It was a bed-sitting room. Even with the curtains drawn, I could make out walls painted salmon pink, cream-coloured furnishings, a pale slab of worktop with a friendly clutter of papers, a feather in a glass vase, a salmon-coloured paperweight. The bed was unoccupied, the duvet straightened, the pillows plumped. This room, I was willing to bet, belonged to Katie.

I wriggled forward, until the bottom of my ribcage pressed into the window ledge. Drew a breath for another push forward and heard in the silence that followed a heavy rush of movement. Someone had come up behind me, out of my line of sight.

It was a male voice, phlegmy, low-pitched.

'What the hell are you doing?'

The tone was pure poison. I could smell cigarette smoke, and sun cream, and sweat.

It crossed my mind just to keep going. To wriggle frantically forward, to collapse on to the floor, to pick myself up and race out on to the street and away. Without speaking, without showing my face. Even if he could make it through the gap between the sash and the window ledge, he'd be far behind me, and if he used the conventional route – down the path and through the tunnel and out on to Great Eastern Street – I'd be long gone before he hit the pavement. Like a child who snatches sweets and then scarpers, I would've been spotted, but I would've escaped.

'You get on your feet right this minute,' the voice ordered.

And I did.

Because, stuck there on the window ledge, my head and chest inside, my hips and legs in the garden, bum sticking up in the air, I felt too vulnerable for flight. All he'd have to do would be to grab my ankle, or some other protuberant part of me, as I tried to wriggle off. I didn't want to encourage that kind of contact.

So I shimmied out backwards and stood up. Turned slowly round to face him.

He was fifty, give or take a year or two. On him fifty looked old. The eyes were pouched, the body slack. For reasons I didn't care to think about, he was carrying a hammer.

'What do you want in this house?' he said. 'You don't look like a burglar.'

I smiled my most honest-looking smile – an important asset in my line of work – and lied through my teeth.

'I'm afraid I've lost my keys. I left them on the kitchen table when I went out this morning, and wouldn't you know—'

'I'm going to call the police,' he interrupted. 'You're not a tenant here.'

'How can you be so sure? Tenants come and go.'

Maybe he was bluffing.

'I'm the landlord,' he said. 'I live next door.'

If it was a bluff, it was a good one.

He was wearing tartan shorts, knee-length, and sandals made of some unnatural material that pretended to be leather. His skin was pale, like the fat on bacon, with red patches beginning to show on the shoulders. His torso was hairless except for a large tuft where his skinny neck joined his skinny chest.

Had this landlord been watching me, I wondered, from behind that elaborate wall? Could I attribute the whispering in the ivy to him, brushing aside the vines so he could get a better look?

'I'll tell you the truth,' I said. 'It's the cat. Katie – Katie Arkwright?'

His bottom lip was pushed out in an expression of mistrust, but he nodded in recognition at the name.

'Well, she's gone away, you see, for a few days. She left a message, asking me to take care of Puss. But she forgot to leave the keys.' I shrugged, a you-see-the-problem sort of gesture. 'I had to get in somehow.'

But he didn't see the problem. Not yet. 'Why couldn't the others feed the cat?'

The others?

'Oh, you mean her housemates? They're away. At a wedding. On the south coast.' For a lie, it had the ring of truth.

His lip retreated to something like a normal position. He was melting.

'So you see . . .'

He put his face to the kitchen window, observed for himself the emptiness. There was a scratching on the inside of the kitchen door, and that wretched mewling sound again.

'Oh, my God.' His voice was anguished. 'The kitten.'

Fumbling now with anxiety, he took a key from a ring on his belt, and unlocked the back door. The long, skinny cat bolted at us, and wrapped herself around our legs.

In the kitchen, next to a lumpy litter tray, was an empty bowl. Next to that was an empty saucer. No food, no water. I checked the back door. No cat flap.

'Follow me,' I said. I led him to the hallway, where a little black bundle of fur huddled beneath the radiator. The kitten was dead.

He carried it outside to examine it in the daylight. It was still dead. He cradled it against his chest. 'She couldn't feed it,' he said, indicating the cat. 'This kitten was the only one in the whole litter that survived. Katie had an eyedropper. She said she'd look after it. She promised,' he muttered, and his bottom lip inched forward again.

That lip reminded me of Jean-Paul Belmondo. Nothing else about him did.

Suddenly, as if the effort of holding the kitten had exhausted him, he placed the animal in my arms and deposited himself heavily into a broken deckchair. He scrabbled in his shorts pocket, pulled out a packet of Silk Cut, took one out and lit it up. He leaned his head back and dragged deeply. Smoke dribbled out of his nose.

I ran my thumb gently down the kitten's back, feeling the tiny vertebrae under the fur. I was torn between pity and revulsion. The corpse had gone past the lovable stage.

'I'll bury it,' I said.

I fed the cat, with a tin from the cupboard and the remains of a pint of milk from the fridge. I found a shoebox under the stairs, lined it with tissues, and prepared a coffin. I poked around. On a noticeboard on the kitchen wall was pinned a cryptic schedule.

Monday, Wed. – B
Tuesday, Friday – K
Thursday, Sunday – C

A cooking rota presumably. Katie had disappeared on Wednesday evening. She'd been due to cook on Friday.

And I saw a note scribbled in purple biro.

Katie: Going home. Got to finish this essay. See you Sunday evening. B. PS I've borrowed your blue scarf. You weren't going to use it?

It was attached to the fridge with a magnet wrought in the image of Michelangelo's David. He wore a tiny pair of Calvin Klein boxers.

The landlord – whose name turned out to be Charlie Thresher – sat slumped in the deckchair, smoking.

I did a quick tour of Katie's salmon-pink room. There was a card propped on the dressing table, the kind that florists include when they deliver a bouquet. It said, *Beauties for a beauty, J.* Not an original sentiment; but even clichés can, I suppose, be heartfelt. There was a broad bookshelf. It held the usual stuff – ring-binders with lecture notes, textbooks, a folder containing essays, and stationery. All very neat and orderly. She'd got A's for her last two assignments. There were T-shirts and sweaters and underwear in the chest of drawers. There was a leotard hanging on the back of the door. There were toiletries and medications in a basket on a shelf, skirts and trousers and shoes and a suitcase, new and inexpensive, in the wardrobe.

There was nothing to indicate that Katie had packed for a long stay away. Nothing to suggest that her departure was premeditated.

There was no white dress.

In the garden, the ground was dry and hard. I dug a hole. It was, as cowgirls say, hot and dusty work. Charlie Thresher roused himself once, stood up from the deckchair and stared over my shoulder at the deepening depression. I offered him the spade, but he sat down again as if he hadn't seen, and lit up another cigarette. I buried the kitten.

He couldn't really talk until it was over. I offered to make him a cup of tea – there was still a drinkable pint of milk in Katie's fridge – but he preferred the anaesthetic effects of nicotine. We sat in Katie's back garden – on broken deckchairs, carefully – and smoked and talked. He smoked. I talked.

There's nothing like a death to bring people together.

'How are they as tenants?' I asked.

He blinked. 'I really thought she loved animals. That's why I let them have the place. Don't normally rent to students, but she

68

had that cat with her, and so . . .' He lit up another cigarette. Gave a spluttering sort of cough. And finally answered my question. 'Not bad,' he said. 'They moved in last January. They're quite pleasant girls. But some of their friends . . . I suppose you expect that with young people nowadays.'

'Anyone in particular?'

'Nah. I don't get involved.' He took another drag on his cigarette. 'You know Katie Arkwright well?' he asked.

'I wouldn't say we were close,' I said, 'though we know a lot of people in common. In fact – actually, I don't know if it's fair to ask you this.' He looked morosely at the loose pile of earth at the edge of the garden. I continued. 'I've been thinking and thinking, but I can't work out where Katie's gone. Any ideas?'

He looked up from his cigarette, and checked me out through narrowed eyes. 'I thought she asked you to feed the cat?'

'A message on the answering machine. She didn't say when she was leaving, or where she was going, or why. Kind of funny, don't you think?'

After ten awkward seconds, he spoke.

'Last time I saw Katie was Wednesday evening. She went off in a taxi. Round about six thirty. Bright daylight still. I don't know where she was going but she was dressed to the nines.'

'Wearing a white dress?'

'And what a dress!' For the first time since we discovered the kitten, he showed some animation. 'It fit really close, all the way down – figure-hugging, you might say.' He ran his hands down his baggy torso to demonstrate what figure-hugging meant, in case the whole idea was new to me. 'A sleeveless bodice, low-cut at front and back. Draped at the neckline.

'White,' he continued, shaking his head. 'Not white like a bride. More like Jean Harlow,' he said, 'out of Donna Karan.'

What a description. The surprise must have shown on my face.

'I'm a photographer,' he said, with pride. 'Portraits – naturalistic, not studio. Gritty stuff. But I've also worked on fashion catalogues. It helps to know what you're dealing with.'

'Women, you mean?'

'Clothes,' he said, looking truculent again.

Digging a grave had made the afternoon race by, and my appointment with the Senior Tutor at Bart's was looming. I slipped my feet back into my loafers, and prepared to go. 'Thank you for your help, Charlie,' I said. 'Listen, about that cab. You didn't by any chance notice the name of the taxi company?'

He cleared his throat, chasing phlegm. 'CabCo,' he said.

'Any other passengers?'

'Nope. Just the one. Just Katie.'

'And she never came back, as far as you know?'

Charlie Thresher lifted himself slowly out of the deckchair. 'Got to go,' he said, by way of explanation. 'Nope. Haven't seen hide nor hair of her or any of her friends since then. Somebody came knocking for them late last night – round about eleven. Made an awful racket. But he went away again without getting an answer.'

'Do you happen to know who it was?'

'All I could see from the window was it was a young guy. Wearing jeans and a denim jacket. He didn't look like he was any too sober.' He shrugged. 'There was always men coming round. That's what you get when you rent to girls. Specially young, pretty girls. Like cats on heat, they are. Attract every tom in sight.'

I guessed from that remark that he liked cats a lot better than he liked women. 'And how about you, Charlie? Katie looked like Jean Harlow, you said. Did you fancy her?'

It wasn't entirely a serious question. The thought of his pouched eyes and gaunt grey face in close proximity to Katie Arkwright was a bit like imagining Aristotle Onassis with the original Shirley Temple. We're talking here about the kind of gap in age and experience that even a shipping fortune couldn't bridge.

'Not my type,' he said. As if he had considered the idea seriously, and rejected it.

'Too blonde?' I asked.

'Too female,' he said, and shuffled off towards his own garden.

70

Chapter 6

Some of my friends and colleagues – Sonny, for example – have an elastic notion of time. I'll be there at eight means: if I can find my clean shirt – if the phone doesn't ring – if I don't have to stop for petrol – I'll see you within an hour. Not me. I lean the other way. Can't bear to be late. I've been known to show up for dinner parties while the hostess is still in the shower. My friends make jokes about it.

But it's not every day that you bury a kitten.

The funeral threw me off balance. The ceremony was brief – brief and tasteful, Thresher said. Even so, by the time I'd dug the excavation and filled it in again, I had a blister on my right palm and a strong need to sit awhile.

That's why I clocked in for my five o'clock appointment with Stephen Fox – Senior Tutor, St Bartholomew's College – with only seconds to spare.

The distance from Great Eastern Street to the main entrance of Bart's, on Maid's Causeway, is little more than a mile.

But what a difference a mile makes.

St Bartholomew's occupies an oblong of land to the north of New Square and just to the east of the Four Lamps roundabout. The site is central enough; it's diagonally across from Jesus College, and only a minute's walk from the bus station. But Bart's is regarded, nevertheless, as out of the run of things. Few people – certainly few tourists – take the trouble to look past the austere wall separating the college from Short Street to the beautiful buildings beyond.

This neglect is their loss. In architectural terms, St Bartholomew's is one of the most impressive of the Cambridge colleges. Its most striking features – the colonnade that fronts Maid's Causeway; the austerely beautiful Brandon Library, where only the deeply coloured bindings challenge the cool restraint; the Great Room with its magnificent dome – are among the finest examples in England of the neo-classical tradition. Its buildings are perfectly adapted in scale and line to the compact site. The design greatly enhanced the reputation of Thomas Leverton, an architect of the eighteenth century who had been in the middle rank before St Bartholomew's. Among people who know about such things (and in Cambridge, there are always people who know), it's argued that the technical knowledge and the aesthetic inspiration were supplied by Leverton's drawing assistant, Joseph Bonomi. I don't lose sleep over that sort of detail; it's enough for me to know that, whoever is responsible for the Bart's design, it clearly outclasses its rivals. Its style manages to be less slavishly Greek and more spontaneous than, for example, Downing College, built only six years later on a much more grandiose scale.

I welcomed the drop in temperature when I stepped into the elegant entrance hall. The room was cool and pale and restrained, except for the dome, which was richly decorated in gilt and turquoise. Opposite the entrance, a staircase coiled to the left, its sinuous shape underlined by a wrought-iron balustrade. From the hall, lobbies opened in two directions. I followed the route indicated on a plaque with gilt lettering. It pointed me back along the colonnade, up a smaller staircase and past the Tutorial Office, which opened on to the first-floor landing. The Senior Tutor's room perched in isolated splendour at the top.

I rapped on the heavy door.

Stephen Fox must have been waiting nearby. The oak swung back within seconds of my summons. I recognised him from our brief encounter at the St John's May Ball – not only the thick white hair, the well-toned complexion, the direct blue eyes, but also, perhaps particularly, the cool, acerbic air.

He stepped aside to let me in, and then craned his neck to check the staircase. It was empty. No people. No pets. Not even a ghost. He closed the door.

'Sit down,' he said, 'over there.' He gave no sign whatsoever of recognition.

The Senior Tutor's office was as cluttered and busy as many an undergraduate room. All around were signs of activity, of things picked up and put down, of work tasks and leisure, intertwined. There were stacks of books, higgledy-piggledy, on a side table, with a vase of flowers past their prime and a scattering of CDs. In a basket by the fireplace, on top of a stack of magazines, was a cricket bat and a pair of pads. The wall showed framed photos from university events, contemporary etchings, a mounted poster of a woman bathing from the Bonnard exhibition at the Tate. On a hook behind the door hung an academic gown. There was a pair of hiking boots too near the ancient radiator for their own good. It all looked chaotic, outgoing, vital.

The central feature in the room presented a much more rigid image. Stephen Fox's desk was solid and broad, as befits a Senior Tutor. The surface was scrupulously tidy. It held only a yellow legal pad, a leather writing case with matching pen holder, and a photograph frame which was angled away from me. There were three chairs: for the Senior Tutor, a captain's chair, the kind that bounces on a spring mechanism set just above the pedestal; a wing-back with frayed arms and a deeply-padded seat; and an upright chair with a ladder-back that looked as if the vertebrae of a sitter would clash with every rung. Death by ladder-back would be a nasty way to go.

Fox directed me to the ladder-back chair. This happens sometimes to private investigators. People shy away from making them too comfortable. I wondered what you had to do to deserve the wing-back.

Fox didn't waste a moment on preliminaries.

'Philip Patterson has asked me to fill you in on events at St

Bartholomew's. Events concerning Katie Arkwright. I take it Miss Arkwright is still missing?'

'No sign of her yet,' I confirmed.

Stephen Fox shook his head in disapproval. It was an ambiguous gesture. It might have been directed at students – whatever will they do next? It might, equally, have been intended for me. Twenty-four hours, he could have been thinking, and she still knows nothing. And there was always the possibility that it was just a nervous tic.

Except that somehow I couldn't believe that nervousness was part of Stephen Fox's repertoire. His composure was too chilly, too armour-plated, to admit of any doubts.

What he said was: 'St Bartholomew's, like most colleges in the University, has a number of drinking clubs.'

'More than most, if rumour is anything to go by.'

I knew, of course, of the Blue Bloods – who didn't? – who prided themselves on drawing the line against students from state schools. Most members of the University considered them to be antiquated and obsolete; their displays of arrogance threatened attempts to convince the rest of Britain that access to Cambridge is meritocratic, that the relatively small proportion of students from state schools is a historical legacy rather than a result of skewed selection procedures. The Blue Bloods sailed close to the wind, but were tolerated, for the moment, by college authorities.

There were the Muses, the first drinking club to cater for women – lady members, they are quaintly called. I had heard of feminists who considered the existence of a ladies' drinking club to be a victory for women's rights; but victory was an odd term, I thought, for what I knew of the Muses and their antics.

There was even rumoured to be a drinking club in Bart's called the Excommunicants, which had been disbanded by college authorities for particularly disgraceful behaviour, but whose members chose to wear their dissolution as a badge of pride. The Excommunicants were renowned for an annual dash through college in the buff on the final day of exams.

'Hmm.' Stephen Fox spoke across my thoughts. 'Well, it was six months ago that the Dorics held a dinner . . .'

'Dorics,' I mused. Rumour hadn't stretched this far. 'They take their name from the colonnade?'

'Precisely,' Fox replied. 'The columns there follow the specifications of the Doric order from ancient Greece. One of the finest examples in Europe.' He paused, and his sharp blue eyes issued a challenge. 'If I may continue?'

Clearly, the Senior Tutor didn't approve of interruptions. I gave Dr Fox a go-ahead gesture and wriggled my spine against the rungs of the chair.

'The dinner began outside college, in the Cambridge Arms, on King Street,' he said. 'They drank substantial quantities there. They drank enough, I understand, that the landlord was more than happy to see the back of them.'

He paused. I flexed my shoulders in an attempt to reduce discomfort, and kept my silence.

'They arrived back in college at seven thirty. Forty of them altogether. Fifteen were old boys, graduates who had returned especially for the occasion, and twenty-five were current members.'

'All men?' I asked.

'Of course,' he said smoothly. 'The Dorics have never admitted ladies. As I was saying, they returned to Bart's for dinner. Tables had been set up by special arrangement in the Echo Room, above the main staircase. The catering manager had hired extra staff for the occasion.' Stephen Fox's face looked tighter, somehow, as the story went on – as if he had sucked on something distasteful. 'The Dorics were reasonably restrained as they passed through the entrance hall. But once they reached the dining room – out of earshot of the porters – their behaviour went distinctly downhill.'

'Perhaps you could be more specific?'

'I beg your pardon?' he said.

'Bad behaviour covers a pretty broad range. What precisely did they do?'

With a you-asked-for-it tone, and a frown, he obliged me.

'Right, Miss Principal, if you want specifics, I'll give you specifics. The Dorics threw food around the Echo Room. Bread rolls. Butter. Spoonfuls of soup. Mashed potato, racks of lamb, red cabbage. Every dish that was set on the table eventually appeared on walls and floor.'

I had seen the Echo Room on one occasion. I could understand his outrage. 'I suppose they were sick?'

Fox's face was grim. 'It is part of their tradition. One or two began as soon as they arrived, with a ceremonious dumping of the contents of their stomachs – the alcohol they'd consumed in the Cambridge Arms – in a corner of the Echo Room. To make space for dinner. As the meal went on, others followed suit.' He paused, then said portentously, 'They played Fines.'

'The undergraduate game?' I struggled to recall. I'd been in one or two gatherings where Fines was proposed, but Newnham didn't go in for these things in a big way. 'Where individuals are accused of a misdemeanour, and take a drink to redeem themselves?'

Fox nodded grimly. 'Except in this case, it wasn't a drink. Each accused man had to stand up and drink an entire bottle of red wine at one go.'

'The mind boggles.'

'And other parts of the anatomy.'

The stiffness was unknotting. We were beginning to have something of a dialogue here.

'There are other events too disgusting to recount,' he continued. 'Suffice it to say that some men who'd overindulged deliberately made themselves sick in order that they could continue stuffing themselves. Some urinated in the room. It made little difference,' he said, bitterly, 'as by then, the carpet was awash. The entire room had to be redecorated, Miss Principal. The Bursar doubts that we'll be able to restore the Echo Mural to its former glory.'

I waited – doing my impatient best to keep interruptions to a minimum – but Fox seemed to have forgotten the issue that had brought me here. 'And Katie Arkwright?' I asked at last.

'Ah, yes. Katie Arkwright.' He paused. 'There were four staff designated to assist in the Echo Room that evening. A young man, a regular member of the catering staff, was in charge. There were three girls recruited for the occasion. They were not regulars, though one of them had worked for the college before. Their names were' – he reached into his desk drawer and took out a folder, opened it and ran his finger down the page – 'Candace Masters. Beverley Stebbings. And, of course,' he said, closing the folder and catching my eye, 'Katie Arkwright.'

I had done more than a few shifts of waitressing in my day. In most cases, though you work your socks off, it's companionable; there's pleasure in a job well done. But not like this. I pondered aloud.

'What must it have been like, for a nineteen-year-old girl to enter a room with forty drunken men? Men whose lack of self-restraint would put Viking raiding parties to shame?'

'Intimidating, to say the least,' Fox volunteered. 'And she was eighteen.'

'Katie?'

'Yes. Eighteen years old when this incident occurred. But age isn't the crucial thing. Her entry to the Echo Room, and that of' – he glanced again at the contents of his folder – 'Candace, and Beverley, was greeted with hoots and calls of – well, Miss Principal, you can imagine.'

I could. The vocabulary of vulgarity: get 'em off, whoo-ahh, tits out for the boys.

'That was the beginning,' Stephen Fox explained. 'I'm afraid it got worse. The girls complained to the assistant manager. He might have gone to the porters earlier on for assistance, but he was relatively inexperienced; he didn't want anyone to know that he'd let it get out of hand. So he didn't intervene, and things came to a head.'

I waited for Fox to continue.

'When the girls brought in the desserts, the situation became very disagreeable.' Fox began to fiddle with his pen holder, turning it round and round on his desk.

'What happened?'

'Miss Arkwright was . . . Well, two of the young men held her fast. They disrobed her. There followed an unpleasant assault.'

My mind recoiled from the scene, retreated to the serene beauty of the buildings. I thought of the entrance hall, the dome, the light, the cool colouring. Thought of Katie Arkwright, trapped, in that beautiful room. 'By how many?' I asked. 'How many of the Dorics were involved?'

'Two, centrally,' he said. 'There were two ringleaders. The others mostly just stood around.'

'*Just* stood around?'

Just – as in 'merely'? 'Simply'? 'No more than'?

They *just* stood around and watched an eighteen-year-old girl be stripped against her will?

'It was a disgraceful episode,' Fox said, primly. 'They've paid dearly for it.'

He described the judicial process that had been brought to bear. The penalties that had been imposed. The ringleaders were rusticated for two terms – banished, in other words, from the University and the city; not that such a ban can easily be enforced. The drinking society was disbanded. Each Doric was required to pay a sum of money in compensation. Some of the money went towards the restoration of the Echo Room; the bulk of it was to be divided among the three waitresses.

'Hush money,' I said. 'To keep the girls from going to the police, or to the papers.'

Stephen Fox's rejoinder was as smooth and sticky as a mud pie.

'The money couldn't, of course, make up for what happened. But it demonstrated the determination at St Bartholomew's to stamp out behaviour of this kind. We all agreed – the girls agreed – that nothing would be gained by going to the police. That it was best for everyone concerned to let the whole thing die.'

78

'But the girl who was attacked in this incident has gone missing. Don't you think the police should be consulted now?'

'Do you have evidence of a crime, Miss Principal?' Fox sat as stiff as a plank. He was every inch the representative of the college.

'Apart from what happened in the Echo Room? No. So far it seems that Ms Arkwright left the ball of her own accord. But the sequence – Katie is attacked; the attackers are punished; Katie disappears – is just too neat to be coincidence. I need to speak to the men who were rusticated. To ask whether they've seen Katie Arkwright since Wednesday evening.'

'I don't think so.' Fox rearranged the penholder in its original position on the desk. Looked towards the door.

'You don't think what?'

'I don't see any need for you to question the undergraduates involved. Whatever Dr Patterson thinks, these are quite separate matters. Punishment has already been meted out. I have no authority to release the names of these two men to you. Your job, as I understand it, is to find Miss Arkwright and satisfy yourself that she is safe. Forty-eight hours have gone by—'

I broke in. Professional integrity was at stake. 'Twenty-four since I was hired.'

'Then I suggest you get on with it.'

I examined his features. He was sixty, at a guess. He was very vigorous-looking for his age. And he was rattled, or beginning to be so.

'Dr Fox, tell me this. Were your colleagues unanimous about the penalties that were dished out to the Doric members? Or were there strong differences of opinion?'

'Miss Principal, we're speaking here about college procedures, procedures that have evolved over hundreds of years to ensure fair play. And that is what they do. You would do well to consider the girls themselves, of whom you know nothing, before you speak. Katie Arkwright was . . .' He hesitated, at a loss for words. He seized his bottom lip between his teeth and gnawed at it.

79

'And as to difference of opinion,' he continued, 'of course there were strong feelings. Some fellows seemed to feel it their duty to deplore the damage done to the girls by this experience. Like Carswell,' he muttered.

There was a light tap at the door. Fox pushed back his captain's chair swiftly, and stood. The chair, propelled by the force of his movement, rolled back a few millimetres of its own accord.

'Carswell?' I reminded him.

'John Carswell,' he declared, with an expression on his face rather like a sneer, 'was – downright eloquent. A regular crusader.' He strode to the door and opened it swiftly.

On the landing stood a gawky young woman, wearing Lycra jeans, flat shoes and a hand-knitted cardigan. Her face was shiny and free of make-up, her features small and unremarkable. As she came shyly into the room, shepherded by Fox, I could see that her only point of beauty was her long ginger hair. It was held in an intricate plait, tumbling to the middle of her back. She was, I assumed – taking into account her appearance and her age – mid-twenties, maybe late twenties, certainly not more. Probably a postgraduate student.

Fox did not introduce us.

He ushered her to the comfortable chair with the padded seat. She sat down shyly, her eyes on the floor, and began to rummage in her rucksack.

Fox fixed me with a steely glance. 'You will have to go now, Miss Principal. I have other appointments today.'

I strolled towards the dark pools of shadow that enveloped the door. Fox walked just behind me, as if to make certain of my departure. At the door, I whirled around, and faced once more into the room. The student in the comfortable chair looked sideways at me, curious.

'One more thing,' I said. 'What was it you were going to say about Katie Arkwright? You were speaking in defence of college procedures. *Katie Arkwright was*, you said, and then you paused. I can't help but be curious.' I offered him my most unthreatening smile. 'Katie Arkwright was – what?'

Stephen Fox looked at me, and for the first time in my presence, he smiled. The smile had in it something of the chill of the polar ice cap. Then he answered, in a low, deliberate voice.

'Not blameless,' he said. 'Off the record, of course. Katie Arkwright was not blameless.'

He glanced back towards his student.

'Good afternoon, Miss Principal.' And he shut the oak door, heavily, quietly – oh so firmly – behind me.

Chapter 7

When Stevie had disappeared the morning after the May Ball – got into a strange car, Helen claimed, with camping equipment strapped to the roof – I hadn't turned a hair.

Stevie is, for one thing, a woman who can take care of herself. She hasn't got the politics of a survivalist, I'm glad to say, but she comes pretty close on the skills.

For another, she and I had a date. Friday evening, Arts Cinema. Stevie had twisted my arm into signing up for all the films in the Vietnam season. We'd yawned our way through *The Deerhunter*, *Platoon*, and *Apocalypse Now*; tonight was DePalma's *Casualties of War*, and I was damned sure she wasn't going to destroy a perfect record by failing to appear.

Besides, Stevie wasn't the type to stand a friend up. Wherever she'd gone early on Thursday morning in her brown sequinned dress, she'd be back. And, after the cinema, maybe I could persuade her to come with me to Wildfell. So what if Sonny was in Amsterdam, chasing his dream of expansion? So what if Helen had taken Ginny to London for a shopping expedition? The weather forecast for the weekend was warm and sunny. Stevie and I could sit under the apple tree, sipping iced lemonade, and catch up on our reading.

But when I arrived at the cinema – a little later than intended – the tunnel at the entrance was packed with people, none of whom looked like Stevie. There was a trio of women academics, straight from an examiners' meeting, briefcases in hand; a mixed group of undergraduates in muted mood, probably coming down fast from the high of the past few days; a few individuals, poring through the summer programme, trying to avoid the embarrassment of making eye contact with strangers; and a good-looking couple, who whispered together in an intimate way that was just this side of snogging.

I craned my head towards Market Passage, fully expecting to see Stevie striding along, with her characteristic grin. Great expectations, swiftly dashed. I wriggled through the crowd to the box office, retrieved our tickets, and shouldered my way back down the tunnel, now on the edge of annoyance. 'Excuse me,' I muttered to the smoochy pair who were blissfully, irritatingly oblivious to the fact that they were obstructing part of the tunnel.

'Where've you been?' the woman said. Speaking to me.

The woman was Stevie. With a man I didn't know. Maybe, for that matter, this was a Stevie I didn't know.

She looked different somehow. As though she had a secret, and was working hard to prevent herself from blurting it out.

'You're wearing a new jacket.' I was searching for something that would account for my not having recognised her earlier.

The jacket in question was leather, cut close to the body, and trendy. Designed to recall the sixties for people who'd missed them the first time around. Not the kind of thing Stevie usually wore.

'Camden Market,' she said. 'We got some amazing bargains.' She spoke to me, but her eyes clung to her companion, and as she said 'we' she reached out and fingered his jacket. 'Look,' she said. It was almost identical to hers.

He moved a couple of inches further away from Stevie, to give me a better view, but he didn't take his arm from her waist.

'This is Geoff,' Stevie said. 'Geoff Leggatt.' She sighed happily, like a child who has reunited her warring parents. 'You two meet at last.'

I looked at Geoff properly for the first time. Not just at his arm, still around Stevie's waist. Not just at his leather jacket, which Stevie continued to stroke. But at him.

Geoff Leggatt was tallish, with the kind of muscles that owed something to genes and as much again to the gym. Not an academic, I concluded. They might have the height but never the shoulders. His sandy-coloured hair was beginning to pull back from the temples. He had grey-blue eyes and a face that relaxed easily into a smile.

He grinned at me now. 'I'm really pleased,' he said, removing his arm from around Stevie so that he could grasp my hand. 'The way Stevie goes on about you, I was beginning to be nervous about meeting, but now that I see you—'

'I'm nothing to worry about after all?' I hadn't intended the edge, but there it was, tainting the air between us, putting a damper on his enthusiasm.

'I didn't mean it like that,' Geoff began.

'Sorry, Geoff,' I relented. 'Glad to meet you, too. I like your jacket.' There was an awkward pause. 'Look, Stevie, the film is about to start. Do you want to . . .?' I didn't know quite what to suggest with Geoff standing there, clinging to Stevie like a limpet to a rock. Did she intend to unhook him long enough to watch the film?

'Don't worry about me,' Geoff said. 'I've got things to do. I'll pick you up, Stevie, after the film. On Jesus Lane? Eleven fifteen?'

'Thanks, melon,' Stevie said. She stood on tiptoe. She kissed him. He kissed her back. I looked at my shoes.

'Goodbye, Geoff,' I said.

Melon? Somewhere deep in my mind, an unacceptable joke from aeons ago struggled to the surface. The punchline was: *Melons for pure delight.* I couldn't help but wonder whether that lay behind the nickname.

Stevie gazed after Geoff as he loped away down Market Passage. Then, with only the smallest of sighs, she took my arm. 'Let's get in there, Laura. I don't want to miss the opening sequence.'

We squeezed our way into row N. In front of us was a party of Italian students. Their complexions were beautiful; their voices too uninhibited for an English cinema. They talked all the way through the ads; Stevie did too.

'So what did you think?' she asked, excitedly, like a chef who's just served up a new soufflé.

'Come on, Stevie. I only spoke to him for a minute.' She looked crestfallen. I slipped in my question about Katie Arkwright and the May Ball, giving Stevie the problem in skeleton form. She had noticed Katie at the gate and had let her out early because she seemed unwell. But she couldn't tell me anything about Miss Arkwright that I didn't already know.

'Geoff has a nice smile,' I said.

That was all the cue she needed. For the space of four minutes – while ads for Bacardi and XXXX lager and bath products from Boots flashed by, while even the frontmost seats of the tiny cinema filled, while the language students sent one of their number on his way with loud and cheerful *ciaos* – Stevie sang the praises of the boyfriend. She detailed Geoff's accomplishments, his kindnesses, his commitment to her.

What could I do but cross my fingers? Stevie's luck with men has been, up to now, in inverse proportion to her qualities as a person. The better she gets, the less reliable her men. I hoped that Geoff Leggatt might alter the trend. But whether or not Geoff was Mr Right, I had to admit that Stevie looked terrific on this new relationship. On the evening of the May Ball, I'd assumed it was the sequinned dress that gave her that special glow. Now I could see that the radiance came from something altogether more personal. Even in her narrow jacket, with its unflattering retro shape, Stevie looked the business.

The film didn't suit me. Not that I expect any film about Vietnam to be cheerful. But a number of the scenes – in which a young woman is abducted from her village by an American military squad; in which two women (her mother? an aunt?) plead for her, weep for her; in which the girl is tormented and gang-raped; in which her attackers justify their behaviour by denouncing her as a VC whore, as if either of those identities, Vietcong or whore, could justify man's inhumanity to woman – were too much for me. They brought unbidden the image of

85

Cindy Sinful, the Saucy Schoolgirl, stuffed into the boot of a BMW.

Had the man who shredded Cindy's face with his knuckle duster – the punter who hired her body for so-called love-making and then beat it to a pulp – shouted *Whore!* as he hit her? Had he believed that she deserved this pain, this mutilation? That he was entitled – no, *required* – to administer it?

And, by an unwelcome chain of association, I thought too of Katie Arkwright, trapped in the Echo Room of St Bartholomew's College with forty men, two of whom were intent on her humiliation, while thirty-eight had a different agenda. They were content *just* to observe.

After a certain point in the film – after the Vietnamese girl had shuffled her wounded way along the railway track, after she'd been executed – I abandoned DePalma.

I tuned out and dwelt instead, though not much more happily, on what Stevie had said. That she and Geoff had got together a fortnight ago. That they shared an interest in outdoor pursuits. That they had been away, briefly, camping at Grafham Water.

That they were planning to go off, that very evening, to Wildfell.

'That's if you don't mind, Laura,' Stevie had said. She was obeying the unspoken rule: Any one of us – Stevie or Helen or me – is free to take a companion to Wildfell Cottage as long as it doesn't interfere with the plans of the others. It's not that friends and lovers are unwelcome at Wildfell, far from it; but they are expected to take second place to the regulars.

'Mind? Why should I mind?'

Only that I'd be alone all weekend. Nowhere to go. Nothing to do.

Only that I felt bereft already because of Sonny's departure for Amsterdam.

Only that I'd been hoping that Stevie and I would come out of the film tonight and she would say, as she so often does, *How about it, Laura? Fancy a quiet weekend at Wildfell?*

Well, obviously Stevie fancied a weekend at Wildfell. Quiet or not.

But not with me.

'How about you, Laura? You want to join us?'

I entertained the thought for only a demi-second. Then I swept aside the veil of self-pity and saw what I really wanted.

'Off you go, Stevie, and enjoy yourself. With the lovely Geoff. I've got things to do this weekend,' I said.

And I meant it.

I'd find out what had happened to Katie.

Histon – separated from Cambridge proper by the merciless traffic of the A14 – is one of several villages that fringe the city of Cambridge. Histon's population is eclectic. It includes the suburbanites, who fled from dingy Cambridge terraces to more spacious accommodation. It includes a hearty group of incomers whose motives are tinged with green – who treasure the opportunity to wake up to the sound of a skylark, or, at dusk, to watch rabbits feeding in the surrounding fields. And then there's the core of old-timers, who grew up within a stone's throw of the duck pond, and still conceive of Histon as the centre of the world.

Rosemary Arkwright was an old-timer. I tracked Katie's mother down to a modest house in a modest close of unassuming homes. A ten-foot laburnum tree occupied pride of place in the front garden, its long sprays of yellow flowers casting a graceful shade over much of the lawn.

The blue sky was cloudless, the sun strong and confident, as I pulled up in front of her house, but even without these clues there was no mistaking it was summer. I stepped out of the car into air laced with the bright perfume of newly cut grass.

A Ford Escort was parked on the concrete driveway. I squeezed past and rang the bell. The first few bars of the theme song from *Cats* jingled through the house. It didn't predispose me to like Katie's mother.

The woman who opened the door was five foot two inches tall

in her fluffy slippers and scarcely more substantial than a stick figure. 'Yes?' She looked up at me with anxious, soulful eyes.

'Mrs Arkwright?'

She nodded. But it was more than just a nod. In that movement, there was a mark of defeat, the mark of a woman facing the inevitable. If her gestures were anything to go by, Rosemary Arkwright spent much of her life braced for bad news.

I began gently. 'I'm looking for your daughter, Katie.'

Rosemary rushed to put me right. 'Katie isn't here. Doesn't live here, I mean. No, she's lived in Cambridge since – I can give you her address. It's not that far – do you have a car? Oh, yes, I see.' She spotted my careworn Saab parked by the side of the road. 'Her house, it's not in a very nice area, but then rents are so steep in the city, aren't they?'

No one would argue with that. If my ex-husband and I hadn't renovated from scratch some years ago – turning a decaying terraced house into a workable home with as much outlay of effort as of money – I'd be working my butt off today just to pay rent. Instead, I'm in the happy position of working my butt off to pay a mortgage.

'No one's told you?'

'Told me what?'

'Katie went to a May Ball on Wednesday evening, but she left, suddenly. Her friends haven't seen her since. College officials have asked me to check that she's all right.' I introduced myself and handed Rosemary my card. 'May I come in?'

'Katie's missing?' Rosemary Arkwright's brow furrowed more deeply, and tears glossed her dark-grey eyes. Her small frame seemed to tremble.

I shepherded us both into the sitting room. A sofa with slip covers patterned with roses sat opposite the television, occupying one whole wall of the room. I urged Mrs Arkwright on to the sofa, and placed myself in an armchair near her elbow.

'There's no reason for alarm, Mrs Arkwright.' I hoped I was speaking the truth. 'Katie might simply have gone to visit friends.'

'Was she with that boy?'

'That boy?'

'Jared something. Some double-barrelled name. Was she with him when she disappeared?'

'Why do you ask that, Mrs Arkwright?'

Rosemary looked up at me in alarm. 'Nothing,' she said. 'I mean, no reason. It's just that – do you mind me saying this? I'm not sure he was good for Katie.'

'Have you met him?'

'No.' Rosemary shook her head with unaccustomed vigour. 'No. Katie mentioned him once or twice. Over lunch. She seemed very taken with him. But she wasn't eager to arrange a meeting. I thought – well, I wondered whether she felt I would let her down.'

'Why should you let her down, Mrs Arkwright?'

'Well, we're the sort of family – I'm the sort anyway,' she corrected herself, 'who don't really mix with people from the University. Not socially. We haven't got that sort of background. Katie is the first person in our family – mine or Robert's – to go to university. And Jared's family are ever so well-to-do, that's what Katie said. They even have a tennis court in their garden.' Rosemary paused. 'Katie said that Jared was rather – well, particular.' She looked down at the thin fingers, folded in her lap, and her voice dropped to something near a whisper. 'I got the impression he might have looked down on me.'

'And that has something to do with why he would be bad for your daughter?'

Rosemary Arkwright gazed for a moment in the direction of the large double-glazed window. She faced the laburnum tree, but her eyes were unfocused. 'Don't you see, Miss . . .?' She leaned over to pick up my card from the coffee table. Her thin fingers were shaking. She fumbled. 'No one,' she said, her voice still whispery, 'no one should have to be ashamed of who they are.'

She smiled weakly in my direction. Her voice lost its ghostly quality and filled with apology instead. 'I should have offered you something to drink, Miss Principal. A cup of tea?'

'Please call me Laura,' I said, reaching out and taking her small cold fingers in mine. 'A cup of tea would be lovely.'

She took a deep breath and stood up. I watched as she made her way to the kitchen. She wore stone-washed jeans – size eight, or less. She was in her mid-fifties – maybe fifty-five? – but she had yet to show any signs of middle-aged spread. In spite of the warm promise of the morning, she wore a bulky emerald-green sweater in fluffy angora. Its big shawl collar didn't disguise how extraordinarily thin was her neck, the lines of the larynx clearly visible. The odds are that Rosemary Arkwright is anorexic, I thought.

I followed her through to the kitchen. The door was ajar. Rosemary had made a line of tablets on the counter in front of her. Behind them were prescription bottles and an array of health food products. She glanced up at me, startled, and rushed to explain.

'Vitamin C,' she said, pointing first to an orange-coloured tablet. 'And gingko. And calcium. This one's B6, for my nerves,' she said. 'You can't be sure of getting the right nutrients from food these days,' she explained. 'So many additives, and lots of the goodness has been taken out by modern processing. Don't you think?'

Her last few words were undercut by heavy footsteps from outside. The back door suddenly burst open.

A man stood in the doorway, a man in his late fifties with a neat, spare body and a heavy-boned face. The look he gave me was an amalgam of surprise and suspicion. Then he transferred his attention to the owner of the house. The tang of fresh grass was overpowering.

'I'm off now, Rosie,' he said.

She glanced at his hands. They were muddied and streaked with grass stains. 'Would you like to wash?'

He shot another wary look in my direction, shook his head, and turned to go. She intercepted him.

'Thanks, Harry,' she said softly. She hesitated a moment, then kissed him on the cheek. He ducked out the doorway, and I followed the sound of his footsteps as he moved towards the side of the house. The engine of the Ford Escort started up. Harry – whoever he was – drove away.

'And those ones?' I asked, drawing Rosemary's attention once more to the tablets.

'Anti-depressants,' she said. 'And tranquillisers.' She looked apprehensively at me, hesitated, glanced away. 'Sometimes, you see, I find it hard to cope. But I can manage, that's what Katie says, as long as I have my fix.'

Rosemary Arkwright's smile, like the rest of her, was small and self-deprecating. But she had the kind of face that's made more beautiful by anxiety – hauntingly lovely eyes, cheekbones to die for. Even the fine lines around her eyes and mouth were heart-moving.

She arranged a linen rectangle on a tray. Everything was done just so – silver teaspoons were rubbed with a polish cloth and wiped with a clean towel, milk was poured into a small flowered jug, the tea pot was swirled with hot water before the tea was made. Even the Café Noir biscuits were arranged in a water-lily pattern on the plate.

I carried the tray into the sitting room and set it carefully on the coffee table next to a small silver-coated ballet slipper. While Rosemary poured the milk for me and added the tea – hers was, of course, taken black – I retrieved my notebook and pen from a jacket pocket and started with friends.

'Close friends?' Rosemary repeated part of the question. 'There's only Deborah Cook. She and Katie both went to St Mary's. You know it? They were inseparable.'

I knew it. A private school, a girls' school, in Bateman Street. They wore funny little striped cotton dresses in summer.

'Have you got an address for her?'

'Deborah's reading English at Cambridge. I don't know where she's living. In college, I guess – her parents are abroad. She and Katie still see a lot of each other, as far as I know.'

'Are there others? What about the girls she shares the house with?'

Rosemary picked up the tiny silver teaspoon and stirred her tea restlessly. 'I've never met them,' she said wistfully. 'I don't really know much about the people Katie spends time with now.' She looked with distant longing at the plate of biscuits.

'Mrs Arkwright, are you and your daughter close? Do you get on, would you say?'

The sadness in the room was almost palpable, as if the lights had been permanently dimmed. As if a little cloud of depression hung over the roof of Rosemary Arkwright's house. Maybe the weight of that unhappiness was one of the things that had made Katie reluctant to arrange a meeting between her mother and her boyfriend. I felt a pull of sympathy for Rosemary; but at the same time, I longed to step outside, to sniff the grass, to stand in the sunshine again.

Rosemary fixed her gaze on the little slipper that graced the centre of the table. She paused before speaking. Her voice came out once again as a whisper.

'Katie was always graceful, even as an infant. She moved like a little moonbeam – that's what her father used to say. But she set such high standards for herself, and they never quite worked out. Her first performance, when she was six, at the King Slocombe School of Dance – she was in the chorus line. At the front of the stage. They had to point their toes, and pirouette, and curtsey – first to the left, then to the right, and finally, straight ahead. Anyway, she turned the wrong way. Katie ended up eyes front, when everyone else was facing sideways. After a second or two, she realised she'd made a mistake – and instead of just carrying on, she burst into tears. Ran off the stage. She cried all the way to bedtime. *I'm so sorry*, she kept saying. *I did it wrong.*'

Rosemary picked the delicate slipper up, off the table, and held it tenderly. 'Laura,' she said, 'I'd give my life for my daughter. But I don't have – the knack – of making her happy. She's so vulnerable. But she says she wants to make her own mistakes, to live life her own way.' Rosemary finished with a helpless shrug. 'That's why she moved out.'

'But, as you said, accommodation in Cambridge is expensive. Do you pay for her house?'

'You'll want to speak to Katie's father,' Rosemary said.

I looked towards the kitchen. 'That wasn't him, then?'

I knew, of course, that it wasn't. But any PI worth her salt has to cultivate curiosity. More than enough to kill the cat. Enough to make the feline species extinct.

'No, That was Harry – Harry Gage, my brother. He helps me out from time to time. Katie's father – Robert Arkwright. Bob,' she said, and her face relaxed a little. 'He lives on the outskirts of Fulbourn. Off the Balsham Road.'

Rosemary settled the slipper on the arm of the sofa, and leaned across it to a side table. 'Here,' she pointed, showing me Bob's location on a Cambridge A–Z. She took a small address book from a drawer in the telephone cabinet, and jotted down the phone number for me. 'Katie might go to him, if she needed something.' She adjusted the shawl collar around her neck, and settled back on the sofa.

'How long ago did you two separate?'

'Bob moved out last summer. After Katie finished her A levels. It really hit her hard, somehow. She's not been easy with him since.'

'She blamed her father?'

'She blamed both of us, really. But she took it out on him. I think she felt he'd abandoned her. That it was her he was leaving, rather than . . .' She didn't say 'me', but it hung in the air all the same.

'Did Katie ever mention something that happened to her when she was waitressing at St Bartholomew's College earlier in the year?'

'Of course she told me. They call themselves gentlemen, those men who assaulted her. Gentlemen! Animals, would be more like it.' Rosemary picked up the slipper again, and stroked it. 'My poor little Katie. I don't think she meant to tell me, but she was so distressed – traumatised really – that she couldn't keep it to herself.'

Suddenly she started as the implications of my question reached home. Her hands began to tremble in agitation. 'How did you hear about that? Has something else happened?'

'No, no, nothing at all. It's over, believe me. I talked to Dr Fox—'

'Dr Fox?' The lovely dark eyes were beginning to take on a sheen of alarm. The initial effect of the tranquilliser must be wearing off.

'The Senior Tutor at St Bartholomew's, Stephen Fox. The man who chaired the inquiry into the incident. Anyway, he gave me the details. It must have been dreadful for Katie and her companions.'

'I didn't want her to be a waitress. Didn't want her to do that sort of thing. Wanted her to find a decent job. But she insisted.' Rosemary wiped her thin fingers fiercely across her face, but a tear remained, glistening on her cheekbone. She said something, so softly this time that I barely picked up the words.

'My baby,' she whispered. And cradled the little slipper closer to her chest.

Chapter 8

At first I thought the racket must have come from the Earl of Stamford public house. Voices raised over a lunchtime pint. One voice was a woman's, fierce and insistent; another was high-pitched, pleading, whining.

And a male voice: venomous. Familiar.

Then a hammer flew though the open door and bounced on the pavement of Great Eastern Street. It hadn't come from the pub.

It came from Katie's house.

As I moved closer, keeping an eye out for missiles, a man shuffled backwards out of the darkened corridor, into the sunlight, holding his palms up in a defensive gesture. I edged aside to make room for him. He was surrounded by a wreath of smoke, but as he set foot on the pavement, he flung his cigarette to the ground and crushed it with the heel of his sandal. I moved my toes from the line of fire just in time.

'And pack your things,' he shouted into the doorway. 'You too, Miss Stebbings. I want you and every one of those blasted little animals out of here as soon as possible.'

It was Charlie Thresher. And in spite of the aggression in his voice, he was in full retreat. A second later, I understood why.

The woman who appeared in the doorway was in her early twenties but slim and strong, with arm muscles taut in a sleeveless black T-Shirt. She was built like an Amazon. Balancing on the balls of her feet on the door sill, she towered over Thresher. And the force of her outburst reduced his shouts to peevish rantings.

'We'll be delighted to get away from here,' she shouted. 'You're a worm. A maggot. You're a maggoty worm!' The childish words were dignified, magnified, by anger. 'And in the meantime, if you so much as brush against our door, I'll tell the whole neighbourhood about you. I'll spray-paint your dirty secrets all over the walls of the railway bridge.'

The railway bridge on Mill Road used to be a favourite site, in more political decades, for public denunciations of date-rapists and wife-batterers. This Amazon clearly knew her Cambridge.

Thresher's dignity was undone. He fumbled a key from the pocket of his shorts. Then, without turning back to face her, he beat a retreat into the house next door.

In one loose movement, the Amazon bent and scooped up the hammer from the pavement. That was when she noticed me. 'Spoils of war,' she said, as cool as baked Alaska. 'Come in.'

She led me down the unlit hallway. After standing in the midday sunshine, I felt now as if I were stumbling in the dark. She paused to bang the hammer two or three times, hard, against the wall that abutted Thresher's, so that only the wallpaper prevented chunks of plaster from flying to the floor. 'Keep out of my way, creep,' she shouted, and then continued down the corridor to the kitchen.

By the time we reached the back of the house, my eyes could penetrate the gloom. Could see, through the window, the unkempt garden where the previous afternoon Thresher and I had buried the kitten. Could see every detail of the cheerfully untidy kitchen, with the cooking rota – *Tuesday, Friday – K –* still attached to the noticeboard.

Could see – and this was new since yesterday – a blonde woman crying in the corner.

She had a long feather-cut fringe, and shiny pink cheeks that coursed with tears. She shook out a tissue and blew her nose as if it were a trumpet. This was less a musical offering, I suspected, and more a bid for attention.

Amazon wasn't impressed. 'Take no notice,' she advised me. 'Beverley's always in tears. If she were a genuine softie, I might

96

be concerned, but underneath that wobbly exterior, she's as hard as nails.'

The Beverley in question was at least four years Amazon's junior. She was dressed like Olivia Newton-John in *Grease* – in pastel leggings and a matching mint crop-top. She looked as sweet as candy, but she wasn't prepared to accept Amazon's account without a fight.

'Hard as nails? Look who's talking!' she responded, jumping up from the stool she'd been perched on. 'You're completely insensitive, Candace. You're a – a brute, that's what you are.'

Brute? I felt as if I'd stumbled into a Mills and Boon romance.

Beverley flounced across the kitchen floor, sniffing with resentment, and ran water for the kettle. She gave a sly glance in my direction. 'Anyway, Candace,' she declared with a tinge of triumph, 'you haven't even offered your guest a cup of tea.'

'Too hot for tea,' the Amazon countered. She turned to me, but didn't raise the topic of refreshments. 'I'm Candace Masters. And that' – she made *that* sound blasphemous – 'if you want to know, is Beverley Stebbings. And it's out in the garden.'

'I'm Laura Principal.'

Beverley Stebbings took the card I proffered, and held it four inches from her eyes. It didn't require an optician to tell that she would've been better off with spectacles.

Candace Masters, on the other hand, shoved the card in her pocket without so much as a glance.

'What's out in the garden?' I asked.

Candace raised her eyes and looked at me straight on for the first time. She was leaning against the wall near the cooker, one leg lifted, the sole of her bare foot resting on a chair. She had skin with faint traces of acne scars under the brown glow; striking features, including a wide, generous mouth; long, tangled dark-brown hair, with plaits that poked out at odd angles. Her clothing – army camouflage trousers and tight black T-shirt – made few concessions to the summer weather, and did nothing at all to disguise a remarkable figure.

'You've not come to buy the bike?' she asked.

I pointed to her pocket. Candace fished out the card I'd given her. 'Private Investigator,' she read. She watched me as if I was in danger of exploding. 'So you've come about Katie,' was what she finally said, in a small, still voice.

Candace fell silent at that point, but the lacuna was filled immediately by Beverley Stebbings. Beverley had nipped out of the kitchen while the kettle boiled, and when she returned, the marks of her tears – for that matter, all distinguishing features – had been wiped off her pink face by an energetic application of make-up. She returned to the kettle, put instant coffee in a mug, and poured and stirred, all the while muttering questions that were intended, presumably, for me.

'So where *is* Katie, then? Tell me that. She lands us in this mess – doesn't even give us any warning of what's coming – and then she's off. How can I concentrate on getting a job when I'm house-hunting?' She took a sip of her coffee, set the mug down on the counter, and burst into tears again. 'It's all Katie's fault!' she wailed.

'Beverley, for Christ's sake,' Candace shouted. 'How can you talk such rubbish when Katie's disappeared? You're the one who upset her, anyway, with your stupid remarks. If it's anyone's fault, it's yours.'

Beverley picked up her mug and escaped towards the front of the house. 'If you want to *interview* me,' she said, with an injured glance in my direction, 'I'll be in my room.'

Once Beverley had made her exit, clicking down the hallway on kitten-heeled sandals, Candace's anger dribbled away. She seemed to deflate. She leaned more heavily against the wall, removed her foot from the chair, then slowly sank down, until she was sitting on the kitchen floor with knees drawn up in front of her.

'What was all that about?' I asked.

Candace said, 'There was no one here to look after the kitten – I imagine Katie assumed that one of us would do it. But Beverley went home to work on an essay, and I sloped off to London.'

'So your landlord—'

'According to Charlie, we killed the kitten with our neglect. He's chucking us out.'

'And Beverley thinks it's all Katie's fault?'

'She always blames someone else. Do you believe in the idea of fixed human nature, Miss Principal?'

'No,' I said. 'Do you?'

'Only in Beverley's case. Beverley has an essential nature, and you spell it B-I-T-C-H.'

I wondered how people with such mutual antipathies came to share a house in the first place.

Candace laid her arms on her knees, and her head on her arms, in a gesture of defeat. That magnificent anger was partly bravado. Then slowly, with difficulty, she lifted her head. 'Is Katie going to be all right?' she asked.

'Any reason why she wouldn't be?'

In the silence that followed my question, an enormous bumble-bee stumbled into the kitchen, tested the air in the middle of the room, and then began to bump its way unevenly along the large window that overlooked the garden. I was about to repeat my question when Candace spoke.

'I was with Katie in the Echo Room,' she said.

I pulled a kitchen chair nearer and straddled it, so that I could lean my forearms on the back and watch Candace's eyes. Not that I saw much of them. In the account that followed – delivered in a deadpan, halting monotone – Candace tended to look at the floor, at the darkened corridor, at the past. Anywhere but at me.

'You were at the Dorics' annual dinner? I'd like to hear about it. Were you frightened?'

'Well, nervous. I was nervous about the job. They were all so disorderly, constantly getting in our way. Katie was concerned the soup would be cold before we finished serving. That sort of thing.'

The long, skinny cat came trotting into the room and pressed her face against Candace's leg. Candace scooped her up, and settled her on her lap, before she continued.

'Near the start of the dinner, while we were putting out the

99

bread rolls, one of the men said, "Show us your tits." I told him to shut it. He did. He laughed; he left me alone. The president of the club – some freckled guy who looked embarrassed about the whole set-up – came over to apologise. Said the Dorics were a little excited. Said things would calm down when they got some food inside them.'

'So you weren't frightened.'

'Not then, I wasn't. But after a while, the atmosphere changed. You could feel the difference. There we were, filling glasses, serving vegetables, pouring gravy – dodging men who were vomiting in the corner – and we started to feel this sense of menace. Something new in the air. Something ruthless. Like some decision had been reached, you know?'

I nodded. Somehow I did. 'Then what happened?'

'One of the men turned to me as I was filling his glass and he put his hand right up my skirt. I mean – right up. He was clawing at me. I yelped and jumped away. I was really, really shocked.'

For a moment, Candace laid her cheek against the cat's warm body, and when she lifted her head again, there was a tear trembling in the corner of her eye. As she spoke, it trickled down, and splashed on to her sun-browned shoulder. 'And do you know what they did then? The men in that room?'

I didn't dare make a noise. I didn't dare interrupt her flow. She might leap up and turn into Action Woman again – trying to banish fear with a fearless stance. I shook my head. No.

'They laughed. Can you believe it? All forty of them. They saw how humiliated I was. How frightened. They heard me whimpering. And they laughed. With pleasure. With a kind of – anticipation. Do you know, Miss Principal—'

'Call me Laura, please.'

'Well, sometimes, Laura, I can still hear that very laugh in my dreams. And I see them all over again. One by one, in slow motion, I see their faces close-up. And every last one of those men is licking his lips.'

Candace turned her brown eyes to me for the first time in this discussion. 'That was the turning point for me, that laugh. That's when I knew we were in trouble. That's when I became afraid.'

Outside, I could hear the traffic trundling past on Mill Road. Candace couldn't hear it. She was a mile and a quarter away, in the Echo Room.

She was watching Katie.

'I saw them move towards Katie,' Candace said. 'She was bending slightly – in that way you do when you're serving food, trying to get close enough not to drop the sauce into someone's lap, but far enough away that you don't brush against them – and they came up on her from behind. Two of them. With exaggerated creeping motions, like the villains in a silent film, they sneaked up on her. And all the while, behind her back, they were signalling to the men around the table. Inviting them to watch, to join in the fun. I tried to catch Katie's eye. She didn't look at me – not until the last second. But I could see from the way she held herself – all tight and rigid – that she sensed something was about to happen. I could tell she was terrified out of her wits.'

The cat rose and yawned and stretched its back in an elaborate arch, then did a 360-degree circle on Candace's lap. Candace waited until it had settled down again and tucked its nose in the crook of her elbow. Then she cleared her throat.

'That moment seemed to last forever,' she said. 'With Katie tensed and those men creeping up behind and everyone around the table staring hungrily. And only Katie not aware of what was coming. But once they grabbed her, all hell broke loose. Those men leaped up from the table and surrounded Katie, and all I could hear was that laughter. Then they began to chant.'

'To chant?'

'Get 'em off,' she said in a small, sad voice. 'Get 'em off.'

Then her speed picked up, and the volume too, like the sound of a runaway train going steadily faster.

'Get 'em off, get 'em off, get 'em off, get 'em off, get 'em off, get 'em off, get 'em off, get 'em off . . .' Suddenly, her voice faded.

The echo of the clatter of a real train died away eerily on the nearby tracks.

'Candace, where was Beverley while this was happening?'

'I don't know – cowering in the kitchen, maybe. She left the room shortly before the attack. I never saw anything more of her until afterwards, after the porters had broken it up, after the college nurse had seen to Katie. Beverley was too scared to stay in the room, I think, but she didn't want to make a fuss. Didn't want to put future jobs at risk. So she hid.'

'And you? You must have been very frightened.'

'Frightened?' Candace asked, as if it was a new idea. Then she told me something about herself. One of those things that once you know it, you know everything. She told me she'd always been the big sister in her family. When she was a kid, she'd looked after her younger sister and brother while her mum worked.

'So I've always thought of myself as brave,' Candace said. 'Responsible. But something happened to me in the Echo Room. When I saw those men coming for Katie, I stopped being the big sister. Stopped being the girl who could look after others. I became nothing. A deer, frozen in the headlights.'

She petted the cat with solemn strokes as she took up the story again. 'Once they'd snatched Katie, all I could see of her was – for a few seconds – her face in profile. Do you know what a horse's eye looks like – when it's scared?'

I knew exactly what she meant. How the white gets bigger and bigger. How the eye rolls around wildly like it's trying to escape from the socket.

'Well, that's how Katie looked. I could see the terror. That terror got inside me, somehow, and I froze. Couldn't do a thing to help. All I could think was that maybe, maybe, if I kept very, very, very still, they'd overlook me. Maybe they'd go away.'

'There were forty men, Candace. Not good odds for even the biggest, bravest sister.'

My bland reassurance didn't help. Candace's voice moved up an octave, became agitated. 'And today, Thresher tells us to move out, and Beverley says that it's all Katie's fault.' She looked at me, pleading, and the tears welled up again in her dark eyes.

'What is it, Candace?'

'Nothing is Katie's fault. How can I make people understand? Nothing.'

I needed a glass of water, urgently. I was running the tap, flushing out the ancient pipes, when there was a clunking sound from the front of the house. By the time I took my first thirsty gulp, a slightly built girl had appeared in the doorway to the kitchen.

'Whew,' she breathed. 'Too hot to wear a helmet.' She dropped a hand-knitted cardigan on the floor next to Candace and ran her fingers roughly through blunt-cut auburn hair. 'Any news?' she asked.

Candace shook her head. 'Not a word. This is Laura Principal. She's a private detective, and she's looking for Katie. Laura – Deborah Cook. She's at St Bartholomew's. In fact, Deborah's the one who told us that there was a job going at the Dorics' dinner.'

'For which I'll never forgive myself,' Deborah said, extending a hand. 'I'm Katie's oldest friend, by the way. We went to school together.'

She was pretty and intelligent-looking and fragile, like Demi Moore without the muscles.

'Did you by any chance know Matt Hamley?'

She looked surprised. 'Sure. Katie and Matt went out for a short while. Now *there's* a nice guy,' she said. She and Candace exchanged nods.

'Compared to Jared Scott-Pettit? Is that what you mean?'

Deborah reddened. 'I'm not very subtle, am I? I didn't mean to—'

Candace couldn't hold back. 'Come on, Deborah. Why shouldn't you dislike Jared? Jared's a prig,' she said, addressing me. 'A total bore. He wants to control Katie – how she dresses, who she sees, what she does. Getting ready for a big party is bad enough, I'd have thought, without someone like Jared breathing down your neck, checking on the colour of your accessories.'

Candace's voice became hectoring, pedantic. *'Let me say it a second time,'* she intoned, *'there is no excuse for sloppiness.'* She was imitating Jared.

Deborah laughed. 'Come on, Candace, can't you just tune him out when he gets going?'

'You like him, then?' I asked. 'You think he's good for Katie?'

Deborah paused and thought. 'Between you and me, Katie's never had an ounce of sense where men are concerned. The men who want her – there's no shortage of them – she loses interest in. The men who make her life hell – they're the ones she goes for. Jared? Well, she's had worse. He's genuinely fond of her, I'll give him that. But he gets on my nerves. Always telling her what to do. And he's desperately concerned about status.'

'Meaning?'

Candace snorted. 'Meaning, he introduces Katie to his friends as a Girton girl. He's ashamed to go out with a woman who isn't a student at Cambridge.'

'What makes it worse,' Deborah explained, 'is that Katie would have given her right arm to study at Cambridge. She thought it would impress her father – make him feel he'd got his money's worth for the school fees. It was hard on her when I got into Cambridge and she didn't. Katie's a bright girl – she's getting good grades at Anglia – but the fact that Jared can't be proud of her as she is doesn't do much for her self-esteem.'

Deborah put her hand on Candace's arm. 'Listen, I'm meeting a group at the Fort St George in quarter of an hour. You want to come?'

'Oh, Christ.' Candace glanced at her watch and jumped up. 'No pubbing for me tonight. I'm supposed to be at work in ten minutes.' She dashed out of the room.

A moment later, we heard the water running upstairs, as Candace prepared for work. Deborah answered questions about Katie. The couple of times she'd spoken to Katie over the past fortnight, the other girl had seemed sort of edgy. Deborah had put it down to the pressure of end-of-term assessment.

'You can't hazard a guess as to why she might have run away?'

'Haven't got the faintest,' Deborah said.

'Or where she might have gone? Her mother hasn't heard from her.'

'I'm not really surprised about that. Mrs Arkwright means well, I think, but she's always trying to clamp down on Katie. Always worried that Katie will come to harm. Katie tries to tell her that times have changed, that women don't go about wrapped up in cotton wool any more, but Mrs Arkwright can never seem to relax.'

'I guess that's why Katie moved in here when she started university, instead of staying at home. But how she could afford it, Deborah? Do you know? The rent on a house like this, in Cambridge, plus bills, would come to a lot of money.'

Deborah shrugged. 'Maybe from her dad. Have you spoken to Mr Arkwright? That's the only thing I can think of.' She had the look of a girl who hasn't often had to wonder where the next pound is coming from; Deborah Cook wasn't much interested in the cost of living. 'And I don't know where else Katie might be. But I wish you'd find her.'

Candace strode back into the kitchen, in a short black skirt and white shirt. Her hair was constrained by a scrunchy. 'I've got to run. You'll tell me, Laura, the minute you hear from Katie?'

Deborah clamoured to be kept informed as well. I gave her my card. She and Candace piled on to bicycles and set off towards town.

Suddenly, there was just me and the cat.

And in the front bedroom, Beverley Stebbings.

'Do come in,' she said, waving me entry as if I were stepping through the portals of Buckingham Palace. But the room had more in common with London Zoo. Every surface bar the desk – the bed, the shelves, the wardrobe top – was chock-a-block with animals. There were Care Bears. Fluffy ducks. Toy tigers. Mousy things with bright black eyes. I'd wondered what Thresher had meant by Miss Stebbings' *blasted little animals*. Now, God help me, I knew.

I sat gingerly on the edge of the bed, feeling a tad uneasy about having all those furry little feet lined up against my kidneys. Beverley perched on a chair, crossed one mint-green knee over the other, and took the lead.

'I'd never met Katie Arkwright until the accommodation office brought us together,' she declared. Her chin was in the air, as if fending off an accusation. 'And when we move out of here, at the end of the month, I expect never to see her again.' For someone with a room full of cuddly toys, she was surprisingly poised.

'Do you mean to say that Katie's difficult?'

Beverley gave her head a quick shake. 'Difficult? No, Candace is the difficult one. Candace is like a volcano; you never know when she's going to explode. That's not Katie. Katie has this nice-as-pie air about her. She can pull the wool over anyone's eyes – like that bloke Jared.'

'What do you think of him?'

'Of Jared? She's damned lucky to have found him. He's quite a catch.'

'In what way?' After Candace and Deborah's reaction, I was curious about Jared's good points.

'In every way,' Beverley declared. 'He dresses well. He has a bit of money. And he's at John's, so she gets to go to good parties.'

Women in the mining communities used to describe a good husband in similarly modest terms. *He doesn't drink*, they'd boast. *He's a good earner. He doesn't beat me.* But I'd somehow imagined that contemporary girls – students, too, with the world opening up in front of them – would want a little more from their partners than that.

I couldn't resist pushing it further. 'Wasn't Katie bright, beautiful, well turned out? Wasn't she – your term – nice as pie? Maybe Jared was lucky to have found *her*.'

'Him, and lots of other men,' Beverley shot back. As quick and cutting as acid reflux.

'Meaning?'

'There were phone calls. From different men. Some of them,' she said with distaste, 'old enough to be her father. And all expecting to go out with Katie. For money. If you know what I mean.' She said the last sentence coyly, as if there might be some doubt.

'You took some of these calls?'

'Three or four.' Beverley shrugged. 'After that, I told her I wouldn't act as her pimp any more. Katie could answer the phone herself.'

'Did any of these men leave a name?'

'Ben, was it? Or Jack? I don't remember.'

'You didn't save any of the messages?'

'What do you take me for? Of course I didn't save them. They were disgusting!'

'Did Katie save any of them? Did she make a note of the numbers, for instance?'

'Now you're asking,' Beverley said. She uncrossed her knees and crossed them again the other way. 'No, Katie always acted the innocent. Pretended the calls had nothing to do with her. But when I suggested she ring the police, or the BT helpline, she didn't do it, did she?'

'You didn't believe her?'

'What, believe Katie? That the calls were nothing to do with her? Miss Principal, in my home town, a girl who got branded as a slag was more or less finished. Socially, I mean. So I make sure that no one – repeat, no one – has anything on me. I avoid compromising situations. That's why I have a good fiancé now, and that's why I'll get married as soon as I've got my degree. I learned from an early age to protect my reputation.'

'And Katie?'

Beverley crossed her arms with an elaborate flick of her wrists. 'No smoke without fire,' she said.

'Does that apply to the Dorics' dinner as well?'

'Beg pardon?'

'To what happened at St Bartholomew's? In the Echo Room?'

Beverley sat very still on her chair.

'Oh, that,' she said at last, airily. 'It was nothing really. Undergraduates in high spirits. When you get forty men on an evening out, of course they'll let off steam. Katie should have anticipated it better.'

Beverley noticed that I looked askance. 'Oh, I know, the committee sided with her. She did her nice-as-pie act again. Even I felt sorry for her, for a time. But not any more. Not now I know the truth.'

'You know the truth, Beverley?'

Beverley uncrossed her legs and rose from the chair. She'd been holding a folded sheet of paper. She placed it in my hand. 'See for yourself,' she said.

The paper had been ripped from a shorthand notebook. The script was shaky, as if the author had balanced the book on a shaky surface in order to write.

The words were anything but shaky.

You little whore, Katie. How much are you charging now for blow-jobs? I'm still waiting for you to call me. And the longer I have to wait, the better you'll have to perform before I'll be happy again.

I recoiled from the harsh words. My glance landed on the shelves where files of furry animals – full of Disney cuteness, with none of the grit of the wild – asserted their owner's innocence.

'You see?' Beverley said. 'How would *you* feel about sharing a house with *that?*'

Chapter 9

The Echo Room was much as I remembered it. My eye went first to the vaulted quadrants of the coloured ceiling, with its ribs of delicate stucco work, and then to the painted wall decoration. The colours of the mural may be fading with time, but there's no diminishing the drama. The nymph Echo was as exquisite and as wilful as before. Narcissus was as cold-hearted in his indifference, Hera as threatening in her anger. The shepherds who – goaded by Pan – ripped Echo limb from limb were every bit as frenzied in their assault.

But there was something else now – some resonance of evil, some reflection of sorrow. Like the sound of quiet weeping, quivering in the corners of the room.

'Filth,' had been Beverley Stebbings' description. For the notes that came initially – or so she suspected – in envelopes, for Katie's eyes alone. Beverley had observed Katie's shock and alarm when she opened these letters; Katie was terrified, Beverley said, of discovery. But in recent weeks, envelopes had been dispensed with. Each note had dropped naked through the letter-box. Each had landed like a time bomb on the bare boards of the corridor. Inviting anyone who approached to attend to, to leer at, the message it contained.

Inviting everyone to know, as Beverley put it, 'what Katie did'.

'Thank you,' I said, to the porter who'd unlocked the Echo Room for me. He'd worn a jacket in spite of the heat, and had stood patiently by.

I returned to the entrance hall, and climbed the other stairway to Stephen Fox's room. Past the Tutorial Office, which was closed for the weekend.

All the way to the top landing.

When I'd rung Dr Fox a short time earlier, his line had been engaged. But now, the outer door to his room was firmly closed. This could mean that the Senior Tutor was in a meeting. It could also mean that he'd taken the normal Saturday afternoon course of action, and headed home. Beguiled by the sunshine, he might have strolled to the river, or maybe he'd even joined in a cricket match on Parker's Piece. I recalled the bat in a basket near the fireplace, and found it not at all difficult to envisage the Senior Tutor strutting his stuff in cricket whites.

There was no answer to my first knock. Or to my second.

I was just about to retreat, when someone fumbled with the knob. The door creaked open. The first thing I saw was panic-stricken eyes. It took me a few seconds to identify the man who groped for my arm, brushing my skirt as he did so. His presence was as unexpected as his demeanour of alarm. It was John Carswell. He pulled me into the room.

There was dread in his tone. 'Here. Over here.'

He drew me towards the desk, and pointed to a spot behind it.

At a distance from the desk stood the captain's chair. In front of it was a worn oriental rug woven in black and blues. And lying on the rug was the Senior Tutor of St Bartholomew's. His leg was twisted at an unnatural angle, splayed sideways from the knee. He must have torn a ligament as he staggered forward. I winced when I saw it. But the head was worse.

Dr Stephen Fox's vigorous stand of hair was instantly recognisable.

You couldn't say the same about his face.

Stephen Fox's face had been compacted. Its nose broken, its distinctiveness erased. Where the temple should have been there was instead a mess of shattered bone and oozing tissue.

And there was a staggering quantity of blood. Blood in amounts that left little hope of life.

Fox lay chest downwards. His face was twisted to the side, its collapsed profile hideously apparent. Blood had surged across his temple in waves of scarlet. It had tainted his hair and trickled down the tender hollow behind his ear; it had streamed over his browbone and flowed along the curve of his cheek. The blood had pooled beneath him, framing his face in scarlet. It had soaked back up into his shirt, shadowing its innocent blue; even after death, Fox's clothing continued to act like a wick, sucking his life's blood back up again on to his lifeless frame.

That was before the blood began permanently to congeal.

I knelt as close to the body as I dared and touched my fingers to the outflung wrist. The arm, considering the heat of the day, was cool. I held on longer, hoping for a pulse, and as I did so, there was a movement from Fox's body – a quiver, a vibration, a buzz. Then a great black fly, its wings gleaming obsidian in the summer light, helicoptered up from the ooze around Fox's face and made its lazy way to the window.

It was only then that I noticed the four fingerprints etched in blood on my forearm. The thumbprint on the underside of my wrist. Took note of the streak of blood across the hip of my skirt. Turned back to look at John Carswell.

He stood as still as twilight, staring down at me. There was horror on his face, and – perhaps – pity. And something else, some other emotion, that I couldn't interpret. His arms were held away from his sides, as if he knew instinctively – he seemed, at that moment, beyond calculation – that his hands were swathed in blood.

Carswell didn't have a handkerchief. Neither did I. And no tissues cluttered the immaculate surface of Stephen Fox's desk.

Turning my back on Carswell, I lifted the hem of my skirt and draped it carefully over the handset of the phone, using the soft cotton as a barrier. I dialled 999.

Then we abandoned Fox's room – left the body, left the blood-soaked rug, left the great lazy fly that was still ambling its way towards the window in a shaft of sunlight.

We went downstairs to the Porters' Lodge to await the police.

*

When the porters learned that there had been a death on college premises, their impulse was to rush to Fox's rooms, to confirm it for themselves.

I didn't have to restrain them for long. A squad car arrived within minutes of my call, and two constables set about securing the scene of the crime. Their movements were practised, their procedures sure. They checked the body, radioed the station and summoned the police surgeon. They confirmed Fox's identity, took down my details and those of John Carswell, and then – imperative, this – they called for cups of tea.

The porters complied. The porters were of late middle-age, while the first police constables on the scene were almost indecently young. But despite generational differences, they acted as allies. They shared the delicate task of preserving order. They shared a style in which unflappable and keep-the-lid-on were key components.

Don't worry. Leave it to the experts. Everything will be all right. Just be patient. Please.

John Carswell seemed to benefit from the wait. When he'd opened Fox's door to me, he'd seemed like a man in shock. I'd wondered whether to contact his doctor. But there in the Porters' Lodge, sitting next to me on a mahogany settle, he soon snapped out of it.

'No need,' Carswell assured me, and I could see for myself that the moment of crisis was past. 'I'm sorry, I must have seemed a bit of a fool.' He smiled. It was a gesture of such sweetness, even in the circumstances, that any link I might have made between him and foolishness flew away. 'It was just the jolt of finding him there, like that.'

I reassured him. 'What kind of person can take a body in their stride?'

'What kind of person would want to?'

I looked at him more closely. Carswell had something there. What would it mean to distance yourself from the grim feelings that go hand in hand with death? To deny the force of the fact that someone who once was, isn't any more? To refuse to be shaken by the fragility of a hold on life? Here was Stephen Fox – a man of vigour and intelligence, a man who wielded, within his narrow institutional compass, a degree of power. A man whose room spoke of a rigid approach to work and an ardent embrace of leisure.

But a man no longer.

'I didn't much like Fox,' I said. During our brief encounters, I had sensed in Fox a defence of territory, a closedness. I imagined him to be someone who didn't take risks in his work, someone who followed procedures to the letter, who used precedent as a gag. Who did so because he couldn't bear to be wrong. But even my mild antipathy was grounded in the assumption that Fox was an ongoing proposition. That whatever else happened, he would continue – continue to be as cold, as irritating, as superior in his manner as he had been on first acquaintance.

I added lamely, 'But of course, it hadn't occurred to me that within a matter of days, he would be dead.'

'It never does,' John Carswell said, and for a moment there was the spectre of grief in his eyes. But he pushed it away, and focused again on me.

Looking at him now, I was reminded of the assessment Helen had made in Browns Restaurant. She was right. John Carswell was more than attractive. His face was pleasantly sculptured, with lines that rescued it from vanity, made it look lived-in; his eyes were not just blue, but the greenest of blues; and most of all, he had a way of looking at a person who spoke to him – a very direct look – that made you feel that each of your utterances was important. In conversation with John Carswell, I felt flattered. Enlivened. Maybe, even, a little flustered?

Flattered and enlivened were OK. Flustered made me nervous. Time to get back to business.

'Did you have an appointment with Fox, Dr Carswell?'

'No appointment, Laura.' He smiled. 'I think, after what we've just been through together, I must call you Laura, don't you? And you must call me John.'

He waited until I'd murmured, 'John,' in agreement.

113

'Anyway, I was passing through the courtyard and saw Fox's window open. I've been concerned about one of my students. Wanted to get Stephen's opinion. His door was ajar, so I rapped and pushed it wider, and then . . .' John looked at me with that direct cyan gaze. 'You saw what I saw.'

Only too clearly. A face framed in blood is not a sight you're likely to forget.

'John, did you touch Fox's body? Anything in the room?'

'Why, yes. Of course. I touched his shoulder. To see if he was warm. And I checked whether he was breathing, by placing a finger on his lips. But that was all. I was only there for a matter of seconds before you knocked.'

I watched him uneasily, wondering if he would explain the closed door. If you wander in through an open door, and think at first there's no one in the room, then to push the door firmly shut – as it was when I arrived – is not the obvious thing to do. And if you see a body, it's even less so.

'Ah, Laura,' he said. 'You're thinking of the door. Ever on duty.' He smiled. 'Why did I close it? As far as I can remember, it was an automatic gesture. Precisely what I would do – what I do every day – when I enter my own room. Step inside, and shut the door. Firmly. Before the student hordes awaken to the fact that I'm there.'

'And when you came up the staircase? Did you see anyone else?'

John brought his eyebrows together in concentration. 'Do you know, when I started up the top flight, I noticed a sound behind me on the landing. A kind of shuffling, outside the Tutorial Office. I thought it was peculiar at the time – whoever made that noise must have retreated back into the shadows as I went by.'

'You didn't actually see anyone?'

'Not a soul.'

He turned further towards me and put an arm along the back of the bench. It was odd that the constables, who seemed so efficient in other respects, hadn't taken steps to separate us. But I wasn't about to tell them their business.

He lowered his voice. 'This wasn't an accident, was it, Laura? Fox was attacked, wasn't he? Murdered?'

I replied like a politician. 'There's a small possibility that he fell, maybe bounced off the corner of the desk. Damaged his face in the process.'

'But if you were the betting type?'

Politician no longer. 'My money would be on murder.'

Quick, authoritative footsteps echoed through the entrance hall.

'That's the CID,' I said. 'We'll know soon enough.'

The rapid disciplined movement of the police across the stone floors was like the approach of a dozen foot-soldiers. Not because of any thundering or shaking, but because of a sense of purpose that swept the air in front. Because of a quick succession of commands and instructions, issued in a low voice, that whispered back, and back again, through the crannies of the marbled hall.

They appeared, one by one, in the Porters' Lodge. There were, in fact, only three of them. The first was a small man with curly brown hair. His light linen jacket was perfect for the weather but inches too long in the arm. He checked the Porters' Lodge as if expecting trouble. Detective Constable Trueblood, I later learned to call him.

He was joined by a uniformed constable with a lazy, swaying gait, whose name I never heard.

And then they both stepped aside to make room for a woman who seemed to crackle with energy. She wore a simple trouser suit, but her thick, unruly hair – it was a blue-black shade rarely seen on Europeans – flipped crazily up on one side and down on the other. She stopped in the doorway for a couple of seconds. Then, without so much as a glance at John and me, she moved rapidly towards the area where the porters waited.

John leaned towards me. His shoulder brushed mine. 'She's the governor, don't you think?'

I looked at her well-defined features. Took in the air of certainty. The decisive way of moving.

'You better believe it,' I said. And smiled.

'You know her?'

'We go back a long way.'

Nicole Pelletier, in an earlier incarnation, had been a student at Anglia University (or Eastern, as it then was called) in Cambridge. I was her tutor. I'd registered her bouncy manner, her mateyness with her peers, and her passion for netball, but with one hundred and fifty students spread amongst my various classes, Nicole hadn't made much of a mark on me. Until, that is, her mother died. The timing was grim – shortly before final examinations. The gutsy way Nicole coped with that death made her more than just another student to me.

'Her name's Nicole Pelletier. She's a detective inspector. I don't think she'd mind me telling you that I kept her on the straight and narrow at university,' I summarised. 'And when I switched to this line of work, she gave me a leg-up. We're even now. Sort of.'

'Young for the job, isn't she?'

'She's a high-flyer.'

I made no claims to have seen it coming. Oh, I'd known Nicole was bright all right; she could come at a new text with a fierce critical intelligence that showed no mercy. And I knew that when something sparked her competitive spirit, heaven help her rivals. Nicole didn't like to be outdone.

Doesn't like to be outdone, I corrected myself.

But intelligence and ambition will only take a girl so far. Nicole read a lot at university; little of it, as far as I could tell, was relevant to her programme of study. She wrote a lot – pieces for the college newspaper, satires, spoofs – but disdained to tackle any essay until the deadline loomed.

On the evidence available to me as her tutor, I would have sworn that Nicole lacked the application, the determination, that would generate success.

I was wrong. And Nicole has been busily demonstrating just how wrong ever since.

'You're – Dr Laura Principal?' asked the ambling constable,

checking his notebook for the name. 'The Inspector would like to see you in the Tutorial Office, upstairs. It's—'

'Thank you. I know where it is.' I turned to complete my conversation with John.

The policeman cleared his throat.

'Yes, Constable?'

'Right away, Dr Principal.' His complexion took on a faint pink glow. 'It's Inspector Pelletier. Immediately, she said.'

John Carswell gave me a questioning look.

'Inspector Pelletier has never forgiven me,' I explained, 'for knowing her in her humble student days. This summons is a reminder of who's in charge now.'

All friendships have their awkward bits, I reckon – the things that are swept under the carpet in the good times and become the object of tug-of-war in the bad. Ours is competition. Nicole needs this competition with me to fuel her, to bury her sense of inferiority; she's never quite forgiven me for being witness to her vulnerability at the time of her mother's death. I put up with it because I know at heart she cares about me. And – let's face it – sparring can be fun.

I unfolded myself from the bench, stretched, and gathered up my shoulder bag. 'Not to worry, Constable. I'll be there before the Inspector can put you on report.'

But in fact, when I reached the Tutorial Office, there was no sign of Nicole. The office was hot and stuffy. Left to my own devices, I checked through the pigeonholes. Stephen Fox's tray was empty. I opened a window that looked out on the courtyard, and leaned on the ledge, catching a breeze and watching the scurry of activity below. I watched as police cars entered sedately from the direction of New Square. Watched as official visitors – pathologist, forensic scientist, scenes-of-crime officers – took directions and fanned out into the college buildings. Watched as cameras were unloaded, and fingerprint equipment, and mobile telephone units, and all the other paraphernalia of police work.

Watched as a gawky girl with a beautiful plait was settled sobbing into a police car.

117

Nicole swept in at that moment. She closed the door and came straight over to the window. 'Laura? Are you all right?' she asked. Her examination of my face showed genuine concern. Finding corpses was not an everyday thing for either of us.

I waved her concern aside with a gesture of indifference. 'Bodies, shmodies,' I declared in my best Groucho Marx accent. 'You?'

'No problem.' Nicole's a DI now; she doesn't admit to need. She gave me a quick kiss on the cheek.

I turned back to the window ledge.

'That girl was one of Fox's students?' I asked. 'She's taking it hard.'

Nicole glanced out of the window at the courtyard below.

'That girl,' she said, with an ironic emphasis, 'is Fox's wife. Beg pardon, his widow. Three months they've been married. Her name is Rachel Hunneyball.'

'You're serious?'

'About her name?'

'About the whole thing. He's old enough to be—'

Nicole shrugged. 'There was probably a touch of that in the relationship. Her Ph.D. was supervised initially by someone called Vogel. She switched to Fox. Shortly after, married him. It seems he was everything to her – mentor, supervisor, father-figure, husband.'

'That's a lot to lose at one blow.'

'Mmm.' Nicole swept her hair away from her face, locking it into place behind her ears, and looked at me suspiciously. 'You've met her, Laura?'

The tall, gawky girl in Fox's room. Who made me think – why? – of a ditty from my childhood. About crabs that walk sideways and lobsters that walk straight.

And how a lobster can't take a crab for its mate. La-la-la. I half-sang the final line.

'Laura?'

'It's an old Bristol tune. Harking back, I suppose, to the days when Bristol was an important harbour. It's about marriage taboos.'

Nicole sighed with impatience. She'd become sharper since her student days – more persuasive, but also more demanding.

'OK, Nicole, I've seen Rachel Hunneyball. In Fox's office. She seemed shy. She walked a little sideways, as if to hide her face. She kept looking at me out of the corner of her eye. Fox didn't introduce us. I thought that was odd at the time – odd, at least, for a man who was so correct about business matters.'

'Maybe she wasn't business, as far as he was concerned. And speaking of business, Laura, what was yours, with Fox?'

'I had to consult him, about a case.' I treated her to my picture-of-innocence smile.

'I want more than that.' Nicole beckoned with her finger to underline the demand.

'You've heard about client confidentiality? I've got a reputation to protect.'

'I know a legally minded sergeant down at the station who would love to debate client confidentiality with you. At length. It wouldn't do a lot for your social life to spend the rest of the weekend there.'

See what I mean? Nicole's powers of persuasion are definitely expanding. I gave in.

'In a nutshell, I'm looking for a nineteen-year-old named Katie Arkwright. She left St John's College on Wednesday evening, during the ball, and hasn't turned up since.'

'I'd heard that you'd checked with the desk about a missing person. But she disappeared from John's. What are you doing stalking the Senior Tutor of Bart's?'

'Substitute talking for stalking and I'll tell you. The link between Katie and Bart's is an incident that took place here in the Echo Room, last winter. Does that ring any bells?'

'There were rumours down at the station. But I never heard the details.'

I treated Nicole to the full story of the Dorics' dinner. From soup to nuts. From the first bread roll that was thrown across the Echo Room to – months later – Candace Masters' tears.

I had to stop at last. 'The girl who was assaulted was Katie Arkwright.'

'I still don't see—'

'Everyone is aware that a big scandal was averted by a hair's-breadth. If Katie had pushed it—'

'If she'd come to us, for instance—'

'Yes. The college name would have been dragged through the mud.'

'So Laura Principal was hired to make sure that Katie Arkwright is not only safe, but happy as well.' Nicole smiled cheekily. 'PIs don't usually trade in happiness. Have you got anywhere?'

'I've met an old boyfriend. And a current one. Talked at length to two housemates – one who cares about Katie and one who is only a whisker away from wishing her ill. I've spoken to her oldest friend, Deborah Cook – who is, incidentally, a student at Bart's. And her landlord. And her mother.'

'And what does all that add up to?'

'Not a lot. None of them knows where Katie might be. No one knows for sure why she left the ball. Katie has an unhappy past. Maybe a shady past, as well.' I took the plunge. What's the good of going a long way back with a police inspector if you can't ask questions? 'Nicole, where around Cambridge would I find girls who are involved in prostitution?'

Nicole laughed. 'Problems with business, Laura?'

'Business is booming. But you know the old girl guide motto. Always be prepared.'

'Well, you're practically on the site of Cambridge's old red-light district, did you know that? Not so long ago, St Bartholomew's undergraduates didn't need to go far beyond the colonnade to find pliable female company. The Four Lamps district was the main hangout for working girls right up until the middle of this century.'

'Today?'

'Things are a little tighter nowadays. There was the brothel on the corner of Newmarket Road and East Road where the girls used to sunbathe naked on the roof between punters. The uniformed boys often dropped into the nearby engineering works during their lunch hour. They'd stand by a top floor window, and dial the brothel just for the fun of watching the girls leap up to answer the phone.'

'But that's gone now, hasn't it? The developers have demolished the building.'

'That's progress, Laura. Most of the girls work solo now. Or for escort agencies. Some have followed the bigger bucks to London. At the moment, Cambridge is, you might say, between brothels. But hang on, where's all this heading? You didn't come to see Stephen Fox in the hope of tracking down a hooker, did you?'

'No. I came to ask him about the aftermath of the assault in the Echo Room. I can't help believing it's connected to Katie's disappearance.'

'If we're talking connections, Laura, there are better places to start.'

'The murder, you mean?'

'Think about it. A missing person on Wednesday. A murder on Saturday. Neither of them particularly common occurrences in this city. And it turns out the two people concerned knew each other. Had professional dealings, so to speak.'

'More than coincidence? Is that what you suspect?'

Nicole stood up abruptly. She had that interview-over look. 'Keep me informed.'

'Yes, ma'am,' I said, tipping an imaginary cap.

Nicole smiled.

With satisfaction.

Chapter 10

He answered on the third ring. He sounded, as I knew he would, warm and relaxed.

He sounded as if he might have been expecting my call.

John Carswell had no objection to going over some of the events of the previous day. He was willing even to reprise what he knew of events that had taken place in the Echo Room.

But he insisted on surroundings more summery than those of St Bart's.

So that's how I found myself on Sunday lunchtime wearing a set of borrowed leathers that bulked through the torso, and riding on the back of a motorbike. As I swung myself up on to the sun-warmed seat behind John, I felt a twinge of unease. But that faded after the first sharp turn into Victoria Avenue. I relaxed, started leaning into the curves. I closed my eyes as we sped along the lane to Madingley and let the flashing of sun through the aspens play on my eyelids. The buffeting of the warm wind made me think of holidays. Of my one exhilarating attempt at water-skiing. Of those crazy, lazy, hazy days of childhood.

Let's go early, John had recommended. Beat the crowds. But when we eased into the parking lot of the Three Horseshoes, in Madingley village, it was clear that the crowds had beaten us. Within the pub's low-ceilinged interior, the queue was three blazers deep for bar snacks. Half of comfortably-off Cambridge seemed to have turned out for lunch, and the conservatory at the back rollicked to the sounds of an anniversary party on its umpteenth bottle of champagne. The air was pungent with Pimm's and lager and Chanel No. 5. We ordered, and escaped with our drinks to a round table on the deep green lawn, to await our food.

'Beat the crowds?' I teased.

'Well, at least we won't bump into half the Senior Combination Room here. Cheers, Laura.'

John was no more right about this than he'd been about the crowds. No sooner had we clicked glasses than a barrel-shaped man wearing an elaborate waistcoat approached. He spoke only to John, his agitated voice hovering inches above a whisper.

'Have you heard the terrible news? About Stephen?'

'I'm afraid so.'

John drew attention to me by placing his arm lightly around my shoulders. 'Laura, may I introduce Humphrey Vogel? He's another St Bartholomew's man. Humphrey, this is Laura Principal. She was with me when I found Stephen's body.' John tossed me a small conspiratorial smile, as if to say: *what does a minute or two matter between friends?*

'You? You found the body? John, how perfectly dreadful.'

Humphrey was accompanied by a woman. She stood quietly behind him, taking in the conversation. He appeared to have forgotten her. John's gesture recalled him to his duty.

'I'm sorry. Miss Principal, allow me to introduce Mrs Talbot.' John murmured, 'Shirley,' and nodded.

She was small-boned, red-haired and smartly dressed. I would have known somehow that she was an American even before she spoke. 'Shirley Ann,' she said, in a soft Californian accent. 'You're not at St Bartholomew's, are you, Miss Principal?'

Humphrey replied for me. 'No, no. She's a – what do you call it? – a private investigator. She does security work, that sort of thing.'

He turned back again to Carswell and continued the conversation. 'Have you any idea how Stephen died? If you saw the body, John, you must know. Was it his heart?'

'Too early to tell,' I said, as if the question had been addressed to me. 'The pathologist is probably looking at him now. But accident seems much more likely than heart attack.'

I might have added: *and murder more likely still.*

Humphrey looked at me rather severely, as if he were thinking of rebuking me for speaking out of turn.

I got in first. He hadn't explained how he knew my line of work.

'Have we met before, Dr Vogel?'

'Not met, not exactly. You were pointed out to me at a May Ball. Head of security, someone said.' His tone was more mocking than respectful. A trivial title for a trivial person, was the implication.

'What took you to a ball at St John's College?'

'Why, half of Bart's was there, didn't you notice? I bumped into poor old Stephen Fox at that ball, as a matter of fact.' Vogel turned back towards John. 'And, of course, you, Carswell. And that young biochemist.'

John supplied the name. 'Greenfield.'

'Yes, yes. And a few of the undergraduates – you know, Hardingham, Bhachu, Duff. I managed to avoid them.' He rolled his eyes at John, suggesting a lucky escape. John smiled blandly back.

I broke in again. 'It was at that ball that I first came across Dr Fox. But he hadn't brought Rachel Hunneyball with him, had he? Wouldn't he normally bring his wife to an event like that?'

I hadn't forgotten that Fox was at the ball purely in passing – that he had come, like John, as a guest of the Master after a meeting. But my simple question seemed as good a way as any to bring Rachel Hunneyball into the conversation.

The question might have been simple; the reaction was anything but. Vogel – with cheeks suddenly empurpled – fixed me with a hostile gaze. He seemed to fill up with indignation. John looked distant, almost pained. Shirley Ann Talbot turned her attention anxiously to Vogel. She put out a hand, apparently in restraint, but he was off.

'I am sorry, Miss Principal, for the sudden death of Stephen Fox. I wouldn't wish any fellow to die before his time. But that does not change one iota the fact that Stephen Fox behaved with complete impropriety where Miss Hunneyball was concerned. To come between a student and her supervisor, when that supervisor has taken extraordinary pains to get her research established; to entice her away; to disrupt the career of one of the most promising students of the past decade – it is unforgivable. *I'll make her my wife; what can be wrong with that?* That's what Fox said when I taxed him with it. And now where is she, I ask you? Now she's a widow.'

Vogel's face wore a look of grim triumph, as if being widowed by violence was the predictable outcome of marriage. Or at the least, of marriage to Fox.

John eased him into a seat, blocking the glances of people at the adjoining table who were clearly amused by his outburst.

Shirley Ann shot me an apologetic look. 'I'll get us some drinks,' she said.

'I'll come with you.'

We were jockeying for position along the bar, trying to catch the barman's eye, before Shirley Ann referred to Vogel's flare-up.

'I hope you can forgive Humphrey,' she said.

'I take it he used to supervise Ms Hunneyball's Ph.D.?'

'Yes. He is deeply convinced of her talents. He and Stephen Fox, on the other hand, have been intellectual rivals for a number of years. When Rachel switched supervisors, from Dr Vogel to Dr Fox, Humphrey was wounded. Humiliated, I think you could say. He blamed Fox. He denounced it in graduate teaching committee as poaching. It was very unusual – very public. And very impassioned.'

I finally caught the barman's eye and ordered drinks and a bowl of olives. Vogel and Shirley Ann weren't planning to eat. The barman set a tray on the towelling mat and began to assemble our order.

'Dr Vogel was sweet on Rachel, wasn't he?'

Shirley Ann shifted uncomfortably, and came at my question the long way round. 'He's not a bad man, underneath the affectation,' she said. 'He was unusually considerate to me when I first arrived. We've been friends of a kind since. But I don't think I'm telling tales that aren't perfectly obvious to the world if I say – how shall I put it?'

Shirley Ann pursed her plum-coloured lips, cocked her head, and searched for the right words. They weren't quite what I'd expected.

'You might say that, for him, the sun shone out of Rachel's ass. And Humphrey rather hoped to build a tan, by basking in its rays.'

Then she picked up the tray, steadied it, and pointed her petite self towards the door.

'Coming?' she said, with a mischievous smile.

As we stepped out into the garden, Shirley Ann came to a halt. I just escaped bumping into her.

'A word before we rejoin the men, Laura. I run the Tutorial Office, and information circulates pretty quickly. I hear you're looking for a girl called Katie Arkwright.'

We edged off the path to make room for some incomers.

'You know something?'

'I don't know if it's relevant. Here, can you take this? My arms are getting tired.' She passed the tray carefully to me, and continued. 'At the beginning of last week – Monday evening it was – I had to pop into the office because I'd left something behind. As I reached the landing, someone was coming down. I was the official recorder at the disciplinary inquiry, you see. That's how I recognised her.'

'Pardon?'

'It was Katie Arkwright.'

Monday. So Katie Arkwright had visited Stephen Fox two days before her disappearance. Five days before he died. 'Perhaps there were some loose ends from the inquiry. Is that possible?'

'Not that I know of.' Shirley Ann shrugged. 'All of Dr Fox's college appointments go through me. He definitely didn't have a meeting arranged with Katie that day – not an official one, anyway.' She glanced towards the larger swath of lawn, where the corner of our table was just visible around the edge of the conservatory. 'The men will be thirsty. We'd better take these drinks to the table.'

'Did Katie Arkwright speak to you?' I asked as I followed her back to the table.

'No. She didn't seem to recognise me. Girls of her age don't really notice middle-aged women.' She smiled over her shoulder. 'You'll see how it is, one day.'

'Did you mention this to the police?'

'The Inspector asked me about Dr Fox's visitors. I mentioned Katie. She seemed interested.'

I'll bet she did.

When we handed drinks around, the purple had faded from Vogel's cheeks. He was his normal prickly, voluble self. He and John were still discussing Stephen Fox, but the conversation had turned towards Fox's more distant family and friends. The state of mind, the reaction to the death, of someone named Gillian was their current concern.

Shirley Ann joined in. 'Of course Gillian must be deeply sad,' she insisted. 'However angry she was with Stephen, there's a long history there.'

'Gillian?' I asked.

Blank looks. They were so used to discussing college matters among themselves that it had scarcely occurred to them that one of the company might not be in the picture. John filled me in.

'Gillian Fox. John's ex-wife. Mother of his children, Richard and Fenella. Our college nurse.'

When I was an undergraduate, I couldn't afford to eat outside college very often. But when I did, it would be in a pub. The usual fare was a Ploughman's Lunch – a dry section of baguette, rubbery Cheddar, Branston pickle and a hamster-sized portion of iceberg lettuce. The fact that this was seen as a pleasant change tells you something about the standard of college food.

But pub food – some pub food – has advanced since then. My risotto was light and moist. John's chicken fillets looked good enough to eat, and he did. Humphrey and Shirley Ann took their leave before we tucked in. With our heads in the shade of the umbrella, and our legs – stripped of leathers – projecting into the sun, we carried on the conversation long after their departure.

'So,' John said, pushing his near-empty plate away and leaning towards me, so he could speak in a lowered voice and still be heard, 'Stephen is dead. And you've been introduced to Humphrey Vogel, the rival; to Shirley Ann Talbot, the loyal administrator; to Rachel Hunneyball, the current spouse; and – in spirit at least – to Gillian Fox, the spurned wife. Who's your suspect?'

So he was another one – I meet them all the time – who couldn't resist playing party games with a death.

'I'm opting for Colonel Mustard. In the kitchen, with the candlestick.'

'Seriously, Laura—'

'Seriously, John – we don't even know he was murdered. It could have been an accident. All right, all right, that battered face doesn't look much like an accident. But even if Dr Fox was helped on his way, I'm not investigating. It's not my case. I'm a *private* investigator. Stephen Fox's death belongs firmly in the hands of the police.'

John warmed to the challenge. Leaned further across the table, took both my hands in his. I let him – just. 'I know this isn't your case, Laura.'

He smiled, a knock-you-out smile that must work on television to devastating effect. It certainly made an impact under the shade of an umbrella on a Sunday afternoon.

'But I never get a chance to be involved in anything as exciting as an investigation. So why don't we pretend?'

'If we're going to investigate, let's do it on behalf of the case I am involved in. Let's think about Katie Arkwright.'

'In what way?' John's playful air had slipped away. Stephen Fox's death might be turned into a game; but he didn't do the same to Katie Arkwright's disappearance.

'You were on the disciplinary committee that considered the incident in the Echo Room, weren't you? What impression did you get of the events? From the statements, I mean? Is there any way that Katie Arkwright could have seen the thing coming? Any action she could have taken to avoid it?'

'Laura, there were statements at that hearing from the catering staff, from the porters, from the college nurse – that's right, Gillian Fox – and also from the forty members of the Doric Club. And the story that emerged was perfectly coherent.' John kept his eyes on the table as he spoke. There was no sign now of that special smile. His forefinger found a knothole on the table and circled the rim of it, slowly, relentlessly, as he spoke.

'She was young,' he said, 'and very, very pretty. I saw her flit past at the ball, and in her long white dress – it looked almost silver – she was like a ray of moonshine. But way back in the disciplinary hearing, she had no shine at all. She was merely pale. Ghostly. Ghastly, maybe, with anxiety and humiliation and pain. It hurt one to see her.'

It clearly hurt John to see her. It was the first time I had heard him use 'one' in that distant way. As a form of protection.

'It was frightening, too, for the other girl – Masters?'

'Yes.' I nodded. 'Candace Masters. Go on.'

'But she managed to escape the worst of it. And the third girl—'

'Beverley Stebbings.'

'She left the room before the worst of the assault and later tried to pretend that nothing significant had happened.'

'Why did she do that?'

'I thought at the time that here was a girl who had to earn a living. If she faced up to the awfulness of the event, she wouldn't be able to play the confident waitress in public again.'

'Beverley Stebbings was in denial?'

'That's what I thought. Still think, I suppose. But it's only a guess.'

'And Katie?'

John worked harder on the knothole than before. He didn't raise his voice. He didn't have to. The depth of feeling was there in the tone. In the words. In the downcast glance.

'What they did to Katie – terrifying her, degrading her – was nothing short of wicked. She is scarcely more than a child. But they thought – you could see it in their eyes, during the hearing – they thought it didn't matter. That she was just a little waitress. Someone hired for their amusement. Someone to serve them. Someone who didn't have the same sensibilities, the same need for security and privacy, that they'd expect for themselves. Or for their sisters.'

'A double standard, is that what you mean? Linked to status? Where some women have to be treated with respect, but others don't have a reputation – or a set of feelings – worth protecting.'

'Just a bit of fun, they said. But underneath, there's something that they don't dare say.' John looked up at me, suddenly. His pensive stare was gone. His green-blue eyes were hot with rage. 'To some of those men – well, how big a line is there, they ask themselves, between the waitress and the barmaid? Between the barmaid and the tart? Katie was there to serve them. In their minds, that made her little better than a whore.'

He brought himself under control. Then he asked, out of the blue, the question that had been bothering me.

'Do you think there's any connection between this and Fox's death?'

'I don't know.'

Stephen Fox had insisted that Katie Arkwright was not blameless; I should consider the girls themselves, he'd said. I knew nothing whatsoever about them.

But one thing I did know. I should have pressed him harder on that 'not blameless'.

Chapter 11

John Carswell and I ended our day with a conversation about responsibility and guilt. It was a strange discussion – on the surface, an exchange of views. An intellectual exercise. But underneath, there were currents of feeling. Things at stake that mattered. For me, at least.

And probably, I thought, for John.

I blame it on the sunshine. It encouraged, as it often does, a risky kind of openness. On top of that, there was the effect of the beer, and the warmly insinuating presence of my companion. I had been lonely lately. And loneliness, before it hardens a woman, makes her vulnerable. Before the afternoon was out, I had admitted to having no firm leads on Katie Arkwright's whereabouts. More than that, I'd admitted to feeling guilty about the failure.

His impulse was to reassure. 'But it's only been – what? A few days?'

'Three since I was hired. Four since she disappeared. But when it comes to missing persons, the early days are the crucial ones. After that, the trail gets cold.'

I had Rosemary, the mother, on my conscience, I confessed. It wasn't clear to me that this fragile woman, who used rituals of consumption – this tablet now, that tablet later, this morsel of food – as a bastion against her fears, could survive prolonged uncertainty. Rosemary Arkwright seemed as insubstantial as air; it felt to me that without her daughter there, in the background, to ground her, Mrs Arkwright might simply fade away.

'Of course, that gives you a reason to put your back into the case,' John agreed. 'But aren't you being too hard on yourself?'

'In what sense?'

'In this sense. Missing persons must be among the most difficult of cases, especially if the person concerned has opted to be missing.' John caught my eye. 'Which is the case here. Right?'

'Appears to be the case,' I amended.

'So finding her, Laura, may be beyond even your formidable talents. You can't always demand the impossible of yourself. You've got to judge yourself in terms of what's attainable.'

This sounded like pussy-footing to me. Wriggling out of responsibility, rather than taking it.

'You're sounding like a bloody lawyer now, John. You tell me. What would be a fair and efficient discharge of my responsibilities in this case – other than finding Katie?'

John remained as calm as a clear blue sea. He replied, mildly, that finding Katie was not the measure of responsibility – it was a bonus.

'In this kind of case, you can't guarantee a happy ending. All you can do is to give it your best shot. Leave no stone unturned.'

That's when I became uneasy. When – in spite of the quiet murmur of birdsong from the stand of trees at the side of the garden, in spite of the exquisite sensation I got when I slid my bare toes into the thick lawn, in spite of the fact that it was Sunday afternoon – I knew I had to work.

Because there was a stone unturned. I'd dialled the telephone number several times, and the phone had rung and rung in a house where no one answered. But I'd not yet spoken to Katie's father.

I knew only isolated titbits about Robert Arkwright. Knew that he and Katie's mother had separated, not much less than a year ago. Knew that Katie thought the world of him, hoped he'd take her with him, was crushed when he left. Knew that Katie wanted to study at Cambridge to impress her father – to make him feel he'd got his money's worth for the school fees, Deborah had said.

There was every reason to think that Katie might have been in touch with her father since she left the ball. Might have confided in him, told him she had plans to go away, asked him for money. Maybe even – my heart leaped up at the thought – maybe even moved in with him for a while.

'I'll take you there,' John said. 'You can check it out for yourself. Where does he live?'

I described the circuitous route that I'd been shown, tracing it in my mind. 'Through Fulbourn, out on the Balsham Road, up a hill, turn left at Fleam Dyke Road.'

We togged up again, and set off. How easy it is to work with a partner, I thought. To have someone else to decide with you, for you, how to proceed. To relax and sit back.

Or rather, to lean forward, to wrap your arms around a broad back – and let him do the driving.

Treacherous thoughts. Since when did I need taking care of? I had managed perfectly well, thank you, for the past several years without anyone else taking decisions for me, or chauffeuring me around.

And I had a partner already.

Sonny might be distracted at the moment. He might be overwhelmed by his ambitions. He and I might be going through a bad patch. But he was still my partner. He was still the man who'd had faith in me when I started out in investigative work. Who saw beyond the bookish exterior to someone who could do more, and do it well. Who agreed that we were talking partnership here, not prison.

And Sonny was still the man I loved to find beside me on weekend mornings, his head buried tortoise fashion under the pillows. Who shared my adolescent love of punning. The man whose brave attempts to overcome his own devils, to feel pride in himself despite his father's disapproval, touched my heart.

Having thought these thoughts, which came and went in a rush of feeling, the sun on my back suddenly felt a little different. I thought of other summer Sundays. How the afternoon drifts on and on until it's evening. Until what was bright and light and teasing becomes something else, a little huskier, and night falls and the people involved move seamlessly from basking in the sun to curling up on the couch, and to intimacies more intimate still. And how – though the sequence is perfectly predictable – you can always pretend to yourself, to each other, that you never saw it coming.

Except that anyone who has fallen in love in the summer knows the sequence by heart.

The motorbike drifted to a stop at the roundabout near the Backs. On my left was Westminster College, on my right the leafy expanse of Queens' Road. I tapped John on the shoulder, spoke loudly over the growl of the motorbike into his helmeted ear.

'Can you drop me off at home, please, John?'

This time, Robert Arkwright answered the phone on the third ring. He had the scratchy voice of a thirty-a-day man. Had to clear his throat before he could tell me that he'd heard the news from Rosemary.

'But I haven't seen Katie for over a week,' he explained. 'I've got a big contract, over Godmanchester way – long hours. I keep worrying that she might have rung while I was out. Where could she be?'

'I was hoping you might have some suggestions, Mr Arkwright.'

But he didn't. Concern for his daughter – anxiety, even fear – was woven through his questions. But he knew little about Katie's everyday life – about how she spent her time, who she hung out with. Or where she might go if she ran away.

'What about the new boyfriend?' he asked. 'She seems very keen on him. I haven't met him yet.'

'I've met him,' I said. I spared Bob Arkwright an account of Jared Scott-Pettit. Kept to myself Jared's view that the Arkwrights were not really from 'our' sort of circle. 'He's as perplexed as you.'

When I tried to sign off, Arkwright interrupted.

'And Rosemary? My wife?' he asked. 'How's she holding up?'

'Forgive me, Mr Arkwright, but I thought that you and Rosemary were divorced.'

'Oh, no, not divorced. I wouldn't divorce Rosemary. Never. I love her, you see.'

You don't come across that kind of loyalty often these days. Till death us do part. For ever and ever.

Neither truly together nor truly separate.

Like Sonny and me?

I pushed the disloyal thought aside, and settled down to some serious housekeeping. Person-keeping, too. Washed my knickers. Sewed a button on the waistband of my indigo sarong. Re-potted a begonia, even though the season was wrong. Made myself a crisp salad of apples and celery and pecans and mayonnaise. Listened to a new CD by Diana Krall. And went early to bed.

Sonny didn't phone.

Tomorrow is a new day, Scarlett, I said to myself as I turned out the light.

And it worked. Because I slept. Not quite for ever and ever, but it felt like that.

Amen.

Even though Parkside Police Station was only a hop, skip and jump from St Bartholomew's College, the incident room had been established on college premises. Routine police inquiries would involve questioning every member of college, from the marketing officer to the Master. Easier to organise this at Bart's. And better in the long run for college/police relations, Nicole and her superiors had decided. If a stream of academics were lined up at the reception booth at Parkside Police Station, complaining about time-wasting – allowing their disdain for the police to show through – tempers would certainly fray on both sides.

The incident room was on the first floor, above the colonnade. The porters pointed the way for me. Third door along the corridor, they said.

The first door concealed a storeroom of some kind; the

disinfectant odour suggested that cleaning materials might be kept there.

The second was fitted with a neat, unostentatious plaque. THE NURSE, it read, in bald capital letters. Gillian Fox.

The incident room could wait.

The walls of the nurse's surgery were painted with buttermilk emulsion. A small posy of flowers perched on the corner of an ancient desk. From an adjoining room, its door an inch ajar, I heard a murmur of voices. Three minutes later, a young woman hobbled out, with a fresh bandage on her ankle. The nurse bustled out behind her.

'Morning,' she said. 'Be with you in a tick.' She brought her notes up to date, tucked them out of sight, and turned to face me.

She was dark and tall and rather splendid, with twists of stiff grey curls among the brown hair, and a dash of something Mediterranean in her bearing.

'What can I do for you?'

Her composure was what you would expect from an experienced nurse – an unflappable air and a studied reassurance. But her smile had an ironic twist I didn't associate with SRNs. Nor did she look the part of the grieving wife.

I introduced myself. 'I didn't expect you to be open for business today, Mrs Fox. Not after what happened on Saturday. I was one of the people who found the body, you see.'

'But I'd understood that John Carswell found the body.'

'I arrived within minutes. And I'm sorry to say that Dr Fox was already dead.'

She looked at me, quizzically, for a moment, as if it were a struggle to decide whether or not to speak. Then she swallowed, hard.

'Tell me about it.' No hint of irony now. I could see that her eyelids were rimmed with red. Mrs Fox sensed my hesitation.

'For Christ's sake,' she said. 'Not you too. Everyone in Bart's avoids speaking of it. They mean to spare me. As if it were the case that if they didn't mention Stephen's death, it wouldn't cross my mind. And perhaps because they don't know what to expect

136

of an ex-wife. Should I mourn? Or should my anger at his treatment of me insulate me from grief – make me indifferent, perhaps? Even triumphant?'

I told her about it. I described how I'd entered the Senior Tutor's room. Recounted the position of her ex-husband's body. How he had lain on the rug, his leg twisted under him; how his shirt had been soaked in blood. I touched on the wounds to his face and head. I didn't mention the fly.

And as I spoke, moisture trembled on the surface of her eyes. She blinked rapidly – clearing her vision, I believe, because she watched me closely as I spoke, fixing this moment in her memory. Tears flowed then over her cheekbones and glistened on her upper lip.

When I finished, she closed her eyes, and bowed her head.

After a moment, I broke the silence. 'How long were you married to Dr Fox?'

'Almost thirty years. And I'd thought I was done with crying. He could be so cruel.' Gillian blew her nose on a tissue strategically placed on the desk. 'Do you know what he said to me? When he took up with her – with Rachel Hunneyball? When I humiliated myself, begging him not to go? When I cried like this, in front of him?'

I couldn't begin to imagine. What do people say to other people in those circumstances? When they have lived together for thirty years? Sure, there are fifty ways to leave your lover – but how many of those can a person live with comfortably afterwards?

'He looked all solicitous. Like he had only my welfare at heart. His tutor look, I used to call it. And then he advised me to give up work. *It would be easier for you, Gillian, so much easier, my dear, if you didn't have to bump into me in college. Why don't you leave your job? Find something else? Take it easy for a while?*'

So Stephen Fox recommended that his wife of thirty years remove herself from his sight. That she give up her a job at an age when employment is almost impossible to find. Not enough that she should lose him, and their family life, all at one go. She was to lose her career as well. Her professional identity. Her colleagues. Her only source of income. And she was to do this, he claimed, for her own sake.

Gillian Fox's tears stopped flowing for the moment. She drew herself up to her full height, took a deep breath, let it out, and spoke more forcefully.

'I didn't leave,' she concluded. 'He went instead.'

Was that 'went' a reference to Fox's death?

'You mean—?'

Before I could finish phrasing the question, the door to the surgery flew open. A man – a large young man with dark curly hair – stormed into the room. He addressed Gillian Fox before he'd even closed the door. He spoke loudly, and waved his arms about. At first I assumed he must be a student. But his position – within inches of Gillian – knocked that notion on its head. So did the things he said.

'They questioned me for hours. Since nine thirty. Someone had told them that I'd refused to see him. Was I angry? they kept asking. What did they expect me to be – elated, after he'd abandoned us? Tickled pink? Anyway, why ask me? Why didn't they ask all the other people Father had injured. Why aren't they questioning that Hunneybum? Or Vogel? Or Carswell, for that matter? Why in God's name pick on me?'

He continued in this vein, in a voice both angry and petulant. Gillian focused on him throughout, looking up into his eyes – she was tall, but he was taller – moving his hair off his forehead, stroking the nape of his neck, and shushing. *Shh, Richard; shh, shh. It'll be all right. Shh.*

At last he was stilled. He put his arms around his mother, and leaned his cheek against her hair. They stood like that, comforting each other, for a brief while. This time it was he who cried.

Eventually, he straightened up. She wiped his face tenderly, he kissed her cheek and left the room, with only a furtive glance at me.

She was quiet for a minute, apparently thinking about what

had just occurred, before she commented. 'Some people think nineteen is grown up,' she said. 'But it's not, not really. He has tried so hard to be the man of the family. To look after Fenella, to look after me.'

Nineteen was Katie Arkwright's age.

'Your son mentioned John Carswell. Carswell was angry with Dr Fox? What was that about?'

Gillian waved a hand of dismissal. 'That's just Richard. He often gets the wrong end of the stick. You may have heard, Miss Principal – everybody else knows – that John Carswell and my husband weren't on the best of terms. When they were younger, apparently – before my time – they were friends. But somewhere along the line, they had a falling-out.'

'You don't know the reason?'

She pondered for a moment, as if it was something she hadn't thought about before. 'No, I don't. John was always the perfect gentleman in our company, but Stephen was very cold to him. Hostile, even. If you'd heard some of Stephen's remarks, you might have said that he despised John Carswell.'

She said this in a tone of voice that left a question mark. As if she didn't herself endorse this view. It was like a 'but', hanging in the air.

'But?'

'But.' Gillian shrugged. 'Stephen's attitude seemed to me to be largely bravado. It crossed my mind, Miss Principal, on more than one occasion, that he might be afraid of Carswell. Deep down, I mean.'

I must have registered some surprise, because Mrs Fox nodded. 'Yes,' she said. 'Afraid.' She checked her watch. 'That's all I know, Miss Principal. Now, if you'll excuse me . . .'

'One minute, if you don't mind. You told me that when your husband talked about divorce, he made that callous suggestion that you should quit your post. You said to me, *I didn't leave. He went instead.* Will you tell me what you meant by that?'

'Ah,' Gillian said. 'I suppose that could sound suspicious. What did I mean?' She shrugged and smiled, a matronly, reassuring smile. I almost expected to see an injection ready for use in her right hand. 'Nothing much,' she repeated, thinking about it. 'Only that it's strange how things work out. A few months ago, I felt my world had ended, because of Stephen. Saw him making a fresh start, saw his life opening up in front of him. But now he's gone. And I am the one with a new life. Only that.'

'Did you have anything to do with his death, Mrs Fox?'

'Do I look like a killer?' she said.

Chapter 12

The incident room was large enough, but barely, to hold civilian clerks and police officers, along with all the equipment they needed to control the communications, monitor the data and feed the information from the murder inquiry into the Home Office computer database. It resembled any other incident room I'd ever been in – except for two things. The first was the row of windows, wider than they were tall, with elegant cross-pieces, that studded the outer wall. The second was the view: a deep landscape over Midsummer Common, with chestnut trees swishing at eye level, and the twisty roofline of the Fort St George pub on the river front barely visible in the distance.

'She had to nip out,' a constable said, checking his watch. 'If you want to wait, she shouldn't be long. She's due to interview someone' – his eyes moved involuntarily to the row of seats behind me – 'at ten o'clock.'

I took a chair, and scanned the person sitting to my left. He was young – twenty, twenty-one – with a bony forehead and a pugnacious set to the jaw. He occupied as much space as he could. His hands were clasped behind his head, elbows akimbo. His legs stretched out across the floor, forming serious obstacles to movement to and from the filing cabinets. I wondered how long it would be before one of the officers would bark at him to sit up straight.

At ten past ten Nicole bustled in. In a smart suit, she looked alert and ready for business. Only her hair hinted at trouble. She'd pulled the sides back into a large tortoiseshell clip at the crown of her head, but one wavy strand broke free as she came into the room and bounced off her temple as she walked. She gave her head a shake of irritation, but carried on.

Until stopped by the outstretched legs that blocked the crowded floor space. She halted in front of the young man. Looked down at his legs as if there were something to be learned from close scrutiny of a pair of chinos. Looked up at his face. Calculating.

'You're Duff?' she asked.

'At your service.' The words were chivalrous. The smile held a definite challenge.

DI Pelletier glanced up then, beyond the legs, and noticed me on the bench.

'I'll see you at half ten,' she told him.

He leaped up in protest. 'But you said ten o'clock,' he objected. 'How dare you keep me waiting like this!'

'Thank you,' she replied, brushing past him, as if he'd jumped up with no other purpose but to clear the path.

She beckoned me through an oak door, into an adjoining office. The office had a door on to the corridor as well, and so allowed for some degree of privacy.

One of the constables followed her in. With a respectful *ma'am*, he set a folder on the table in front of her, and departed.

'Well, well, well,' I said, when she had closed the door. 'Two firsts in one morning. Nicole late for work.'

'Not late,' she grumbled. 'I was here at six a.m., if you need to know. But I had to pop off home for an hour. Having a new bathroom suite put in. Would you believe the plumber has ruined the damned cork tiles while getting the old bath out? Did I want to install new tiles? he wanted to know.'

Her teeth were gritted. 'No, I bloody well don't want to change my tiles. You ruined them. You can fix them for me.' She banged her fist down on the table.

I groaned in sympathy. 'I'll never forget the weekend you laid those tiles. I thought you'd need care in the community by the time you finished the area around the pedestal.'

'But they looked so good when they were done,' she sighed. 'Well, not any more.'

She was seated by now. I stepped up behind her, undid the tortoiseshell clip, combed the errant lock of hair into place with my fingers, and fastened the clasp. It all stayed in place. Then I sat down too.

'The other first,' I said. 'You've seen me right away.'

Nicole put the plumber behind her, and grinned her thanks. 'It's not your charm, Laura. I just couldn't bring myself to be nice to that little thug out there.'

'Is he a student at Bart's?'

'Yes and no. He's been rusticated – sent down – for two terms. Supposed to keep himself out of Cambridge. As far as I can tell, the only thing he keeps out of is the lecture room, and there's nothing new about that.' She paused, waiting for the penny to drop.

'Yes,' she confirmed, when she could see that I'd twigged. 'Katie Arkwright. He was one of the men disciplined for the assault.'

'Do you mean to say there's been a complaint to the police at last?'

'Nope. No complaint. The assault remains a college matter. Roger Duff's here because I want to interview him about the murder.'

'It's murder now?'

'Official. Stephen Fox was killed by a blow, delivered from above, from a blunt instrument.'

'The wound to the temple. But wasn't there another blow? It looked to me like his nose had been smashed too. Do you have any idea what the blunt instrument might have been?'

'We picked up a cricket bat, splattered in blood, on the landing below. It's being examined at the lab now. Fox's nose suffered a separate hit. Or maybe it was smashed when he fell. He might have hit his face on the desk as he went down. They're still checking.'

'Nicole, there was a cricket bat in Fox's office the first time I was there. But not, as far as I recall, when I found the body. Do you reckon Fox might have been done in with his own bat? And then the killer tossed it away on the landing?'

'There's a sporting chance,' Nicole said.

I rolled my eyes.

Sometimes she goes too far.

'Doesn't that suggest that the killing wasn't premeditated? Someone comes to see Fox. There's a row. They look around, snatch up the cricket bat, and boom. Fox goes down. If the killing had been planned, the person concerned would've brought a weapon with them.'

'Unless they knew the cricket bat was there. That would include anyone – student, staff, friends, family – who had visited Fox's office before. It would even include you, Laura.'

'Thanks, Nicole. For your open-minded approach to justice.' A shuffle of footsteps in the passage outside brought me back to the issue at hand. 'So, tell me, Inspector – what do you want with Duff ?'

'Pure routine. Since Saturday, we've talked about Stephen Fox to dozens of people in this college. And Roger Duff's name was bandied about by several of those people in response to the traditional question about enemies. Seems he shoots off his mouth – about everything and everyone. One of the everyones was our murder victim.'

'What's his complaint? Does it have to do with the disciplinary hearing?'

'Of course. He says the Senior Tutor had it in for him. That's why, Duff claims, he was rusticated.'

'Attacking a girl wasn't reason enough?'

Nicole shrugged out of her jacket, and arranged it carefully over the back of a chair. 'I don't think it'll lead anywhere myself. He's one of those huff and puff boys, if you ask me. Claims he'll blow your house in, but hasn't really got the steam. So, meanwhile – anything on Katie Arkwright?'

I felt the gloom settle in. 'I'm getting nowhere fast. Don't suppose I could sit in on your interview with Duff? Given the connection?'

Nicole laughed. 'Never hurts to ask, Laura – but of course the answer's no. Tell you what. Give me a ring and we'll have a drink at my house one of these evenings. I'll show you the new bathroom. If you have any space in your busy social schedule.'

Oh, I had space all right.

'Done.'

I wrote a note, placed it in the student pigeonholes, and made my way towards Midsummer Common. As soon as I was outside the cool corridors of the college, sweat leaped to my forehead. Only mid-morning, and already it was muggy. There were patches of wet tar on Maid's Causeway. I swung over the top of the wrought-iron fence and down on to the common, where I removed my sandals. Keeping an eye out for cowpats, I barefooted my way through the long grass, en route to the Fort St George.

The Fort St George, on the river side of Midsummer Common, is the closest the city of Cambridge comes to a traditional country pub. The central part of the building harks back to earlier centuries, with its picturesque roof and low ceilings and aphorisms in elegant lettering painted on dark-stained wood. It has a choice location: backing on to the River Cam, opposite the boathouses, and facing forward on to the breadth of Midsummer Common. On warm evenings, university and language school students spill out of the pub's bars and on to the Common.

But in spite of its cultivated quaintness, in spite of its popularity, the Fort St George has had its share of trouble. There was the landlady who was beaten up in her first week on the job – leaped on by a customer who had too many chemicals in her bloodstream. She raged in from the patio, pulled the astonished manager to the ground, and kicked and punched her. All in the job, the landlady said.

A good place, I'd decided, for a quiet meeting.

So early in the day, the Fort St George was peaceful. The bar adjoining the dining room was empty. Except for a tottery old chap watching cartoons on a telly set high up on the wall, the public bar was empty too. The snug, by contrast, was busy. On stools at the bar, with a map of Cambridge spread out in front of them, were middle-aged twins. They wore shorts and backpacks. They debated destinations in relaxed Australian accents.

And in a shadowy corner, nursing a Pimm's, was a man of twenty or so, with a long, arched nose, a pale complexion and curly black hair. He was thin enough that he could do with some feeding up, as my mother would say; and good looking enough that he probably had girls queuing to cook for him.

I recommended Kettle's Yard Gallery to the twins, and ordered a coffee. When I turned around, I met the eyes of the good-looking guy in the corner. He didn't turn away. Just allowed himself a small, seductive smile. And though he was a baby compared to me, he was a beautiful baby. My return smile came involuntarily from somewhere that doesn't measure age.

I carried a dose of caffeine outside to the picnic table nearest the river. I sat there following the course of a triangle of cygnets who rippled their way downriver under the watchful eye of their parents, until my attention was taken by someone striding across the common. He was on a beeline from St Bartholomew's College to the Fort St George.

It was Duff. He must have been released at last by Inspector Pelletier. He was moving swiftly in spite of the heat. He made straight for the bar, like a man in a hurry. He didn't glance in my direction, didn't notice me sitting there. I waited for him to approach me, but in vain.

When five minutes had passed, I drained the last drop of coffee, took my sunglasses off, and strolled back inside the dimly lit bar.

Duff was sharing a table with the thin, good-looking bloke. They were deep in conversation; the words flew between them quick and tight. Their chairs were well apart, but Duff tapped his finger on the other man's shoulder, in a gesture that was curiously intimate. Something about this tableau made me uneasy. Something about it wasn't quite right.

I remained just inside the doorway, watching them, until

finally Duff looked up. His jaw jutted out aggressively. 'Who are you? What the fuck do you want?' he demanded. He didn't seem to notice the looks of disapproval that his language earned from the Australian twins. His companion's mouth curved once again into that seductive smile.

'Aren't you going to introduce me to your friend?' I asked Duff. He pushed his chair back noisily and headed towards me.

Most students jump at the offer of a drink. But not Duff. When I told him I was buying, he stabbed his finger at my throat as if he intended to skewer me with it.

'Outside,' he growled. It was more a threat than an invitation. 'We can talk outside.'

I shrugged, turned, and led the way towards the river. I swung myself on to the bench attached to the picnic table. After a split-second hesitation, he settled himself in on the other side.

My note to Duff had explained, more or less, who I was, but I went over it again. A private investigator, I said, trying to locate Katie Arkwright, who'd been missing since the John's May Ball.

Duff was scornful. 'Don't know why you're interested in that little whore. Missing, you say? That type'll do anything to get attention.'

Anything? Like get assaulted, maybe, by a gang of drunks?

I looked up at the hazy sky. Counted to five. Wondered how long it would be before there'd be thunder. When I spoke, my voice was moulded into mildness.

'Do you know, Roger— Listen, you don't mind if I call you Roger, do you?'

Instead of speaking, Duff lowered his chin and looked up at me through angry eyes, like a bull readying for the charge.

I continued in the same mellow tone.

'Have you noticed, Roger, how a lot of people slip from "woman" to "whore" when they're pissed off? Automatically? You can see why, can't you? Because in a sense, it doesn't matter what a woman does. Whether she plays the innocent and keeps sex at a distance, or whether she goes wild and meets men on their own terms, it doesn't really matter, does it? The Catch-22 is that all women are, potentially at least, whores. Yes?'

He didn't answer. The glare deepened. The teeth gritted. The chin dropped further. Smoke didn't issue from his nostrils, but I wouldn't have been surprised to see it. And he didn't even have a cigarette in his hand.

But for all the facial signals, Duff said not a word. He left it to me.

'I guess it wouldn't be fair to blame you, personally, for this,' I said. 'It's part of the culture. But the trouble with seeing women as whores is that a detective like me has a hard time distinguishing a serious accusation from a chance remark. You see my problem?'

If he saw my problem, he gave no sign of it. He glanced over his shoulder, in the direction of the snug. He'd left his pal for a little too long. He started to rise.

Without thinking, I leaned across the table and pressed his wrist into the rough wooden surface, putting my full weight and all the strength acquired from years of rowing into the grip. If it hurt him, all to the good.

'You listen to me, Duff. The girls who know Katie best – her housemate, her best friend – think the charge of prostitution is a load of cobblers.'

Duff stared in astonishment at his wrist. It was seconds before he finally put all his effort into the struggle and managed to break free.

'A load of cobblers, is it?' He rubbed his wrist and spoke to me, at last, through gritted teeth. 'You keep your eyes open, Miss So-Called Detective. You'll see Katie Arkwright for what she is. And it won't be a pretty sight.'

'Duff,' I whispered to his retreating back. 'It wouldn't be you who sent those obscene messages to Katie, now would it?'

I'm sure he heard me. But he didn't turn back.

Flash, flash, flash. The first thing I saw when I pushed open the door of my home on Clare Street was the indicator light on the answering machine. Three messages.

I should have thought work. Should have thought Katie Arkwright. Or Stevie, filling me in on a new case.

But instead I thought: *Sonny*. Surely this would be Sonny, saying he was sorry he'd been tied up. Saying that he loved me. Saying he was coming home.

I felt so sure of it that I couldn't bear to listen. Couldn't bear the prospect of proving myself wrong.

I went upstairs, washed my face, doused it with moisturiser. Put on a sleeveless top. Came down again. The light continued to blink.

The house was stuffy. I distanced myself from the answering machine, and propped the back door open to let a breeze through. The scent of lilac drew me outside.

The area behind my home consists for the most part of an uneven patch of lawn, infrequently cut, with a taller fringe of grasses along the fence. Little here to earn the name of garden. But snuggled up against the house in a position that collects the afternoon sun is an irregularly shaped patio made of stone. It is home to terracotta pots collected over the years, to trailing ivy, to dishes of stones retrieved from the Suffolk coast. There are parsley and basil plants. There are tall clumps of fennel and a scattering of Michaelmas daisies whose pale faces shine out even at dusk. I picked up a flat grey stone and felt its smooth warmth against my palm, strong and sure like the flank of a horse. Then I plucked three daisies and arranged them in a handpainted blue jug, settling them down next to the answering machine.

That did it.

Ready at last.

The first message was from Stevie. She was back in London after a great weekend with Geoff at Wildfell Cottage. I was to ring her when I had a moment, she said, to catch up on all the news.

The second message was from John Carswell. He hoped I wasn't too shaken up by the motorbike ride the day before. Had I managed to contact Robert Arkwright? And how about dinner sometime this week?

The third was from Rosemary Arkwright. Please call me, she said.

I got through straightaway.

'Any news?' I asked. Couldn't keep the eagerness out of my voice.

'Good news, that's why I've rung.' Rosemary's telephone voice matched her appearance. Slight and hesitant, but with a streak of something beautiful running through it. 'I spoke to Katie on the telephone this morning. She rang just after breakfast. You'll be pleased to know she's safe and sound.'

I was washed with a sunrise sensation – a surge of energy – that must have been relief. 'That's wonderful, Mrs Arkwright. Where is she? What's she been doing?'

'She's in London, that's what she said. She's got a job and somewhere to stay. She'll come to visit, in a while, when everything's sorted.'

'If you give me her address, Mrs Arkwright, I'll pop down and have a word with her. Check how she's doing. On behalf of the college.'

There was a pause on the other end of the line.

'Mrs Arkwright?'

'I don't have her address.'

'But surely she—'

'She didn't give me one.' Rosemary cleared her throat – a small, anxious sound – and continued in a firmer voice. 'Anyway, I want you to leave my daughter alone until she's ready to come home. Give her some space.' There was a note of strain in her voice that sat oddly with the assertiveness of her words.

'Don't you want to know where she is? And why she ran away? You can't seriously mean that you're happy to leave things as they stand?'

'Happy?' repeated Rosemary, as if it were an alien word. 'Who says happiness has anything to do with it?'

The conversation was over.

The minute Rosemary rang off, I dialled through to St John's College and asked for the Master. Rosemary Arkwright might be Katie's mother, but Philip Patterson was my client.

He'd already spoken to Rosemary that morning, and he seemed to share her view. I proposed switching the search to London. He responded with less enthusiasm than a reluctant mother who discovers she's carrying not one foetus but four.

'Not a good idea,' he said.

'But that's why you hired me in the first place. To check that Katie's well – that nothing's troubling her.'

'Dr Principal, Katie's mother is very insistent that the inquiry be dropped. Now that the girl's safety is ensured, there's no need to look for her, she says. The college has no real authority in this matter, and further investigation would be an invasion of privacy. That's Mrs Arkwright's view. And, I have to tell you, I'm inclined to agree.'

'But that's absurd. A phone call doesn't prove anything. Doesn't prove Katie's safe. Why don't I just—'

'No. You'll drop the case, Dr Principal. Rosemary Arkwright was most emphatic. You will drop the case, immediately. Do you understand?'

'Why would—'

'As far as I'm concerned, the case is closed. So is the subject. If you would care to leave a list of your expenses, my secretary will draw up a cheque. Good day.'

Like most people who work successfully on a freelance basis, I've dedicated a corner of my brain to intercepting actions that might alienate important clients. There's a little fist of tissue – that's how I imagine it – lurking somewhere to the left of the hypothalamus gland. It makes me report back to customers when I'd rather tell them to stuff it. Requires me, sometimes, to set aside an intriguing new case in favour of a dull-as-dishwater delivery. Prevents me from smart-mouthing a rich-but-despicable corporate client.

This mechanism swung into action when Philip Patterson

gave me the brush-off. Against my better judgement, it forced me to choke out something that sounded like goodbye.

Chapter 13

Fulbourn is a village some four miles south-east of Cambridge, near enough for commuting comfort, far enough away to have a life of its own.

But when people in Cambridge say of a neighbour, 'He's been taken to Fulbourn,' they don't mean that he's been whisked off to visit friends who live on one of the village's picturesquely named streets – Greater Foxes, perhaps, or Fulbourn Old Drift. No, nine times out of ten they have in mind the colder and bleaker image of Fulbourn Psychiatric Hospital. In spite of enlightened care programmes – in spite of its sheltering conifers, its outlook over the pale-yellow fields of summer – Fulbourn is burdened still with the stigma that defined mental illness in earlier eras.

I passed the hospital on my way to find Robert Arkwright, Katie's father, and pulled over on a grassy verge to consult my map. But my mind strayed away from the route and off to Katie's mother.

A woman as delicate as Rosemary Arkwright might have been forced, decades ago, to spend part of her life in Fulbourn Hospital. Today, with anti-depressant medicines, Rosemary functioned perfectly well on home territory. Though she might be in pain, the pain was her own, and it spilled over scarcely at all into the community.

Was Rosemary's depression, I wondered, of recent origin? Did it have any connection to the breakdown of her marriage? Or, perhaps, to Katie's leaving home? Rosemary might be the type of woman whose sense of purpose comes from caring for a child. Who is resourceful and tender in raising that child, but finds –

once the daughter declares independence – that it's more difficult to care for herself. Or did Rosemary's depression have other roots – a physical illness, perhaps, that sapped her emotional stamina? A hardship that she'd tried, but failed, to forget?

Behind me, a tractor chugged out of the lane leading to a nearby farm. I dropped my speculation and edged back on to the road just ahead of it. Guesswork of the crudest kind, I chided myself. And beside the point. Delicate Rosemary might be, but she'd mustered sufficient strength to persuade the Master of St John's to abandon the search for her daughter.

Maybe Robert Arkwright would know what that was about.

Katie's father lived beyond the village. The map led me past a nature reserve, past a public footpath, and out on to an open stretch of road. The road cut a swath between fields as straight as a die; I could see its progress a mile or so away to the crest of the next hill. On either side, the green fields were dusted with bright-red poppies. The scene was poignant with the lushness of summer. Further along, there was a border of young poplars, and as I drove slowly up the slope, their leaves silvered and shimmered in the late-afternoon sunshine.

Almost at the crest of the hill, the landmark I'd been looking for popped into view: a sign pointing left to Fleam Dyke Pumping Station. I turned off and rolled the Saab to a halt. There were no other cars to be disturbed by my stopping.

Fleam Dyke Road was like nothing I'd ever seen before, nowhere I'd ever been. It was dead straight, like a Roman road, and bordered by high hedgerows of spiky hawthorn that spun webs of shadow, even on this summer's afternoon, on to the surface of the road. The hawthorn was impenetrable; you couldn't see through it, or above it, to whatever lay beyond. It created the odd impression that after entering Fleam Dyke Road, there'd be no way out – no openings, no exits, no escapes. The impression of a never-ending tunnel, with a smooth tarmac surface, towering walls of prickly hawthorn, and a roof of flat blue sky.

But that impression – like something out of a De Chirico

nightmare – proved to be false. There were exits and entrances on to Fleam Dyke Road – three, to be precise. A narrow driveway led to a line of lock-up garages; two gates further on gave access to fields. But in each case, because of the height of the hawthorn, the opening was invisible until I'd drawn abreast.

And the lane was not dead, like a tunnel; it was alive. I put the Saab back in gear and crept slowly along, and as I did so, I was accompanied by a tremendous whisper and buzzing from the hedgerow, by the day-songs of a million tiny insects, by a wave of sound that broke, then started up behind me again, as I edged by.

And at the very end of the road, set well back beyond lawns of an incongruously dark green – a green so rich, so aqueous that it looked out of place in the summer countryside – was a collection of tidy buildings. The pumping station – property, a sign announced, of the Cambridge Water Company. It was protected from intrusion by wrought-iron fencing.

The only houses that fronted on to Fleam Dyke Road were tall, and of red brick. They formed a semi-detached pair, right where the road shouldered up to the pumping station. With their neat front gardens, and the lush lawns of the pumping station as a backdrop, it looked as if I'd stumbled upon an isolated, immaculately kept hamlet.

Immaculate, except for the fact that one of the houses had been boarded up with plywood sheets. You wouldn't have thought there could be many vandals in a backwater like this, but I suppose an empty building anywhere will eventually attract its share of trouble.

I approached the other house, edging my car in behind a two-year-old Volvo with a high-polish paint job. It made me feel sorry for the pitted surface of the Saab. As I parked, someone stood at the bay window, staring out. Visitors here must be rarer than hitchhikers in the Himalayas.

That was when it started. An eager barking, from inside the house. A loud, insistent, let-me-at-'em kind of bark.

The figure at the window didn't move. I was watched, as I locked the car, dropped the keys in my jacket pocket, swung the jacket over my shoulder. I was watched – and the dog still barked – as I made my way to the front door.

There were panels of glass shaped like comets' tails in the upper part of the door. Behind them, when I reached the top step, a shadow shifted. And then the door was opened, by a man in a semi-crouching position. His fingers were looped through a dog's collar. The retriever strained forward, yelping still.

'Hey, Redknapp. Shh now. It's all right. Want to go out?'

The dog turned an eager snout towards his master, and seemed to forget me entirely. Arkwright let go of the animal's collar. I pushed back against the door frame to make way as Redknapp scuttled past, and within seconds, he was locked in a tussle with a large piece of wood he'd retrieved from the middle of the lawn.

'He's gnostic,' Arkwright said.

Gnostic? Wasn't that some kind of religious sect? I'd never before come across a dog with a religious affiliation.

Gnostic was what I thought he said. But then Arkwright pointed, with affection, to the dog, and to the piece of hardwood fencepost with which the animal was doing battle.

'Redknapp loves that piece of wood,' he said. 'We brought it with us when we moved from Histon. He wrestles with it, talks to it, goes to sleep with it between his paws. He chews on it so much, I call it his gnawstick.'

Oh.

Introductions took no time at all. Katie's father Robert – Bob, he insisted – invited me into the kitchen straightaway, fetched two Cokes from a plentiful stock in the refrigerator, and poured mine into a glass. It was nice of him. It would have been even nicer to be offered a beer. It didn't seem to occur to Bob that on a hot afternoon, a lager would be more refreshing – even for a driver, even for a woman – than a case of colas.

I was relieved when he led the way out of the kitchen. It had that just-passing-through look I've seen before in the homes of men who are single, but not by choice. Neat and clean, with food in the fridge, but few signs that the house is a home. I'm not a

Homes and Gardens type; but being in that room gave even me ideas. I wanted to pinch out the ivy that straggled on the windowsill, to take the stiff corner-to-corner pile of bills and put them where they could relax in a basket. I wanted, above all, to frame some pictures for the walls.

We moved into the sitting room, where Bob filled the empty corners by talking, candidly and proudly, about his daughter. How, when Katie was little, she was a mischief – always fiddling with things she shouldn't, going where she wasn't supposed to. How she had calmed down in adolescence. Had her sulks, of course – what teenager doesn't? – but became more pliable, he said. Serious-minded. Clever.

'I'm a contractor,' he told me, tapping his cigarette on the edge of a metal ashtray. 'I clear construction sites – you know, like the work on Parkside swimming pool – before the actual building begins.'

And did reasonably well from it, I thought, if the Volvo and the school fees were anything to go by.

Bob recalled fondly how Katie used sometimes to accompany him to the building sites.

'Look at her there.' He had drawn a cloth-bound album from a chest of drawers and opened it carefully on my lap. Turned the pages one by one, stopping finally at a photo of Katie, aged twelve or thirteen. She was perched on a pile of timbers, reading a very fat book.

'That book had twelve hundred pages,' he said with pride. 'A story set in the American Civil War.'

'*Gone with the Wind?*'

'That's it,' he said. 'Takes after her mother. Always reading.'

I turned the pages of the album while he spoke. It had been lovingly, painstakingly put together. Each photo embedded in triangular paper corners, the old-fashioned way. Each inscribed underneath with dates, places, names – *Rosemary Louise Arkwright. Robert Timothy Arkwright. Katie Deanna Arkwright* – in a calligraphic hand.

Most of the photos were of Katie. The ages varied.

Katie astride a stick on a patch of lawn, with wispy hair. She wore yellow dungarees and an expression of grave concentration.

Katie clinging to Rosemary's chest like a baby chimp, skinny legs wrapped tightly around her mother's waist, face buried in her neck, as if she'd just had a fright. Rosemary stared straight out of the picture, her beautiful eyes passionately protective.

Katie, seven or eight years old, dressed to the nines in a posh coat and patent-leather shoes. There was a bow in her now-abundant blonde curls, and a vast smile on her face. She reached greedily towards the camera.

He paused in his anecdotes, and I saw my chance. 'You don't have any idea where she might be now, Bob?'

He shook his head: no. 'You see, love' – I'd gone from 'Laura' to 'love' in a matter of minutes – 'Katie's not quite got over my leaving Histon yet. She refuses to confide in me. She won't even let me help her,' he said, sadly. 'I sent her some money – you know, for living expenses. It's not much. Scarcely more than I used to spend on school fees. But – well, she sent it back. Her way of declaring independence, I suppose.'

Bob shifted heavily in his armchair. He lit up again, using the stump of one Benson and Hedges to set the next one alight. Gave a great sigh. 'Rosemary says Katie's in London. I don't know anything more than that.'

There was a long pause. I wondered if he'd have something to add. But when he spoke, blowing out of cloud of smoke, it was a switch of topic. 'Katie always tried to get me to stop smoking, you know. Even bought me some of that Nicorette. Horrible stuff. I tried it, for her sake.'

As if to erase the taste of Nicorette, he took another puff.

'May I take one of these photos of Katie? One of the recent ones?'

Bob jumped up, fetched a handful of photographs from a drawer. 'Sure,' he said. 'Here's some loose ones. Choose whichever you like.'

I selected a black-and-white close-up of Katie, seated on the grass with her arms wound around her knees. Her face was square on to the camera. Even if she changed her hair, that heart-shaped face would stick in the memory.

'She's beautiful, your daughter,' I said.

'She is,' Bob said. 'And modest with it. Some girls are pretty, they get a big head.' He looked in my direction, pointedly. 'I expect you know about that, Laura.'

He may have meant it as a compliment. I decided not to probe.

'They wrap the boys around their little fingers. Swan about like the Queen of Sheba. But not our Katie. If you ask me, she doesn't even believe that she's attractive. *Oh, Daddy*, she says when I compliment her. As if I've said something embarrassing.'

He paused. Contemplated the glowing tip of his cigarette.

'That's another way she's like her mother. Rosemary always felt small, somehow. Insignificant. I suppose that worked in my favour.'

'Pardon?'

'If Rosemary had known how beautiful she was, she never would've hitched up with an ordinary fellow like me.'

Bob Arkwright's description did him a disservice. He was some years older than Rosemary – maybe early sixties. He had broad shoulders and an abdomen that was only just beginning to crowd the waistband of his trousers. His sandy hair had retreated from the centre of his scalp, but it was balanced by bushy eyebrows, and a complexion coloured by outdoor work. He was pleasant-looking in a bluff sort of way. Not someone you'd notice straightaway in a crowd; but once you did notice him, you'd expect to like him.

'Rosemary was the most beautiful girl in our village. Radiant, she was. In spite of herself, if you know what I mean. She kept a bit of a distance from boys, like she was shy. I was older than her, and no great catch, but I couldn't help myself. I knew she was the girl for me. So I just kept on at her. And then one day, out of the blue, to my great surprise, she said she'd marry me. Just like that.' He smiled.

159

'You left her last year. So the marriage wasn't quite happy ever after?'

'You love someone enough, Laura, you don't always ask if it's happy. For a long while, just having her there was enough. And after Katie was born, we were a family, you know? But last summer . . . I don't know if anyone else can possibly understand this, but I found that I just couldn't take it any more.'

I waited while he struggled with some kind of pain.

'I would've done anything for Rosie, you know, Laura. Anything at all. But I just couldn't bear any longer to see her so desolate. And to know there's not a single thing in the world I can do to make her happy. Maybe, I thought – maybe on her own, without me, Rosemary could find some kind of peace.'

'Your wife suffers from depression?'

'That's what the doctors call it. Just plain unhappiness might be a better description.' He wriggled in his chair. Kept his eyes fixed on his cigarette. 'And Katie – well, Katie didn't relish the idea of being alone with Rosemary. Begged me to let her live here with me while she attended university. But I couldn't do that, Laura. Couldn't take Katie away. Katie is the thing – the only thing, really – that matters to Rosemary.'

Bob must have seen my raised eyebrow. He rushed to explain. 'Oh, Rosemary loves me. But she identifies with Katie. She *is* Katie, in a sense. Taking Katie away from Rosemary could destroy her.'

Bob had not looked at me during this speech, which was haltingly delivered. I had the impression that he'd only begun to articulate his feelings since living on his own. That I might be, perhaps, the first person to whom he'd spoken of these solemn things.

Now he looked up, his misery apparent in his face. Breaking the silence hadn't brought relief. 'I'm sorry, love, I shouldn't have told you this. Rosemary would be so ashamed if she knew I was spreading stories about her. She's a very private person.'

'Who am I going to tell?' I asked. And then went to the heart of the matter. 'Do you know what she's done, Bob?'

He looked at me with surprise. 'Rosemary?'

'She insists that I stop looking for Katie. She's convinced the Master of St John's College to take me off the case.'

Arkwright sat very still for a moment, absorbing this news. Then he leaned over, and moved a coaster into position on the side table next to his arm. With elaborate precision, he set his Coke down, and lined it up so that it sat exactly in the middle of the coaster. And all the while, he avoided my eyes. When he finally looked up, he had a small, sad smile on his face.

'You want another Coke?' he asked.

'I've got to be going soon. But tell me, Bob, why would Rosemary call off the search for Katie?'

'I don't know. Maybe . . .' Bob shook his head. 'No, I don't know. You tell me, love,' he said.

The sun was low and red when I left Bob Arkwright's house. I drove off down the lane, thinking, and drinking in the splendour of the evening. And as I did, something white flashed in the hedgerow to the right-hand side of the track.

I braked and peered into the spiky growth that separated Fleam Dyke Road from the open fields beyond. All I could see was the hawthorn and the metal fencing it had twined around, and the grasses that fringed the base.

The flash was repeated. Then there was a shadowy rush across the track, and another. I slowed and watched in delight. Wild rabbits, pebble-brown, moving in an erratic stop-go-go pattern. The flash I'd seen had been the white blaze of an upturned tail. Once I was tuned in, I realised that the sides of the lane were alive with rabbits. There were dozens of them, enjoying their evening feed.

I peered through the gloom until I reached the first of the gates that gave access to a field. I backed the car into the opening. Then I sat quietly and watched the rabbits taking their evening meal, the sun drifting downwards all the while in my rear-view mirror.

But the pink-red of the sun recalled to me the scarlet of the blood on Stephen Fox's temple. The maroon of the sticky surface it formed on the oriental rug. The brownish-red where the blood defeated the crispness of his shirt.

Stephen Fox was dead. What did that dreadful fact have to do with Katie Arkwright? With the girl who clung to her mother in childhood – who fled from her later on? With the girl whose beauty seemed to give more pleasure to other people than to herself?

Why would Rosemary Arkwright call off the search for Katie? For Katie, her child – the only thing, according to Bob, that she really cared about.

For her baby.

'You tell me,' Bob Arkwright had said.

But he knew the answer. Knew *an* answer, at least. Knew it as well as I did.

Rosemary Arkwright would call off the search only if she didn't want her daughter found. Only if she wanted to hide Katie. From Bob Arkwright? From Philip Patterson? From me?

The sun had dropped so low that I could no longer see its disc in the rear-view mirror. The hedge to my right blocked out the little remaining light of day. Everything had taken on the loud silence of late evening. When I'd first parked the car, there had been a tractor grumbling in the distance. Now the only sound was a wayward breeze that riffled through the hedgerow. And, briefly, in the distance, a thudding. I leaned out of the open window, trying to identify the sound, but it had ceased.

I closed my eyes, the better to follow my train of thought. It was too shadowy now anyway to make out anything beyond dim shapes. If the bunnies were still stop-starting their way along the grasses at the edge of the road, I couldn't see them. They might be standing on their heads, for all I knew, giving me the V-sign.

And, looking inward, rather than outward, I asked myself again: why would Rosemary Arkwright want to hide her child? Why would she push Philip Patterson to renege on his commitment? It didn't make sense – unless, that is, Rosemary knew that Katie was implicated in Fox's murder, and was keen to keep her out of the way until the whole bloody mess had blown over.

Katie and Stephen Fox.

There were links. But they were loose.

Katie knew Stephen Fox; so did hundreds of other people. A senior tutor is one of the best-known figures in the college world – a person to be reckoned with by colleagues, university officials and students alike.

Katie's disappearance and Fox's death had occurred only a few days apart. As Nicole had pointed out, this was a coincidence that could bear looking into. But a coincidence doesn't make a crime.

Katie had been seen coming from Fox's office in the week in which he died. Her name wasn't in the appointment book and she had no official reason to be there.

None of these connections on its own amounted to a call for action. But blended together, they meant that there was more going on than met the eye. That Katie and Fox were almost certainly linked in some manner that went beyond the formal and the known.

And when this likelihood was added to Rosemary's insistence – her uncharacteristically assertive insistence – that Katie should not be found, my curiosity was raised to full revs. I was gripped by a sharp anxiety on Katie's behalf.

But I no longer had a client.

Suddenly, there was the scuffing noise of boot on clod. The car gave a tremor, like the quiver of a horse's flank when a fly alights. I knew instantly that someone or something had touched it. I reached across the passenger seat, and flicked the lock. Began frantically winding up the window with my left hand. Wished not for the first time for electronic windows.

In two strides a man was alongside, looming over me.

Bob Arkwright.

'I was taking Redknapp for a walk,' he said, 'when I spotted the car. Were you watching the rabbits?'

'You're a lucky man.' I took a deep breath and tried to pass it off as an inhalation of fresh country air. 'You get them every evening. But the rabbits have retired now, and it's getting too dark for scenery.'

Something about the darkness now and the silence had shifted from soft to sinister. Or maybe it was just my dislike of having someone stand alongside the car when I was sitting inside. Made me feel vulnerable.

'So,' I said, starting the engine, 'I'll be on my way.'

Bob Arkwright bent over so that his face was level with mine. The dog jumped and made a low growl. I released the handbrake.

'Redknapp,' Arkwright said. 'Quiet, boy.' He stared at me with an intensity that hadn't seemed part of him when we were back in that unlived-in-looking house.

'Katie's just a child,' he said. 'She looks grown up, but she's been sheltered. Doesn't know her way around. She won't manage on her own. You've got to find her, Miss Principal. Whatever Rosemary says.'

'But Mr Arkwright' – I couldn't call him Bob, not after the start he'd just given me – 'I was hired by St John's College and they've ordered me to abandon the case. I haven't got a client any more.'

Bob Arkwright stood up and pulled on Redknapp's lead, bringing the dog back from where he'd been sniffing a trail at the base of the hedge. He stepped away from the car.

It was dark; I couldn't make out his features. But I heard every word.

'Let me be your client,' he said.

Chapter 14

The primary principle of investigation is to rule out the obvious. To scan the straightforward options first, before exploring anything more fanciful.

That's why the police, when a child's reported missing, begin by searching its home – by checking the cupboards, the garden shed, the attic, for a baby who might simply have curled up and gone to sleep. Checking, at the worst, for a corpse.

That's why I made my way back to Histon, where Rosemary lived. But Bob, my new client, had been adamant: leave Rosemary alone, he had said. So I parked the car on Rosemary's street, out of sight of her laburnum tree, and knocked on doors.

'Rosemary Arkwright's not in,' I said. 'Anyone know where I can find her? And' – as an afterthought – 'how about Katie?'

Well, they all knew who Katie was. A girl like that lights up the neighbourhood. Her comings and goings become a matter of note. But there hadn't been any comings and goings – not from Katie, not around here – in recent weeks.

OK, I thought. Just checking.

Of course, I didn't get away quite as lightly as that. A man watering his rose bushes in defiance of the hosepipe ban treated me to a rehash of the trouble on Grantchester Meadows during May Week.

'Terrible, isn't it?' During his monologue, he monitored me out of the corner of his eye, making sure that I agreed, that I wasn't one of those university types who make excuses for undergraduate excess.

I reassured him with a neutral answer. 'Drunkenness isn't pretty,' I said.

And conflict between town and gown is not, apparently, dead.

The heavy-set woman next door was unloading shopping from the boot of her car. She found the topic of our conversation irresistible, rested her bags on her hip and joined in.

'Don't think we don't know what we're talking about,' she insisted. 'Half of us around here have worked for the colleges at some time or another. George here was a gardener at Peterhouse for forty-eight years. And those students wouldn't have had clean sheets on their beds if it wasn't for me and Pat and Louise and Edith. We could tell you a thing or two. Isn't that right, Edith?'

She pounced on a woman who had poked her head out of an upstairs window to see what was going on.

I used that moment to wriggle out. I'd seen *Upstairs, Downstairs*. I knew the storyline already.

Besides, I had housekeeping of my own to do.

It took me the best part of the afternoon.

I looked with a critical eye, an outsider's eye, at the mess that had accumulated in Clare Street while I'd been living like a bachelor girl. At the flotsam and jetsam that drifted across the coffee table. At the spent matches on the mantelpiece. The dirty glasses by the side of the bed. The assortment of trainers and shoes that had been commandeered for foot duty, and never returned to their rightful place.

And having noticed the mess for the first time in weeks, I responded like my mother's daughter. I shifted and sorted, discarded and filed.

My efforts weren't only on the surface. I cleaned as well.

I washed up all the dirty dishes. Polished my favourite pair of antique wine glasses – a gift from Helen – until they gleamed. I put fresh linen on the bed. And, though it rarely got lifted these days, I even remembered to clean the underside of the toilet seat. It was a selective attack rather than a complete spring-cleaning, but the effect was a minor transformation. And all afternoon, while discarding and filing, and shifting and scrubbing, I kept the doors and windows propped open. The musty odour that the house had acquired in recent days gradually lifted. The scent of honeysuckle trickled in and that of must trickled out.

And then, fortified by the scent of flowers and the shine of the floorboards, I went to work on myself. I washed my skin and my hair with a potion that left me smelling of cucumber. I filed the calluses off my heels, and layered on lotion from neck to toe, until my body was as smooth as a baby's bottom and much less smelly. I finished off with clothes that were casual enough to appear unconsidered – a crisp pair of jeans that fitted like a dream, a fresh white T-shirt, a wide belt that did wonders for my waist.

And I made provision for hunger. Laid in stuff that could be munched while we did whatever other things might take our fancy.

There were pistachio nuts and slices of smoked salmon, marinated olives and raspberries and ripe avocados. There were oysters, fresh from the coast. Not very subtle, the oysters; but it wasn't subtlety I was after.

There was wine chilling in the fridge. Cold but not icy, that was how he liked it.

All I needed now was Sonny.

Sonny's plane was due in at five o'clock. The half-hours ticked away. He didn't arrive.

I became anxious. At seven, when I heard what I thought was a taxi pull up outside, I rushed to the door. I'd doubted him – doubted he would actually come – and now he was proving me wrong. Who would have thought that being wrong could feel so good?

There was a smile on my face of pure pleasure: welcome home, Sonny, it said.

Wrong again.

It was John Carswell on the doorstep, not Sonny. He responded to my glad greeting with such obvious delight that I hadn't the heart to put him straight.

'Just for a moment,' I said, inviting him in. 'I'm expecting Sonny back from Amsterdam, you see.'

'Ah.' His voice was grave, even mildly mocking. 'The boyfriend.'

I was tempted to respond by insisting that Sonny was far more than just a boyfriend. Boyfriend sounds so trivial. Partner, I could have countered. Long-term lover. Sonny's not someone I have a date with, I could have said, he's someone who shares my life.

But for some strange reason, I didn't.

'Look what I've found for you,' John said.

The object was rectangular and heavy and firm. It was wrapped in a Heffer's bag. You didn't have to be a private investigator to figure out that John Carswell had brought me a book.

I looked up at him, curious now. He was studying me carefully, those astonishing green-blue eyes waiting for a reaction.

I slipped the book from its bag. It was a slim hardback, the faded dustjacket foxed with brown. There was a sketch of an undistinguished-looking building, and above it, the title: *The Spinning House: 1635–1894*. The author was J. Digby Critchley. He might be an historian, as the title page suggested, but I'd never come across his name before.

'What is it?' I asked. Meaning: why this particular book? Why for me?

'I found it second-hand, going for a snip. There were only ever two hundred copies printed. Thought you might be interested.'

I had set aside my work as a historian years ago, and even in my academic days, it wasn't monographs on local history that set the pulses racing. I struggled not to let my disappointment show.

'It's about prostitution in Cambridge,' John explained.

'No, you're mistaken,' I said minutes later, after I'd thumbed, enthralled, through the early pages. It wasn't about prostitution in Cambridge. Not really. There was little about the corrupting effects of a university peopled with men alone. Nothing about the undergraduates, who – denied access to women of their own class – sought the company of others whom they could never take home for tea. Nothing about the dilemmas of those women who had to supplement uncertain earnings as laundresses or pickers with periodic spells of prostitution.

There was no discussion in Critchley of the hypocrisy that sliced along lines of sex and class. Nothing about the tightrope walked by respectable young women of the town. About the way they might be flattered by the attentions of students – might be wooed and indulged – only to be dismissed as tarts if they responded with smiles and kisses. No sowing of wild oats, no experiments in love, for local girls; moments of abandon were marked for men alone.

Nothing about the cruel line drawn between women who were offered only two options: will you be pure as the driven snow, my dear? Or will you be a whore?

No, I thought, as I leafed through the old volume, increasingly absorbed. J. Critchley Digby had written not about prostitution in the city, but about the University's response.

John leaned over my shoulder and pointed to an engraving, which showed an austere building with rows and rows of tiny windows.

'The Spinning House,' he said. 'A truly dreadful place.'

I raised an eyebrow.

'On St Andrew's Street,' he explained. 'Part workhouse and part gaol. Dedicated, by 1750, to the punishment of women.'

With sixty cells the size of cupboards, I read. With iron shutters. With no heat, no water, little light, little air.

The Spinning House, where women suspected of lewd conduct were imprisoned.

Where the Town Crier was paid, from time to time – on instructions from the Vice Chancellor – to whip the women and girls.

Somewhere in the course of my reading, I arranged myself

169

cross-legged on a cushion on the floor. John Carswell opened the wine – cold, but not too cold – and poured us each a glass. He noticed the contents of the fridge. 'Help yourself,' I said. And, joking, 'What's mine is yours.'

He ferried smoked salmon, and avocados, and raspberries into the sitting room and pulled up a cushion facing me.

'It's amazing, John. I've lived in Cambridge ever since my own undergraduate days, and I've never before heard of this place. How can that be? It disappeared less than a hundred years ago.'

'Simple.' John shrugged. 'Ancient universities love tradition – but only as long as it makes them look good. Powerful institutions don't relish reports about their less savoury pasts.'

'But J. Digby Critchley—'

'J. Digby Critchley was never appointed to the history faculty, was he? I imagine this volume did little for his career.'

Even in June, it can become nippy by nine o'clock. I was stretched out full-length on the polished floorboards, facing a flickering fire, when another knock came. John had stood to fetch more bread. He headed for the door. At the last moment, I tried to call him back.

Too late.

I heard Sonny's startled murmur. Saw John step aside so that the door opened wider, saw him gesture towards me. I was already on my way.

'Sweetheart, what kept you?' I didn't mean the question to come out as a complaint, but that was how Sonny took it.

'I've been working,' Sonny retorted. Indeed, he looked as if he had. His jacket was crumpled, his chin stubbled, his face lined with fatigue. He tore his gaze away from John. Swept the room, taking in the side-by-side cushions, the mostly empty bottle of Chablis, the remains of our supper. 'The delay hasn't been too much of an inconvenience, I see. You obviously haven't waited.'

John, looking mildly embarrassed, and fresh beside Sonny's exhaustion, interceded. 'It's my fault,' he said. 'Laura's been doing some research. I insisted she have something to eat while she was at it. Can I get you a plate?' He headed in the direction of the kitchen.

I appreciated John's tact. And wished like hell he wasn't there at all.

Sonny and I stood, facing one another. There was a long silence, as each of us tried to find a way to cross the breach. Tried, and didn't succeed. I reached out a hand towards him. 'Sonny,' I whispered. But I felt him stiffen, felt a pulling-away, and I couldn't go on.

Sonny accepted the glass of wine that John handed him, but refused a cushion near me. He sat in an armchair at a daunting distance. He managed, with his usual gusto, to eat a stuffed bagel. He even joined in the conversation for a while.

'What's this research?' he said.

At that moment, I didn't feel like talking about the Spinning House, any more, I suppose, than he felt like asking. But it was marginally better than silence.

I told him about the lock-up. About the sixty women who were imprisoned there at any one time. About the outrage felt by the townspeople of Cambridge. How the coach belonging to the Proctor – a University official – was often pelted with stones as he carried girls away.

And how, by the nineteenth century, resentment had become national.

'Look at this, Sonny.' I showed him a passage in Critchley's book. 'See? The *Daily Telegraph* led a national campaign. Against what it termed "the Abominable Spinning House".'

Sonny got into the spirit of the thing at last. 'And even in 1860,' he pointed out, 'the *Telegraph* wasn't a paper that shrank from demanding punishment where punishment was due. A question, Laura. Why were the good people of Cambridge so opposed? Surely they weren't keen to have prostitutes prowling along Petty Cury?'

John broke in. 'Arrests were rather indiscriminate, it seems. Proctors were likely to pounce on any woman alone – and certainly, any girl walking with an undergraduate. As the people of Cambridge saw it, their womenfolk were being imprisoned without trial, and their reputations ruined.'

'Not to mention the danger to their health from conditions inside.'

'Plus,' said John, 'the fact that the girls were tried in the Vice-Chancellor's secret court, without representation, meant that there was no opportunity to put mistakes right. People of the time detested the secret court, detested the Proctors' powers of arrest. Saw it as an example of feudal privilege. The *Morning Chronicle* referred to the Spinning House as the "University Bastille".'

'They saw it,' I butted in, 'as an insult to the people of Cambridge, whose police and magistrates should be the ones to keep order in the town.'

'And, I suppose, they were right,' said Sonny, shaking his head. 'You couldn't find a clearer example of town versus gown.' He looked at John in a calculating way. 'Would I be wrong in thinking that you're a don? A representative of that very gown?'

John took it in good part. 'Guilty as charged. But in my defence, the Spinning House was closed some seventy years before my appointment. I can hardly be held responsible.' He offered Sonny that winning smile.

'No?' Sonny refilled his glass, leaning across me as he did so. 'Isn't that what they always say? *It wasn't me, guv, it was the organisation?*'

'Sonny.' This was getting a bit out of hand.

He didn't respond. His eyes were locked on to John's.

To my surprise, John seemed to flinch. A cloud dulled the colour of his green-blue eyes, and he looked distinctly uneasy.

I put my hand on Sonny's arm, and spoke again.

'Hey, you. Sonny Mendlowitz. Anybody home?'

His attention wavered, and his eyes flickered in my direction.

'How are you doing on the Cindy Sinful case?' I asked. 'Did your guy do it or not?'

'Apparently not.' Sonny was focused on me now. 'The owner of the BMW sent me to his snooker club, and I turned up a new witness there. A man who claims to have been drinking with Trevor when Cindy was being driven towards the motorway. I persuaded him to make a statement.'

'Well done, Sonny.' Why had I jumped to conclusions before about Sonny protecting a guilty man? 'So he's innocent, after all.'

'Not necessarily,' Sonny said.

John stood up. 'Laura?'

'Not necessarily?' I asked.

'I don't believe the witness.' Sonny shrugged. 'Even though I had to persuade the guy to make a statement – or so he made it seem – I had the feeling when I walked into the snooker club that he knew exactly why I was there. That he'd been expecting me.'

'That means that the defendant put him up to it?'

'You know it, girl. And I know it. Now I've got to show it.'

John cleared his throat. 'Shall I nip out and get another bottle, Laura?'

'No need. There's another one under the broccoli. Bottom of the fridge. Do you mind opening it, John?'

Sonny stood up. He gave me a small, tired smile. 'Not for me, Laura,' he said.

I stood too and put my arms around him for the first time since he'd entered the room. Touched my cheek to his crumpled jacket. Felt the familiar contours of his chest, his shoulders, his back. Felt his right arm go around me. It was tentative, but it was there. And then it tightened briefly, so for seconds, in our moment alone, he held me close.

'I'm sorry, Laura. I really am. I have to go. To London, to pick up some stuff from the office, and then back to Amsterdam for an early-morning meeting. I wanted to see you for a few minutes. To tell you in person, that's all.'

'Shall I come with you? I could be ready in ten minutes. I could give you a hand . . .'

He disengaged. 'Not this time. Soon.' He looked in the direction of the kitchen and away again. 'Be a good girl,' he said.

He kissed me briefly on the lips and was gone.

*

I don't know whether or not John hung around in the kitchen deliberately, to give me time to recover from Sonny's departure. Don't know whether he witnessed our goodbyes. But I was grateful for a chance to compose myself. I plumped up my cushion, tidied the remains of our supper, and poked the fire. I closed J. Digby Critchley's history of the Spinning House, and folded it back inside its carrier bag.

I put a B.B. King recording on the CD player and turned up the volume. I'd rather hear about B.B.'s sweet little angel than talk.

I sat down, not on the floor cushion, but in the armchair that Sonny had deserted.

John set a fresh glass of wine near me, and took his place quietly. If he'd spoken, I might've asked him to leave.

But instead, he listened to the music. His first words didn't come until four tracks into the album. By then, I'd been restored to some kind of equilibrium.

Still, John was a few sentences into his story before I realised that he was talking not just about the Cambridge Folk Festival, but about his wife.

'She was sitting cross-legged on the grass – like you, Laura, on that cushion before.' John's face was warm with memory. 'Someone was playing a mournful kind of guitar piece, and Vivienne was listening as if her life depended on it. Bent forward, so her long hair made a veil around her face. All I could see was her hair and the curve of her back. I waited for minutes to see her face. Finally, the music ended, and Vivienne uncoiled, and she shook her head backwards, long, languid shakes. Stretched her beautiful face to the sun and smiled.'

He looked up at me. His expression was apologetic. 'I'm sorry,' he said. 'I can never hear a blues guitar without thinking of that moment.'

'What happened to her?'

'I loved her solidly, for twenty years.' He passed a hand over his face, as if to conjure himself back to the present. 'But she died.'

'Tell me,' I said. 'Tell me how she died.'

John glanced up, as if to check that I actually meant what I said. Then he told me.

Vivienne had been driving home one night from Colchester, in her green Toyota. She was late and may have been travelling a little too fast for the winding A604.

'In the hilly area near Stoke-by-Clare, her car went off the road.' He paused. 'At first, they assumed it was an accident. Later, we learned that another car had collided with her from the back – twice. Had bumped the Toyota off the road, into the adjoining field. Whoever it was didn't stop. Left her alone and injured.'

I didn't say I was sorry. That would require John to say something to comfort me, and I didn't want to put him in that position. I slipped out of the armchair, took up a seat once again on the cushion next to him, and placed my hand on his arm.

'The car wasn't spotted until daybreak. It probably took her hours to die.'

'They never found the other driver?'

'No.' John shook his head. 'Even today, whenever a car comes up too fast in the outside lane of the motorway, I find myself thinking: were you the one? The one who killed her?'

'No arrest. No conviction. There's bound to be a sense of unfinished business. Of something left undone.'

He laid his hand over mine, and traced the outline of my fingertips. 'Perhaps that's why I'm intrigued by your job,' he said. 'Being a PI means working towards that kind of closure.' He squeezed my hand, as if he'd just thought of something. Lifted it gently and kissed my fingers.

I half wanted to pull away. And half didn't.

'Laura?'

I felt drawn to John. Wanted to comfort him. Wished I hadn't had quite so many glasses of wine.

Thought of Sonny, who, only half an hour earlier, had kissed me, almost on this very spot, so tenderly.

Be a good girl.

The telephone rang. I sprang up and answered it.

'Who is it?' John whispered, looking at his watch.

'Shh,' I whispered back. 'I think it's Deborah Cook. Katie Arkwright's friend.'

Her voice was distorted, choking, as she tried to speak. At first, I thought it was laughter. Then I realised she was on the edge of panic.

'What is it, Deborah? Are you hurt? Is it Katie?'

'No, it's me,' Deborah sobbed. 'You've got to help me. I think I've found a body.'

Chapter 15

Deborah Cook's room in St Bartholomew's College could have been a student room anywhere in England. There was a black-and-white poster of a young River Phoenix – a still from the film *Stand by Me*. There was another poster, of Kurt Cobain. In earlier times, it might have been James Dean hanging up there. The reckless deaths, the suicides, the lost boys, tough-looking but vulnerable. The perfect way to snare a young girl's heart. *I could have saved him . . .*

There was a wooden chair, the seat and back strewn with the paraphernalia of a student life. A copy of *Varsity* open to a page showing highlights of the club scene. A screwdriver and some worn screws. A pair of jeans that looked wide enough to go twice around Deborah's slight frame. A flute in a cracked leather case.

The central light fixture cast a bright circle on the thin carpet and touched the corner of the bed. On the bedside table was a lava lamp. I toggled the switch. Darker corners of the room shot into view.

And in the extended sweep of light, I saw a bundle wrapped in newspaper lying on the floor. It was shaped like a rugby ball but much, much larger. The knot that had held the packet together had been unpicked. The paper was stripped back, layer upon layer, as if someone had been peeling away – *he loves me, he loves me not* – the petals of a flower.

As if someone had been playing Pass the Parcel. But if this were Pass the Parcel, it would have been a very macabre game indeed. Not at all the kind of party game you'd want for your child's birthday.

For, as a glance revealed, it wasn't jelly tots or miniature chocolate bars that were secreted inside the parcel. What was tucked away in its darkened heart was a bundle of bones.

Using my Maglite, I eased the opening, edged it wider still. Inside a shell of newspaper, stiff and yellow, there was a cavern, as if a papier-mâché structure had been built around a balloon. The base was filled with bones. Peering into the hollow, I thought I could pick out a characteristic pattern – skull at one end, ribs collapsed on vertebrae, pelvis, thighbones, tibia and fibula. Some of the bones were loose, their cartilage attachments worn – or torn – away. The hip bone wasn't, in this case, connected to the thigh bone. But it was a skeleton nonetheless. About eighteen inches long.

One bone lay by itself, on the carpet.

Deborah sat on the bed. She had drawn herself as far back as she could. She was pressed against the wall, legs drawn up beneath her. Her forearms made a defensive cross over her chest; each hand gripped its opposite shoulder. Her chin was tucked down, resting on her wrists.

I looked in the direction of the isolated bone and back again at Deborah.

'I couldn't help it,' she protested. 'It just fell out.'

'Show me where you found the parcel.'

Deborah struggled up off the bed, her movements heavy with shock. She led me to a tall alcove next to the fireplace. The bottom portion had been filled in by a cupboard. It was painted two tones darker than the institutional beige of the walls.

'Here,' Deborah said. As well as shock, there was apprehension in her glance. Her words began to flow out in a smooth stream, with little room for breath between. 'I noticed that the floor of the cupboard was made of a kind of plywood, and it was higher than the floor of the bedroom, and I was tidying and I lifted the plywood and underneath it was this – this—'

She turned and gestured helplessly.

'It's too small. It can't be a person. Can it?'

'You sit down again,' I said. And when the girl was settled, and breathing normally again, I examined the bones, without touching them or the strange wrappings in which they were enclosed.

'I'm no expert, Deborah. But this could be the remains of a baby.'

I watched her face carefully. She was pale, her eyes were unsteady. But the moment had passed when she might collapse.

'Deborah, why did you ring me? Why not the police?'

'I had your card and you – you're a detective, aren't you? I thought you would know what it is. Know what to do.' She looked not at me, but at the alcove cupboard. 'I'm pretty upset. Maybe – maybe you could take the – the skeleton – to the police? Tell them you found it somewhere? I don't think I can deal with them. I'm too upset, you know?'

There was a kettle in a corner of the room. I found the necessaries, and made tea. Added powdered creamer at her nod, and sugar without asking. I handed her the mug and perched on the end of the bed.

'Deborah.' I surprised myself by adopting the tone of a midwife I know – firm but kind. 'Deborah, I'm going to ask you some questions. I want you to think about your answers carefully, and tell me the absolute truth. Unless you do, I won't be able to help you.'

The girl nodded, bending forward over her mug of tea. Her face was obscured behind auburn wings of hair.

'Do you know anything – anything at all – about this? The skeleton's identity? Where it came from? Who put it there?'

My questions were met with vigorous headshakes.

'Was there anything else inside this parcel when you opened it? Anything at all?'

'No.' She was positive – emphatic. She took another sip of tea and looked up. Some of the tension had gone out of her body. She looked almost relieved. She balanced her mug carefully to avoid spills and began to wriggle her bottom off the bed.

'Just a minute,' I said. 'One more question. Rummaging about under the floor of that cupboard – what were you doing, Deborah? Were you looking for something in particular?'

Deborah's thin face tightened in alarm. 'No. No. I wasn't looking for anything. I was just tidying the cupboard, and—' Suddenly she burst into tears. Her eyes reddened, and instantly, the prettiness was erased. Drops of tea slopped on to the unbleached cotton covering. 'You know, don't you? How? How did you know?'

I stood up and took the mug away from her. Offered her a handful of tissues. And pointed to the chair.

'Oh.' She sniffed. 'The screwdriver.'

'The false floor of that cupboard had been screwed in place. It takes effort to dislodge a fitting like that. And the effort would be worth it only if you expected to find something.'

Deborah blew her nose.

I offered her a second option. 'Or if you intended to hide something. Something illegal?'

She sat quietly now, with downcast eyes.

'And seeing as you were so keen to avoid the police, I figured you might have been after a hiding place for drugs.'

She didn't disagree.

'Get them for me.'

Deborah turned her back and rummaged in a drawer. From under the socks and the knickers, she brought out a couple of dozen small plastic envelopes, each containing a tablet. She handed them to me.

'What are you going to do?' she asked.

'Shhh. I'm thinking.'

'I wasn't dealing,' Deborah pleaded. 'These were just for me. Honest, Miss Principal.'

Did I believe her? Deborah had enough money; she didn't need to deal. But since when did affluence stand in the way of greed? And it might be – how did a dealer I once knew put it? – a social thing. A way of being cool.

From her desk, I picked up a pair of scissors. Cut the tops off the envelopes. Walked Deborah to the loo, and watched while she dumped the lot into the bowl and flushed. Three tablets bobbed back to the surface. I flushed again. They were gone.

We went back to her room and contacted Parkside Police Station. While I waited for Detective Inspector Pelletier to ring back, I called Deborah away from the dressing table. She'd been reapplying her make-up, smoothing a mask of foundation and blusher on to her pale face.

'You'll tell them?' she asked.

'No, you'll tell them,' I said. 'Every detail. Except, of course, that one.'

'And what shall I say about . . .?'

'Oh, say you were doing a spot of do-it-yourself, Deborah. Enlarging the cupboard.'

'They'll never believe me.'

I shrugged. 'Depends how good an actress you are.'

And later, while we waited for the arrival of the police, I knelt on the thin grey carpet, and peered again, more closely, at that single bone.

I'm not an expert, but this was almost certainly an arm bone, withered, darkened, dried. I tried to imagine it as it might have been. Not the muscles and tendons and joints, I don't mean that – not an anatomical reconstruction.

No, I tried to imagine it with flesh on. With the pale, plump flesh of a baby. Or with the powdery creases, the blotchy, tender skin, of the newborn. Tried to imagine the tiny hand, the blind fingertips. To envision the way those fingers might clutch at an adult, the way their grasp would become surer day by day as the infant strengthened its delicate hold on life.

Tried to imagine, not just the fingertips and the dimpled knuckles and the floppy wrist and the tiny forearm, but the little person of whom they were a part. Struggling to make sense of the world. Looking hungrily towards a mother, a father – an adult who would keep him safe, offer him protection, until he could fend for himself.

A little person. Somebody's little treasure. Somebody's love.

And in the middle of my imagining, I opened my eyes. Was

struck by the glint of metal inches away. On all fours, like a baby myself, I crawled nearer to the gleam and impaled it on my torchbeam.

It was a tiny bracelet, two lengths of silver chain and a small metal disc. There was some lettering on the tarnished surface, but without picking the bracelet up, it was difficult to decipher the diminutive script.

'Laura?'

Deborah. I'd almost forgotten her.

'Laura, shouldn't we have contacted the college authorities? They're supposed to be the ones who summon the police.'

'Stuff the college authorities,' I said.

How would the college authorities feel when they learned that, for the second time in a fortnight, I'd reported the presence of a body in St Bartholomew's?

And, for that matter, how did I feel? *If a body meet a body . . .*

I sent Deborah on a search.

She returned a minute later with a magnifier borrowed from a biologist who had a room nearby.

Deborah held the torch for me. I returned to my awkward position, bum in the air, nose inches away from the arm bone. I angled the magnifier over the name-tag. The engraving was in italic script, with elongated letters. I expected a single word, or two words – the baby's name.

Instead, there was a curious jumble of letters. It took a moment for my brain to unpick them. To make any sense.

Ofme Notofme, it said.

Deborah Cook was a quick-change artist. While I'd been wondering whether I could maintain my composure – *need a body cry?* – she had put on her make-up, and with it a whole new persona. All the panic had gone down the toilet with the drugs.

And if Nicole suspected that there was an unstated reason why the screwdriver had been borrowed, why the cupboard had been tampered with, she opted not to know.

'You don't think Deborah Cook had anything to do with this baby's death, do you, Nicole?'

I meant *you* collectively. The police. The fuzz. The Old Bill. It was unlikely that Nicole would be in charge of this case. One murder investigation per inspector at a time, that's how it's played.

But whatever mystery writers say, suspicious deaths rarely happen in college. And when two bodies turn up in one college, links between them can't be overlooked. Detective Inspector Pelletier was the person most likely to liaise between the two cases.

'No.' Nicole took a roundabout way of explaining. 'As soon as the scenes-of-crime officers finish, the skeleton will go off to the forensic scientists for dating. We'll try to discover when this baby died.'

'But surely the newspaper—'

Nicole's headshake stopped me in mid-sentence.

'Whoever put the body there snipped off the headers. There's no date on the paper to narrow things down. But we'll figure it out sooner or later.'

'And Deborah?'

'Come on, Laura, look at the colour of the bones. The corrosion. The tarnish on the bracelet. Ten to one this baby died before Deborah herself was out of nappies. Maybe before she was born. She's not a suspect.' Nicole fixed me with a fierce gaze. 'For that matter, nor are you. Though maybe you should be.'

We were sitting in the incident room in Bart's. An extra room on that corridor had been commandeered, in light of the new discovery. Even now, approaching midnight, there was a steady movement of police officers, in and out of the corridor, moving furniture and setting up equipment.

I marched to my own defence. 'Coincidence, Nicole. With a capital C.' I did my best, as you must for a good defence, to anticipate the prosecution's point of view. 'OK, so we've had two deaths, in one college, in less than a week. And I've been present more or less at the finding of both the bodies. A strange coincidence, I agree. An unlikely one. But I can assure you, it's a case of what Ripley used to call strange but true.'

'The word on the street is that Ripley faked his material. You don't expect me to believe, Laura, that these two incidents are absolutely unrelated?'

'*Absolutely* would be going too far,' I conceded. 'There are links – but they're all above board. I met Deborah because Katie Arkwright disappeared; for the same reason, I tried to see Fox in his office and turned up his body instead. Believe me, that's the only thing that links me with corpses one and two.'

Nicole wasn't going to make this easy for me. 'So the connection is Katie Arkwright?'

'I wouldn't put it quite like that. The link is my *professional* inquiry into Katie's disappearance.'

When doctors, psychologists or lawyers find themselves in trouble, they always invoke the concept of a profession. Why not private investigators too?

'Speaking of that *professional* inquiry,' Nicole said. Her face was as much the picture of innocence as a senior policewoman – who's been everywhere, seen everything, and found little of it heartening – could make it. She put an emphasis on 'professional' that showed she knew exactly what I was up to. 'Remember you were asking about brothels? I've put the question to one or two of my male colleagues. Interested?'

'*Certainly.*'

Nicole obliged. 'If you're looking for prostitutes, they say – you can imagine the ribbing I got, Laura – there's a small flat of working girls in Cherry Hinton at the moment, and another even smaller one in Milton. The former has mainly black girls, and the latter mainly Chinese. They swear blind there's no young blonde in either. And no one under twenty-five years of age.'

'And your colleagues' connection with these working flats is . . .?'

'Purely *professional*, of course. Are you getting anywhere with Katie Arkwright?'

'Thanks for the info, Nicole – sorry about that ribbing. And as to Katie – it depends what you mean by anywhere. I've spoken to the parents. To the housemates. To various friends.' Even, I thought, to one or two enemies, though I didn't want to mention Roger Duff to Nicole. 'But none of them can provide details about where Katie might have got to. Or why she might have gone.'

'You think she's all right?'

I pondered that for a moment. Faced the thoughts that I'd put behind me up till now.

'No, Nicole. To be frank, I don't. I've only got suspicions to go on, but they are suspicious suspicions, if you know what I mean.'

'I'll know when you tell me.'

'Well, there's the fact that when she left, she didn't take any of her things, as far as I could see. She hasn't gone back to her house, and she hasn't communicated with anyone since. Except her mother. Katie rang her mother – maybe – to say she was all right; didn't say where she was exactly or why she'd gone.'

'I don't understand the maybe.'

I shrugged. 'When Rosemary reported this to me – and told me to call off the search – she was more than a little odd. I'm not sure that she was telling the truth when she said she didn't have an address for Katie. For that matter we've only got Rosemary's word for it that her daughter rang at all. It's not inconceivable that Rosemary made up the call in order to justify abandoning the search.'

'Why would she do that?'

'Heaven knows.' It didn't seem a good idea to discuss my suspicions just yet about a connection between Katie and Stephen Fox. 'Anyway, my point is that Katie had a good life here. She was popular, a successful student. She had family and friends.'

'And,' Nicole interjected, 'she was in love.' Her dry tone suggested that she remembered only too well what I'd said about Jared Scott-Pettit.

'That, too. Why run away? It's the kind of inexplicable thing that makes me all uneasy.'

Nicole nodded. 'What else?'

'There's her state of mind immediately beforehand. On the evening of the ball, she was exhilarated. Then, quite suddenly, she began to behave like a girl with something to fear.'

'She might have been a girl who only *thought* she had something to fear,' Nicole shrugged. 'Surely you would have come to me before if there were actual signs of violence? Or abduction?'

'True enough, Nicole. I don't know which nags at me more – the possibility that Katie has been harmed. Or the chance that she's harmed herself.'

'Harmed herself? Why do you say that?'

'State of mind, again. Katie looked on the surface like a girl who had everything going for her.'

'But?'

'All her acquaintances – from a fellow called Matt, who used to go out with her years ago, to her best friend, Deborah—'

'Our Deborah?'

'She of the skeleton in the closet.' I nodded. 'They all mention how little Katie valued herself. If Katie has had a shock of some kind, she's the sort of person who might not have the resources to shake it off.'

'So you're planning to do – what, precisely?'

'I have to warn you, Nicole, I'm running out of standard options. Moving on to the section of the manual reserved for desperate measures.'

'I don't recall what's in that section,' Nicole said. 'Care to fill me in?'

I shook my head. 'Nope, not at the moment. Not unless it pans out. Anyway, Nicole' – I looked at the bags under her eyes and the coffee stain on her lapel – 'there's Stephen Fox. And these poor wee bones. I reckon you've got enough on your plate.'

It was past midnight. I didn't want to go home.

Didn't want to walk into my sitting room. Didn't want to see the cushions, side by side, on the floor I'd polished earlier that day. Didn't want to see the empty wine glasses, to smell the charred embers of the fire.

Didn't want to be there alone.

The porter looked askance when I asked him to admit me to the Echo Room, at something past the midnight hour. But he had to go over that way anyway to check on some noise in the west wing, so he indulged me.

'Ever since the police installed that equipment we've had a problem,' he grumbled, 'with the electricity.' He pointed out the fuse box, at the bottom of the staircase. A precaution, he said; in case the lights went out before his return.

I had dreaded going to Clare Street on my own. Yet the moment I was alone inside the Echo Room, I experienced a sense of release. The last week had rushed past in a blur of activity – first the May Ball, and then, before I could recover from my all-night tour of duty, there had been interviews with Katie's friends and housemates and family. There'd been the shock of finding Stephen Fox's body. There'd been the discovery of a baby's bones buried in an alcove.

And as if all that weren't enough to make a girl feel overloaded, there had run in parallel, like a slip road to disaster, the emotional ups and downs of my life outside work. The chaos of what was happening – or what was not happening? – with John Carswell and with Sonny.

All these shifts and changes had been so compressed in time that I hadn't had the chance to make sense of them. Things had occurred that were significant, I knew that much; but I hadn't worked out exactly how they were significant. I was like a skier, who hears a roar and feels the ground tremble, but is too busy watching her footing to ask: hey, what the hell was that?

The moment I re-entered the Echo Room, I began to get a grip. I shut the door, dumped my shoulder bag on the floor, and knew that this was the right place. That I was on the edge of understanding.

I adjusted the ancient dimmer switch so that the room was blanketed in a dusky light. Made my way around the perimeter, searching for the best vantage point. Eventually positioned myself at the farthest point from the door. The Echo Mural rolled out on the long wall to my right.

The contradiction between the vicious events depicted in the mural, and the idyllic scenery – the contradiction that gave this painting much of its power – was muted now. In the dim light, the fluffy white clouds above the cypress trees lost their gleam; they melted into a greying sky. The only white that still glinted and glittered was the white of Echo's eye, as the nymph, sensing the shepherds' murderous approach, recoiled in alarm.

I felt closer here to Katie than anywhere else.

Closer than I had, for example, in the company of her boyfriend. Jared Scott-Pettit might have been fond of Katie, might have admired her beauty, but he was busy remoulding her. He wouldn't see the real Katie. In Jared's company, she'd be acting a part.

Closer certainly than at her former home in Histon. Growing up there, within the sweep of her mother's anxious presence, Katie tried to play the part of the dutiful daughter; but she hadn't felt at home when she was at home. That was why she'd moved out. Why she'd made a bold attempt to go beyond the fearfulness that defined Rosemary's life. I couldn't help but feel sorry for Rosemary – sorry for the fact that she had been compelled to try to straitjacket Katie. Sorry for the fact that, though she loved her daughter, she seemed to have lost her in the end. But I couldn't blame Katie in the least for wanting more.

And as for understanding Katie, I hadn't felt close to her at her father's home in Fulbourn either. Bob was apparently a generous father, and an admiring one; but he'd refused to rescue Katie from Rosemary's anxious grip. The photos I'd seen there tantalised with their clues to Katie's identity; how much remained in Katie still, I wondered, of the determined toddler, of the girl who clung like a monkey to her mother for protection, of the beautiful and beloved child clutching greedily at life?

And how much had been battered out by circumstance?

And I couldn't feel close to Katie in her rented house. Her

bedroom was prettily decorated. But the room gave little away. It was almost as if – like Katie herself? – the smooth appearance had been designed to please the eye, to prevent the onlooker from asking what lay beneath the surface. And the public spaces of the house seemed more than fully occupied by the roisterous energy of Candace Masters. By the tight and spiteful presence of Beverley Stebbings.

Candace was loyal at least. She knew what Katie had suffered here, in the Echo Room. She had seen the moment of dreadful suspense before the Dorics pounced, and the even more horrible moments that followed. Candace had been a faithful witness to Katie's terror. More than that, she'd felt in her own stomach the sickening build-up of tension, the weight of abasement. Candace – eldest child – would, if she could, have tucked Katie under her wing. Would have protected her. But in the event, when Katie needed her most, Candace was unable to intercede. *A deer*, she had said, *frozen in the headlights*. She understood how terrible was the surrender of dignity, the loss of power to act. She'd been throttled by her own fear.

But there the similarity ended. Candace hadn't shared Katie's specific humiliation. Hadn't felt those fingers ripping her clothes, baring her flesh to uncaring eyes. Was not encircled by men, men who pressed in, who threatened to crush her by their bulk, who blocked her breathing with their sour breaths. Candace did not feel, as Katie might have felt, her body split off under their callous, casual hands. Feel it become a disassociated lump of flesh, giving off sensation still – registering every prod and poke – but no longer recognisable as a part of her self.

I had been gazing at the Echo Mural, my glance resting on the brutal shepherds, on the gleam of blood-craze in their eyes. How odd, I thought, that it should be shepherds who tore Echo limb from limb. Shepherds are, after all, among the most solitary of men. And the most nurturing. The good shepherd protects his flock from predators. He shelters them against the weather, he carries the newborn lambs to safety, he provides milk for the motherless young.

But my random thought was interrupted by a shuffling on the landing outside. Probably the porter passing again on his way back from the west wing.

I called out to let him know I was still inside.

No reply. Maybe I'd imagined that shuffling, just as I'd imagined the scene at the Dorics' annual dinner.

And that made me think, in turn, of some of the judgements that had been passed on Katie.

There was Matt Hamley, who found her too needy, too complicated, too desperate to belong. There was Charlie Thresher, with his oblique complaint about cats on heat. There was Deborah Cook, who had said Katie fell, perennially, for the wrong kind of man. There was Stephen Fox, who had insisted that Katie was not blameless.

Matt Hamley, who was fascinated by Katie's good looks.

Charlie Thresher, who had hidden behind the ivy that covered his wall, and watched me pick my way through Katie's garden.

Deborah Cook, who had found the remains of an infant hidden in her room.

And finally, Stephen Fox. Who was dead.

And at that moment, the door on the opposite side of the room opened a crack and closed again.

Suddenly I was aware, in a way I hadn't been before, of the time. Almost one a.m. May Week was over; most of the students had gone home; the conference season wasn't fully underway. All of which meant that St Bartholomew's was largely empty.

'Who's there?'

My call was met with silence. The Echo Room was quiet as a tomb. A faint buzzing noise from the dimmer switch was the only thing, other than my own suddenly harsher breathing, to pierce the silence. I set myself to listen. Nothing. No sound. Not even traffic in the distance. Maid's Causeway was nearby, but at this time of night, there'd be few cars and fewer lorries, and not many sounds would penetrate anyway all the way into the windowless hall.

And, I supposed, not many sounds from inside the room would

reach the corridors of the college. A person could make a noise here, could clap their hands, perhaps – could scream – and never be heard.

There was no sound from the landing. There were no footsteps on the stairs.

I took a deep breath and headed for the door, but I'd only taken half a dozen long strides when I stopped.

The lights went out. I supposed that's what had happened. All I knew was that one instant there was a soft, dusky light – light that muted the images in the Echo Mural, light that gave a warm glow to the walls. The next instant there was nothing but black.

Not warm, living black. Not liquorice black, skin black, loam black, coal black, rich and dark and complicated.

But empty black. The black of nothingness. Of caverns. Of cellars. Of being buried alive.

To run forward into this blackness would be like driving a motorbike fast into a pitch-dark tunnel. Bracing for the crash against the concrete pillar. I couldn't do it. I moved forward instead with painful slowness, hesitant foot after hesitant foot, arms outstretched in front of me, hands groping for the door.

Step by step by step, listening all the while. And I heard things, or thought I did.

Thought I heard a squeak of hinges, felt rather than saw a movement, heard a swish and a rustle.

Sensed something slip-slide, slip-slide, along the floor.

And then – and there was no mistaking this – a metallic scrape. A click. My hands collided with a solid sweep of oak. I fumbled for the doorknob. Grasped it and twisted and pulled. Pulled it again. It didn't shift at all. Not a millimetre of movement.

I had been locked in, in the dark, in the Echo Room.

I shouted. I thumped with my fist on the oak. 'Open this door. Let me out.' I wrapped both my hands around the knob and shook it back and forth, with all my strength, so that it rattled. Banged once again on the door.

Nothing. No reply.

I stopped then – suddenly aware of another possibility.

Cocked my ears for sounds inside the room. Stood still for seconds. For one minute, two minutes, three. Made certain there was no one and nothing in with me. No sound of heavy breathing. No rush of blood through someone else's arteries.

I guess that was a good thing.

I was locked in.

But at least I was alone.

Chapter 16

It was twenty minutes – twenty long minutes – before the porter unlocked the door of the Echo Room and set me free.

Twenty minutes before he approached the landing and heard my muffled shouts.

Twenty minutes before the lights went on again, making me blink. Before I could confirm what I'd earlier inferred from my fumblings in the dark.

My shoulder bag had been stolen. Someone had cracked open the door and spotted it nearby. That same someone had disabled the lights at the bottom of the staircase and crept back up. With one swift movement, they'd slid my bag out into the corridor and turned the key in the lock, trapping me in the flat black of the Echo Room.

In the dark, I hadn't seen the arm that had snaked my bag away. All I knew was that the someone who had done it was agile – able to race to and from the fuse box in record time – and quick-thinking. And that this agile, quick-thinking person had my bag.

And with my bag, of course, went a great deal of the stuff of daily life. Keys: for the car, for the house, for the office in London. Credit cards and money, chequebook and cashcard. Addresses and diary. Ticket for the dry cleaner, where my DJ from the May Ball waited to be collected. Nothing that counts as a catastrophe. The kind of things that can slow a woman down if they're gone.

The porter had been chatting to two constables in the west wing. He hadn't seen a soul. He was, fortunately for me, one of those people who approach retirement age with hearing intact, and he'd picked up the trace of my cries for help as he headed back towards the Lodge.

Who says that more police on the streets would reduce the levels of crime? Since the discovery of the second corpse, St Bartholomew's College could boast a concentration of police personnel matched only by the station itself. It certainly hadn't deterred the person who'd stolen my bag. I found Nicole and her colleagues in Deborah Cook's room, where an attendant was in the process of removing the skeleton. The faces that met me there were as blank as they were weary. The police had seen nothing, heard nothing.

Nicole roused herself enough to issue a few straightforward instructions.

'Constable,' she said, addressing an angular young woman who hovered by her elbow, 'ask the porter to show you to the Echo Room and wait there until you're relieved. Make sure nothing is touched. I'll have prints taken off that doorknob when we're finished here.'

I was warmed by her concern. 'You're going to follow up a bag-snatch, Nicole? When you've got so much else on your plate?'

Nicole pulled her gaze away from the skeleton. She placed a hand on either temple and massaged her fingers along her scalp, from forehead to crown, raking the hair off her face. Within seconds, her obsidian waves had sprung back into place.

'I can't overlook the possibility,' she said, 'that the person who locked you in might be linked to all of this.' Her arm waved vaguely towards the bundle that contained the skeleton, and then towards the incident room.

All of this. A baby's bones. The corpse of Stephen Fox.

She looked me straight in the eye. I could see the concern. 'You all right, Laura?'

I took stock. 'Shaken, I suppose.' The sensation of being locked in is unpleasant, even when you're not in danger. When you're probably not in danger, I amended. 'Surprised – it happened very quickly. And bloody pissed off at the loss of my bag, Nicole.' I laughed. 'In short, right as rain.'

'Go home, then,' Nicole ordered.

'Bossy-boots,' I said. And left.

I'd had enough of St Bartholomew's College to last a lifetime, and quite enough of the police.

Back in the Porters' Lodge, the porter told me that the second key for the Echo Room was missing from the key cupboard. It had been on its hook when he'd shown me upstairs; someone had pocketed it while he was in the west wing.

He pressed a ten-pound note into my palm. In case of emergency, he said. I turned to scribble a note in my diary to remind myself to repay him – then remembered that my diary was in my shoulder bag, and my shoulder bag was missing.

I trudged home in the dark across Midsummer Common, across Jesus Green, and up the hill to Clare Street. It was not the least frightening; though the sky was black, it was a warm, summer black, loam black, espresso black – rich, engulfing, soothing. I found my spare key where I always kept it, under a stone. Let myself in and staggered into bed.

In my fatigue, I didn't even notice the floor cushions side by side, the dirty wine glasses, the charred embers in the fireplace.

I fell instantly asleep.

I dreamed fitfully of a lamb, with panicked eyes, trapped in a darkened hollow. Of a shepherd, with features cruel and cold. I struggled to hold on to a pouch containing something precious, but the shepherd used his crook to rip the pouch out of my resisting arms.

The next day, I stayed at home, cancelling my credit cards, pottering around with paperwork and gradually stripping off. As the temperature soared, I shifted from a shirt and waistcoat, to a shirt, to a waistcoat alone.

Helen called after lunch. 'It's too nice a day to be indoors,' she said. 'I'm picking Ginny up from school and we're punting down to Grantchester. You coming with us?'

She didn't have to ask twice. Filing tax receipts can't hold a candle to an afternoon on the river. We arranged to meet by the boatyard in Granta Place at three forty-five.

I was a quarter of an hour late.

'Sorry, girls,' I said, enveloping Helen's daughter Ginny – whom I hadn't seen for weeks – in a bear hug, and planting a kiss on Helen's sun-warmed cheek. 'Just as I was leaving the house, someone rang from the police station. Invited me to pop in to identify a bag.'

Ginny had already secured a punt, so we saved further conversation until we were adrift on the river.

Helen loaded a canvas bag carefully into the boat. 'Our tea,' she said. From the way the bag clunked when it connected with the bottom of the boat, there was something besides sandwiches in there.

Ginny was keen to take her turn at punting, but she let me do the honours until we were out of the busy area around the Mill Pond.

'You can take over at Crusoe Bridge,' I said to Ginny. 'It should be quieter there.'

The stretch of river beside the boatyard had the kind of crowds you'd expect for a warm summer afternoon. There were parties of locals like ourselves, preparing for an outing. There were more punts still with visitors. Some were chauffeured by students in striped shirts and boaters, playing up to the Cambridge image. Others were steered ineptly by giggling groups of young people. The result was the customary chaos.

I waited my chance. Waited until two punts that were on course to bump each other had bumped, and were lodged near the riverbank. Waited until a laughing group of tourists had zig-zagged their boat back into the safety of the dock. Then, with a length of river temporarily free, I pushed off.

It always takes a minute or two to get the rhythm right. To lift the pole in one swift movement, so that it doesn't stick in the mud on the bottom of the Cam. To swing it to its new position further ahead, without spraying river water over the passengers seated in the bottom of the punt. To drop the heavy pole smoothly, let its weight slip through your palms, to lean over and press down at the moment of impact – propelling the punt onwards. And then to begin the cycle over again.

After a minute, we were free of the crowds and moving at a stately pace. Gliding towards Grantchester.

When it had all become more or less automatic, Helen reopened the conversation. 'The bag they found was yours?'

'Mine all right. Picked up by a papergirl first thing this morning.' According to the police, she'd flicked a copy of the *Daily Mail* on to a doorstep; as she turned, she'd seen my bag stashed among the bushes. It was only a hundred yards or so from Bart's.

'And the contents?' Helen asked.

She ducked, as I steered a little too close to an overhanging branch, then reached for the paddle and used it to help me get the punt back into the mainstream.

'Sorry,' I said. 'I'm obviously out of practice. What's worrying, Helen, is that the contents had been selectively stripped. My house key is missing, and my address book. And of course, the cash. But they left the credit cards and the car keys.'

Helen understood the implications right away. 'Not a professional job.'

'No. Not someone who knew how to make use of stolen credit cards; not someone who was experienced at driving away. Worse than that, I'm afraid. Someone with an interest in me.'

Ginny was trailing a hand in the water, scooping up fronds of river weeds, and watching them as they dripped off her fingers. She was all ears.

'Will you have the locks changed?' Helen asked.

'Mr Sparkes is booked and my next-door neighbour's on duty. By the time I get home this evening, my door should be fitted with a shiny new lock.'

We'd been going only a few minutes, but already we'd passed the back of the Fitzwilliam Museum.

'Hey,' Ginny said. 'My turn.' She stood and stepped forward

carefully. 'Don't know why I'm taking such trouble to keep my balance. In this heat, a swim would be a relief.' She stood beside me for a few seconds, catching the rhythm, and then took the pole from me. Her wobble was short-lived. We quickly picked up a smooth pace again, and skimmed beneath the traffic on Fen Causeway.

'She's good at this,' Helen said, as I eased myself down alongside her in the bottom of the punt. Her tone was proud but bordered with faint surprise – *hey, look what my baby can do*.

We were stretched out, more or less, facing Ginny, with our backs resting against the wooden seat.

'Hey, Ginny, watch out behind. There's a punt overtaking. Do you want—?'

But before I'd finished speaking, Ginny had the situation under control. Helen and I let her take charge – finally – and drifted into our own conversation. She told me about her current project, shifting library resources away from monographs and towards the Internet. I told her about Katie.

'Horrible,' Helen remarked with a shudder, as I recounted Katie's ordeal in the Echo Room. 'But not entirely out of character. Bart's has a reputation as one of the randier colleges around. They used to hire young women as bedders – one of the few colleges to do so – if older women from the same family worked there as well. I imagine Katie's not the first girl to suffer in this way.' She glanced at my face. 'Hey, Laura, shall we break open the wine? Before it gets warm?'

I shook my head. No. Not that I had anything against a glass of wine; just that drinking in a punt had a touch too much of *Brideshead Revisited* about it for my taste.

'Helen, have you heard of the Spinning House?'

She screwed up her face in concentration, distracted from the wine. 'Myrtle – do you remember, Laura, that energetic pensioner who used to baby-sit when Ginny was in nursery school?'

I nodded. Myrtle had looked about two hundred years of age, but she had a calm energy that suited her to the task of caring for a toddler, and an endless well of good humour.

'Well, Myrtle used to say when Ginny misbehaved, "Naughty girls get taken to the Spinning House." I never knew what she meant by it. Do you?'

'Someone gave me a monograph about it the other day.' I didn't feel like talking about John Carswell yet, even to Helen. Maybe especially to Helen. 'Local girls were locked up there if university officials thought they'd been soliciting.'

'A gaol, you mean? In Cambridge? When was this?'

'It was closed down after a scandal in the 1890s.'

'For prostitutes? You've got to be kidding.'

'Well, ostensibly for prostitutes. There was no public trial, no evidence presented, no legal representation, so I guess we'll never know whether they were prostitutes or not.'

'And what does this have to do with Katie?'

'I'm not absolutely sure, Helen. But Stephen Fox – before he was murdered – hinted that Katie had brought the Echo Room episode upon herself in some way. *Katie Arkwright was not blameless* – that's what he said. And other, less reliable witnesses' – I was thinking here of Thresher's ambiguous comments about cats on heat, and, of course, Roger Duff – 'have made similar remarks. So I've been thinking.'

'Thinking Katie might have involved herself in a spot of prostitution?'

That's Helen. Hitting the nail on the head.

'Thinking: what could a girl do to support herself while she attended university? A beautiful nineteen-year-old girl? There's no student grant to speak of. Her mother has no money; she refused her father's help. Where would she get the funds for accommodation – especially at Cambridge prices – and tuition and books? For the white satin dress and the silver high-heeled sandals and the classy-looking outfits that her boyfriend so admired?'

'She could work in a massage parlour,' Ginny said.

There was not a break in her rhythm, in the steady up-and-down movement of the punting pole. She was a hell of a lot cooler than Helen and me.

'How do you know about massage parlours?' Helen asked. Trying to sound casual. Not entirely succeeding.

'From your magazine,' Ginny said. 'What do you call it— Hey, I think I need a break now. My shoulders are sore.'

'*Marie Claire*?' Helen said. She stood and made her way to the front of the boat. 'My turn, Ginny. There's some soft drinks there if you're thirsty.'

Ginny plunked down next to me. I massaged her shoulders, while she rummaged in the bag for a drink. 'So what did *Marie Claire* have to say about massage parlours?'

'Don't really remember,' shrugged Ginny. 'Oh, that felt good, Laura. I'm not even sure it *was Marie Claire*. But there was this girl, she was like – eighteen – and she had a baby. She moved to London. She started out in a massage parlour and then she moved to another kind of brothel. It sounded awful to me, but it was better than social security, she said.'

The riverbank was opening up now, the trees on either side pulling apart to reveal scruffy meadows. Helen was punting silently. Her face was a picture of concern.

'Ginny,' she said. 'You wouldn't ever think of—'

Ginny interrupted. 'No way, Mum.' She was offended by the question. But I understood. There are things a mother can't allow to pass.

Helen flushed. Only partly from embarrassment.

'Hey, Helen.' I caught her eye and began to recite. 'Mother, may I go out to swim? Yes, my darling daughter. Hang your clothes on a hickory limb—'

Helen joined me for the punchline. 'But don't go near the water!'

'What are you two on about?' Ginny sounded a little touchy still.

We laughed, with something like relief.

Just as we reached Grantchester, with Trumpington Hall and the Eight Acre Wood on our left, and the path leading to the Orchard on our right, we came head to head with another punt.

I'd heard their voices, their high-spirited banter, even before I saw them. Then the punt came into view – a party of people in their late teens and early twenties, wearing shorts and T-shirts. As the punt took evasive action, and steered an expert course to our right, I saw brown legs dangling over the side and champagne glasses raised in celebration. Then something started them laughing again, and the man with the punt pole missed his stroke. Their punt drifted on, back towards Cambridge. The pole remained in the river, obstinately upright, one end projecting out of the water, and the other secured in the mud at the bottom of the Cam. A pair of brown legs, followed by a body, slipped into the water. He swam with confident strokes to retrieve the pole, while the laughter of four others rang out over the water.

Our boat slid alongside the pole before the swimmer got there. I stood up and dislodged it from the mud, then laid it flat on the surface of the river and floated it back towards the swimmer. For a second, before the movement of our boat carried me away, our eyes locked.

'Hello, Jared,' I said.

One end of their boat had come to rest against the riverbank. I checked out the other four occupants. Three of them – two women and a man – were strangers to me. But the fourth – a large, curly-haired fellow, the youngest of the party – looked familiar. To my surprise, and Ginny's, he hallooed Helen and she waved back.

'Who's that, Mum?' Ginny asked, before I could get a word in.

'His name is Richard,' she said. 'He worked in the library for part of his gap year. Richard Fox.'

No wonder I hadn't immediately connected the face and the name. When I'd seen Richard, he'd been ranting furiously to his mother about being interrogated by the police. And here he was, looking as if he hadn't a care in the world.

Ginny steered us into our chosen spot seconds later. We unloaded our things on to the meadow, found an area in the shelter of a line of bushes to spread our picnic cloth, unpacked the sandwiches and the cakes and fruit and – at last – uncorked the wine. We didn't care that it was warm. Ginny wandered down to the river's edge to see if there were any cygnets around, and Helen and I settled down on a blanket to soak up the last of the afternoon sun.

I must have fallen asleep – certainly the sun looked lower in the sky the next time I opened my eyes. But I'd been aware, in some semi-conscious way, of the light breeze that licked the trees from time to time, and the shouts of children playing football. And then, somewhere on the other side of the bushes, of Ginny's voice, saying, 'You mean Laura? She's over there.'

I struggled up on to my elbows as his footsteps approached and checked that I was decent – that the buttons on my waistcoat were fastened. I looked up as he loomed over me. I had to squint into the sun. It formed a halo round his head. The angel image could have been misleading, but I recognised the voice at least of Jared Scott-Pettit.

I stood up beside him, and brushed myself off, straightening my clothes. I beckoned him a few steps away from the blanket, so as not to awaken Helen.

'It's funny seeing you on the river,' he said, 'because I was planning to ring you today.'

I interrupted, and started to warn him that there was no real news of Katie yet. But he waved me aside.

'No, it's not that, Miss Principal. It's just that I've found something that belongs to her.' He held out an elegant black wallet. 'The night of the May Ball, Katie put this in my room for safe-keeping. It must have fallen down behind the futon. I've only just found it this morning.'

I took the wallet from him, and began to open it. 'Anything of interest?'

Jared had, he claimed, been too fastidious to check it out. Somehow, leaving it to a private investigator seemed more – well – seemly to him. I had no such qualms. I counted the money – sixty pounds, in twenties, plus coins. 'That's not all her money,' Jared said. 'She had a few more notes tucked inside her bra.'

I checked the key compartment which held one key, a house key by the look of it. I also found a library card, a student card,

202

membership of a fitness centre, two credit cards, and – lo and behold – a slip of paper with a phone number on it. A number for Greater London.

'What's this?' I asked, holding the slip of paper up.

Jared squirmed. He looked for a moment as if he might deny any knowledge of it. Then he relented.

'It belongs to an outfit that calls itself The Heavenly Twins.'

So he had looked.

'And? Do they know anything about Katie?'

Jared managed to look both indignant and embarrassed at the same time. 'Well, I was hardly going to ask them about her, was I? She wouldn't have anything to do with a place like that!'

Jared needed someone else to do the dirty work for him. I kept the telephone number and changed the topic. After a couple of minutes of small talk, he took his leave.

'Just a minute, Jared,' I said, changing position slightly so that I had a better view of his face. 'How long have you known Richard Fox?'

Jared brightened. Here was a topic that didn't trouble him. 'I know him from the rock-climbing club. His father is – was – the Senior Tutor at St Bartholomew's College. He's the one who—'

'Was murdered,' I said. 'Yes, I know.'

The office was in London, near Baker Street, just off the Marylebone Road. The walls were painted a jazzy shade of fuchsia. The woman behind the curved desk wore lipstick to match.

'You'll do,' Angela said. Her motherly smile took the sting out of this remark. 'You're older than our average. Most men like 'em a little younger, but we occasionally get a client who insists on someone more mature. Someone – if you know what I mean – who knows her way around.'

I was pretty sure she didn't mean orienteering.

She made notes on the computer, read them through and then nodded again. 'You'll do.'

I had begun in a roundabout fashion, by asking Angela – she

introduced herself only by her first name – what precisely the agency expected of the girls they provided as escorts. She was absolutely clear. As cheerfully as a scoutmistress detailing the kit for the Easter camping trip, she reeled off a list: perfect grooming at all times, smart clothes, absolutely no denims, and above all, lady-like behaviour.

'Our clients,' she stressed, 'are gentlemen. We even get the occasional diplomat. They want someone who speaks properly, who knows how to carry herself. In other words, a lady.'

Other requisites: punctuality – clients were never, *but never*, to be kept waiting. Discretion – no gossip about clients away from work. Anonymity – girls to use their own names, but not to give out addresses or phone numbers.

'Anonymity protects our girls,' Angela said.

'Anonymity also means, doesn't it, that any request for a specific girl has to go through your office?'

'Of course,' she said.

The list of duties so far had a glaring omission. Like a job specification for a boxer that went no further than etiquette in the dressing room.

Angela seemed to me to be skirting around the central issue.

'But what does a girl have to *do?*'

Angela fixed me with a concerned glance. She had a very fat, very beautiful face and impressive composure. Her eyes were wide and knowing, her body soft and full. She reminded me of a pampered Persian cat.

'*Do?*' she asked. 'What do you mean, *do?*' The question displeased her. 'This isn't a massage parlour, Miss Principal. It's not a cleaning agency. Our girls don't *do* anything. Our girls simply *are.*'

'Are what?' I persisted.

'Are exceptional companions. They *do* nothing at all, except make interesting conversation. Our clients appreciate a woman with ideas. A woman who studied, as you did, at Cambridge or Oxford.'

'So let me get this straight. Men pay you – and you pay the girls—'

'Generously. A hundred and fifty pounds a session, as I said.'

'To take a girl to dinner. The man pays for the meal?'

'Of course. The meal is taken discreetly, in a private room. The man certainly pays. And in return he can expect two hours of sparkling conversation, with an attractive woman. No strings attached.'

'How did you dream up that name?' I asked. 'The Heavenly Twins.'

Angela looked at me appraisingly.

'What are you really here for?' she asked.

So much for subtlety. I opened my briefcase and took out the photo: Katie Arkwright, slim and fragile, seated on the grass with her arms wound around her knees, staring straight into the camera. I passed it to Angela and made my confession.

'I heard about The Heavenly Twins from my niece,' I said. 'Katie. One of your girls, I believe?'

Angela took the photo. Her voluptuous lips pressed tightly together.

'Katie Arkwright,' she said. She spun her chair round, and, without rising, selected a file from a trolley beside the desk. Scanned the contents.

'Katie Arkwright signed up in March. She saw four clients for us. All of them satisfactory, though two of them complained that she was a little reserved.' Angela snapped the file shut. 'Then she broke the cardinal rule.'

'Anonymity?'

'Worse than that. She failed to show. A donor to a medical charity, visiting from Hong Kong. The charity administrator had arranged company for him, on the evening before he went home. He waited for over an hour. Your niece never showed up.'

'What date was this?'

Angela ran a fat, beautifully manicured finger down the file. 'June the fifteenth,' she said.

The night after the May Ball.

'Angela, I assume you get to know your girls pretty well. Have you any idea why Katie failed to show up?'

Angela squared her shoulders. Tried to look severe.

And only half answered my question.

'It's a matter of professionalism,' Angela said. 'I always explain to our girls: you've got to have pride. If you show – by the way you present yourself, by your way of speaking – that you are a lady ... well, you'll be treated properly in return.'

More than this, she wouldn't say. I left feeling uneasy.

On the way out, in the spartan lobby, a man was fingering his way through the contents of one of the metal letter-boxes that lined the left-hand wall.

'Excuse me,' I said. He gave me a suspicious look. 'You're a tenant here?'

He pulled at his tie. 'MGM Software,' he said. 'Second floor.'

'Do you know anything about The Heavenly Twins agency?'

Suspicion was chased away by a glint of amusement. I think I preferred the suspicion. The man studied me with greater interest. He was short, but even so, his height didn't justify the focus on my breasts.

'You work for them?' he asked.

'No,' I said quickly. 'I'm checking it out for my niece. Is The Heavenly Twins above board?'

He chortled. 'Heavenly Twins – above board. That's a good one. Tell your niece that as long as she has great tits, she'll do fine. The girls go out with guys; take off their blouses and bras and sit there, through dinner, naked from the waist up.'

My distaste must have shown in my face, because he gave me a glance that was almost apologetic.

'You really didn't know, did you? Sorry, love, but all you had to do was use your head. Where did you imagine they got that name?'

My heavenly twins and I strolled out of the building with as much dignity as we could muster.

I resolved to take a refresher course, some time, on the English *double-entendre*.

*

A person could be forgiven for thinking that my answering machine was on a direct line to St Bartholomew's College. Apart from a brief hello from Stevie, all my most urgent messages came from Bart's. From John Carswell, who wanted to see me. From Deborah Cook, who wanted to see me. From DI Pelletier.

She wanted to see me, too.

I made a lazy morning of it, and reached the college round about midday. There was a small group of Spanish visitors in the entrance hall, listening to a guide deliver a joke-encrusted account of college history. I sidled past them to the Porters' Lodge and returned the ten-pound note.

When I arrived at the incident room, the constable who admitted me was in furious form.

'How can we conduct an investigation? Most people are away,' he grumbled. 'Seems as if the lecturers and supervisors just bugger off when the exams are over. How's that for a job? Eight weeks a term, three terms a year – that leaves how many weeks free?'

'Twenty eight,' I said. 'More than half the year.' I launched into the standard explanation. 'But that's not taking into account all the time that tutors dedicate to research. And all that extra marking after term ends. And committees. Oxbridge academics work far harder than an eight-week term suggests.'

'If you say so,' said the constable, and showed me in to Nicole's office.

It was seventy-eight degrees outside in the shade. In the small office that Nicole had set up for herself, with one ill-placed window and no blinds to block the glare, you could up that by ten degrees.

Nicole's olive skin, trapped in the heat of the room, had taken on a russet glow. Sweat beaded her upper lip, and her black eyebrows glistened. But her outfit seemed to make no concessions to the heat. She wore a tailored trouser suit of stiff black cotton. Sure, the sleeves were only elbow-length. But every button was done up on the double-breasted jacket, and – in an implicit challenge to the wimps on the force – a long viscose scarf was draped around her neck.

I immediately stripped down, and settled my own short-sleeved jacket on the back of a chair. 'How can you work in this oven, Nicole?'

'Try to rise above it.' Nicole grinned. 'You know the saying: if you can't stand the heat . . .'

'But you're the one who summoned me, oh mistress of cool.'

'So I did. But for someone who doesn't like the temperature here, Laura, would it be fair to say you spend an awful lot of time in Bart's?'

The bit about time spent in Bart's was a question. The rest was a dig.

I rose above it.

'Listen to this, Nicole. Katie Arkwright worked for an escort agency – The Heavenly Twins. Most of their employees are Oxbridge students. Bright girls, like Katie.'

'But Katie's not—'

'I know. I guess she lied. Or maybe she's so pretty that they didn't care. The key thing is this: the girls go out to dinner with men lined up by the agency. They take off their tops. They sit with their breasts bared and make scintillating conversation. Now, what do you think of that as a way to put yourself through college?'

Nicole tried not to wince, but I saw a muscle dance in the corner of her cheek. 'It's self-destructive, if you ask me. With a no-hoper, a girl who has nothing to look forward to, I can just about understand it. But these girls? They're on the edge of a good career; they have a chance of making something of themselves. Don't they have any self-respect?'

'It's a far cry from a Saturday job at Woolies,' I agreed. 'But I keep asking myself: where's the harm? Compared to Woolies, it's better paid. The hours are shorter. And they get a first-class meal to boot.'

Nicole glanced towards the door, which was still open a crack. Stood up, took two strides towards it, toed it shut. As she did so, I saw that my earlier assessment had been mistaken. Nicole had made concessions to the weather. Under the desk, her feet had been bare. Bare of shoes, anyway. Each toenail was filed in a neat ellipse, and painted a look-at-me red.

She plonked herself down again. 'It's the punters that worry me,' she said. 'What pleasure can they possibly derive from dining with a woman who's there only for the money? A woman who shivers the evening away, boobs flopping in her entrée, while he tests out his views on Kierkegaard or cricket?'

It sounded as if Nicole had thought this through before.

'You have to conclude,' she concluded, 'men are weird.'

'Some men,' I said.

She ignored me.

'And if you ask me, Laura, if the agency supplied just any pretty girls, it wouldn't be so bad. Just another case of male mammary-fixation – nothing new in that. But this is more insidious.'

'What are you on about?'

'Come on, Laura. Doesn't the insistence on well-educated women give the game away?'

'Well—' I began. But Nicole wasn't waiting.

'It's obvious. These clients are frightened by women with minds of their own. They're not paying to look at naked breasts – they're paying to cut intelligent girls down to size. To make them look ridiculous. To turn them back into bodies.'

I got it at last. 'You mean they enjoy seeing highly educated girls being degraded?'

'I mean,' Nicole said, 'that their motivation isn't admiration of women, it's fear. Maybe worse than fear. If I were Katie, I wouldn't touch it with a bargepole.'

'If you're right, Nicole, maybe we ought to find out what clients Katie saw. Angela – who runs the show for The Heavenly Twins – says she had four "dates". Could you check whether any of them showed a specific interest in her? Asked for her again, that sort of thing?'

Nicole looked for half a second as if she were considering my request. Then she thought better of it.

'I've nothing to do with the Arkwright case, Laura. And quite enough to do here. I've got a murder on my hands – you haven't forgotten Stephen Fox? And now there's this skeleton. By the way,' she said, tapping her finger on a pile of papers sitting square in the centre of the desk, 'it's a baby for sure. And it was hidden in the alcove decades ago: 1961, to be precise.'

'The forensics people can date bones to the year?' It was the first I'd heard of it.

'To hell with bones,' Nicole said. 'It's the newspaper they were wrapped in. It carried an ad for a closing-down sale at an outfitter's near Mitcham's Corner. We chased up the date – April the thirteenth, 1961 – when the shop went out of business.'

'Anything else?'

'One interesting thing. That room – Deborah Cook's room, where the skeleton was found? – has had more than its fair share of non-accidental deaths.'

'Murders?'

'Suicides. Both in the late 1950s. One, a young theology student, in the second week of his university career. The other, a mathematician, after completing final exams. He was convinced he'd disgraced himself in the examinations; as it turned out, he would have received a first.'

'Did they hang themselves?' I asked and then realised my mistake. 'No, it would be gas, wouldn't it? In the late 1950s.' Cambridge was one of the first British towns to be converted from the old type of gas, which was toxic, to the newer non-toxic variety, precisely because of student deaths. I'd heard that eight or nine students killed themselves in Cambridge alone in the year before conversion, which happened sometime in the swinging sixties.

'Yup. Gas.' Nicole nodded. 'Blocked up the flue, lay down on the floor, turned on the taps.' She shook her head glumly. 'One good thing about the job today – we don't have to deal with that mess any more.'

'Are drug-related deaths any prettier?'

'You're a little ray of sunshine, Laura, aren't you?'

'Listen, it's not possible, is it, that one of the suicides placed the skeleton in the alcove? Then killed himself in remorse?'

'That'd be a trick. He'd have to wrap the corpse in newspaper printed after his death.'

'Who occupied the room in 1961?'

'That's the odd thing, Laura. Apparently it was locked. Waiting for the whispers about suicide to die down. College officials didn't want to risk installing some sensitive new boy in a room where the two previous inhabitants had snuffed it. That room was empty in 1961.'

There was a knock. A constable stuck his head around the door. 'The girl you wanted to see is here, ma'am.'

'Thank you, Constable. I'll be through in a moment.'

She stood up. A gesture of dismissal.

I stayed where I was.

'What we were talking about before, Nicole. The Heavenly Twins. What if one of these – clients – knows what's happened to Katie – and we never even check it out?'

Nicole pondered for thirty seconds. Then I heard a shuffle under the desk. When she stepped out from behind it, there was not a glimmer of pillar-box red. Nicole's feet were shod in smart black loafers.

'Leave me the address,' she said. 'I have to do a court appearance in London next week. If the case ends early, I might have a word with Angela on my way back.'

I left Nicole's office via the incident room and almost crashed into Deborah Cook. She was standing aside, making room for me to pass by. When she realised it was me, she clutched at my arm.

Her face looked positively thin now. Pinched, rather than slim.

'You look as if you haven't slept a wink,' I said, checking out her clammy skin. 'Are you all right?'

'Laura,' Deborah whispered, and burst into tears. 'I've got to get away from here. That baby – I keep seeing that baby. Not the bones, but how it must have been, before it died.'

'Shall I have a word with the housekeeper? Surely they can find you another room.'

'I can't bear to be alone,' Deborah wailed. She cast a sideways glance at Nicole, who was waiting for her near the door, watching our interaction with undisguised interest. Deborah clung more closely to me.

'Tell you what,' I said, disengaging her hand as gently as I could. 'You have your talk with the Inspector. And after that, go back to your room and pack some clothes. I'll collect you in an hour. I'm sure I can sort out somewhere better for you to stay.'

She cast me a glance of unalloyed gratitude.

They look sophisticated, some of these students, but they are oh so young.

Chapter 17

'Dr Carswell?' the porter repeated. He had taken off his shapeless grey jacket and rolled up his shirt-sleeves in deference to the heat. 'Certainly he's in. Saw him not ten minutes ago. He collected the key to the Echo Room.'

The porter looked at me with an appraising eye. This wasn't the man who'd pressed a ten-pound note into my palm after my bag had been stolen. This was a more cynical colleague.

'Guess you're going to look for him there, eh? Want me to go with you?'

'Not necessary,' I said. 'But thanks.'

I turned towards the staircase. The porter called after me. 'What is it with this Echo Room?' he asked.

When he saw he had my attention, he continued. 'For years, it's sat empty. Not counting special occasions, that is. And now, there are fellows swarming all over it; you get yourself locked in; the police dust it for fingerprints. Suddenly, that room's like Piccadilly Circus.'

Like Piccadilly Circus? He was thinking of the traffic, I suppose – the whirl of cars and black cabs and double-decker buses careering around the peninsula where the elegant arc of Regent Street collides with the razzle-dazzle of theatre land. Where the brash neon of Tower Records talks back to Shaftesbury Avenue, the new popular art forms issuing a challenge to the old.

Or perhaps he was referring to the crush of people – the tired-eyed tourists, disgorged from the underground, riffling through racks of postcards. Pounding the pavement outside Planet

Hollywood. Fanning out towards Liberty's or Fortnum's or Mappin and Webb. Was that what drew the comparison?

Or maybe he had in mind the statue – too fragile for its heavy base – of Eros, Greek god of love and passion, that hovers over clusters of visitors and rent boys. The son of Aphrodite, according to some; but in other, earlier, accounts, the child of Chaos. Eros, whose coy silhouette can seem incongruous compared with the commercial chaos of the area – but is, on deeper reflection, quite in keeping.

Or was he thinking – as I was – of the streets of Soho, to the north? Where you can eat the best Chinese or Italian meals in London, or join the dirty-mac brigade at the seediest shows. In places where they give you – give men, that is – a hank of toilet roll or a strip of towelling on the way in. Where love and commercialism are synonymous.

Where there's no passion that isn't paid for.

I took the stairs two at a time, not wanting to think along these lines a moment longer. Granted, The Heavenly Twins – where Katie had earned £150 a session for stripping and eating – was, as DI Pelletier pointed out, an uncomfortable concept. Granted, Katie's experience in the Echo Room rested on a similar strand of misogyny. But that was as far as comparisons went. St Bartholomew's College was a far cry from Soho. When you begin to pursue parallels between the sleazy dives of Soho and one of the most venerable universities in the land – well, forget it, I told myself. Stick to the facts.

There were footsteps in the Echo Room. They ceased the instant I opened the door. John Carswell had been walking – long strides, hands in pockets, head bowed – as if, deep in thought, he'd been making his way home along Market Hill. He'd been walking the length of the room, along a central line. Pacing, probably. Back and forth, back and forth, back and forth.

He was facing away now, halfway between me and the far wall. He straightened his shoulders, but didn't swing around.

'John. Are you all right?'

I couldn't say precisely what made me ask that question.

Something about the set of his shoulders, about the way his hands were pushed into his pockets, gave cause for concern.

He brought a hand up, and rubbed his face. And when he turned towards me, it was with an expression of bland welcome. But by the hesitation, if nothing else, I knew the welcome was feigned. He didn't want my company. Not now, anyway.

'Laura,' he exclaimed. The heartiness of the greeting didn't ring true. 'I was just seeing how the mural has survived the toings and froings of our constabulary friends.'

I let it pass. He was casually turned out in a soft white shirt, loose linen trousers and an expensive belt. His equally pricey briefcase lay where he'd dropped it by the door.

'My bag was sitting there when it was nicked,' I said.

'I heard about that, Laura.' Remembrance of bags past seemed finally to recall John to the here and now. 'Tried to ring you last evening, but—'

'I was in London. Visiting an escort agency that specialises in girls from Oxbridge.'

'And you found . . .?'

'I found traces of Katie.'

John listened intently while I told him about The Heavenly Twins. 'Vivienne would've been horrified,' he said. 'She was active in the women's movement during that period when any sex work smacked of rape. I guess now,' he said, looking to me as if for guidance, 'things have changed.'

'Now,' I said, 'the questions are different. Is sex work inevitably degrading? A coercive option, into which vulnerable women – abused teenagers, women with kids to support, women in the thrall of drugs or pimps – are pushed? Or – the other side of the coin – is sex work a legitimate and honourable choice? Akin to waitressing or cleaning or shop work, and often better paid? Is sex work tainted only by our society's attitudes towards sexually active women?'

'You know the answer to that, Laura?'

'I know the questions. That's a start. And I've got a question for you, John.'

No, I didn't ask him why, several years after Vivienne's death, he still hadn't remarried, though it was on my mind. They say that remarriage is a compliment to the first partner – proof that the marriage was happy. So why had an attractive man like John Carswell, who'd apparently adored his late wife, remained single?

Instead, I asked him about Katie. 'In Katie's bedroom in Great Eastern Street' – Katie's salmon-pink room – 'there was a card propped on the dressing table, a florist's card. *Beauties for a beauty*, it said. It was signed with a single initial. *J.* Did you send flowers to Katie?'

If John's unconvincing show of welcome was a measure of his ability to dissemble, then he was completely taken aback by my question. His look of surprise was so persuasive it bordered on the comic. 'Why would I do that? I hardly even knew Katie Arkwright.'

'I don't know. Maybe because you felt so strongly about what happened to her. You did feel strongly about her case, didn't you?'

'She's young, she'd been deeply injured. And it happened here. Yes, that bothered me. As a senior member of the college, I felt a kind of indirect responsibility. But I wouldn't send her flowers,' he insisted. 'Sending flowers would be more of the same.'

'More of the same?'

'Intrusive. Pushing myself at her. Wouldn't it?'

'Yes, I can see that.' I thought for a few seconds. 'How long have you been at St Bartholomew's, John?'

'I came here as an undergraduate in the late 1950s. Those were the days,' he said, with a ghost of a twinkle. 'We never had it so good.'

'So I heard.' *You never had it so good* had been an electioneering slogan in the period of rising consumption in the late 1950s. It had struck a chord with millions. 'You lived here, in college, in 1961? Stephen Fox as well?'

Carswell's curiosity was piqued now. He wondered what I was driving at. But he answered freely enough. 'Yes, of course. We both lived in college as undergraduates. And came back afterwards, as research fellows. Why these questions, Laura? The Spinning House is one thing. But I would've thought you'd find my personal history rather less fascinating.'

'Why? Just that things get more and more convoluted, John. Forgive me if I'm prying unnecessarily. But you see – another body has been found. Did you know?'

'A baby's skeleton. I heard. Horrible,' he said, with a fastidious shudder. 'Let's go, Laura. Have a drink, shall we?'

'The room the remains were in had been the site of two successive suicides. Were you here when they took place? Did you know either of the men who died?'

'One of them occurred during my second year. Shall we pursue this sombre topic over coffee?'

'I'm sorry, John, not today. I've promised to find somewhere outside college where Deborah Cook – Katie's friend – can stay. It was she who found the skeleton. She's pretty shaken.' I tried again. 'Did you know him – the student who died? Was he a friend of yours?'

'Knew him, yes. Everyone in college knew everyone else in those days. Gerald Chichester was his name. He was a gregarious bloke. It was a complete shock when he gassed himself. And very sad. But he wasn't a particular friend.' He paused and considered. 'Did he have anything to do with the baby, do you think?'

'No,' I said. 'The baby wasn't placed there until after his death. That's why I was asking about '61.'

'After Gerald's death?' Carswell murmured, and he turned abruptly away again, and returned to pacing the room.

The house on Great Eastern Street hadn't changed in any fundamental way. The back door was open, and through it I could still see the trellis heavy with honeysuckle. The bicycle with the For Sale sign still lingered near the door. The time to sell a bike in Cambridge is October, when the academic year begins; in June, abandoned bicycles are to be had for the asking.

But there was one difference: the hallway, and the kitchen were littered with cardboard boxes and carrier bags. Some were stacked up higgledy-piggledy, waiting to be of use. Others were half-full of clothes, or linen, or odds and ends.

'You're sure I won't be in the way?' Deborah asked. She looked uncertainly around her. She peered in the top of a carrier bag that was tipping its contents on to the linoleum, and shook it gently upright.

'That's mine,' Beverley shot back. The eye she cast on the carrier bag was proprietorial, but her tone was not unkind. 'It goes here. The Beehive bags belong to Candace. Who'll be back soon, by the way.' Beverley gestured towards the end of the room nearest the garden. 'You can put her things along that wall.'

Deborah responded well to orders. She set to work, shifting things from one side of the room to another.

Beverley approved. 'You're welcome to camp in Katie's room until we move. In fact, you can pack her things. Mrs Arkwright will send Katie's uncle over to pick them up as soon as they're ready.'

'I'll be glad to,' Deborah said. Putting belongings into boxes must have seemed like child's play compared to turning a skeleton out of a cupboard.

I had no intention of helping, so I plugged in the kettle and looked on contentedly as Debbie and Bev – they quickly addressed each other so – worked. Bev had replaced the mint-green outfit with Lycra shorts and a bra-top in blue. She wore trainers, slouch socks and a blue band in her hair. She was no longer disappointed to be leaving this house, she explained, wrapping her few pieces of china with elaborate care in cast-off pages from the *Sun*. She had found something much better. *With such nice girls*, she said. *Girls who really look after themselves.*

Beverley would have got on well, I decided, with my mother's sister. *You look after yourself, my girl*, Aunt Verna used to warn.

In Verna's lexicon, the opposite of looking after yourself was letting yourself go. Letting yourself go had serious consequences; we were left in no doubt of that. Women who didn't work at feminine ideals of beauty – women who put on weight, who let the tiredness that came from long days at the factory show on their faces – were taking grave risks. We would hear about Mrs Carter, whose husband Alf had taken off with a girl fresh out of school, leaving Mrs Carter to raise all the little Carters on her own. *Well*, Verna would say, shaking her head, *what do you expect? She let herself go.*

Letting yourself go had a darker set of meanings too. It covered a wide range of acts – acts that were shameful because they were dangerous, and dangerous because they were shameful. A woman who drank too much in public or who danced too exuberantly, one who laughed too loudly or in any way appeared to abandon herself to pleasure could be accused of letting herself go. The consequences took a grim turn: they were made known to us, in hushed tones, in stories of women found dead in alleys with needle tracks up their arms.

And yet, and yet . . . Letting yourself go had a sweet sound, too – the sweet sound of the forbidden. It had an exotic, seductive ring, like *she upped and left*. Or *turning your back on everything*. Or *throwing caution to the winds*. I wondered if Verna – if Beverley, for that matter – ever heard that siren call. If they were tempted ever to let themselves go.

Beverley, in defiance of the heat, had closed the front door. An opportunistic thief might otherwise dash inside, she explained, and make off with one of her boxes. She was taking no chances. Where doors open directly on to the pavement, you have to think about these things.

Just as she accepted a mug of tea from me, someone knocked on the door.

Beverley dusted off her knees and went to answer. As she trotted down the corridor, the knocking was repeated, more urgently. I heard a man's voice, calling.

'If we shift this table a little to the left,' Deborah said, 'we'll have room to move about.' She was busy clearing odds and ends off the kitchen table.

Reluctantly, I set my mug of tea down and went to help.

The voice was louder, and the words were slurred. I couldn't make out what he was saying, but it was clear that he was agitated.

'Move your end a little to the right,' Deborah said, intent on the job at hand.

Beverley let out a shriek. Then a high-pitched whimper. Feet thumped and shuffled. Voices growled.

By the time I managed to drop the table and reach the corridor, Beverley was doubled over in the doorway, in furious struggle with a man who had one fist meshed deep in her hair. He gripped her neck with the other. He was doing his best to pull her towards him, out into the street.

Beverley flailed about desperately, finally clamping on to the door frame as if her life depended on it. I couldn't get at him. She was blocking my way.

'Let me pass,' I hissed in Beverley's ear.

She released her grip on the door frame, and the moment she did, I rushed at her attacker, swinging the side of my hand up sharply to his face. I hit him at the base of his nostrils as hard as I could.

There was a crunching sound.

He blinked, then shook his head. He abandoned Beverley, and stumbled backwards, off the pavement, into the road. Blood began to flow in a rich stream from his nose. He looked bewildered.

I almost felt sorry for him.

Then he was staring, his face contorted with hatred, at Beverley. In his confusion, he seemed to think she was the one who'd hurt him.

'You little slut,' he croaked.

So much for sympathy.

He was about thirty years of age, I reckoned, thin and wiry and reeking of beer. I couldn't take full credit for the way he swayed in the road, oblivious to the Mini that had to skirt around him. He'd spent most of the day in the pub.

'You all right, mate?' the driver asked, seeing the blood.

Beverley's attacker wiped his nose on the hem of a dirty

T-shirt, turning the blue to a dark purple. 'Fucking whore attacked me,' he shouted, gesticulating wildly in Beverley's direction. 'She attacked me. All I wanted was some pussy.' He fumbled in his jeans pocket, struggled to extricate his hand again, came up waving a card. 'Says she's up for anything, and then she does this.'

The Mini zoomed off.

I stepped up to Beverley's attacker, keeping well clear of the blood, and snatched the card from his hand.

'Where did you get this?' Now, after the fact, I was trembling with fury. I grabbed him by the shoulders, and shook him, taking care to keep him at a distance. 'Where? Where'd you get this?'

He blinked at me through a haze of alcohol. Then he waved an impatient arm in the direction of the Earl of Stamford public house, and sat down abruptly on the edge of the pavement.

I stuck my thumbs roughly in his armpits, forcing him up again, and propelled him towards the entrance of the pub. Steered him through the front door, and left him to collapse over the nearest table. Blood dribbled down his upper lip and plopped on to the carpet.

The landlord was rearranging glasses on the shelf behind the bar. He looked up at us in alarm.

'Where's the men's toilet?' I asked.

'Back there. Past the fruit machine.'

I headed for the back of the room. 'What about him?' the landlord said, plaintively. 'He's bleeding on my carpet.'

'Try ice and a towel, for starters,' I said. 'To stop the bleeding. Then black coffee. And after, when he's sober enough that anyone will allow him in their car, call a taxi and send him home.'

The men's loos were permeated by a floral smell, mainly sweet pea. It overlaid the reek of urine. In my jaded condition, I might have preferred urine.

The cubicle was clean, but could have done with a root-and-branch redecoration. Paper was beginning to peel off the walls. Someone had started refurbishment in a unique way – by arranging a medley of cards over a patch where the paper had been stripped away. Five cards altogether. On closer inspection, five identical cards. All bore the same message.

I'll make your dreams CUM true. Anything – that's my motto. Front, back. With, without . . . It's up to you.

Call on Katie, at 90 Great Eastern Street. I'm waiting for you . . .

I had just stepped out of the pub on to Mill Road, when – over the traffic noises – I noticed the sound of someone running along Great Eastern Street. Running softly, on the balls of their feet.

I spun around sharply. There, tearing along from the direction of the house, was Candace. Her haystack of a hairdo bounced around her face as she ran.

'Shhh,' she whispered, a finger to her lips. 'Don't want the others to hear. Can I speak to you? In private?'

'How's Beverley?'

'Pretty shaken up, I think. Her scalp's raw in spots. He yanked some strands of hair out. But Deb says it'll grow back.'

Candace had, apparently, returned to the house before the blood had dried on the pavement. 'Do you know, Laura, when Beverley showed me that card – you know the one – she didn't make a single complaint against Katie. She just kept saying, over and over again, "What'd I do? Why did he attack *me*?"'

A bit of a shock for Beverley. All that looking after herself – and still she was vulnerable.

There were half-moons of sweat under the arms of Candace's black T-shirt. Her forehead was sharp with perspiration.

'Let's go somewhere cooler,' I said.

We strolled the back way through to Coleridge Rec, where we bought ice creams, and waded solemnly through the paddling pool, our heads towering above those of crashing, splashing toddlers. Their noise and ribaldry returned a sense of normality. It took some of the sting out of what had gone before.

'It happened in March,' Candace said. 'Katie and I went to London to do a bit of shopping. She'd not been in a good state for weeks and I thought it might cheer her up. But though she tried to be good company – encouraging me to buy things and the like – the crowds on Oxford Street seemed to draw the life out of her. She wasn't short-tempered or anything, only listless.'

We spotted an opening on a bench underneath the chestnut trees and sat down. Candace extended her brown legs, still damp from the paddling pool, into the sun. Our heads, our shoulders, were wreathed in glorious shade.

'Katie was listless,' I reminded her.

'Until we were heading home. We caught a bus and somehow got the route wrong. Had to get off and walk back to King's Cross station. Then she saw someone she knew.'

'At the station?'

'No, on one of those sooty roads nearby. Leaning into a car, she was, talking to the driver. Katie was very excited. *It's Vanessa*, she whispered. *She used to live in Histon.* I have to tell you, Laura, I wasn't really keen to speak to Vanessa from Histon, even if she and Katie had gone to primary school together. Vanessa – well, she was clearly prostituting herself. And I didn't know if it was safe, or what.'

'But Katie insisted?'

Candace nodded. 'Katie said afterwards, on the train, that it was like the solution to a mystery. Vanessa had been in some kind of trouble at home – Katie didn't know exactly what. No one had seen her since she was fifteen, when she ran away. And now there she was, Katie said, safe and sound. Hardly safe and sound, I said; selling herself to men in cars. But nothing I could say put Katie off. She was fascinated. Vanessa looks all right, she kept saying. She looks healthy enough. Not like those junkies you see on television, with faces like death. Vanessa looks OK.'

'Was she distinctive-looking?'

'You could say that. Eyes rimmed with black. A ponytail of bleached hair that started on the crown of her head and came all the way down to the middle of her back. Maybe it was a hair extension,' she added with a shrug. 'Gold hoopy earrings. A denim skirt that only just covered her bum. And black suede boots up to the knee.' Candace gave a reluctant chuckle. 'Vanessa Savage. Apparently, that's her real name.'

'All ponytail and thigh, huh?' I'd seen her double on the streets many times. 'Why didn't you tell me this before, Candace?'

Candace inspected her legs, flexed her feet up and down, up and down, in the sunshine. 'It was Beverley,' she said. 'She's such a vindictive little cow. I didn't want to give her any more reason to be suspicious about Katie. But now that you know, Laura—' She paused. Her black eyes searched my face. 'Do you want me to come with you?'

'You've got some serious packing to do, Candace,' I said. 'Anyway, you've been watching over Katie for a long while. Maybe it's time now to begin' – I used that phrase in what I hoped was a different way from Aunt Verna – 'looking after yourself.'

Chapter 18

King's Cross station has gone up in the world in recent years. The fruit seller on Platform 8 offers quality produce. W.H. Smith has been revamped. Café Select offers one of the liveliest spots for commuter-gazing in London. It's not Covent Garden, but it's less of a dump than it used to be.

The one thing that hasn't altered, though, is the toilets. They're to be found in a subterranean corner of the station, down a steeply banked flight of stairs. There's an entry fee – designed, or so I've been told, to inhibit certain classes of users. To act as a deterrent to drunks who might fall asleep in the cubicles. To make junkies think again about shooting up there. To prevent the cubicles being used as trysting places by the least discriminating of punters and the most desperate of tarts.

Most of the street prostitutes have pushed on to Paddington or Shepherd Market. But in the King's Cross loos, precautions remain. There are vivid yellow containers for the disposal of needles in the cubicles. There is a spyhole at eye-height in every door.

Some passengers shiver at the sight of those toilets, seeing in them, apparently, all that the careful traveller – the traveller who looks after herself – might wish to avoid. But the King's Cross toilets are clean; and the women who keep them so have, over the years, done a valiant job of nudging the facility in the direction of cosy. They've hung reproductions of paintings, in ornate wooden frames, on the wall. One shows a shipboard scene from the 1880s. Two young ladies, modestly dressed – servant girls, perhaps – stand with eyes cast down and covert smiles, while sailors in their Sunday best try to amuse them. The colours are soft and muted, like the ancient lighting in the loos – gold and faded greens and ivories. And sometimes, there will be vases of flowers, too; I've seen chrysanthemums there, bold and robust; and bundles of blue and violet straw flowers. And, often as not, there'll be music. On a soggy London day, Ella Fitzgerald does a lot to dispel the gloom.

I didn't have to visit the King's Cross toilets. Could have held out for a facility somewhere else with brass taps and a money-no-object clientele. But I can't help liking King's Cross ladies' toilets for the way they represent a triumph of hope over experience. They're proof that it's sometimes possible to build a refuge in even the most unpromising of places.

When I thought of Katie Arkwright, I took comfort from that.

I set out from the station in the late afternoon, armed only with a London A–Z. Traced myself a route, so I wouldn't miss any streets out of carelessness or boredom. Began to walk it. This search was a long shot, and I knew it. But if you're going to attempt a long shot, you might as well do it whole-heartedly.

I'd checked with Stevie first, of course, for advice. She had shrugged. 'You'll be lucky to find her,' she'd said. 'So many of the girls have gone off-street now. To brothels. To working flats.'

'It's illegal, of course – for the brothel-keeper, anyway. Whereas street-walking isn't.'

'Who cares about illegal?' Stevie said. 'It's a hell of a lot safer and the police don't give you grief.'

So in the absence of better information, I criss-crossed the area. The undersides of over-passes. The busy streets that channelled traffic down towards the centre. The side streets, leafy and green. The alleyways that snaked between disused warehouses, now boarded up, or revived as discount outlets.

I checked the pubs along my route. 'Anyone seen this girl?' I asked, offering a pint of best beer to lubricate their tongues. They looked. They always looked at Katie Arkwright, seated on the grass in black and white with her arms wound around her knees. Her face wasn't so much beautiful – it wasn't that that made them linger – as it was moving.

But no one was moved to recognise her.

And then I asked about Vanessa Savage. I'd describe her – the short skirt, the knee-length boots, the hoopy earrings. The long fall of platinum hair. And they'd shrug.

Seen lots of girls like that, they'd say.

But not lately. Not here.

And so it went. The traffic fumes made my head ache – now that's a danger from street-walking that the tabloids don't tell you about. But I wasn't yet ready to say die.

Just before half past six, I fuelled up with fish and chips. Relegated the A–Z to my backpack for the time being, and concentrated on eating the hot, glistening chips without burning my tongue, on wolfing down the battered fish without smearing grease on my clothes. And in the course of my mobile feast, I came across a phone box with a card that invited passers-by to have the time of their lives.

With Vanessa.

When I'd finished the fish, and wiped my hands on a meagre portion of napkin, I rang the number on the card. I was hopeful, really hopeful, for the first time in days. The scenario was there in front of me as I fumbled with the receiver ... Vanessa from Histon would answer. She'd know exactly where Katie was; Katie might even be lodging with her, an innocent visitor from childhood, reading a book in the second bedroom while Vanessa did what she did in the first. Katie, bored out of her skull and tired of the game, would leap at the chance to come back to Cambridge.

But the Vanessa who answered had the voice of a woman in her forties. She was a Welshwoman, born and bred in Llandudno. Never been to Histon in her life.

At that point, some people might have called it a day. Might have said: *enough of carbon monoxide fumes and dirty pavements; I'm going home.* But the food had fired me with fat and protein and fish jokes. *I'd haddock up to here, but I was determined to carry on.*

Good Cod, I declared, *you can't give up now.*

And in this frivolous vein, I combed my hair, shoved open the door of the call box, and stepped out on to the kerb.

Stepped almost into the path of an oncoming car.

The phone box was situated near the freight depot, at the edge of a busy thoroughfare. A black Montego suddenly switched lanes and pulled hard to the left, as if someone had spotted the BT sign at the last moment. It was a manoeuvre with a whiff of recklessness about it; one or two other drivers gave hoots of half-hearted protest. Someone alighted from the passenger side. 'Ta-ta, love' she said, cheerfully enough, but without a backward glance. The car sped away with as little concern for other drivers as it had shown on stopping. The passenger headed for the phone box, rummaging in her shoulder bag.

She was chubbier than I'd imagined; looked seventeen rather than nineteen. But she had the overly made-up eyes, the black suede boots, the denim skirt, and the ponytail. Vanessa Savage, or a damn good imitation.

She dialled a number. I waited while she chatted and tutted and listened. At one point, she noticed me standing outside and flashed a just-a-minute signal through the glass. When she stepped out, I hailed her.

She paused, and checked me up and down.

Vanessa Savage had smooth pink cheeks and a scar at the edge of her eyebrow. It lent her face a comic twist.

'You rang?' she asked in answer to her name.

I told her I knew people she knew, from back home in Histon. Told her I needed a private word.

She scratched the back of one leg thoughtfully with the toe of her other boot. When both feet returned to the ground, she'd made up her mind.

'All right,' she said. 'But you'll have to stand right there.' She guided me to a position away from the kerb. 'No punter's going to stop if he thinks we're deep in conversation. They worry too much about being brushed aside. Some of them,' she said, dropping her voice to a whisper, 'are so nervous, you'd imagine it's a date they're asking for. What do they think?' She giggled. 'They got the money, I'll turn them down?'

She was so relaxed, she might have been selling cigarettes. If it was an act, it was damn good.

'You don't mean that,' I said. Just to be clear.

When Vanessa was taken by surprise, it made the scar in her eyebrow dance. 'Mean what?'

'That you'd go with any bloke who had the money.'

There was a second's hesitation. Then she waved the exchange aside. 'Course not,' she said. The lighter tone was gone. 'You have to size 'em up first. Make sure they're not angry. Make sure they're not mean.' She looked at me, as if sizing *me* up. 'And, of course, make sure they're not after things you don't do. You've got to get everything agreed in advance, before you go with them.'

I thought of that photograph Sonny had shown me, at Stansted, days ago. Of Cindy Sinful, after she'd been rescued – but just – from the boot of a car.

Thought of the seven prostitutes who've been murdered in Glasgow in the past six years. No sign of a serial killer. The truth is probably worse, police say – that there's an awful lot of men out there who see prostitutes as easy prey.

'How do you know, Vanessa? That they're not angry, that is? Or mean. How can you be sure?'

'Oh, you can just tell.' Vanessa was tiring of this conversation. She affected a knowing look that made her appear younger still. 'Most blokes are friendly enough. And as for the weirdos – well, nine times out of ten, their eyes will give it away. It's all down to experience.'

You could just tell. Their eyes give it away, she said. Nine times out of ten.

I didn't much care for those odds.

Vanessa was gazing down the road now, eyeing up the oncoming traffic. She arched her back, stuck her bosoms out.

You knew right away that this wasn't just the inadvertent display of a teenage girl, high on her own sexuality. This was different. Vanessa looked like what she was. Young. Pretty. Unthreatening.

And for sale.

I spoke to her from behind, like a conscience.

'Vanessa, where's Katie Arkwright?'

The skinny tail of hair was like a satin cord. It trembled. 'Who?' she asked. Her eyes remained fixed on the traffic.

'You know who I mean. You went to primary school together. Katie spoke to you here, a few months ago.' Still no answer. Her foot tapped nervously on the pavement. Not an easy thing to do, foot tapping, when your boots have platform soles.

I tried once more. 'She's disappeared, Vanessa. All she's left is this card.'

Reluctantly, Vanessa took the card. Skimmed the text. *I'll make your dreams CUM true. Anything – that's my motto. Front, back. With, without . . . It's up to you. Call on Katie, at 90 Great Eastern Street. I'm waiting for you . . .*

The colour vanished from Vanessa's cheeks. 'Is this where she lived? Great Eastern Street?'

'She shared a house there with two other girls.'

Vanessa didn't so much hand the card back to me as fling it away. She looked shocked. 'It's not right,' she said. 'It's filthy. No self-respecting working girl would make promises like that. And to put her address on for anyone to see – it's crazy.'

For the first time, Vanessa's voice was tinged with suspicion. 'Why are you showing this to me? I don't believe Katie gave you this card. Katie wouldn't say those things. She wouldn't!'

Her vehemence told its own story.

'You've seen her.'

Vanessa whirled around to face me. The anger was gone as quickly as it had come. 'No. Not since that day she stopped to talk.' She softened. 'Do you know, it made me feel real funny, seeing Katie like that, out of the blue. I recognised her straight away, but it made me feel funny. Like I was back in Mrs Hooper's class at primary school. For a few seconds I thought . . .' Vanessa swallowed. Shrugged. 'I thought I was a kid again.'

The temperature couldn't have fallen much below nineteen degrees, but Vanessa shivered. Feeling like a kid again had taken the warm glow off the evening. Vanessa was one of those children for whom the streets of London hold fewer terrors than the family home.

'Vanessa?' I touched her arm. 'Vanessa, why don't you work inside, like so many of the other girls? Wouldn't it be less dangerous?'

'I tried it,' Vanessa shot back. 'You work in a brothel, for a boss – well, you do what she says. Work the hours she dictates. Take the clients she gives you. Give freebies to the people who offer protection.' The inflection she put on *protection* would have burned your fingers.

She shrugged again. 'I'd rather be my own boss. Keep my earnings for myself. I've got plans, you see. I don't stick myself with needles, like some of those girls on Goods Way. I don't snort my money away. And one of these days, I'm going to have money in the bank, enough for a down-payment on a flat. And then I'm going to have a proper home. Somewhere nice, away from here,' she finished, solemnly. 'Somewhere with hedges.'

A man was walking towards us from the direction of the canal. He was taking his time. His hands were thrust deep into his pockets.

'Shh,' Vanessa said, silencing me. 'Get out of the way.' She turned off the main road, and walked towards him, tossing him what was intended as a sultry smile. I thought she looked fetchingly comical, rather than seductive; but then, I wasn't the target.

'Vanessa.' I followed her, lowering my voice to a whisper. 'Where can I reach you if we need to talk again?'

'Shut up,' she hissed between clenched teeth. The man noticed the clenched teeth. He looked confused.

'I need an address. A phone number.'

She stepped towards the man, who was staring at her now, his eyes hooded and hopeful. He looked ready to bolt.

I snatched at her shoulder bag. Slid my card, with a twenty-pound note, into the top compartment. 'Call me,' I said. 'If you hear anything at all about Katie.'

She looked back at me one last time. 'Sure, sweetie. Now piss off.' She wasn't being unfriendly. The girl had a job to do.

I didn't stay to see her negotiations with the man. Didn't watch her link her arm through his and walk towards the corner. In her suede platforms, she was two inches taller than him and a whole lot more attractive.

Instead, I headed back towards the station. Or what I was thought was towards the station. The encounter with Vanessa had disoriented me just a little, but I couldn't be bothered to retrieve the map from my backpack. I was too troubled.

Troubled by the fact that Vanessa was only nineteen – Katie's age – and already she could tell, or thought she could, which blokes a prostitute could trust. *It's all down to experience*, she'd said. What kind of experience do you need before you know that men who look like this, who talk like that, will do you harm?

Troubled by her vulnerability. By the desperation that must have driven her to this work – work that cut her off from other women. From the company of decent men.

But how the hell did I know that? Katie, for one, had been keen to speak to Vanessa. How could I be sure that Vanessa didn't go home at night to a flat full of friends – to people who thought the world of her. *Salt of the earth, our Vanessa*, they might say. *She's a good kid.* Was it just my own prejudices that made me assume that a prostitute was beyond the pale?

And what grounds did I have to describe Vanessa as desperate? To say that she'd been driven into prostitution? Maybe she'd weighed up the alternatives, and come to a rational decision – that waitressing was a mug's game, that cleaning was exhausting, that shop work was dull. That street-walking was her best available option. Who was I to assume that prostitution represented a last-ditch stab at survival? How would I know?

I hadn't, after all, asked Vanessa herself.

I hadn't walked for long, but I'd been buried in thought. I was suddenly unsure of my way. Perhaps I'd come full circle, around the block. There were no street signs on the scruffy buildings that lined the road. Nothing to help me get my bearings.

I listened for the rumble of trains, calculating that if I could make my way to the back of the buildings on my left, I should be nearer the station. There was an alleyway that headed in that direction. I peered into the gloom, into a warren of small connecting lanes. With luck, I'd be able to cut back almost to where I had begun.

I trotted off into the empty back streets, past rows of dustbins. Past carrier bags, their sides ripped apart by predators. Past a cache of cardboard panels, and an old sleeping bag, home to someone who was probably out on the main road at the moment, working up the change for a can of cider. Past several alcoves whose rank odour testified to their function as toilets.

Turned the corner into another alley, narrower and more rutted. When I looked to the left, I could hear traffic in that direction, flowing more smoothly now that rush hour had ended. That must be the way back to the road where I'd left Vanessa. I glanced to the right.

Saw movement. Looked more closely. Wished I hadn't.

The setting was stark. A short stretch of alleyway, once roughly paved, now rutted with the wear of years; a massive wall of dark-red brick; a rusty fire escape. One of the warehouses that lined the sides had a loading door, pitted with dry rot, high up on the wall.

Below the door, an old Ford Escort had been abandoned. It had been torched; the paint on one side was blackened and blistered. The windows were shattered. Fragments of glass were scattered around.

All this I took in in a flash. But it was only background.

What caught my attention – what had held me in place, like a hand gripping my collar, whether I wanted to look or not – was a woman.

233

She wore a denim skirt that barely covered her bum. She wore black suede boots with platform soles. She was on her knees in the dirt. In the half-light, the pale skin of her arms turned to grey. The skinny cable of hair gleamed silver down her back.

Her shirt was unbuttoned, the sides tucked into her waistband. Her soft breasts bounced in the open air as she moved. In and out, in and out, in and out.

Her head was bent towards the crotch of a man who stood, or rather leaned back, his weight against the car. His eyes were closed.

I stood there for seconds only.

He, wrapped in the reactions of his body, didn't notice.

She did. She jerked when she saw me – a reflex: of embarrassment? of fear? And then she turned away, very deliberately, and gave her full attention again to the task in hand.

This was a commercial transaction. She was for sale. He'd paid, she'd accepted. Business was business. However startled she was by my sudden appearance, Vanessa from Histon would finish the job.

She was young. She was pretty. On her knees, in an alley.

I guess it was a choice. Of sorts.

Chapter 19

That evening, I went to the office in Camden Town in search of comfort. A down-to-earth exchange with Stevie would be best, but if Stevie wasn't there – and why should she be? – I'd settle for a trawl through yesterday's post. Anything to delay the anonymity of the train journey back to Cambridge.

At least until I'd put that scene in the alleyway behind me.

Our office, above the Satay Palace, at the top of the third flight of stairs, consists of a single large attic room, with dormer windows and sloping ceilings. There were plans once to build partitions, but we've long since evolved into an office that is euphemistically described as open-plan. Besides filing cabinets and a stationery cupboard, our furnishings run to four large desks – school surplus – that have taken on a patina, even a glamour, with the passing of the years. They're approaching the point where cheap and dated mutates into antique. There's an ancient armchair with a canework frame. And the walls are painted a thick caramel colour that gives the room a warm glow even on a cold day.

I took the stairs quickly, two at a time, testing my aerobic capacity. Stopped short on the top landing, outside Aardvark Investigations. Bent forward to catch my breath and stretch my hamstrings.

Saw a glimmer of illumination at the base of the door. The lights were on. The door was unlocked.

I went in search of comfort, and I found it. On the far side of the room, wearing a light mackintosh as if he'd just come in, and standing by the desk as if just going out, was Sonny Mendlowitz.

He held the telephone to his ear. For a second he didn't notice me, so intent was he on his conversation; and then he looked up, caught my eye, and gave me a no-holds-barred smile.

'Laura's just walked in,' he reported into the mouthpiece. His eyes didn't leave mine. 'Make it four.' Then he replaced the receiver, spread his arms in invitation, and waited.

If I'd thought about it, I might have held back, but I didn't. I just let myself be bundled up, as if there'd never been a distance between us.

Sonny left no opening for small talk. He stepped back a little and studied my face. 'Something's got you down,' he concluded. 'Is it to do with Katie Arkwright?'

That would do for now. 'I've picked up a trail. Katie did some freelance work with an escort agency here in London – The Heavenly Twins. Kept her activities secret from her friends.'

'The Heavenly Twins.' Sonny rolled the name around on his tongue. Fished out some fragment of memory. Couldn't resist a smile. 'Isn't that the agency that sends Oxbridge girls to dinner with—'

'—their tits out. That's the one.'

'Then I don't understand the long face, Laura. Airing her boobs over dinner won't damage Katie, will it?' Sonny chuckled. 'After all, students are expected to—'

I could see the joke coming a mile off, about keeping abreast of things. 'Spare me, Sonny, please.'

We heard footsteps, one light set, another heavier, making their synchronised way up the stairs.

Sonny bent his head for a solemn inspection of my face and waggled his eyebrow, trying to elicit a smile. He played straitjacket with me, encircling me from behind. He caught me up again, when I wriggled away, and kneaded my ribs with his fingertips. By the time Stevie arrived, I was reduced to undignified giggles. It wasn't the same thing as feeling good, but it was a start.

She came with Geoff, trailing the aromas of ginger and garlic, cardamom and coriander. Bengali takeaway. Thoughts of Katie went on to the back burner. It felt like days since I'd downed that fish and chips.

Sonny fetched the oilcloth from the cupboard. He spread it out over his desk, just as it was, so that – beneath the plastic surface – the piles of papers, the mounds of pens and Post-its, created a landscape of chaos. Geoff unloaded cartons from the paper carrier bag and arranged them deftly amongst the hills. I unpicked cardboard covers and prised open a bag of naan bread. Stevie flicked the tops off bottles of Cobra beer.

Stevie had brought more than enough for four. We loaded our plates with rice and dansak and chicken tikka and tarka dall, with onion bhajis and bhindi and chapatis, and there was still enough on the desk for another round. Each of us pulled a chair over to the table. Four plates were balanced on four laps, four lengths of paper towelling passed around, four pairs of legs were carefully raised and four pairs of feet were settled firmly on the desk.

'Cheers!' Geoff declared. He leaned over gingerly, picked his beer up off the floor, and toasted us all.

'Cheers!' we repeated. I was a beat behind the others. Then we tucked in.

There wasn't much in the way of talk until we'd polished off the first round. Then Stevie went straight to the point. 'What's wrong with you, Laura?' she asked. 'You've not got a lot in the way of sparkle today. Has something happened?'

'No sparkle says it in a nutshell, Stevie.' I felt like a bottle of tonic water that had been left with the top off overnight.

I told them about Vanessa Savage, selling lonely acts of un-love to a stranger in a strange place. So that she could some day purchase a home of her own, with hedges.

Stevie didn't think much of her chances. 'Not bloody likely,' she said.

'Pardon?'

'Prostitutes talk up their plans for the future to justify being on the game. Ask them how much they're actually saving, and you get a different story.'

'But with someone like Vanessa – who's not a junkie – where would the money go?'

Stevie shrugged. 'On costumes for work – no prostitute wears the same clothes at home that she puts on for clients. On little extras for the kids, to make up for the fact that Mummy's never there at bedtime. And increasingly, as the months go by, on stuff to ease them into work – and I don't mean KY jelly.'

'Drugs?'

'There's hardly a woman out there who doesn't have a good long joint before she hits the street. Or a stiff drink or two, or three. Or temazepan. And maybe, at the end of the shift, something stronger, to help her forget. How otherwise is she going to live with the shame? With the sheer hard work?'

My puzzlement – where did she get that? – must have shown on my face.

'Drop-in centre,' Stevie explained. Ah, yes. I should have remembered. A three-month stint in Manchester, before she came to work for us.

Sonny went for a more optimistic account. 'I'm not convinced,' he said. 'In Amsterdam, I talked to a high-class hooker who made a packet and retired early. Martina didn't care a fig for any shame. Said her money paid for meals in swanky restaurants as well as anyone else's.'

'The hookers for whom it's a light-hearted little earner – the Cynthia Paynes of the profession – are one in a million. Believe me, Sonny, to make a packet in prostitution, and get out again – undamaged – you need to be a special kind of person. Good with money. A hard-headed manager.'

'How about youth or beauty?' Geoff asked.

'Not as important as self-confidence – so you can resist all the shit that's thrown at you. But what you really need is luck.' Stevie turned to me. 'What about it, Laura. Is Vanessa lucky?'

'I hardly know her.' And then I realised that Vanessa was like most of the prostitutes I'd come across. 'The truth is, Stevie, if Vanessa was one of the lucky ones, she wouldn't be working in King's Cross.'

Stevie squeezed my hand, and did her best to change the subject. 'And what about that girl who ran away from the May Ball? That what's-her-name?'

'Katie,' Sonny said, watching my face. 'Apparently, Katie Arkwright's been hanging out at some fancy escort agency.'

'The Heavenly Twins is already old news, I'm afraid. Katie's in deeper now. She's selling more than scenery.'

I dug in my pocket. Retrieved the card that had been pinned to the toilet wall. 'She was using this to advertise in Cambridge, just before she disappeared. I suspect she's here in London now.'

A sharp intake of breath, and then another, as the card – *Anything – that's my motto* – was passed around.

Followed by heavy silence.

Then Geoff leaned forward with a quizzical expression. 'I can understand, I guess, about Vanessa Savage. But this Katie – she's a student, isn't she? Why would a girl with a good education throw it all away?'

Sonny jumped in. 'You've got to get with the times, Geoff. In the eighties, prostitutes were girls from the north who'd been thrown out of work. Another factory closed; they'd get on the train, come to London in search of a job. Never get further than King's Cross.'

Geoff nodded. 'Sure. We used to call them Thatcher's girls.'

'Now,' Sonny said, 'it's the turn of their southern sisters. Don't you read the papers? A cabinet minister's daughter, studying at London University, caught picking up punters at the Café de Paris. Brighton massage parlours providing computers so that undergraduates can work on their assignments between clients.'

'Everywhere you turn,' Stevie concurred, 'there are stories about student prostitutes. And a rash of novels that make it almost sound like fun. Plus the demand's there. Escort agencies, massage parlours – they all recruit kids from university now.' We could see it in her face, hear it in her voice; Stevie had turned a corner into anger. 'Students are popular with the clients. Make the punters feel like benefactors. When they pay for a fuck, they're not buying drugs for some junkie whore, they tell themselves, they're helping a girl through college.'

This monologue produced an awkward silence. Geoff jumped into the opening. 'Let's do something about this mess,' he said. He started to clear away the remains of our meal.

Katie's card sat on the table, stained with grease, next to what was left of the cauliflower bhaji. I leaned over and picked it up.

Front, back. With, without . . .
Call on Katie, at 90 Great Eastern Street.

Suddenly I remembered Vanessa's reaction when she'd seen the card. She'd been shocked – shocked, presumably, that Katie would work without condoms. There are boundaries, Vanessa had implied. Things a self-respecting working girl just wouldn't do.

Katie was short on self-esteem. But timid as she was, would Katie really have volunteered to do the things that other whores refused?

Was her self-loathing really as deep as this?

And if it was, what else – what worse – might Katie Arkwright do?

And then there was that other thing. That bit about the address.

'Laura?'

Sonny had taken a mango out of a bag. He used his penknife to strip away the thin skin. Carved off thick golden pieces of perfumed flesh, one at a time.

'Thanks, Sonny,' I said absent-mindedly, accepting the last slippery slice. 'Listen – something Vanessa Savage said. About Katie. When she saw the card. She said, *No self-respecting working girl—*'

Geoff took the offensive now. 'A contradiction in terms?' he asked. 'Self-respecting prostitute?'

Stevie remonstrated with him. She could see he'd gone too far.

I was overcome suddenly by the need to do something.

'I've had it with all this discussion,' I said. I saw Sonny's eyebrow go up a fraction. 'It's all beside the point.'

'And the point is . . .?'

I stood up and began to pace the room. 'I need to find her.'

No one argued with that. Not even Stevie. But Sonny did push me further than I'd meant to go.

'Tell me, Laura – why are you so hooked on this Katie thing anyway? This search is more than simply business for you, isn't it?'

'Of course it is.' I wasn't afraid to own up. 'There's a bit of me that fears that Katie will become another Vanessa. I can't let that happen without talking to her at least. Seeing if there's another way.'

'As long as you don't get your hopes too high,' Sonny said, softer now. 'The sex trade is massive.' He had done his homework for the Cindy Sinful case. 'Do you have any idea, Laura, of the extent of the industry in London alone?'

I shook my head. Didn't fancy a round of *Mastermind*.

Specialist subject? Statistics on the Sex Trade.

'Pass,' I said.

A mere pass wasn't going to slow Sonny down. 'Try a higher annual turnover than London Transport.' He reached for another bottle of beer. 'Try eighty thousand punters every week. Eight thousand kerb-crawlers. Five thousand hookers – that's currently working.'

'And don't forget,' Stevie threw in, 'most of the five thousand are squirrelled away in massage parlours, and working flats, and escort agencies, where it's hard to dig them out. It won't be easy to find a girl in that crowd.'

'Like looking for a needle in a haystack,' Sonny agreed cheerfully.

Stevie corrected him. 'An orange pip in a pile of shit,' she said.

Then she relented. 'Laura, what were you trying to say before? When Geoff' – he blushed; she grinned at him in reassurance – 'so rudely interrupted. You got as far as "self-respecting working girl". Now what was all that about?'

I fingered Katie's card again. *No self-respecting working girl would put her address on for anyone to see.*

Told Stevie how Vanessa had flung the card at me. Told Stevie what she'd said.

'And I've been thinking. It's absolutely true that Katie hadn't a very high opinion of herself. And it's true that self-loathing is one of the factors that propels girls into prostitution. But maybe that isn't the explanation here. Maybe, in this case, self had nothing to do with it.'

'Lost me, Laura. What are you trying to say?'

'Maybe this card wasn't Katie's creation at all. Maybe someone made it for her.'

I could see the light of understanding flickering in Stevie's eyes.

'Without her permission,' she said.

That night I went back to Sonny's flat, with Sonny.

To the stone steps leading up to his front door. To the Victorian tiles in the hallway. To the bedroom. I knew every inch of the place.

To Sonny's body – the line of his back, his cold toes, the confident way he moved.

All so distant. And yet so familiar. The way your home town looks after a long absence. You recognise everything – every shop, every patch of grass, every bus shelter – but it's coloured by a veil of new experience. And you know you'll never see it in quite the same, unselfconscious way again.

And you wonder: can it still be my home town after all that time away?

Chapter 20

I didn't sleep well, in spite of having Sonny alongside me to chase away the blues.

He'd told me, between our takeaway meal in the office, and our more intimate time at home, about Cindy Sinful. Told me that the case had ended. That another prostitute had received the same injuries as Cindy, more or less, from a man who went by the same description and used more or less the same MO.

It wasn't a copycat attack; the impact of the signet ring had never been mentioned to the media. And since it had happened two nights earlier, while Trevor Wallace was still in prison awaiting trial, he would soon be off the hook. The police would have to begin all over again to search for Cindy's attacker.

Sonny provided a basic description of the prostitute who'd suffered the beating this time. She wore a tracksuit and trainers and was in her mid-thirties.

Not Vanessa Savage, then. But the attacker was still free. Roaming the streets, as the saying goes. I shivered for Vanessa. If she could avoid the bad guys, nine times out of ten, then I hoped that her next client would be one of the nine.

And I shivered for any other girls who might be out there. Any less experienced girls, especially – who couldn't yet tell the decent from the dangerous where clients were concerned.

I left Sonny, reluctantly, and early. Left him with the duvet tucked around him, his head burrowed under the pillows. He looked as if he wanted to fight off the morning. To linger in the night.

I would have liked to linger too, but the thought that had

gripped me the previous evening woke me up, more than once, in the night. In the morning, that same thought forced me back to Cambridge.

I found a seat on the seven forty-five Cambridge Cruiser next to a man wearing an Arsenal jacket. He offered me a piece of his chewing gum. I lent him my copy of *The Times*.

At eight forty I stepped on to Cambridge station with Katie's card in hand, and quickly discovered that the number of printers in Cambridge and the villages around exceeded thirty-five. It seemed excessive for a city of this size. But then the presence of two universities, and a population awash with graduates, makes it a wordy sort of city; and where there is a surplus of words, some of them are bound to find their way into print.

I decided to hit city outlets first, travelling by means of my trusty trainers. If that didn't work, I'd get behind the wheel of the Saab, and take a tour of Sawston, Linton, Cherry Hinton, Foxton – all those villages, encircling Cambridge, with Anglo-Saxon names and contemporary cottage industry.

The route I took from the station was twisting but logical. First Masterprint, on Tenison Road; on to CopyColour in the old Dale's Brewery building, Elitian Printers on Mill Road, and two chain shops – Kall-Kwik and Presto Print – on Regent Street. I walked swiftly and enjoyed it. After the back alleys of King's Cross, the streets of Cambridge seemed blissfully quiet. Picturesque. Even – aside from the traffic – peaceful.

But in Cambridge, I never allow myself to forget that appearances can oh so easily deceive. These streets must have appeared even more peaceful and quiet back in the 1970s. That was the period when the Cambridge Rapist had mounted one brutal attack after another on women in their own homes, and then, having left them desperately injured, trundled off to watch telly – peacefully, quietly – with his wife.

And, coming closer in time, it was within the compass of these peaceful streets that Beverley had been attacked by a man on her own doorstep. That a baby's bones had been found encased in newspaper, like the remains of a fish and chip dinner. That

Stephen Fox, Senior Tutor of St Bartholomew's, had had his head caved in.

At each of the printers, I began with a prologue. With a story about the person who had, ostensibly, given me this card. How this person had subsequently disappeared; how I needed to find them quickly, before I left the country, to repay a debt. Not a word of the tale was true. It was a white lie, not a cruel one. You can't just burst in and hand a youthful manager a card that offers to make her dreams CUM true. Not, at least, without preamble.

But in spite of my efforts, they were taken aback.

No, they said. Not us.

A Chelsea bun from Fitzbillies helped to fortify me for a further attempt. The independent printer on Trumpington Street had eschewed the brash look-at-me lettering of the big printing chains in favour of thin gold script on a background of subdued green. Too up-market for my purposes, I reckoned; but my systematic self made me have a go.

Inside, it sounded like all the other shops I'd visited so far. There was the breathy rhythm of copying machines – thrum, thrum, thrum – the crackle of paper, the buzzer that signalled the end of a process. There was a heady smell of toner in the air.

Opposite the service counter, shielding the main work area, a set of open shelves held paper in different dimensions and colours. The manager trotted round from behind.

'Mr Mercer,' he announced. I looked over my shoulder, expecting to see a man behind me, before I realised that the print shop manager had just introduced himself.

'And what can I do for you, young lady?' It was a curious affectation. He was my age, or younger.

I decided this time to dive straight in.

'Did you make this card?' I asked.

He had a quick smile that was withdrawn almost the instant it appeared – a smile like a darting tongue. The sleeves of his shirt were rolled up to the elbows. Underneath one rolled edge, I spied the tail of a tattoo.

He took the card from me. Held it gingerly, by its edges, as if it were a compact disc. Studied it slowly. Tugged with his free hand at the gold stud in his left ear. You didn't have to be an expert on body language to know that he viewed this card, as had most of the others who'd looked at it, with distaste.

He turned the card over and glanced at the reverse side – blank – and finally spoke.

'Not what you'd call an artistic job, is it?'

'Design?' I asked. 'Or content?'

'Layout's terrible,' he said. 'Top margin's too small; words all crammed in the centre. And as for the text – well! Some people have a funny sense of humour, that's all I can say.'

I took the card back and inspected it again. *Anything – that's my motto.* It didn't make me laugh. 'What makes you think it's a joke?'

The manager looked affronted. As if I was challenging his integrity, instead of just wondering what I was missing.

'I just can't see the joke myself,' I said. And my friends – faced with my puns – have been known to suggest I could do with a little less jocularity.

'Well, it doesn't look funny to me either,' the manager complained. 'Which just goes to show. No accounting for taste, is there? But it was meant as a birthday joke. That's what he told me.'

'You mean . . .?' Sometimes I can be as dense as treacle.

'These cards were made up here, couple of months ago. The young man came in with a template – the words already written out on a slip of paper. Why he didn't just run it off on his computer, I don't know. Anyway, if it had been serious, I would have refused. We run a respectable business here. But he said it was a joke, so I did it.'

At last. On the trail.

But I hadn't hit it off right with the manager. He'd come from the back of the shop with that friendly introduction, and I'd been slow to respond. Now he was miffed. He was backing away.

What we needed was some common ground.

I pointed to his arm. He glanced at it, blushed, and hurriedly began to roll his right sleeve down. 'No, don't,' I said. 'May I take a closer look?'

He was uneasy at first. But when I told him that I was thinking of getting a tattoo – I didn't say where; didn't know him well enough for that – he loosened up.

It was a rose with an elongated stem, twisting around the word 'Glenda'. 'It looks great,' I said. 'Three colours, huh? Where'd you have it done?'

By the time we got back to Katie's card, we'd bonded. It was he who returned first to the subject.

'Why are you asking?' he said, referring to the card.

One good lie deserves another.

'I'm a private investigator.' I flashed my own business card. 'And I need to find this character who had the card made. He's inherited quite a lot of money, from an uncle he didn't know he had; and now he's gone and moved away, without leaving a trace.'

'How very odd,' said Mr Mercer. He was referring to the behaviour of the beneficiary in my tale; he appeared to accept, in spite of its absurdity, the story itself.

He tugged the earring once again and plunged into thought. 'I could probably recognise him, if he came in here again; but there's not much I can say about him. Brownish hair. A solid sort of face. A good jacket. I took him for a student – probably an undergraduate. Ah, wait a minute,' he said. He turned around and trotted towards the back of the shop, behind the open shelves.

Returned shortly after with a ledger. Ran his finger down the page. Came to the bottom of one sheet, went on to the next.

'You've got names there?'

'I keep a copy of each job, for one year. In case the customer wants a reissue. Just let me find it. Then we can check if it's the same guy.'

He located the card that matched mine, wrote down a number, and then shifted to the computer. 'Here we are,' he said. His voice had a flourish of pride. 'Got it.' He jotted the name on a square of paper, and handed it to me. 'Funny thing,' he said, rubbing his earring again. 'Would that be a Ph.D.? Or an MD? I could have sworn he was too young to have a doctorate. But then that's one of the features of getting older, isn't it? Everyone else looks younger. My dentist doesn't look old enough to be in long trousers.'

I took the scrap of paper. A name was written there in the tattooed man's crabbed hand.

Dr Stephen Fox, it said.

'Is that him?' he asked.

'You bet.'

The tattooed man grinned his fleeting grin, pleased to be of help. 'You'll find him now,' he said proudly. 'Stephen Fox is based at St Bartholomew's College.'

Not any more, I thought.

The minute I saw that name – Dr Stephen Fox – I knew what I needed next. But it wasn't until I'd made my way down King's Parade and through the grounds of King's College; wasn't until I'd bought an ice cream from the vendor near the gates; wasn't until I'd licked half of it away, strolling along the Backs in the direction of home, that I knew where I might get it.

I raced back to Clare Street, as quickly as my trusty trainers would carry me, rescued my car from its parking spot, and fought my way through traffic along Mill Road. A lorry with a load too wide for Cambridge streets gave me cause for pause. For one still moment, from the peak of the railway bridge, I looked down on Great Eastern Street.

The street had the same somnambulant air as on my first visit. Katie's house, however, looked different. The madras cotton that had covered the window had been replaced by a blind with a scalloped edge. The girls were gone.

The blue paintwork on Charlie Thresher's door glistened in the sun. When I rang the bell, he didn't respond.

A wheelie bin propped open the garden gate, as if someone had dragged it dutifully this far, and then said to hell with it.

I made my way down the path that ran behind the houses. Past the unkempt garden with the magnolia tree. Past the rows of runner beans. Past the shed with the blacked-out windows.

Came to Thresher's garden. To the elaborate brickwork, the reconstructed wall with portholes and undulating edge. I entered through a wishing-well gate, its little pitched roof vivid with pink roses. Knocked loudly on the back door.

Thresher's shuffling footsteps could be heard almost instantly. He met me with a sour look. 'I suppose you'd better come in,' he said. The speed of his response, and his lack of surprise at finding me here, convinced me of one thing.

Charlie Thresher had been expecting me.

'You were expecting me?' I asked. He stepped aside to let me in and closed the door behind me.

'Me? Expecting you?' Thresher said. Answering a question with a question. Not answering.

He'd soaked up more sun since the last time we met. His shoulders and back were mottled now, with the angry stains, the crackling patches of white, that are left after the sunburn peels away. He wore the same tartan shorts, the same sandals, as before.

'Cigarette?' he asked, pulling some Silk Cuts out of his pocket. 'Cup of tea?'

'Tea would be nice.'

While Thresher pottered around, filling the kettle, rooting out tea bags, I tried not to stare.

To call Charlie Thresher's kitchen a dump would be to flatter it. In places, the ancient lino had been reduced to black powder. The walls – painted, long ago, a sickly green gloss – were splattered with grease and dirt. The few fittings – including a refrigerator with a pair of pliers where a handle should have been – looked as if they had been salvaged out of a wrecker's yard. The room was dark and dingy and dirty.

Thresher rummaged around in the back of the fridge and came

249

up with a carton of milk. He bent his nose to the carton and involuntarily pulled back.

'I'll take mine black,' I volunteered.

I cleared a stack of newspapers off the only chair in the kitchen and sat down. 'Do you mind?'

'You go ahead,' he grumbled, handing me a mug. The string of a tea bag hung over the rim. I took the tea bag out, and set it on the newspapers.

'You don't have many visitors?' I asked.

'Why do you say that?' Once again, he answered a question with a question. But as he leaned against the wall – there was, after all, only one chair – I had the impression he was genuinely perplexed.

We talked back and forth for a while, a desultory conversation – about the long, skinny cat, which he had adopted, about bits of Cambridge gossip. He'd lived in the town all his life, and remembered this area in the time – before BSE, even before Sainsbury's and Tesco – when Mill Road boasted five butcher shops.

'Those were the days,' he said, shaking his head. As if a carcass in the window was a measure of a good society.

I set my mug down. Half a cup was all I could manage. If I drank any more of the tea, I might see what was in the bottom of the mug, and I might not like it.

'Excuse me,' I said, standing up and making for the hallway. Already on my way out of the kitchen door. 'Have to use your loo.'

I took the narrow stairs two at a time, balancing myself as I went with one hand on the wall. I opened the door at the head of the stairs – sure enough, the bathroom, and marginally cleaner than what I'd seen of the downstairs – and closed it loudly. Sped along the corridor as quietly as my trainers could carry me to the front of the house. Opened the door of what should be – if this house was like others of its period – the largest, brightest room in the house.

For a moment I couldn't see. Darkness blinkered me. Then I

tiptoed to the window, and looped up the end of the blanket that had shut out the daylight. Looked around.

It was like waking up suddenly and finding yourself surrounded by faces – crowds of people, peering at you, leaning over your bed. The walls of the room were coated with photographs. There must have been hundreds of them, fighting for space, their edges overlapping. Black-and-white faces in vivid close-up. Bodies, or parts of bodies – a shoulder, a pair of feet, a back. Groups – children skateboarding; two young women mending a puncture; three men, arms around each other's shoulders, staggering home from the pub.

And as I looked – as I adjusted to the indifferent light, and to the sheer volume of images – one or two began to stand out.

There was Candace, clothed in camouflage trousers and a black boob-tube, sitting against the back wall of the house with her knees drawn up to the sun, having a quiet cigarette. She squinted upwards into the light. Her hair was a tangle of plaits around her head, and tendrils of smoke escaped from the edges of her nostrils.

Two girls lying in the garden on an old blanket. They wore bikini bottoms; were naked from the waist up. One, with blonde curls leaking out below a floppy-brimmed hat, rested on her elbows, skimming a magazine, pointing to something on the page. The other girl had turned slightly towards her, following the pointing finger; the photo captured the tender profile of her breast, her wild hair tied behind her back. It was Candace and Katie, in what they must have thought was the privacy of their garden.

There was a woman standing near a door, her face wreathed in honeysuckle vine. Her hand was raised as if she'd only just knocked. The photo captured perfectly that sense of waiting for a door to open. You could almost see her impatience, the tapping of her foot, the moment of decision. And with a small shock, I recognised myself. This photo must have been taken the very first time I came round to Katie's house. Just before I'd tried to slip in through a window. Just after I'd heard a rustling in the ivy.

And I heard a rustling now.

A shuffling rather, in the hallway. I turned.

Charlie Thresher stood in the doorway of his studio, for studio it must be. I could see now the clutter of equipment. There were cameras and tripods and cables and special lenses, laid out with far more care than any of the equipment in the kitchen had been.

'You told me you took portraits,' I said. 'I had no idea they'd be this good.'

'Just the tip of the iceberg,' Thresher said, and his skinny chest swelled with pride.

'Doesn't it bother you?' I asked.

'Beg your pardon?'

'Sneaking around like that? Spying on people, invading their privacy? Taking pictures without their permission?'

Thresher didn't look at all put out. In fact, he looked downright relaxed. Out of his pocket and into his mouth came a Silk Cut; he lit it with a quick flick of a lighter. Standing there in the doorway, with the cigarette resting on his bottom lip, surrounded by his handiwork, he looked completely at ease.

'Sneaking up on people? Invading their privacy, is it?' Thresher repeated. 'You're a fine one to talk. You came here with a cock-and-bull story about feeding the cat; you took advantage when I was upset about the kitten. And then you imply that I'm the one with ethical problems. Hah!' he exclaimed. 'I haven't told a lie. Pictures don't lie. All I'm after with my photographs is a little bit of truth.'

'Me too,' I said. 'The truth about Katie. And you can help.'

He said nothing for a moment. His gaunt face as he looked at me was impassive. Then he shook his head. 'Can't help. She's gone. Probably for good.'

'You can. You can help. Look at these pictures. Some of them were taken out the back. But you also took pictures at the front, didn't you? Out of this window? These girls mending the puncture, for example.'

'So what if I did?'

'So you must have taken pictures of the men who came to the

door. Some of them anyway. The men you said made a fuss. The unpleasant characters. You said the girls were like cats on heat. There were always men after them.'

He stood upright, pulling away from the door frame slowly as if he'd been attached to it with glue. Tore the end of his cigarette off his bottom lip, threw it into a bucket of sand that rested near the doorway. Shuffled over to a chest of drawers on the far wall.

Thresher knew what he was doing, all right. He went straight for the top drawer, tugged it open, and flipped through papers until he came to a large brown envelope. Handed it to me.

'You do the honours,' he said.

There were four photos in here. One was of a man in a shellsuit; he reminded me of the chap from the Earl of Stamford, the one who'd tried to drag Beverley into the street. But it was actually someone else – equally drunk, by the way he was standing, and probably equally offensive.

The other three photos were of Roger Duff.

Roger Duff, at night-time, sliding up to Katie's front door, slipping something through the letter-box. From his air of stealth, you knew he was up to no good.

Roger Duff, banging on the door, with his handsome friend from the Fort St George hanging back over his shoulder.

Roger Duff, standing in the small car park on the opposite side of Great Eastern Street, staring towards Katie's house.

I turned them over. Each photo had a date pencilled on the back.

'May I have one of these?'

Thresher shrugged and stuck his bottom lip out. 'I'm a professional photographer,' he said. The emphasis was on *professional*.

'How much for this one? Five pounds? Ten?'

'For you . . .' He grinned; it was not a pretty sight. 'For you, twenty.'

I paid the twenty. Had to. Thresher didn't care about the money, I reckoned. He just wanted to get back at me for accusing him of spying. He would've refused to sell if I'd haggled.

As I turned to go, two more photographs caught my eye. They were just to the right of the door.

'I'm surprised you didn't notice them on your way in,' Thresher said. 'That's the night you asked me about. June the fourteenth. The May Ball.'

The night Katie disappeared.

Like Jean Harlow, he had said, *out of Donna Karan*. I could see what he meant. The dress Katie wore – a lily-white maximum-visibility dress – was cut low enough at the front to show the first hint of a lovely cleavage. Cut low at the back, drifting down towards her waist. Close-fitting over the hips and thighs, but softened by the way the fabric draped. Flaring out again in pleats at the hemline. A dress made to look, at one and the same time, as sexy as hell and as pure as the driven snow. Madonna and whore in one package. Every man's dream.

Katie stood outside the house, on the pavement, in the warm slanting sun of an early-summer evening. The sun made her dress gleam; her soft curls glow a darker gold; her pale skin shine. She was clutching at Candace's arm. Candace leaned against the door frame and gestured with her free hand. I could almost hear her words.

Go on, now. Get away with you. Don't be silly, Katie. You'll have fun.

In the second picture, there was less to see. A taxi had pulled away from the kerb, heading towards town. Katie sat in the rear. She leaned into the window, looking back – at Candace? – as the car moved off. None of the exuberance of the previous photos showed now in that pale little face. Her eyes were full of misgiving. Maybe even sorrow. She looked fearful and resigned.

White.

But not like a bride. Not like a token of celebration.

More like a lamb to the slaughter.

Chapter 21

Saturday was a good day. I had three breaks in the investigation. Three things that pushed the inquiry forward, decisively; three things that lifted me out of plod.

The first was when I'd guessed that the man who'd visited the print shop in Trumpington Street – that Dr Fox, who'd seemed too young to be a doctor – might actually be Roger Duff. That Duff had used Fox's name – as a joke, presumably; a flash of spite – when he'd had the cards made up. That was a spark of genius on my part.

And I'd risen from mere genius to sheer genius when I'd worked out that if Duff had been harassing Katie, Charlie Thresher would have photographic proof. It stood to reason. Thresher was, after all, a past master at poking around in his neighbours' business, and he styled himself as a photographer in the gritty, realistic mode.

After I left Great Eastern Street, I carried the photo back to Mercer at the print shop. Sure enough. Instant recognition.

'Yes,' he said. 'That's him. Stephen Fox. Looks awfully young to be a doctor, don't you think?'

I certainly did.

But for all my self-congratulation, I was no closer to finding Katie in the flesh. And even further, perhaps, from knowing how and why – and at whose hand – Stephen Fox had died.

And my third break – a choice bit of gossip from Stephen Fox's widow – owed more to luck than to genius.

I was on my way to see Nicole, to find out whether she thought action could and should be taken against Duff for what he'd done to Katie, when I passed the Echo Room. I opened the door.

And, as luck would have it, Rachel Hunneyball was standing inside. Experiencing a solitary moment of grief.

For a fraction of time, I thought of backing off. But then I changed my mind, deciding it would be callous rather than tactful. Leaving the bereaved to mourn on their own can isolate them. Make them feel that, in their sorrow, they're unfit for human company. Force on them an untenable choice – to seek comfort from others or to grieve for the dead.

My approach was tentative. I introduced myself. Asked Rachel if the Echo Room was a good place to remember Stephen. She didn't try to hide the tears that glistened on her face.

'I had no time,' she said, 'to get used to being a wife. And now, suddenly, I'm a widow. Like Echo,' she said.

We looked at the mural, at the fluffy white clouds above the cypress trees. I hadn't noticed before that the furthermost clouds were fringed faintly and improbably with black.

'Like Echo?'

'One minute tripping across a grassy hillside,' Rachel said, 'on a beautiful spring day, confident in her future. Then violence broke into her life and tore her to pieces. That's kind of how I feel, Miss Principal.'

'Torn to pieces.' My voice was a quiet echo of hers.

Rachel took a deep breath, meaning that she'd said enough for now. She adjusted her cardigan and prepared to take her leave. I noticed that she seemed broader somehow than when I had first come across her in Stephen Fox's study. I wondered if grief could make a person stolid.

But as she came abreast of me, she noticed – couldn't help but notice – the black-and-white photograph I was carrying, ready to show to Nicole.

'Roger Duff!' She looked at the photo more closely. 'Excuse me for asking, but why do you have a picture of Duff? Did he have something to do with Stephen's death?'

Now there was a leap. 'Why do you ask, Rachel? Has Duff said anything to you about your husband's murder?'

'No, no, nothing like that.' Rachel Hunneyball was a little flustered now. 'That's just the sort of person he is. Lots of people are scared of him. If you cross him, he never lets go.'

'And Stephen crossed him, in a sense, didn't he? Dr Fox had a key role in the committee that disciplined Duff after that disastrous Dorics' dinner. That's what you're thinking of?'

Rachel looked tired now. She was rubbing her back as if in pain. 'I've got to go,' she said. 'I've got to lie down.'

'Of course.' She did look under a lot of strain. 'Do you need a lift?'

'Thank you, no. I'll be fine.' At the door, she paused. She pulled her cardigan across her chest, as if it were cold in the Echo Room. 'Do you know, he boasted that he'd got rid of that girl. That Arkwright girl.'

For a moment, I thought she meant Stephen Fox.

'He?' I prodded. 'Do you mean your husband?'

A phone rang. The sound came, incongruously, from my shoulder bag. It seemed startlingly loud in the sound-deadened atmosphere of the Echo Room. 'Ignore it,' I said.

After three terse and peevish buzzes, it subsided.

'No, not Stephen,' Rachel replied, with a flash of impatience. 'Him. Duff. He was in the Fort St George with some cronies, towards the end of term. Someone asked wasn't he nervous hanging around Cambridge after his rustication. The disciplinary committee ordered him to keep away, you know.'

'I know. Go on.'

'Well, there's nothing more to say, really. Duff became angry, and started railing against everyone involved. The disciplinary committee. The waitresses. But especially Katie Arkwright. *The little tart*, he called her. That's when he said it. Like he was gloating. *I got rid of her.*'

'What did you imagine he meant by that?'

She shrugged. 'I didn't take him very seriously. He's a nutter. No one believes a word he says.'

'You didn't mention this to the police?'

Rachel shrugged again. 'Please,' she said. 'I've got to go and lie down now. You can tell them if you like.'

I stood for a moment, after Rachel Hunneyball left, trying to decide how deeply Duff might be implicated in this whole sordid affair. He had been one of the instigators of the attack on Katie in this very room. He had visited her house, sometimes in the dead of night, hammering on the door, demanding entrance. Probably he had written those hateful, hate-filled letters. Those letters that had convinced Beverley Stebbings – *no smoke without fire* – that Katie was on the game.

Roger Duff was a veritable little chimney; he'd happily provided the smoke. And as if to drive the point home – the turn of the screw, so to speak – he had constructed crudely worded cards advertising Katie's services, and had posted these in public spaces so that other men could see. He had invited the men of Cambridge to know Katie as a whore. Even worse – as a whore, unlike other whores, who would do anything.

A man who would do that . . . Was there anything that man wouldn't do?

Once again, the shrill, insistent call of my mobile phone.

Would a man like that have gone further? Would he really have got rid of her? Meaning what – killed her? Or stolen her away?

Ringing again. I rummaged around in my shoulder bag, my mind on the problem in hand.

And how far would a man like Duff go to avenge himself on someone who had brought him to book? On someone who had banished him? Denied him the right to finish his degree with the rest of his cohort?

In short, I wondered: could Roger Duff have murdered Stephen Fox?

My fingers grabbed the phone, and plucked it out from the bottom of my bag.

'Laura Principal,' I said.

'Hello,' said a weary voice.

It was a young voice. A woman's voice.

It was Katie Arkwright.

If what you want is sexy surroundings, don't go to a brothel.

Actually, the Pleasure Palace, where I went to pick up Katie Arkwright, wasn't strictly speaking a brothel. It was what's called in the trade a working flat. Only two girls on duty at any one time – not ten or twenty, as in massage parlours. The madam puts in her appearance only to pocket the exorbitant rent.

Set aside any notions you might have of gauzy interiors. Forget ersatz Roman villas or plush red wall hangings. Like most brothels, the Pleasure Palace was chilling in its ordinariness. Like – it came to me in a macabre flash – the ordinariness of that family home at 25 Cromwell Street, Gloucester, where Fred West and Rosemary, his missus, raped and murdered a succession of their own and other people's children.

Imagine a short parade of shops in an unremarkable area between King's Cross station and Clerkenwell.

Imagine an upstairs flat with a small entrance conveniently next to a pharmacy.

Imagine a closed-circuit television camera above the door, a buzzer system on the entrance. One of the things that a decent brothel can offer is a dash of security.

At the top of the stairs, you're greeted by a maid. Not a nudge-nudge, wink-wink sort of maid, with black stockings and bulging blouse and flirty skirt. No, this maid wore corduroy trousers; her baggy sweatshirt bore an image of the Tower of London.

'Hello, Miss Principal,' she said. She seemed shy. Unsure of herself. 'I'm Katie.'

It was a modest set-up. The primary colour in the sitting room was brown. The sofas were new and cheap and impersonal, with plastic protective covers on the back where a visitor might rest his head – sofa condoms, I thought; some comfort with no real contact. There were two telephones, and a fax machine. A television in the corner. A coffee table in shiny yellow pine with coasters for our mugs of tea.

It was tidy. Magazines – *Hello!, Good Housekeeping, Bella,* and a single issue devoted to motor racing – were neatly stacked. A plastic tidy-all kept bottles of nail polish and emery boards in order. That – the tidiness – was part of the maid's job, the least important part. Although the large ashtrays on the coffee table were empty, there was a strong under-taint of cigarette smoke.

It was early evening when I arrived – a peak period, for clients stopping by on their way home from the office. Both of the bedrooms in the flat were in use. Vicki and Rochelle were hard at work. We waited for Rochelle to finish with her client so that she and Katie could say their goodbyes.

The thermostat was turned up way too high. The cloying warmth discouraged conversation. Or maybe it was knowing what was going on behind the thin walls. Katie used the remote to turn the television on. Jerry Springer sprang into view. Two teenagers were screaming at their mothers for embarrassing them in front of friends.

'Gross!' Katie said. I didn't know whether she meant the mothers or the daughters, or maybe, Springer himself.

After two or three minutes, there was movement from one of the bedrooms. A man in a smart navy suit emerged. He was punching numbers into a mobile phone as he moved towards the door, and he gave us a wave.

'Goodbye, Katya,' he said. 'See you next Thursday.'

'Bye, Ben.'

I looked at her, waiting for an explanation.

'I haven't told the regulars,' Katie said. 'I've only told the girls that I'm leaving.'

'He called you Katya.'

'Oh, that.' She giggled. 'It's like – a stage name. Nobody uses their own name here. You save that for real life. These are just clients. That's what Rochelle says.'

Speak of the devil. Rochelle swished through the bedroom

door, cigarette in hand, dressed in transparent baby dolls and fluffy slippers. No wonder the thermostat was on maximum.

She was a heavy-set girl with soft, close-cropped hair, like fur on a seal's head. She was also a bit of a clown. Katie did the introductions, and Rochelle kept us laughing until the next client buzzed.

'That'll be Kevin,' she said. 'I play a naughty schoolgirl. Before you can growl, *what are you doing in the stationery cupboard?* Kevin's finished.' She winked. 'That's the kind of customer I like.'

We prepared to leave, but Rochelle couldn't resist a final tease. She whispered in my ear, low enough that Kevin wouldn't hear, 'Sure you don't want to stay and have a go, love?'

'Gee, Rochelle, wish you'd asked me sooner. I'd have worn my gym knickers.'

Rochelle lit up another cigarette and led Kevin to the bedroom. Maybe he'd catch her smoking behind the bike sheds.

My car was parked a couple of streets away from the Pleasure Palace. We passed a kebab house.

'You hungry?' It was after seven o'clock. Katie was thin, far thinner than she looked in her photos, and could do with some food, I thought, whatever the hour.

But she wasn't in the mood. 'No,' she said, shaking her head. 'Now that we're on our way, I just want to get home.'

I stopped anyway, picked up a doner kebab and a couple of Diet Cokes. Katie might not be hungry, but I was. Once we were in the car, she held the Coke for me, and I ate the kebab, passing it over to Katie from time to time when I needed both hands free. There was little conversation between us as we wove through the London traffic. I'd decided to keep questions to the minimum for now, to let Katie set the pace. I might shake her resolve to return to Cambridge if I pressed her too hard.

But well before we turned on to the M11, Katie began to open up, telling me about the world we'd just left. About the Pleasure Palace and what she did there.

Challenging me not to judge.

'If you were a client,' she explained, 'I'd have to ask you what you wanted. What services. For some of them, they've done it so many times before it's like ordering a Big Mac and fries. *The full works, with costume*, they say; and they already know the price before I give it. I have a list that they can refer to, if they need it.'

'You do all the negotiations?'

'That's the maid's job.' She nodded. 'Once they've paid you, Vicki or Rochelle will take them into the bedroom.'

'Did you find it difficult?'

'Well,' she said, with a grave look, 'there was quite a lot to learn.' I remembered the fierce concentration on the face of the little girl who had ridden a stick around Histon. Like she had to get it right. 'The main thing is putting clients at their ease. I'm quite good at that. And taking phone calls.'

'Is there anything you hate about it?'

She thought for a few seconds. 'The worst thing is the guys who come in, look the girls over – make a choice, you know ...' Katie took a swig of her soft drink and looked at me sideways, checking how I was taking this. 'Then they bugger off.'

'Too scared to go through with it?'

'No, not scared. It's just that seeing a prostitute in the flesh is enough for them. They go away to some corner to wank off.'

Could it really be in these streetwise, upfront, sex-on-offer-everywhere days that a prostitute is still such an exotic creature? That some men can get their kicks merely by spending a few seconds in the same room with her?

'You serious?'

'Sure am. Trying to collect from those ones is really hard,' she said solemnly. 'Believe me.'

I do.

I believe you, Katie.

Katya.

About this, anyway.

After minutes of this, minutes of listening to Katie's clear, high voice elaborating on the bleak business of sex, my resolution broke. That question – *how the hell did you get into this?* – was battering at me.

I could have said: *how can you talk about work in a brothel in this matter-of-fact way? As if it were a part-time job at Pizzaland?*

I could have said: *how could you stand those sordid encounters?*

I could have said: *what's a nice girl like you doing in a place like that?*

Katie was looking at me curiously by now. I tried again.

'Did Vanessa Savage find you the maid's job, Katie?'

No reply.

I glanced at the passenger seat. Katie was staring out of the window at the dark-shrouded fields. A radio mast loomed up. She watched its red lights until it was behind us.

'Yes,' she said. 'Vanessa refused to help me work on the streets. *A girl like you will need to get acclimatised.* That's what she said. She knew they needed a maid at the Pleasure Palace. She said they'd teach me the ropes there. And from then on it would be up to me.'

One for Vanessa, I thought. For sharing her wee bit of wisdom, so hard won.

In the distance, off to our right, a line of brightly lit windows came rushing out of the woods as a Liverpool Street train made its way northwards.

I finished my Coke. Katie reached across and relieved me of the can. 'I suppose everyone will want to know why I left Cambridge.'

She meant me.

'Only if you're ready.'

'Vanessa gave me your card, yesterday evening. I've been thinking about it constantly since then. About why I came here. Listen, Laura – have you ever had a really bad year?'

A really bad year.

How about the year Paul Principal died?

You hear so much crap about death, about dying. About the person who is ready to die, and slips contentedly away. About the lover of life who refuses to go quietly and staggers back from the brink.

And then there was my father. My gallant, beloved father – marked out in life by toughness and fierce loyalty and infectious laughter. How he'd adored my mother. With what tenderness, what pride, he'd loved my brother and me.

Death – not the fact of death, but the prospect – had flattened all that. Had left in place of gallantry an inconsolable peevishness. In place of laughter, a quavering, anxious fear.

It took Paul one hundred and eighty-four days and nights to die. And every one of those days robbed me of a little more of the father that I'd loved.

'Yes,' I said to Katie. 'I've had a bad year. My father died. And I learned that I couldn't live any longer with my husband.'

Katie nodded. 'It felt as if there was a weight always pressing on my heart. I did my best to carry on, not to let my parents down. Did my work at college. But every night when I went off to sleep, I hoped – it sounds silly, I suppose—'

'What?'

'I hoped that I'd wake up dead.'

I swallowed. 'Doesn't sound silly, Katie. I had a friend like that once. Claire found things – difficult.'

'What happened to her?'

For some people, in some circumstances, deception is the best policy. 'She's a successful music producer,' I lied. 'Has a cottage in Northumbria, and two lovely kids.'

'Hope for me yet, then,' Katie said. She knew it was a lie but didn't mind. 'The turning point was Jared. We had such a lot of fun together that I thought – well, I hoped – I could make a fresh start. It was a sort of fantasy. You know. Happy ever after.'

And why not? Why shouldn't a nineteen-year-old girl dream of happiness? Happy ever after may be an illusion. But it's a whole lot better than hoping to wake up dead.

'When you went to St John's you felt good about things? About the prospect of the ball?'

'It was beautiful, Laura. You can't imagine. The lights and the college and the fireworks reflecting in the river. I'd never been so happy. And then, suddenly—'

Then, suddenly, she began to cry. The sleeves of her Tower of London sweatshirt hardly served to stem the flow.

'What happened?' I asked. 'When you were on the dance floor, at John's, what happened?'

'You were there?'

'In charge of security. Go on, tell me.'

'Well . . .' Katie rolled the window down a crack. Breathed in the night air. 'It was such a shock, Laura. I was bopping away, just enjoying the music; and when I turned around, this horrible man was beside me. Roger Duff. *This is for you, whore*, he said. And handed me something.'

She began to cry again, her face revealing in its contortions the anguish of that moment.

'I shouldn't have looked, Laura, I should have just turned away, but I couldn't help myself. He gave me this terrible card with my name on it. *Check out the men's toilets*, that's what Duff said to me.'

'What did he mean by that?'

'Meaning there were other cards – similar cards – in there. And the men with him – do you know Anthony Cocker?'

'A thin, good-looking bloke?'

'That's Cocker. He and the others laughed. And Stephen Fox was standing nearby, watching me, and he was laughing too. I couldn't stand it any more. I had to get away.'

'You were afraid that other people would see the card and believe it? That you'd be branded as a whore?'

'That's what he planned. And Jared – he'd have left me, then and there, I know he would. So I didn't have a choice.'

'You left the ball. You caught the last train to London?'

Katie nodded. 'I thought Vanessa could help me. But I couldn't find her that night, so I had to go to an awful hostel. Next day, we met up. You know the rest.'

'Some of it.'

She was staring out of the side window again. The sniffing had subsided.

'Katie, are you OK?'

'I'm OK.' She smiled at me, a wan, gentle smile.

'Can I ask you another question? You don't have to answer if you don't want to.' I was encouraged by her nod. 'Why didn't you go to your mother or your father at that point? Why run away, on your own?'

'It's hard to explain.' She flipped a switch on the radio and ran quickly through the channels. Turned it off again.

'I felt as if my reputation in Cambridge had been destroyed. Even my housemates doubted me.'

'Beverley Stebbings, you mean.'

'*Christ, Katie, what have you been up to?* That was what Beverley said when she heard a message on the answering machine.' Katie sighed. 'And besides, there's the landlord.'

'Charlie Thresher, from next door?'

'He's really strange. Always watching me.' She shivered. 'I couldn't bring myself to go back to that house.'

'And your mother?'

Katie's tears started up again. She appealed to me. 'You've met her, haven't you, Laura? You must see that I couldn't tell my mother about all this. She'd go to pieces.'

'You feared she might harm herself?'

'She's tried before,' Katie said. 'And my father? Well, I couldn't bear it if Daddy was disappointed in me. Oh, I must seem like such a wimp to you. This is all so feeble. But there were other things, too. Things I don't want to talk about.'

'What you've told me, Katie, is enough to make anyone flee. And I know about the other things. About the men at the door. The notes through the letter-box. And I know about the Dorics.'

'You know?' Katie sounded astonished. Maybe she imagined that these things sullied her so much that no one who knew them could treat her with respect. She was ashamed. She should have been angry.

I found myself getting angry on her behalf.

'You're not responsible, Katie. Roger Duff did it. All of it. That card that he passed you at the May Ball? Duff prepared that card himself. Had it printed. I can prove it. And it was because of those cards that you had men ringing up, coming round.'

'But there were notes that came to the flat—'

'That was Duff, too. He put those through the letter-box. Don't you see, Katie? It's harassment. We can get him for it. But tell me—'

'Get him?' Katie interrupted. The tone in her voice was one of amazement. *Do you mean these people are vulnerable, too? Just like me?*

Which reminded me.

Katie got out the mobile phone for me, and dialled the incident room at Bart's. Nicole was busy. The constable who took the message seemed slower than average. Laura who? Katie who? How can the Detective Inspector get in touch?

'Katie, what's your dad's address again?'

'The Willows, Fleam Dyke Road,' she said. And she threw in the phone number.

I relayed that to the constable. He made me hang on while he jotted everything down.

'We'll be there in forty-five minutes,' I said.

And while the phone was in action, I rang and left a message for John Carswell on his machine. Told him, in outline, where I was heading and why. We'd been due to meet for a drink later that evening. 'I probably won't make it,' I said.

Then I put the phone firmly away.

'Tell me, Katie, why did you mention Stephen Fox being at the ball? Where does he come into it?'

'You understand so much of what's happened to me. Don't you know about Dr Fox?'

And then she told me.

How, a few days before the ball, the Senior Tutor of St Bartholomew's had summoned Katie to his room. She'd gone; something to do with the Dorics affair, she'd assumed.

But when she was in his office, with the door closed, Dr Fox had turned on her with glistening anger. He'd waved a business card in her face.

'He was horrible,' she said. 'He accused me of misleading the committee. Tried to force himself on me. *What's another one?* he said. *You've probably had hundreds.* I had no idea what it was about, Laura. Couldn't understand him at all. Do you think that Duff—?'

'Don't think,' I said. 'Know.' Roger Duff, with boundless malice, must have sent one of the 'business' cards to Dr Fox. His way of saying, *see? Katie Arkwright was a whore after all. What I did to her didn't matter.* 'Did you manage to get away?'

'I struggled, and he let go of me then. But I was shaking like a leaf when I left his office. You don't expect to be leaped on like that by a Senior Tutor.'

No, not in the usual run of things. But nothing was exactly usual about this case. 'And all this happened a couple of days before the May Ball?'

'On Monday, I think it was.'

That was when Shirley Ann Talbot had noticed Katie Arkwright coming down the stairs from Fox's room. A few days before Fox had his head bashed in.

'And when you thought it over, Katie, when you recovered from the shock, what did you decide to do about Stephen Fox?'

'To do? What could I do? He said that if I mentioned this to anyone, he'd produce the card in public. He'd make the whole of Cambridge know what a slut I was.'

'Did you go back there? Did you visit him the following Saturday?'

'No.' Katie spoke emphatically. Too emphatically? Too defensively? Too concerned to deny a visit? 'The following Saturday, I was exhausted. Had to spend the morning in bed. Anyway, why would I go back to Bart's? I never ever want to see Stephen Fox again.'

'And you never will.'

'What do you mean?' She heard the portent in my voice.

'He's dead, did you know that?'

'Dead?' Katie looked as if the very word was alien to her. 'Who's dead?'

'Stephen Fox. St Bartholomew's Senior Tutor. Somebody saw him that Saturday. And whoever it was, they killed him.'

Chapter 22

Fulbourn's not the same after nightfall.

For one thing, the day noises are gone. The sounds of a summer afternoon in the countryside can be almost raucous, like the rising volume of voices at a cocktail party. But by the time Katie and I reached Fulbourn, afternoon had passed into evening, and evening was yielding to night. No more whisperings and buzzings of the bee-loud glade; the butterflies, the hoverflies and the bumble bees had all folded their wings for the night. We could hear the sough of the night breeze, and the hum of our tyres on the tarmac. But the only living sounds were the lonely utterances of the night stalkers: the call of a barn owl, the piping of a bat, the bark of a badger. Apart from the occasional snuffle of a hedgehog, the hedgerows had fallen silent.

The road that led out of the village was as straight as before. It cut through fields as cleanly as before; rose up the same gentle, relentless slope as before.

But darkness makes all the difference. The lights of Fulbourn village didn't seriously dent the gloom of the countryside; Cambridge was just a pale aurora on the horizon. And here, now, in the dark, that lush sense of summer was gone. The fields with their dusting of poppies had disappeared into undifferentiated darkness. Where there had been open vistas, the sides of the road now closed in on us, blanketing out the world beyond.

'I've always been afraid of the dark.' Katie shivered. 'This is such a godforsaken place. As if we're the only people alive in the world.' She pointed up ahead. 'There's the turning,' she said.

In the twilight at the top of the hill, we could see the silhouette

269

of the sign for Fleam Dyke Pumping Station. I took the turning, slowly, and stopped the car to have a look.

Even in the gloom, Fleam Dyke Road was still like nothing I'd seen before. It still resembled a Roman road – ruthless, puritanical almost, in its refusal to go anywhere but straight.

It was still bordered on either side by tall, impenetrable hedges, walls of prickly hawthorn that formed a tunnel. But this time round, night had tossed its black tarpaulin between us and the flat blue sky.

I put the Saab into gear and we made our way slowly towards Bob Arkwright's house at the end of the road. Katie had vetoed a call to her father to warn him we were coming. I would've done it differently; I'm not much of a one for surprises myself.

Katie may have picked up on my unease. She looked away from me, rolled down the window, and breathed in the night air. And then, as if to say, *this homecoming is nothing really, not a solemn occasion; I was never really lost*, she turned on Radio Q103, at ear-splitting volume.

The sound of the night breeze was instantly drowned out by the high-pitched voices of the Four Seasons. *Big . . . girls . . . don't . . . cry . . .*

'Hey, listen, Laura,' she said, with a quirky smile. 'They're playing my song.'

I laughed. And we joined in the chorus.

It may be dark in the countryside, but you can sing at the top of your lungs, with no one to complain.

We launched into song again, ridding ourselves of tension. *Big girls don't cry*. Raucous now. I made my voice husky so I could tackle the bass line. Katie tapped out the rhythm on the dashboard.

And suddenly, behind us, with no warning at all, a huge pair of headlights snapped on.

Our chorus ended abruptly. In the rear-view mirror I could see nothing but blinding orbs of light, no more than a few feet behind the Saab.

The driver – whoever it was – must have been sitting in the driveway that led to the lock-up garages. Waiting in the dark.

Waiting to follow us when we drove by.

I didn't have to tell her. Katie switched the radio off. The sound of the Four Seasons faded away. For the first time, I could hear the engine of a four-wheel-drive vehicle, close behind us. Far too close for comfort.

Katie twisted around in her seat, and clutched my arm. Her voice went screechy with fear.

'They're coming closer. They're going to—'

By God, they were.

Coming straight for us.

I slammed my foot down on the accelerator. In the rear-view mirror, the lights dazzled.

'How many people in that car, Katie?'

Katie wriggled round again, struggling against the seatbelt.

'I can't see. Their headlamps are blinding me. They're like spotlights.'

It flashed through my mind that these lights were abnormally high, abnormally huge. Not like headlamps at all. More like the roof-mounted lights that are used, illegally, for hunting deer. For immobilising prey before the kill.

I avoided looking in the rear-view mirror. Tried to keep my eyes glued on what was ahead. I was going far too fast already for this ribbon of roadway. A second's inattention could be enough to slam us at bone-crunching speed into the hedge.

But still, without looking, I knew the vehicle had edged even closer, knew that we were about to be rammed.

Katie's scream blended with the impact. It was like a giant's hammer slamming on to an anvil. Like metal scrunching and buckling. As if a sheet of aluminium foil had been suddenly, angrily, fisted into a ball.

And the sound of the crash was echoed by a jolt that shimmered through my body. Could teeth break, I wondered – could bones crumble – from this kind of blow?

And what about the car? The Saab was well made, but two more collisions like that, and she'd buckle.

If – which seemed unlikely – we managed to stay on the road.

I pressed my foot down again, depressing the accelerator as hard as I dared. The car spat and leaped. It found its foothold, and ate up the road. It careered through the tunnel – too fast for safety – heading for the houses at the end.

Within seconds, the vehicle had crept up on us again. Its engine gave off an ominous growl. Its lights blazed through our rear windscreen, lighting up the interior of the Saab with their cold glare.

Without trying to look, I saw my own knuckles, white on the wheel.

I saw Katie's face, pale with shock.

And I saw an object on the floor by Katie's feet. I shouted.

'Katie. Pick up the phone.'

I pushed harder on the accelerator, though I feared the Saab would fly out of control. Katie fumbled with the aerial. She looked at me in confusion.

'Dial 999,' I shouted. 'Press send. Tell them we're on Fleam Dyke Road.'

They hit us again. Harder this time. The impact reverberated through my body. I jolted forward, barely able to keep my grip on the wheel. There was a crunch of pain, an excruciating pain, in my neck, and I was swept by sheer terror.

Is this what it's like, is this how it feels, when your neck snaps?

'Laura,' Katie screamed, at the same instant. Her body jerked forward. She flung out her arms to protect herself. The telephone flew from her hands and out of the window.

We're alive. Alive. Where there's life . . . Bob Arkwright's house was almost in sight.

The four-wheel-drive fell back. There was a car's length, two cars' lengths, between us.

'They're slowing,' Katie breathed. 'Oh, thank God, they've given up.'

I wanted desperately to believe her. But within seconds, the vehicle had edged closer again. Only this time, it was positioned differently. Not directly behind us now, but coming up on our left.

Its spotlights were level now with my rear lights. I swerved from side to side, frantically, to block them. But they were gaining on us, inch by inch. Edging up alongside.

They were going to ram us. To slam us sideways, off the road, into a collision with the hawthorn hedge.

We had only one chance. Katie had only one chance.

'Brace yourself, Katie,' I shouted. 'When I stop, throw yourself out of the car. Run to your father. Don't look back.'

I took a deep breath, and cleared my mind.

I didn't look at her again.

'Now!'

I banished thoughts of car accidents. Of people crushed and decapitated.

I banished thoughts of death and dying, and all that crap.

As I saw the vehicle on my left begin to pull sharply towards me on a collision course, I rammed my foot down on the brake. Yanked on the handbrake. Tuned out the screeching and the cranking – the sound of my Saab, falling to bits.

Watched quietly – almost calmly now – as the front of the Saab fell back, towards the rear of the Range Rover.

Watched as, propelled by its own momentum, the four-wheel-drive veered dangerously to the right. Watched it sheer off the tarmac, jounce in the ruts. Heard them apply the brakes, late. Saw the car finally – fifty, a hundred, two hundred yards further on – slide to a halt.

Katie was out of my car before they'd even begun to brake. She fell to her knees on the verge, in an absurd parody of prayer. Picked herself up again, shot a desperate glance over her shoulder—

Go! I urged.

—and staggered off. Limping, fumbling, falling. And finally – after a fashion – running.

There was no sign of light from Bob Arkwright's windows. And something else was missing. There was no sound of Redknapp's bark.

But I hadn't time to think about that now.

Ahead of me, the front doors of the four-wheel-drive swung open. Two men clambered out.

I didn't want them to see Katie. Didn't want them even to think of her, until she'd reached the safety of her father's house.

'Hey,' I shouted. My voice came out in a croak. I tried again. It wasn't much better. 'Hey! Over here!'

I had to use my shoulder to force the car door open. The result was a searing pain.

I had been frightened, while I was driving. But now fear had been overwhelmed by two sharper emotions: anger at the deliberate damage to my car, and relief that I could move.

The pain was bad. But it was only pain.

They were standing on the road, in hot dispute. As I approached, I could hear their voices, though not their words. Anthony Cocker, the thin, good-looking one, spoke in a tone that was barbed with accusation. Roger Duff was more subdued.

At the sound of my footsteps, they wheeled. They rallied. In the face of a common enemy, there was a change of mood.

Duff took the lead. He looked at me but spoke to his partner in crime. 'Well, Anthony.' The voice was sly and taunting. 'What have we got here? It's that little whore's friend. The private detective. How did you enjoy our game?'

My rage was genuine. 'You shits. You tried to kill us.' Now that Katie was out of harm's way, now that I was standing by the roadside, any capacity I'd had for cool-headed action had drained away.

What swept me now was fury. 'Why? Why try to kill us?'

'Look what that little whore did to us!' Duff exclaimed. 'We were sent down for two terms. Do you know anything, you stupid cunt, about how that looks on our records? How that's going to follow Anthony and me for the rest of our lives? And all for what? For a dirty whore.'

He really believes it, I thought. Some of my fury was overlaid by sheer astonishment.

He really believes that he's done nothing wrong. That Katie's the one who should be punished. But punished for what?

And it was then that I heard something scuffing towards us from the direction of Bob Arkwright's house.

Anthony spoke for the first time. He'd held back behind Duff, as if using him as a shelter. Now he stepped forward. Smiled at me, his downward-glancing, mocking, smile. That small, seductive smile.

'Pretty,' he said.

In the pause, in the half-second's silence, I heard Duff's harsh intake of breath.

Heard the soft steps slip-sliding along the road. I craned forward, trying to see through the darkness. Moving my neck brought back that stabbing pain.

'Very pretty,' Anthony repeated. 'Delicious.' He kept his eyes on me, but his words were for Duff. 'Don't you think so, Roger?'

Anthony was flirting with me, I realised with amazement. And Duff knew it too.

Katie shuffled out of the darkness towards me. 'Laura,' she whispered, 'the house is locked. Daddy's not there.' She was dragging a long stick, a fencepost, behind her, as if she'd picked it up and forgotten to set it down again. 'Redknapp's gone. He's left his gnawstick behind. Laura,' Katie asked, in a small, wistful voice, 'what ever shall I do?'

Duff tried for a voice of command. 'Anthony.' It didn't work. 'Anthony!' He pleaded now. 'Don't pay any attention to her. Can't you see that she's trouble? Just like the other one?'

The other one. He meant Katie, of course – in the Echo Room.

Her face now was pale and shocked. Defeat shone in her movements. At any moment, she might crumple, might slip to the ground. Like a princess waiting for a rescue that didn't come, Katie might sink into a sleep of despair.

That was when Duff attacked me. I'd been distracted, watching Katie. I didn't see it coming.

Duff stepped up and rammed his fist into my jaw.

It wasn't a particularly powerful punch, or even very well placed; he was too outraged to go for technique. But it was powerful enough, and the punch jolted my right side where my neck was already in spasm.

I crumpled to the ground. Pain stapled me in place on the grassy verge. Wouldn't let me up.

Duff was over me in two strides. Landed a vicious kick to my ribs. Positioned himself for another.

I groped desperately for some kind of weapon, something to block those sledgehammer blows. I felt myself sinking.

Duff was stopped by a growl. It was a deep-throated growl. It issued loudly and without preamble from pale lips in a pale face topped by blonde curls. Katie's timidity had fallen away.

When she drew herself up to her five feet something inches in height and growled in rage, she was so brimming with righteous anger that even Duff recoiled.

'That's exactly what you told him before,' she snarled. 'He admired me, he flirted with me. You said I was trouble. And then – you attacked me.

'And him—' she jerked a thumb at Anthony, pronouncing the words with infinite loathing. 'He enjoyed it.'

Katie took a breath, and the next bit came out with even greater assurance. 'Roger Duff, you utter bastard. You did it for him. That's why you tore my clothes off. That's why you assaulted me. Because he admired me. You did it to punish me. And to entertain him.'

Seeing Katie's transformation, from terrified girl – like a trapped horse, Candace had said; white eye frantic in its socket – to enraged woman had taken Duff aback. But it was only temporary. Partway through her tirade, he recovered.

'I'll deal with you in a moment,' he barked. And turned back to me. The spasm had seized my neck and shoulder now. No way could I protect myself. No way could I even stand. I crawled, slowly, painfully, towards Katie, with some crazy idea of defending her.

But Duff shouldn't have turned his back on Katie. Her stance held no defeat now. Only coruscating anger.

He drew his leg back once again, and aimed it, not at my ribs this time, but at my head.

Katie dragged up the gnawstick. Raised it into the air. Swung it, like a baseball bat.

Brought it down with a compelling crack across Duff's knees.

And as he collapsed, his face twisted in pain, a police car edged past my Saab and pulled up alongside. Nicole opened the passenger door and stepped out. She brushed down her skirt, and surveyed the scene. Took in Duff writhing in agony on the verge. Me, on hands and knees, unable yet to rise. Katie, looking dazed, with a long piece of hardwood clutched in her hand.

Then Nicole trotted out that multi-purpose police greeting.

'Hello, hello, hello,' she said.

Chapter 23

'She what?'

When I recovered enough to tell her how Katie had leapt to my rescue, Nicole treated me to her best you-expect-us-to-believe-that? tone. I didn't mind in the least.

Didn't mind, because she'd been the soul of patience.

Had contented herself with brief preliminary statements from myself, Duff and Anthony Cocker. Their statements were not completely in accord with mine. Nicole gallantly agreed to leave the work of sorting out the truth until morning.

DI Pelletier felt a little guilty, though she didn't put it quite like that. About the lapse in procedures earlier in the evening. About the constable who'd written down – slowly, laboriously – the details of our destination. Who'd scribbled the place (Fleam Dyke Road) and the people (Katie and me) and the estimated time of arrival in large letters for anyone to see. Who'd shared them, unintentionally, with Roger Duff as he left the incident room after another question-and-answer session with Nicole.

She wasn't taking sides, of course; that would be unprofessional. But in the preliminary search of Duff's vehicle, she had turned up my address book. Had proposed to him that he might have stolen it from the Echo Room in the hope of discovering where Katie Arkwright had gone. 'If only you were as keen on your studies,' she'd remarked, 'as you were on this campaign against the girl.' And as Roger Duff departed to Addenbrooke's for X-rays, she'd added a breezy *now be a good boy* that had – for some obscure reason – got right up his nose. He'd directed a ferocious glare at her as he was driven away. An onlooker might have thought there'd been police harassment here, rather than a mild instance of irony.

And it was Nicole who noticed how close Katie was to collapse. The delivery of that stunning blow with the gnawstick had left her temporarily elated; Nicole saw through the exhilaration to the trauma behind. The police needed to have a lengthy Q&A with Katie, and rather quickly, she pointed out; but she allowed me the chance to make a counter-proposal. I offered to take responsibility for delivering Katie for interview the following morning, and Nicole readily agreed.

'Right then, take her home,' she said. 'Put the girl to bed.'

So Katie and I were chauffeured to my house in a police car. I didn't enjoy abandoning the Saab on Fleam Dyke Road; but if you need a quiet byway in which to park a vehicle until it can be towed, I guess you could do worse. And the pain in my neck, which was duller now but still disagreeable, had muted my interest in driving.

By the time we arrived at Clare Street, Katie was yawning, with shock, as much as fatigue. I told her to wash and sleep in my bed; I'd settle for the sofa. I made her a cup of cocoa; she didn't want anything stronger, though I certainly did. And when I brought the cocoa to her, I noticed the changed look in her eye. Calm. Accepting of something – herself, maybe? I even saw a smidgen of triumph there.

For how long? I wondered. Katie gave no sign at all of having registered the fact that she might be a suspect in Stephen Fox's murder. Would she still have that serene look – that glimmer of exultation – after she'd been closeted with Nicole the next day?

She placed the phone back on the bedside table, taking care not to shake the cocoa. 'Still no answer from Daddy,' she said.

'Perhaps he's gone to visit your mum. Katie, you'll have to ring her sooner or later, you know. Shall I do it for you? Tell her you're back in Cambridge? Tell her you're all right?'

Katie sighed, and smiled just a little. 'Tomorrow,' she said. 'I'll see Mum tomorrow. I'd have to explain everything, and I'm just too tired now.'

'And Jared?'

Katie looked puzzled. As if the name came to her across an enormous distance. Across the last moments of the ball, and the hostel in King's Cross; across surreal dinners arranged by The Heavenly Twins; across the barrier formed by the Pleasure Palace, where sleaze was rendered as mundane as PG Tips. Across the distance of things not shared.

'Jared,' she said at last. The tone was wistful. 'I guess I'll see him tomorrow, too. If he still wants to see me.'

'Everyone will be thrilled to see you,' I said firmly.

Another little lie.

I went into Katie's room – my bedroom – at seven thirty a.m. Took her in a warm slice of French toast – with real Canadian maple syrup, not that synthetic stuff. I also treated her to the best orange in the fruit bowl, conscientiously peeled and trimmed.

The condemned woman gets a hearty meal, I thought guiltily.

Took her coffee and the newspaper.

And tried to find an easy way to break the bad news.

'Thought you might like to take your time this morning.'

Katie cocked an eyebrow at me. With her curls helter-skelter round her head, and an eyebrow at that quizzical angle, she looked sweetly comical.

'Take my time? Don't be silly, Laura. I'm not going to miss a minute of this lovely day. I'll ring Deb and Candace – maybe they'll want to go punting.' She sounded happy. Like someone who hadn't seen a lovely day in quite some time. 'Oh, and of course, first thing, I'll talk to Mummy.'

'Katie, do you remember Inspector Pelletier? From last evening?'

Katie tucked into her breakfast. '*Merci*, Mademoiselle Principal.' She kissed her thumb and forefinger to signify delight. 'Zees French toast is *exactement* the way I like it. Compliments to the chef.' She took another bite and mumbled through the mouthful. 'Or should that be chefette?'

'Not if you value your life, kiddo! Look, seriously, Katie. The

Inspector wants to see you this morning. She wants to ask you some questions.'

'Those two tried to kill us, didn't they? I hope she throws the book at them. I'll tell her precisely what that Roger Duff did, every nasty thing from the Dorics dinner onwards.'

'And about Stephen Fox.'

'Oh, yuck,' she said. 'I mean, I'm sorry he died, but do we have to think about creeps like that on a day like today?' She placed the tray into my hands, and bounced off the bed with the kind of careless movement that reminds me I'm not nineteen any more. On the way to the bathroom, she turned and tossed me another set of questions. 'So should I see this policewoman—'

'Detective Inspector.'

'Police Detective Inspector whatever – this woman – should I see her after breakfast? After I've rung my mother? Or do I need to make an appointment?'

She really hadn't twigged. She thought Stephen Fox was well and truly behind her. She believed he was nothing more now than a nasty moment from the past. Not something that would come back to haunt her, that would throw its dark shadow over her – every day, every minute – for the rest of her life.

I heard the water running in the bathroom and then Katie frisked back into the room and leaped on to the bed. I handed her the tray.

But I chickened out. I didn't confront her with what was coming.

'I thought you might want to have a bath. Maybe wash your hair. Lounge around for a while. I'll go down to St Bartholomew's first—' I stopped, as Katie's eyes widened. Even after all she'd been through, the name of St Bartholomew's still had the power to hurt.

'I'm sorry, Katie. You'll have to go to Bart's. That's where the Inspector has her incident room. Anyway, I'll go first, and talk to her myself. You can follow a little later. I'll be waiting for you there at, say, ten?'

'That might not be enough time, Laura. My mother—'

'Your mother will meet you there,' I said quietly.

My phone call to Rosemary Arkwright had solved at least one mystery. It was the first time we'd spoken since she'd turfed me off the case. She answered the phone with a lilt to her voice, but it didn't last long.

'Mrs Arkwright? Laura Principal speaking. You know, the investigator who—'

She cut me off. It took an effort to get the words out. 'You've – you've found her then? You've found our Katie?' Her voice quavered.

I confirmed that, yes, Katie had been found. That she'd been in a minor accident the evening before – might seem bruised and shaken – but that she was fundamentally safe and well. That she was back in Cambridge, and keen to see her mother.

There was no comment from Rosemary. A silence, instead. It was almost as if the line had been cut.

'Mrs Arkwright?'

An odd sound, a choking sound, but no speech.

And yet I felt she was there, somewhere, on the other end of the line. With her enormous soulful eyes. With her thin body and her heartbreakingly lovely face.

'Rosemary?'

And then I understood. The anguish of the past weeks had found release in silent, agonised sobs.

I heard her speaking at a distance to someone else. Her words were choked with tears. 'They've found her. She's safe.'

And a man's voice, heavy with wonder and relief: 'Katie – safe.'

Rosemary returned to the telephone. 'Sorry, Miss Principal. Robert is here, with me. We're both – well, you understand.' She took a deep breath and continued, speaking more firmly now. 'Where's Katie? Can we see her?'

'I'm meeting her at the incident room at St Bartholomew's College later this morning. Do you know where Bart's is, Rosemary?'

A pause again.

'Rosemary?'

'Yes, Miss Principal. I know.'

'Katie is going to be interrogated by the police. About the murder of a man who was Senior Tutor there. A man named Stephen Fox.'

This time I knew immediately what the pause signified. Rosemary was crying again. I could almost hear the tears.

'Oh, my God,' she said, in a faint voice. It carried like the whisper of birds across a lake. 'Oh, my God.'

I hesitated. 'Perhaps Katie should have a solicitor with her when she's interviewed. A legal advisor. Is there a family lawyer you could bring?'

In the background, Bob Arkwright was speaking, trying to get Rosemary's attention. 'Rosemary, has something happened to Katie? What is it? Darling, what's wrong?'

'Everything's going to be all right, Bob. Katie will be fine.'

No more vapours for Rosemary. No more rush-for-the-tablets, no more just-barely-functioning. Faced now with a tangible threat to her daughter, Rosemary Arkwright was solid.

'Thank you, Miss Principal, for all you've done. We'll be at Bart's as soon as we can. We'll bring a lawyer. A good lawyer,' she said, with emphasis.

Katie was right about it being a lovely morning, at least in terms of the weather. The sun shone as bold as brass. It beckoned me on down the hill towards Jesus Green. Everywhere, people were preparing for a hot English day. Near the iron footbridge that crosses the Cam, there was a group of young women, pushing prams, airing their babies before the midday heat. The pavilion on Jesus Green was open for ice cream; there was a small queue, even though it was barely past breakfast time.

And when I reached the far side of Victoria Bridge, a barman was hosing down the terrace in front of the Fort St George.

I craned my neck, wondering idly whether there would be anyone in the snug this time of the morning. In the room, I thought, where I'd seen Anthony Cocker – that beautiful, skinny boy – with Roger Duff; where Cocker had smiled his seductive smile at me for the first time, and Duff had responded like a raging bull.

I should have seen it then; should have understood. How Anthony flirted; it was part of who he was. Flirted with women, but didn't particularly like them. Did, however, like the reaction he got from Duff – the sense of power that came when Duff rose, as Duff inevitably did, to the bait. When Duff placed himself between Anthony and the girl. Scared her off. Intimidated her.

I should have known that Anthony liked it. Liked it when Duff became jealous. Liked it when the girl was frightened. When her smile of invitation was replaced by a grimace of fear.

Liked it even better at the Dorics' dinner. When he smiled at the pretty waitress, and she smiled back. From the moment that Katie flirted with Anthony – returned his smiles – Duff hated her. Hated her; took advantage of the circumstances to make her suffer. To turn her nervousness into terror. To humiliate her.

And Anthony liked that best.

'Thirsty, love?' the barman asked.

'Bit early for me,' I laughed. 'But don't sell it all before lunchtime, promise? I may need a pint on my way back from Bart's.'

By the time I had tramped across Midsummer Common, in the morning sun, I was warm enough to fancy that pint. But the interior of St Bartholomew's was refreshing, as always. The entrance hall, with its gilt and turquoise dome – exquisitely pale, exquisitely cool – was an antidote to summer languor. It was also perfectly empty. Not a porter in sight. Other than the faint whistle of a tea-kettle from some inner alcove, it could seem as if I were the only person in the college.

Yet, somewhere in the incident room, somewhere in the heart of this building, Nicole and her colleagues were already at work. They were sifting, sorting, classifying information. Preparing questions, comparing answers. Pushing the wheels of justice inexorably on.

No, I told myself, as I began to ascend the staircase to the incident room. Things couldn't just be left as they were. There had to be closure. Things would have to come to an end.

And then I heard it. A soft shush-thump. Footsteps, on the other staircase, the one that led to the Echo Room.

I retraced my steps through the entrance hall and followed without thinking. Past the fuse box, and up again, to the top, to the landing. Turned the handle, slowly, slowly. Opened the door a crack.

The lights were turned on inside the Echo Room, but at their lowest level. Although I could see my way clear into the centre of the room – none of the stumbling blackness I'd experienced before – the corners retreated into shadow. And at the far end of the room, a man was crouched in one of those corners. Sitting, rather, in a cross-legged position, with his head bowed. As if he might be meditating. Or praying.

While I watched, John Carswell slowly, slowly lifted his head. Slowly, slowly uncoiled his neck. As if his head were a massive weight; as if it took all the strength of his back to shift it.

His gaze remained fixed upon the centre of the Echo Mural. But I knew that when he spoke, he spoke to me.

'Something's happening, isn't it?'

I entered the Echo Room and shut the door behind me. Waited for him to continue.

'The college is swarming with police officers. It feels sordid, somehow. Oh, not because the police are here, I don't mean that, Laura. But because they're doing our job. They're sorting out the mess we should have sorted out. So long ago.'

By 'we', he meant, I supposed, the members of the college.

He was pale, too pale for a man with a tan. And sweaty. Now that my eyes had adjusted to the dim light, I could pick out the deep discolorations – bruises of sleeplessness – under his eyes.

'I used to love this room, Laura. There were some aspects of college life – the pompousness, the flaunting of privilege, the sense of superiority – that I could do without.'

'But you didn't do without.'

John continued as if I hadn't interrupted.

'Felt uneasy with them, shall we say. But the Echo Room was perfect. Bonomi's little masterpiece. The proportions are impeccable, don't you think? And it's just so damned beautiful. I used to be able to come here, when things felt wrong. To sit here, in the quiet evening, and find peace.'

'Until the attack on Katie Arkwright, you mean.'

'Since then,' he agreed, 'nothing's been the same.'

'Stephen Fox's death. And the body – the skeleton – in the room in the west wing. That's what you mean?'

John nodded. He unfolded his legs slowly, and stood up. There was an unsteadiness about him that I'd never seen before. He'd always seemed the epitome of vigour.

I walked up to him. It was only when I was a few inches away that I realised he'd been drinking. Rather a lot. The odour of whisky was intense. His eyes were flecked with red.

'Poor John,' I murmured. And slipped my arms around him.

There was a second's hesitation. Then John returned the hug. Gratefully – but tentatively also, as if he expected me at any moment to pull away. Expected it to end.

It was I who ended it. 'John?' I said, leaning back from him, the better to see his face. 'John, why don't you tell me what's the matter? It can't be worse than keeping it to yourself.'

He shook his head, but I didn't know whether it was in agreement with me – *no, it can't be worse* – or in refusal to tell. In any event, he began to speak.

'Guilt,' he said, 'is a strange thing. Is he guilty or innocent? we ask. As if it were a simple either-or choice. X or Y. As if you could assess the evidence and arrive at an unequivocal answer: this person is guilty – this one, and not that. He, and he alone, is responsible. Bears the burden. Deserves the punishment.'

What was it Candace had said? So fiercely, so protectively, from the depths of her sense of failure. From the moment when she'd been throttled – pinned in place, as she put it – by her fear.

Nothing is Katie's fault.

That was what she'd said.

How can I make people understand? Nothing is Katie's fault.

Nothing is a tall order.

'Tell me, John. Speaking of responsibility. When you were undergraduates – why did you stop being friends with Stephen Fox?'

We had been standing close, facing one another, my hands held in his. It might have looked, to someone coming into the Echo Room, seeing us from the doorway, as if we were just about to dance. To lift our knees and scuttle across the room in a polka. To slide into the stately rhythms of a waltz.

But instead of leading me on to the dance floor, John's shoulders bent forward, in a gesture of defeat. 'Laura,' he said, 'you don't really want to know.'

'Want doesn't come into it, John. I must know. You must tell me what he did.'

'All right, if you'll put your arms around me once more.'

There. That wasn't so hard.

'It was in our third year,' he began, 'shortly before finals. We were close, Stephen and I, as young men sometimes are. We'd gone to the same school. Played cricket together.' He shrugged. 'We were mates. You know?'

'I understand.'

'Stephen had some quirky things about him. I guess so did I for that matter; so did most of us, at that age. But Stephen's worst quirk was women. He was never at ease with women, you know? He always thought they were cheating him or making fun of him; and he always had to get the better of them, one way or another. I didn't like to go out with him – in a foursome, say – because I couldn't be quite sure how he'd behave.'

'So what did he do?'

'There was nothing really serious – nothing that I knew about – until just before finals. There was this girl – little more than a child really. Sixteen, she was. She wasn't one of us. She was a bedder – someone who—'

'I was a Newnham girl, John.' Bedder is a Cambridge term for the women who clean the undergraduates' rooms.

287

'Anyway, she was a sweet girl. Named Louise, I think – last name Sage or Gage, something like that. And as it happens, very, very pretty. Anyway, one day, I found her crying her eyes out. I felt awkward about it, didn't know really how to help. Invited her to talk. She told me what was wrong.'

He looked away, fixing his sights on the furthermost corner of the Echo Mural. Where the last curl of the sun's rays dusted pink on the edge of a cloud.

'Fox had forced her to have sex?'

'She put it in softer terms than that. The reality was, I suspect, even worse.'

'And what happened then?'

'I tackled Stephen about it. He made excuses, said it wasn't really anything. Said she was just a silly girl. The next day, while I was still pondering what to do, he came back to me. He said the episode was all over. Said that they'd got rid of Louise. *What do you mean, got rid of her?* I asked. *She's gone*, Stephen said. *She had to go. She was pregnant.*'

'And you kept quiet? About the rape?'

John turned back to me. The distress in his face almost melted my resolve. 'I let myself be persuaded. I can't explain why. Some of it was youth and inexperience – Stephen was always better at getting what he wanted than me.'

'And some of it was loyalty?'

'Loyalty,' John agreed. He spat the word out. 'Codes of loyalty bind men together, they say. And override their common decency. Their sense of justice. If it helps at all, Laura – I've never stopped feeling guilty about this. About my lack of integrity. My failure of nerve.'

I remembered Stephen Fox's sneer. *John Carswell was downright eloquent*, he'd said. At last the sneer made sense.

'That's why you pressed so hard for firm action against the men who assaulted Katie Arkwright?'

'I had to make sure this time around that justice was done. But of course – I understand more clearly now – even justice doesn't make things right.'

Curiosity got the better of me. 'Did you ever tell your wife about Stephen?'

'Vivienne had more integrity in her little finger than there is in the entire fellowship of Bart's. She always did what was right and hang the consequences. I loved that about her.'

'She wouldn't have forgiven you?'

'Oh, she would have forgiven me, all right. But she never would've looked at me in the same way again. And I – I couldn't bear it. That's why I went on keeping quiet. And you, Laura. You're a lot like Vivienne, you know. Have I lost you too, now?'

I stared again at the Echo Mural.

'I don't know how I feel, John. Probably won't know until this whole thing is over.'

Over, I thought. Is there such a thing as over?

'But there is one thing I know now. I can't make it better for you.'

Chapter 24

'Have you heard the latest? The Senior Tutor left an heir.' Nicole watched me keenly to see whether I was in the know. She saw only surprise on my face. 'You'd no idea, Laura? That Rachel Hunneyball is pregnant.'

I should, of course, have realised. Should have added two and two together the last time we'd met. 'Hard on her,' I said, thinking aloud. 'A wife, a widow, a mother – all in less than a year.'

And a little Hunneyball-Fox. To carry on the traditions of the college.

Nicole was in probing mood. 'You have an answer now to your question?'

'What question was that, Nicole?'

'Why Katie ran away?'

I had made my way from the Echo Room, down one staircase and up another, fighting against a sense of *déjà vu*. Struggling to distinguish the present from the past.

'You looking for the incident room, miss?' a porter had asked me. He pointed the way to the first floor, above the colonnade. Third door along the corridor, he said. But that I already knew.

I'd passed a storeroom of some kind. From behind the door, a disinfectant odour leaked into the corridor.

Passed a room with a plaque on the door that read THE NURSE in bald capital letters. And under that, in smaller script: Gillian Fox.

Arrived at my destination.

Nicole was standing just inside the doorway, swapping notes

with two plain-clothes policemen. She saw me, took a last regretful look at the view of Midsummer Common, and pointed me into her tiny office.

As before, it was hot, and the window was open only a crack. Nicole's main concession to comfort – visible concession, that is; anything might have been happening under her desk – was a massive flask. It sat on a filing cabinet to her left. Enough coffee there, I thought, for half the Cambridgeshire Constabulary.

She didn't offer me any. She slid her feet under the desk, and grinned.

'What's so funny?' I asked.

'I'm waiting,' Nicole said.

I adjusted myself so that my back was straight on the chair and the pain in my neck was muted.

And I told her, as best I could, as best I knew, why Katie had run away.

That, in spite of her advantages – in spite of beauty and brains and a family who loved her – Katie was far from being a confident girl. This was apparent from her early teens at least; maybe from infancy, if some baby photographs were to be believed. Perhaps some of Rosemary's insecurities had rubbed off on her. Maybe Rosemary's depressions, her leanings towards self-harm, made it difficult for Katie to be carefree.

'And Katie didn't have many opportunities to build up her self-confidence *vis-à-vis* the big wide world,' I concluded. 'Her mother was strict with her.'

'Strict as in cruel?' Nicole asked. I've known it in other CID officers. They tend to develop a suspicious turn of mind.

'No, not cruel. Strict as in *be careful, be careful*. Because from Rosemary's vantage point, the world is full of dangers. Because that's the only way, as Rosemary sees it, to keep a daughter safe. Anyway, Nicole, the crucial thing is that in the past year, several things turned low self-esteem into a crisis.'

'Such as?' She wasn't going to let me get away without specifics.

'Such as her parents' separation. Katie had always seen herself

291

as Daddy's little girl. Seen her father as her ally in the effort to win some freedom. When Bob left and didn't take her with him, Katie felt abandoned.'

'Several things, Laura. That's what you said.'

'Katie was turned down by Cambridge University; her friend Deb got in. That didn't help. And we talked about the other things yesterday evening.'

She ticked them off on her fingers. 'The assault in the Echo Room. The notes, the letters, the fake business cards – courtesy of Roger Duff. A young man, you could say, who used his time destructively.'

Nicole paused. Lifted the flask, and two glasses, on to her desk. Gave voice to her doubts. 'But look, Laura, is it really enough? Enough to explain why she would leave home, family, friends, university? Granted, she might have felt down in the dumps, felt dirtied by all this. But why London? Why Vanessa, who wasn't, you said, a close friend?'

'Vanessa's easy,' I started to explain.

'Of course, she's easy,' Nicole guffawed. 'She's a prostitute.'

A cheap shot, I decided. Best ignored.

'Katie had been humiliated, first at the Dorics dinner, and then in the months afterwards, by Duff. No one seemed really to understand. Then she spotted Vanessa. Vanessa, who'd been an apparently ordinary girl when they were growing up, but then became an outcast. My guess is that Katie felt a strong sense of affinity with her – felt that here, at last, was someone who'd understand her humiliation. Would understand what it was like to be victimised by men.' I hesitated. Knew I couldn't not say it, however bad it looked for Katie.

'And, Nicole, there's something else. I've only just realised myself how much the echoes—' Bad choice of word, that. 'How much continuing fall-out there was from the incident in the Echo Room. Last night, at Fleam Dyke Road – you remember me telling you about Katie's splendid defensive action?'

'Defensive?' Nicole interrupted. 'According to Duff, Katie made an unprovoked attack on an innocent man.'

'If Duff is innocent, then I'm Little Bo Peep. You think I gave myself this bruise on the jaw?' I fingered the area just below my ear. It still felt as delicate as eggs.

'But the interesting thing, Nicole, is the change in Katie. When she came back after finding her father's house empty, she was like a dog who'd been whipped. She couldn't even run. Two minutes later, she was Wonder Woman, without the tiara. You would've been proud of her. She swung that gnawstick like a riot cop with a truncheon. When she saw Duff and Anthony going for me — Anthony flirting, Duff punching — Katie suddenly understood precisely what had happened at the Dorics dinner. Saw it in a new light. And, with me lying on the ground, in pain, she was able for the first time to be angry — really, really angry — about what they'd done. Before, when she went to London, I reckon all that anger was turned inwards, against herself.'

Nicole has never had that kind of problem with anger. She can let loose — when it's justified, of course — at the drop of a hat. And since she's never had it, she found it hard to understand.

'I'm not with you,' she said.

'Try this, then. What do you think of Anthony Cocker? His looks, I mean?'

'Drop-dead gorgeous,' Nicole said. 'If he had a personality I could fancy him myself.'

'That's what Katie thought,' I said. 'At the Dorics' dinner, Anthony flirted with her and she responded. So after the assault, she felt—'

'Complicit,' Nicole said. This, she could understand. Completely.

'Yes, guilty. Katie felt as if, in returning Cocker's smiles, she'd issued an invitation for them to hold her fast, and strip her, and assault her. With an audience of forty men.'

Nicole sat quietly for a moment, weighing it all up. Then she hefted the flask, and filled the glasses with something cold and amber-coloured. Handed one to me. 'So, Laura: now Katie's angry, is she? You realise, don't you, that she's a suspect? For the murder of Stephen Fox?'

293

I eyed the iced tea with distaste. With sugar, the stuff sets my teeth on edge. Without sugar, it's pretty well undrinkable.

'You'll have nothing on Katie that could impress the CPS,' I said. 'So what if Katie visited Fox a few days before the murder? Her actions last evening – the courageous way she stood up for me—'

Nicole shot back, 'Her actions last evening prove she's capable of extreme violence. Duff has a fractured knee-cap. Prints that match those in Katie's bedroom were found at the crime scene, all over Fox's office. And – for reasons you've just explained – Katie is a very, very angry girl. It may not amount to a case yet, but it's a damned good start.'

'Come on, Nicole—' I halted my protest before it had barely begun. I'd known when I left Clare Street that morning that Nicole would make this reading of what I said. Knew that she would – how could she not? – weave my little tale into another, more dangerous story. A story for the prosecution.

Knew that Katie's realisation that she wasn't to blame for the Echo Room incident, that she had a right to be angry – Katie's refusal to be a victim – would make her, in the eyes of the law, a more plausible villain.

Knew that hiding the truth at this point would only make it worse.

Knew that Katie, minutes from now, would trip into the interview room and tell Nicole another story – another truth – far more damaging to herself. She would tell Nicole – tell the police – precisely what Stephen Fox had done to her. How, before she ran away, he'd added another plank to her self-loathing. How Stephen Fox had waved a hooker's card at her and demanded sex. Told her – with all the authority of a Senior Tutor – that she really and truly was a whore. That she'd misled the disciplinary committee. That if the committee had known the 'truth' about her, Duff and Cocker would never have been punished.

Katie would tell Nicole how she had, at that moment, hated Stephen Fox.

How – even in death – she hated him still.

What did it matter if I spilled the beans, when the suspect would do it so very well herself?

I exited the door of Nicole's tiny office just seconds before Katie was shown in. She had scrubbed her face since I'd seen her last, and brushed her curls up into a short ponytail.

The thing that had changed most since breakfast-time was her expression – from cheerful, innocent, unshadowed relief to intimations of trouble. Anxiety rippled across her face.

I stuck to safe topics. 'You saw your mum?'

She nodded.

'And your father?'

'They were wonderful,' she said, with feeling.

She looked sideways at Mr Curtis, from Barr Ellison – that was how he'd been introduced – and back to me again, as if telling me in code that something was up. She hadn't realised that I already knew it.

'The policeman found a room for my parents to wait in. Right next door. The nurse's surgery. Will you go and see them? Make sure they're all right?'

I shut Nicole's office door behind me.

Turned around. Almost bumped into a man who was waiting to get my attention.

It was Jared Scott-Pettit.

'Thank you for finding Katie,' he said.

'How was she with you?' My curiosity was genuine.

I couldn't be sure whether Jared's next statement was an answer to my question or not. 'She seems – different, somehow. She doesn't really want to talk very much. About what happened.'

'Give it time,' I advised. Agony aunt has never been my best role.

Jared wasn't ready to give up yet. He lowered his voice to a whisper. 'She told me – that she stayed in a kind of brothel in London. Did you know that?'

'I picked her up there.'

'But she wouldn't say what she did there, exactly. Did she – well, you know?'

'I do know what you mean, Jared. But I don't know whether she did. We didn't talk about it.' I looked at him closely. 'Does it matter?'

Jared squirmed. Took evasive action. 'It might matter to Katie,' he said. 'To how she feels about things.'

'Well, then, your answer's obvious. Let her tell you, in her own time. You wouldn't want to press the issue – make a big thing of it, maybe give Katie the impression that her virtue mattered more than her safe return home – now would you?'

Maybe I could do this agony aunt thing, after all.

And I left him looking uneasily around. In case someone – even worse, someone from *our sort of circle* – might have overheard.

Nicole had borrowed Gillian Fox's surgery to accommodate Mr and Mrs Arkwright. Gillian Fox, to my relief, was nowhere to be seen. Not that I had anything against the woman; she seemed to me a rather splendid person, who'd coped remarkably well with being dumped by her husband. But it would have been less than tactful to provide a place for the parents of a suspected killer alongside the former wife of the man she was supposed to have killed.

I hesitated before opening the door to the surgery. In spite of Rosemary's robust performance on the telephone that morning, I feared that once she registered the extent of Katie's danger, we might be in for a collapse.

And I was wrong.

Rosemary Arkwright sat in an upholstered chair, as upright as the chair back would allow. She wore a pretty cotton sundress that emphasised the wispiness of her figure, and a cornflower-blue cardigan.

'Do come in, Miss Principal,' she said, when I walked through the door. She said it in a tone of welcome, and smiled. Her large grey eyes were as melancholy as ever, but Rosemary hadn't collapsed.

Bob Arkwright knelt on the floor, with his head resting on Rosemary's lap. I could see – before Rosemary wielded a tissue and gently wiped them away – that his face was wet with tears.

He rose. 'Laura,' he said, extending his hand – I came and sat down next to Rosemary – 'thank you for finding our Katie. We were so frightened. Only now—'

I sat down next to Rosemary.

'Hush,' said Rosemary, gently. 'It's going to be all right, Robert.' She patted the seat on her other side, and Bob took his place. Rosemary watched him, smiling sadly, until he was calmer, and then she turned to me and took my hand.

She spoke quietly then, but very clearly, like a little brook. Her voice was soothing, somehow. Made me feel less unhappy. Less defeated by what was going on in the interview room.

'You don't mind?' she said, glancing down.

I shook my head. Somehow, at this moment, it seemed perfectly natural that Rosemary Arkwright should hold my hand in hers.

'You shouldn't be upset,' she said. 'How are you to know who'll turn out to be a murderer? A killer? How can anyone be sure? The important thing is this: Katie's just a child. She's not to blame.'

She spoke with a burnished certainty. An absolute assurance. I heard the door open quietly, behind her back, and it made me nervous. I wondered if Rosemary Arkwright might be just a little mad.

'You'll come to realise,' she continued. 'That nothing is Katie's fault. Sometimes people can't help themselves, that's all. You'll see. Sometimes the provocation is overwhelming.'

'Is that why you pressed me to drop the search for Katie? Did you suspect even then that your daughter could be implicated in Fox's death?'

Rosemary hesitated. 'Not exactly,' she said. 'When Katie rang, well – I hoped that if she stayed away a while longer, the murder investigation would die down. She wouldn't have to tell the police what Fox had said to her. Wouldn't have to relive that awful experience. Wouldn't have to reveal the reason for his murder.'

Nicole was standing behind us now, with every sense alert. It was as if she'd put on a pair of antennae and they were quivering in Rosemary's direction.

Nicole spoke, her tone one of practised authority. Of quiet command.

'You can tell us about the murder, Mrs Arkwright? You can tell us why Katie did it?'

'If you want to know about my daughter's motives, you must ask her,' Rosemary said. 'She'll tell you the truth.'

She rose to her feet. Her five-foot-two-inch frame looked frail still, but somehow taller than before. 'But if you want to know why Stephen Fox died, Inspector, then I'm the one to ask.'

'Rosemary!' Bob Arkwright pleaded. 'Rosemary, there must be another way.'

'No, Bob, only the truth will do. I'm ready for the truth, at last, after all these years. I'm not ashamed any more. I'm ready now to tell them how I murdered Stephen Fox. And why.'

Chapter 25

There's a kind of summer heat, in a temperate country like England, that makes you stand straighter and throw your shoulders back. That's liberating. You feel at home in your body. You smile at strangers. You become aware of new worlds of possibility.

But there's another kind of heat, a claustrophobic heat – like being locked in a cupboard with a three-bar electric fire. It sneaks into your bedroom while you're sleeping; and when you wake up, it is squatting on your chest. Sucking the strength from your bones. Making everything seem like too much trouble. This kind of heat has you looking at other people out of the corner of your eye; you shield yourself against them as a dog guards a bone.

It was this second kind of heat that greeted me when I finally took my leave of the Arkwrights. I stepped from the cooler shadows of St Bartholomew's College into half past two on a humid afternoon.

I had a commitment, but I couldn't face the prospect of a garden party. I rang Helen and asked her to make my apologies. Invent something, I said. The truth was the kind of simple thing that simply isn't said: that the thought of staying in the city that afternoon – even in a garden – was intolerable. That I couldn't face the crowds and chatter. That I might get by with the help of champagne, but I didn't want to face the afterwards, when I'd be flatter than a pancake.

I headed for the river. Bought a bottle of water in the Fort St George. Changed into the spare shorts and the No Fear T-shirt that I store in the boathouse. Carried my scull down to the water.

The Cam was dark and deep that day, the surface not glassy at all but matted by a warm breeze. It was a breeze in training to be a wind. It pleated the surface of the water. It rushed across the towpath, and gave chase to a runaway hat. These gusts hinted at less gentle things to come.

I took it easy. Rowed slowly alongside the eastern tail of Midsummer Common. Steered around a formation of ducklings who were trailing their mother upstream. Eyeballed the inline skaters on Riverside. Exchanged smiles with a man who was planting aubretia on the roof of his narrow boat.

Didn't begin to stretch out, to find my rhythm, until I was abreast of Stourbridge Common. Until I'd slid past a group of scruffy ponies, bracing their backs to the wind. By the time I reached Ditton Meadows, I was skimming at speed over the surface of the Cam. Aware only of my body – my ribcage expanding, my knees sliding up and down. Aware of lengthening my stroke, of getting my second wind. Feeling the sweat break out on my forehead, feeling the breeze dash it away.

It was then that I realised how swiftly the weather was changing. It was hot still, and even more humid, but no longer bright. Clouds of a gun-metal grey were roiling up in the summer sky. The tops of the willow trees leaned first one way, then another, their leaves flashing silver and green.

Then I heard it. Like a military aircraft taking off from Marshall's Airport, with the engine sounds trembling in the clouded sky. But this sound wasn't man-made. It was the first thunder, from miles off. It was the herald of the storm.

I put my back into the stroke. The skies were darkening rapidly now, but I'd try to outrun the storm. Try to make it to Baits Bite Lock before the downpour.

And now, now that I was rowing for all I was worth, the riverbank disappeared from view. My mind retreated back to St Bartholomew's College. Back to the death of Stephen Fox.

It was official now – with the police if not the courts. Rosemary Arkwright was guilty of murder. She had recounted Stephen Fox's last few moments in vivid detail. How the Senior Tutor had turned to retrieve something from the drawer of his desk. He was talking all the while, in that cool, acerbic voice, making fun of Rosemary – belittling her, baiting her. Using sarcasm to put her in her place.

Sometimes people can't help themselves, Rosemary had said.

She was speaking not of Katie, of course, but of herself. Fox's stream of invective had overwhelmed Rosemary. Filled her with an urge to destroy. The minute he bent over, she'd snatched up the cricket bat and crashed it across his temple. Rosemary wasn't strong – far from it. But with Fox peering in the drawer, head down, back to her, she had a height advantage. And she possessed the strength that sometimes comes from the release of pent-up rage.

She'd swung the bat – much as Katie had later swung the gnawstick? – and it had hit, full square, willow on bone. Struck Fox's temple. Cracked Fox's skull. Destroyed the living tissue that had been Fox's brain.

Then – terrified by what she'd done, yet unable to stop – she'd swung the bat again and, as he staggered back, it struck his face. He'd spun on one leg, the knee twisting beneath him, and fell.

No more cool, acerbic air. No more cutting invective. Stephen Fox was dead. Rosemary had fled the room, sped down the stairs. The cricket bat was still clutched in her hand.

'No one saw her? No one heard her?' Sonny asked, when we went over it later.

'It was Saturday,' I explained. 'Few people were around. And the few who were – who might have pointed an accusing finger – had picked up only an inkling of her presence.'

Had nothing more solid than shadows to report.

One of the porters had caught a glimpse of a woman as she'd entered from the colonnade. Whether or not this was Rosemary – and he certainly couldn't be sure – she hadn't paused to speak to him. Rosemary had no need of directions; even after four decades, she knew every turning of every corridor in St Bartholomew's College, and the location of every room.

Minutes later, a student on an errand had noticed a female of the right age group in the vicinity of the Tutorial Office. But her description was so vague, her remembrance so uncertain, that the police hadn't pursued it. What Shirley Ann Talbot had told me on the lawn of the pub at Madingley had proved to be correct: undergraduates really don't pay much attention to a woman of middle age.

John Carswell had had the nearest brush with Rosemary. Ascending the stairs to Stephen Fox's office on the morning of the murder, he'd heard a shuffling on the landing. If he hadn't been so absorbed in his thoughts – if he'd paused to investigate – he would've seen Rosemary Arkwright, shivering with shock. Would have spotted the blood smeared across her dress. But Carswell didn't see her. Rosemary Arkwright had stepped back into the shadows. She was a woman accustomed to making herself small.

Rosemary had left other signs behind, it later turned out. Her fingerprints were on the bat, on Fox's desk, on the drawer from which, after his death, she'd taken the card that Fox had been reaching for. But in the early days after the murder, no one had known to whom these fingerprints belonged. Rosemary was merely the mother of a missing girl, in a quite separate case. There'd been no reason to check her fingerprints, no reason to compare them with those at the scene of the murder.

Rosemary had no direct association – none of which the police were aware – with Stephen Fox.

How could they have known? I'd only begun to string the story together – to understand the who and why of Stephen Fox's murder – shortly before, when John Carswell had told me why he'd fallen out with Stephen Fox. Told me, that is, about the rape of a child of sixteen – a local girl – in St Bartholomew's College, nearly forty years before. How she'd been got rid of, to prevent a scandal.

And he'd told me that this girl – who happened, he said, to be very, very pretty – was named Louise. *Louise Sage, or Gage*, John had said; *something like that.*

Sage, Gage – such similar names. Little to distinguish one from the other. Who could blame John for forgetting such a detail, especially after so many years?

But forgetting is a luxury that victims can't afford. Rosemary Arkwright had never for a moment forgotten Stephen Fox.

Mrs Rosemary Arkwright, that is. Whose brother – Harry Gage – had been mowing the lawn when I visited her house.

Rosemary Arkwright – who'd prepared a photo album for her husband; who'd written the full names of family members under each photo in an elegant calligraphic hand.

Katie Deanna Arkwright, she'd written.

Robert Timothy Arkwright.

And – last, but not least – *Rosemary Louise.*

I could bring that photo to mind, see Rosemary in it (*a very, very pretty girl*) with the name by which she'd been known as a child. Before violence and the birth and death of an infant had cut her childhood short. Had left her with a lifelong legacy of shame and loss. Had made her want to wipe away Louise Gage, and replace her with the older, wiser – always sadder – Rosemary.

But the baby – *my baby* – she couldn't forget. *Ofme Notofme.* The baby she hadn't wanted. The baby she'd mourned all her life.

Rosemary – Louise – had told no one in her family what Stephen Fox had done. In shame and silence, in isolation, she'd endured. Alone, she'd managed, somehow, the agony of labour. A child herself, she'd given birth by herself, twenty-four weeks after the rape. The baby was stillborn. She'd cleaned up afterwards. Spent her savings on a bracelet. Wrapped the baby in a blanket and carried it to Cambridge. She'd taken a pile of newspapers, the little corpse, and the master key for that corridor from her aunt's keyring. She'd stolen into the college, into the room that she knew had been unoccupied since Gerald Chichester (poor young man) had gassed himself. She'd lifted the floor of the cupboard. Her father was a carpenter; she'd often helped with jobs like that. She'd placed the bracelet on the baby's tiny arm. Wrapped newspapers tenderly around. Said a prayer – *though I*

303

walk through the valley of the shadow of death. And buried her baby.

She didn't have another until, twenty years later, Katie was born.

Rosemary had told us all this in clear, quiet tones. Almost serene.

And I told Sonny.

He was waiting for me at Baits Bite Lock.

When I came to my final stretch of the river, I was rowing like an automaton, submerged in thought. Going over and over the last few weeks in my mind. Thinking of the vicious man who was still on the loose in London, waiting to vent his anger on another working girl. Sonny's involvement with the Cindy Sinful case had ended, but the issues would run and run. Thinking of Katie, whether she could plug back into normal life. Thinking, above all, of Rosemary.

But as I passed under the A14, where trucks for Ipswich and cars for Kettering skimmed above the fields, the drone of traffic recalled me rudely to the present. To the tension in the air. I looked over my shoulder. Saw the guillotine-like structure of the lock. Heard the rush of water over the weir.

At that very moment, there was a flash so powerful that the surface of the river became a mirror, reflecting the lightning back into my eyes. I heard, almost immediately, a rich grumble of thunder, and the rain began.

I raced for the bank, steering just past the spot where two anglers nested under a large green umbrella. Struggled to secure the boat and my oars, in the face of the driving rain.

One of the men detached himself and bounded down the bank, his wellies squelching on the grass. He extended a hand to help me up. I seized the long, lean fingers, felt a familiar hand on my elbow, and allowed myself to be shepherded up the bank – danger from lightning notwithstanding – to the shelter of a willow tree. Sonny leaped down the bank once again, and steadied the scull. He picked it out of the water, and turned it upside down on the verge. Then he joined me under the tree.

'Where did you come from?' I asked, astonished. The rain coursed down around us. The tree formed a natural gazebo, sheltering us from the storm.

'I get around.' He laughed a little at my amazement, and ran a forefinger down the side of my nose. 'You told Helen you were heading for Baits Bite, remember?'

We fell quiet, comforted by the deluge that was inches away from our den.

'Penny for your thoughts,' said Sonny finally.

'It's over,' I said.

And then I told him – everything that I knew – about Rosemary Arkwright and Stephen Fox and Katie.

But Sonny didn't wait for the end. 'Why didn't she tell her family – the aunt who worked at Bart's with her? Or have an abortion?' he asked.

I shrugged. 'It was 1961, Sonny. Girls didn't admit to rape. Rape was shameful, for the victim most of all. As for abortion – well, Rosemary had heard whispers about an abortionist in the next village. But she'd no idea how to get in touch, and she wasn't even sure she wanted to. Without a soul to talk it over with, what could she do? She kept the pregnancy a secret.'

I responded to Sonny's sceptical glance by passing on what Rosemary had told me.

'She had a rounded shape when she was sixteen, Sonny – the anorexia came later. She wore smock dresses. According to Rosemary, the pregnancy scarcely showed.'

As if it knew it wasn't wanted, she'd said to me, sadly.

'So she never told anyone? Never broke the silence?'

'Only once.' And, I explained to Sonny, it was crucial to what happened, in the end.

Rosemary had reported the rape to the college. When they'd called her in, to tell her that her services were no longer required, she was so shocked that she'd blurted it out. 'But I've been attacked,' she said, in a quavering voice. 'One of the students – Stephen Fox – did something to me. I'm pregnant.'

She could still see that moment now. The faces of the college

305

officials. Two of them, there were, a man and a woman. Serious. Concerned. Distressed for her. *Yes, my dear*, they'd said. *How terrible for you*, they'd said. *Don't worry, my dear, he'll be punished. But it's best for you – don't you think? – if you keep away from college, at least for a while.* She had nodded, and taken the money they'd given her. She'd supposed it was for the best.

And the one thing, the only thing, that had comforted her all those years, when she woke up crying from a nightmare – clinging to Robert, unable to tell him about the little body that haunted her dreams – the one and only thing that enabled her to carry on was their promise, her belief, that Stephen Fox had been punished.

'Do you know, Sonny, when Rosemary got to that point in her narrative, she made eye contact with me. I wanted to look away but couldn't. I felt almost sickened by the betrayal in her eyes.'

Sonny was the one who looked astonished now. 'So this incident was buried – literally – for almost forty years. Why has it surfaced now? Because of Katie?'

'Not talked about,' I agreed. 'But buried? Not really, Sonny. It lived on in Rosemary's insecurity. In her depression. In the restrictive way she brought Katie up, hoping, I imagine, to shield her from similar pain.'

And it lived on, I thought, in John Carswell's sense of guilt. I remembered the conversation we'd had, John and I, about responsibility. Riding on his motorbike, drifting back from Madingley.

I pushed the memory aside. Focused on responsibility.

'It was me, Sonny.'

'What was you?'

'I'm responsible. I set the whole thing in motion again,' I explained. 'I'm the one who visited Rosemary in Histon. And who, in the course of the conversation, mentioned Stephen Fox.'

Though I hadn't read the signs correctly at the time, Rosemary had been shaken to the core to hear that name again. To realise that Stephen Fox was still at the college – that far from being sent down in disgrace, he'd enjoyed a distinguished academic career.

She'd turned it over and over and over in her mind, after I'd left. And then, she'd made her way to the Senior Tutor's room.

'Laura, I don't understand – did Rosemary intend to kill Fox? Was this cold-blooded revenge? Was it premeditated murder?'

'Don't think so. Rosemary says – and I believe her – that she intended merely to be heard. To make him know how she'd suffered. To vent her distress. But then – when she was there – what he did pushed her over the edge.'

Rosemary had reminded Stephen Fox of who she was; told him that she'd heard of him again because he'd officiated at an enquiry involving her daughter. *Ah, yes, the lovely Katie,* Fox had countered. She'd stormed at him; taxed him with what he'd done to her, so many years before. Shouted at him now, the way she'd been unable to shout at him then.

And at that point, Fox had abandoned his detached stance and turned his vicious side to Rosemary, goading her. *Katie asked for it,* he'd said. *Like mother, like daughter. She's a whore. I can even show you her card.*

And – quoting the words from the card – *I'll make your dreams CUM true* – he'd bent over his desk to fetch the original article, turning his back on Rosemary.

And that's when I killed him, she said.

The rain was so intense now that there was a haze of moisture hanging just above the surface of the river. The path that ran between us and the grassy verge was pocked with puddles, and the umber dust ran in rivulets down the bank. A cyclist raced past, his head and body draped in a plastic poncho, looking like a tent on wheels.

'What will happen to her?' asked Sonny.

'Nicole thinks that if Rosemary pleads guilty to manslaughter, the CPS will accept it. They'll drop any murder charge.'

'So she'll get a custodial sentence, but a brief one. Poor Rosemary.'

Neither of us spoke for a very long time. Myself, I didn't want to break the spell. Didn't want to have to go on, to other things.

Sonny broke the silence.

'Funny about history,' he said.

'History?' I'd been trained as an historian, but not Sonny. Sonny had always been firmly fixed in the present. Mr Here-and-Now, I've called him on more than one occasion – the practical man who keeps me rooted in the world as it is. 'Since when are you interested in history, Sonny?'

'Not history in a big way. The Arkwrights, I mean. The parallels are uncanny. Rosemary Arkwright kept the secret of the rape and the baby's birth and death from the man she married. The secret tore her apart. It cast a constant shadow over the marriage.'

I could see what he was getting at. 'And Katie, Rosemary's daughter, was burdened also by something she perceived as shameful – something that was no more her fault than the rape had been her mother's. Katie couldn't bear that Jared should know about her secret past. That's partly why she fled.'

I shook my head. 'Relationships. God, they're complicated. People kid themselves that it's all a matter of choice, that they can do them in their own way, in their own time. But the past keeps coming back to haunt the present.'

The look Sonny gave me, under the willow tree, was long and searching.

'What is it?' Something about his expression made me feel uneasy.

'Don't you think it's time to talk about *our* past?'

I stepped out from under the tree, and held my hands to the sky. The downpour had dwindled. It drizzled quietly and calmly, drifting past us in a soft spray, cool and fine and wet. 'Let's go now,' I said. 'I'm cold. I need to get changed.'

Sonny put his arm around me. He rubbed my back to warm it. 'Laura, did you hear me?'

I'd heard. But I also realised – it had been sneaking up on me all afternoon – that I'd already gone through partial mourning for Sonny. For the petering out of our relationship. The weeks when I'd pressed for reconciliation – for time together, for a chance to talk – had passed. Now he posed the prospect of a better understanding, and I felt myself chickening out.

'What past?' I asked, sounding – even to my own ears – petulant.

'Well, for a start,' he said, 'there's me. There's the way I've been chasing this project in Amsterdam, regardless of what it did to you and me. Regardless of what it did to the boys. I was with the accountant all morning yesterday, you know, and she assures me we can do it now. That the money will be all right. The Amsterdam thing could work.'

He paused.

I didn't ask the 'but' question. Knew full well he was going to answer it himself.

'But now that it's possible, Laura, I'm full of doubts. What good is a bigger business if it comes between us? I think I must've had some kind of brainstorm – some kind of middle-aged crisis.'

'You're not middle-aged!'

'No. It's the crisis that's middle-aged.'

Sonny looked at me, waiting. I was unable to speak. He picked up the conversation again. 'Laura, we need to talk.'

'What about?' I stalled.

'About us, for a start. About the skeletons in our cupboard. About John Carswell – how you feel about him. How serious it is. No, just listen for a minute, Laura. Why don't we go away? Just you and me?'

'Go away? When?' I felt a rising sense of panic. 'Where?'

'Why not now? Your case has ended, hasn't it? We can be in Wildfell before evening. Sitting in front of the fire.'

'But, Sonny, I promised Nicole I'd pop in tonight and have a look at her new bathroom suite.'

'It'll still be there later in the week.'

'I have an appointment tomorrow with the osteopath. About my neck.'

'So change it. And meanwhile, I'll massage your neck morning and night. Put it on the road to recovery.'

The rain was nothing more than a mist now – wet air, Sonny

said. But rivulets of moisture still ran down the ivy that encased the trunk of the willow tree. Droplets trembled and fell from the leaves. A pair of swans edged over to the bank near us, growling and snuffling as they rooted among the weeds that grew by the waterside.

Then the angler, as if to drown out the sound of the swans – or maybe to drown out our conversation – turned on his radio. It wasn't what you'd call loud; fishing etiquette wouldn't permit that. But we had no problem, from where we stood, picking up the music. It was a deep, sexy soul song, with a strong, slow beat.

Sonny stepped out on to the puddle-strewn path and held out his arms.

'How about a dance?' he asked. He was moving gently to the music.

I hesitated. Then stepped slowly into the circle of his arms, until we were face to face. Until I was staring straight into Sonny's warm brown eyes; until his lips brushed the side of my mouth. Until we were dancing slowly, slowly. Dancing, barely.

Cheek to cheek.

'Do you play?' Sonny whispered in my ear. The fisherman glanced up at us, and looked quickly away. The swans stared balefully through their black masks.

'Do you play?' Sonny asked again. And, for now, I did.